"I have no right to want you."

August said the words almost to himself, as though trying to make them sink in.

He did, though. He wanted her. Leila could read the want in his eyes, and that tormented look made tenderness bloom in her heart again.

Leila had no idea when she'd ended up so close to him, but as she clutched a fistful of his shirt in her hand, she didn't know if she wanted to push August away or pull him closer. Her heart was flying away from her now, bringing her outside of herself. Only one man had ever made it beat like this—frantically, out of control.

"I have no right to want you." August spoke the words with more force this time, but that tone only made her blood rush faster. She could no longer make a sound decision, so she pulled on his shirt, bringing him close, standing on her tiptoes and touching her lips to his.

PRAISE FOR
SARA RICHARDSON

"With wit and warmth, Sara Richardson creates heartfelt stories you can't put down."

—Lori Foster, *New York Times* bestselling author

"Sara Richardson writes unputdownable, unforgettable stories from the heart." —Jill Shalvis, *New York Times* bestselling author

"Sara [Richardson] brings real feelings to every scene she writes."

—Carolyn Brown, *New York Times* bestselling author

THE SUMMER SISTERS

"This is sure to win readers' hearts."　　　　　　—*Publishers Weekly*

ONE NIGHT WITH A COWBOY

"Richardson has a gift for creating empathetic characters and charming small-town settings, and her taut plotting and sparkling prose keep the pages turning. This appealing love story is sure to please."　　　　　　　　　　　　　　　　—*Publishers Weekly*

HOME FOR THE HOLIDAYS

"Fill your favorite mug with hot chocolate and whipped cream as you savor this wonderful holiday story of family reunited and dreams finally fulfilled. I loved it!"

—Sherryl Woods, #1 *New York Times* bestselling author

"You'll want to stay home for the holidays with this satisfying Christmas read." —Sheila Roberts, *USA Today* bestselling author

FIRST KISS WITH A COWBOY

"The pace is fast, the setting's charming, and the love scenes are delicious. Fans of cowboy romance are sure to be captivated."
—*Publishers Weekly*, Starred Review

A COWBOY FOR CHRISTMAS

"Tight plotting and a sweet surprise ending make for a delightful Christmas treat. Readers will be sad to see the series end."
—*Publishers Weekly*

COLORADO COWBOY

"Readers who love tear-jerking small-town romances...will quickly devour this charming installment." —*Publishers Weekly*

RENEGADE COWBOY

"Top Pick! An amazing story about finding a second chance to be with the one that you love." —Harlequin Junkie

"A beautifully honest and heartwarming tale about forgiveness and growing up that will win the hearts of fans and newcomers alike."
—*RT Book Reviews*

HOMETOWN COWBOY

"Filled with humor, heart, and love, this page-turner is one wild ride." —Jennifer Ryan, *New York Times* bestselling author

NO BETTER MAN

"Charming, witty, and fun. There's no better read. I enjoyed every word!"

—Debbie Macomber, #1 *New York Times* bestselling author

Last Dance
with a Cowboy

Last Dance with a Cowboy

A SILVERADO LAKE NOVEL

SARA RICHARDSON

FOREVER
New York   Boston

Copyright © 2021 by Sara Richardson
Bonus novella *Sunrise Ranch* copyright © 2020 by Carolyn Brown

Cover design by Daniela Medina
Cover photographs © Rob Lang Photography; Shutterstock
Cover copyright © 2021 by Hachette Book Group, Inc.

Forever
Hachette Book Group
1290 Avenue of the Americas, New York, NY 10104
read-forever.com
twitter.com/readforeverpub

First edition: December 2021

Forever is an imprint of Grand Central Publishing. The Forever name and logo are trademarks of Hachette Book Group, Inc.

The publisher is not responsible for websites (or their content) that are not owned by the publisher.

ISBNs: 978-1-5387-1720-2 (mass market), 978-1-5387-1719-6 (ebook)

Printed in the United States of America

CW

10 9 8 7 6 5 4 3 2 1

To Erin and Lori
The best research assistants ever!

Acknowledgments

Writing this book required a lot of hands-on research, and I wanted to especially thank the vineyards and wineries of Palisade, Colorado, for their wonderful hospitality. A special thanks goes to Laura and Brandon at Mesa Park Vineyards—I so appreciate them taking the time to show me around and answer all my questions! I loved my entire experience at their beautiful vineyard—especially meeting their mascot, Daryl. The staff at Restoration Vineyards also proved to be incredibly helpful in providing information and answering questions in my quest to learn about growing grapes in Colorado. I learned so much during my visit to their tasting patio. I highly recommend a visit to both these vineyards if you ever find yourself in Colorado.

Once again, I wanted to thank my fabulous team behind the scenes—Amy Pierpont, Sam Brody, Suzie Townsend, and Dani Segelbaum. You are all rock stars and I appreciate you!

A big thanks to Erin Romero and Lori Bowen for joining me on this critical research trip. I can't wait to do it again soon!

This was a tough year for everyone, and I want to thank my family for their patience, grace, and love as I balanced deadlines with life. Will, AJ, and Kaleb, thank you for always being there no matter what.

Chapter One

Strangulation by bow tie wasn't August's favorite way to spend an evening.

Usually, he endured at least a few hours wearing the fancy torture device, but tonight... well, tonight, this black silk bow tie that had likely cost his boss upward of five hundred dollars was going in the trash early. Even though he'd been attending black-tie galas in Napa for well over thirteen years, he would never get used to wearing a tux.

With a few flicks of his wrist, August unraveled the bow tie and tossed it nonchalantly into a stainless-steel trash can hidden behind the pavilion's stone pillar.

"I hope that shirt is coming off next."

August didn't even have to turn his head to know who had spoken. Close to three hundred guests were attending the Kingston Family Vineyards' annual wine club members' gala on the patio overlooking the vineyard, but he would recognize Corrine Laurent's voice anywhere. As the granddaughter of their wine club's longest-standing members, Corrine got special attention at every event she attended, and this one was no different.

"Forrest doesn't like it when I take off my shirt." He approached

Corrine and her friend—Nadia, if he wasn't mistaken—giving both of their sparkling gowns exactly the right amount of attention before grinning. "He says it's not professional." Truthfully, Forrest Kingston would likely tell August to take off his shirt right now if it would make the woman happy, but thankfully his boss happened to be otherwise occupied with a group of investors near the tasting bar. So August was off the hook. For now, anyway.

"I like you better when you're unprofessional." Corrine's blue eyes seemed to sparkle as much as the sequins on her gown. "There's nothing better than seeing you ride your horse in the vineyards wearing jeans and a T-shirt, and your cowboy hat shading your eyes." She gave a quick raise of her eyebrows.

Yeah, the woman seemed to spend a lot of time watching him when she visited the winery, but since she was barely out of college, he'd make sure *watching* was all she did.

"I could picture him riding a horse, looking all hot and cowboy like," Nadia murmured as she appraised him.

"Trust me, I'd rather be wearing jeans and playing the cowboy role tonight." Forrest could take the cowboy out of Colorado and make August manage his Napa vineyards, but he couldn't take the Colorado out of the cowboy. He'd learned to adapt, to be what his boss wanted him to be. But he still hadn't forgotten who he really was.

"Well..." Corrine leaned in with a conspiratorial smirk. "Since you're all dressed up in your fancy suit, can you tell us more about the new cabernet sauvignon coming out this fall?"

"I can do more than tell you." He held out an arm to each of them, easily settling into his role as head schmoozer. "I can give you a sample. As long as you promise to keep it our little secret."

Sharing a look of intrigue, the women linked their arms through his, and he led them to the far end of the tasting bar where he'd stashed the bottle of the special new cab he'd overseen himself.

"Ladies..." He lowered his voice and made a show of glancing around as if afraid someone might overhear. "You two are going to be the first to sip this brand-new creation that's the culmination of years of work." He didn't mention that the work had been mostly his and had happened in secret until he'd finally told Forrest about his labor of love. "We fully believe we have curated the perfect cab." He reached under the bar and presented them with the bottle that had yet to even be labeled. "We selected only the darkest, ripest grapes for this one, which give it mocha notes and aromas. You'll also notice a rich finish with fine-grained tannins, providing a nice backbone."

"Mmm," Corrine hummed. "Nothing sexier than a cowboy speaking wine."

"Are you sure he's still single?" Nadia asked as if he weren't standing right there.

"Well, I've never heard him mention a significant other." Corrine stared directly at August. "But maybe that's because he doesn't want to settle down."

"Oh, I have a significant other, all right." August pulled out two branded wine tumblers and filled each with a generous pour. "At about four hundred acres, she's beautiful but she's also more demanding than any woman ever could be." He slid the glasses across the bar with a smirk.

Corrine took her tumbler with a roll of her eyes. "What will a vineyard ever give you that I couldn't?"

The vineyard had given him a lot. Far more than he could ever repay. After his father had died, August had gotten lost, unable to face going home to Colorado. He'd dropped out of college, sunken into a dark depression, and had all but given up on life when he'd met Forrest Kingston at a bar in San Francisco. He wasn't sure if the man had hired him out of pity or because he was a cheap labor prospect, but the reason didn't matter. This vineyard had healed him. He'd done just about every job in this operation, working his way up to general manager, but spending time in the vineyard was still his favorite thing to do. That was where he'd found himself, in the hard work of tending the vines, babying them along, harvesting the fruits of his labor. August owed Kingston Family Vineyards his life.

But he didn't talk about those kinds of things. Especially not with clients. So, he grinned again. "The vineyard gives me all the wine I can drink." He found another glass and poured himself a taste before holding it up for a toast. "To sharing a glass of the best wine in the valley with two tempting, albeit off-limits, ladies."

Corrine glared at him but smiled and clinked her glass against his. "À votre santé."

"Santé," Nadia chimed in.

Swirling the wine in his glass, August inhaled the robust scent. Even the smell was enough to intoxicate him. He sipped the burgundy liquid slowly, savoring it, letting the nuances of the wine come together on his palate.

"My God." Corrine closed her eyes and took another delicate sip. "This cab is downright sensual."

"Not as sensual as watching him drink it." Nadia sent him a dazzling grin. "You really don't date, huh?"

"I don't need to date." There were women, of course. None from the wine club members' list, however. And none with any staying power. Every woman he saw—every woman he talked to or slept with—he compared to the one woman who had mattered. "I have the life I want." True, he had fallen into this gig in Napa. It wasn't what he'd pictured back when he'd thought he would marry Leila, but that dream had shattered. His life now suited him fine.

"Who said anything about life?" Corrine kept her eyes on him while she took another sip. "I'd be happy with one night."

He laughed like he assumed she was joking, but instinct told him she wasn't. "I assure you...one night with me wouldn't be enough." After years of entertaining the wealthy and elite, he played the part of a Casanova all too easily. That might be his biggest problem. He'd become an actor.

Corrine leaned over the bar. "I'd be happy to test that theory—"

"Darling, there you are!" Corrine's grandmother rushed to the bar. Vivian Laurent was nearing eighty years old, but one would never know it with her styled blond hair and nearly flawless skin.

"You absolutely must come and meet Mr. and Mrs. Deckers. I was telling them all about your trip to France. They'd love to hear the details."

Corrine pouted as her grandmother dragged both her and her friend away. August simply waved a cheerful good-bye.

Phew. He poured himself another splash of the cab. Saved by the granny.

After stashing the bottle back under the bar, he took his glass and wandered to the edge of the stone terrace. This vantage point offered the best view of the vineyards that were nestled into the valley's rolling hills. The sun hovered just over the western horizon, setting the lush green vines ablaze with a surreal glow.

Every once in a while, this place offered him glimpses of home. There were no mountains here, but back when he used to hike around his family's Colorado ranch, he had a spot a lot like this one. A spot where he would climb up to get a view of the Valentino Bellas Vineyards—the much smaller, family-run operation back in Silverado Lake, Colorado. After he'd started dating Leila Valentino, they would hike up there together to watch the sunset while they drank a bottle of wine she'd snuck out of her grandparents' cellar . . .

"It's a little early to be losing articles of clothing." Forrest joined him at the stacked stone wall that could double as another bar area. His boss's gaze centered on the collar of August's shirt where the missing bow tie should be. "I guess I should be glad the rest of your clothes are still on."

"My shirt wouldn't be, if Corrine had her way." August sipped the wine, still staring out over the landscape. He'd learned to play whatever part Forrest wanted him to, but he always felt more like himself when he had his hands in the dirt and on the vines than at any other time.

Forrest chuckled, swirling his own glass of wine. "Thank you for charming Corrine to keep her grandparents happy. Not that you have to put any effort into charming young, beautiful women."

"It's part of the job description." He faced his boss directly.

In some ways, Forrest was a cowboy himself—about the same height as August, but broader across the shoulders. His face had been weathered from years of work in the sun, which often fooled unsuspecting business professionals into thinking the man was more of a farmer interested in curating the vineyards than a shark who'd taken over wineries all up and down the West Coast. "Corrine is easy to charm."

Forrest laughed again, this time shaking his head. "All women love you, August. I'm just glad you don't love any of them back."

August steered his gaze out over the vines, remembering the one woman he had loved. The woman he'd walked away from but had never forgotten. "Maybe I could love one of them back. Eventually."

This time, Forrest laughed loudly enough to draw the attention of two women who were speaking in hushed tones nearby. "You're too much like me." He clapped a hand on August's shoulder. "Married to the job. Why do you think you've come so far since I first hired you?"

Because this job had first become his lifeline and then it had become his life. He inhaled the wine's aroma again, letting it fill his senses before he drank.

"If I had ever been naive enough to fall for a woman, I wouldn't be where I am now." Forrest glanced over his shoulder as though admiring the upscale crowd mingling behind them. "And neither would you."

That was likely true. If he'd married the woman he'd fallen for like he'd promised, his life would look very different. He wouldn't be here pretending and charming clients. He decided not to let himself picture where he might be instead. No use in revisiting the past.

"Speaking of where you are now, I have a new assignment for you." Forrest prodded him out of earshot as though he didn't want any of their guests to overhear.

Well, this ought to be good. "Where are you sending me this

time?" He'd spent most of the last six months revamping an operation they'd bought up in Oregon, and before that, he'd been in western Nevada.

"I'm sending you home." Forrest set his wineglass on the stone wall and adjusted his cufflinks. "To Silverado Lake."

August nearly choked on his wine. "Colorado?" Not this again. Last summer, Forrest had sent him out there to talk to the Valentinos—Leila's family—about purchasing their winery, but the family had clearly told him they were not interested in selling out to a big corporation.

"Leila Valentino contacted me. She found out we'd done a scouting mission last summer and she wanted to talk about a partnership."

"Leila?" He hadn't sipped more wine, but he still felt like he was choking. "She hasn't had anything to do with the winery for years." When he'd visited her grandparents last summer, he'd learned she'd gotten married three years before and was living in Denver.

"She's the one in charge out there now, apparently." Forrest signaled a passing server and exchanged his empty glass for a full one, giving August a few seconds to reel in his shock. Leila was home? With her husband?

"Anyway, the woman proposed a partnership. I told her I'd rather just take the property off her hands, but she went on and on about a family legacy, yada, yada, yada." A roll of his eyes made it clear what he thought about deeply rooted family connections. "The fact is, their operation is in trouble, and she needs a bailout."

It didn't surprise him that Valentino Bellas might be in financial peril. It was a small, family-run business with virtually no distribution channels. Which begged the question . . . why would Forrest even be interested? "I'm not sure it's worth the investment." Might as well be honest with the man. The Valentinos' vineyard was a beautiful place but, compared to the other Kingston vineyards and wineries, it was not at all profitable. "They only have about twenty acres, and the vines are still young. They maybe produce three thousand bottles of wine a year." That would not amount to a profit sufficient for Kingston.

"I'm well aware." Forrest always got testy when anyone pushed back on his ideas. "But there is room for expansion if we can acquire more land, and their acreage right now is low yielding. I have no doubt you can turn things around."

"Me?" The choking sensation returned. "You want me to go take over Valentino Bellas?" So, he would become Leila's new boss? "That's a bad idea. The woman hates me." She had every right to hate him. Before he'd left for college, he'd given her a ring and a promise, and then he'd never gone back home to make good on either.

"I don't care if she hates you," Forrest shot back. "We've done everything we can on the West Coast. I want a new challenge. Colorado is starting to make a name for itself in the wine world, and I want to be on the front end of it."

Right. This wasn't about money for once. Forrest wanted notoriety. He wanted to conquer new territory.

"Besides..." His boss's amused grin turned sly. "This is a huge opportunity for you too. It's no secret you've been working your way up around here. You make this project a success, and I'll add *executive vp* to your title."

August studied the man's expression. Forrest was serious. This offer was everything he'd been working for. It was the next step— a huge step in his career. And yet... Valentino Bellas? How could he even show his face there?

"You're aware of the challenges with growing grapes in Colorado, aren't you?" He couldn't resist trying to argue his way out of this predicament. Leila would likely refuse to work with him, and he didn't want to work with her either. They had too much history. How was he supposed to undo years of silence? "The temperature swings alone make the whole thing a gamble."

"And yet people are finding success there." Forrest's tone had moved beyond subtle annoyance. "Besides, I only agreed to a provisional partnership. If the winery doesn't increase its profit margin by thirty percent by the end of the fall, Kingston takes over completely."

August recognized that gleam in Forrest's eyes. This was all about the man's ego. "So you can basically fire her and send her family packing. She agreed to that?"

Forrest grinned. "I stipulated. Those were my terms, and she agreed to them."

Why? Why would Leila put her family's business in jeopardy? "Does she know I'm coming?" Because he wouldn't be shocked at all if she left town before he got there.

"No, I thought we would surprise them by sending in some reinforcements."

That would go over well. "I can assure you, she won't be happy to see me."

"Well then, it's a good thing you don't have feelings." Forrest clapped him on the shoulder again and started to walk away. "Whether she's happy to see you or not, this is your one shot. I know you won't screw it up."

Chapter Two

Leila gulped down another sip of coffee and struggled to keep her expression neutral as she stared at the screen in front of her. One wrong move—one raise of an eyebrow, one frown, one twitch in her cheek—and her nonna, who was sitting only a few feet away, would ask her what was wrong.

And Leila couldn't answer.

These numbers. God. She didn't dare squeeze her eyes shut to ward off a headache the way she wanted to. She'd known the winery was in trouble—her brother had kept her updated on the early freezes that had decimated the crop a few years back—but she hadn't realized things were this bad. Her eyes moved over the spreadsheet's lines while the partnership she'd made with Kingston sat like a rock in her gut. Her recently earned MBA wouldn't be enough to help them dig out of this hole.

"Do you have any questions, mimma?" Nonna asked, peering over her red-rimmed bifocals.

"Um, no." She understood everything. She simply wasn't sure what to do about their dire financial projections. "Our inventory is going to be very low next year."

"Yes, yes." Her grandmother waved off the statement. "That

happens from time to time. We can't control the weather, you know, but we've always managed." She rose inelegantly from her chair, still stiff from the double mastectomy she'd endured three months ago. "Don't look so worried. Valentino Bellas has been here for twenty-three years and it will be here for twenty-three more."

Leila couldn't look at her and risk giving away her doubts. She'd never been skilled at hiding her emotions, and she didn't want her grandmother to know what she had done. With the breast cancer treatments Nonna had been going through, Leila hadn't had the heart to trouble her grandparents with the financial woes they faced. That was why she'd contacted Forrest Kingston. But the man had driven a hard bargain. While the partnership would be enough to keep them afloat for the next several months, she had no doubt he'd completely take over her grandparents' legacy and kick out both her and her brother if she didn't prove she could make this place profitable.

Noticing her grandmother's curious stare in her direction, Leila pushed out a smile. "I'm not worried." She didn't have the time or the mental capacity to worry. She simply had to get things done around here. Worry was a distraction she couldn't afford. "But we're going to have to make some changes—"

Their barn cat interrupted with a loud meow and crawled out from the open desk drawer where she'd been napping. Regina hopped up onto the desk and stretched regally before marching right across the laptop keys.

"Hey!" Leila shooed the cat down. "I thought Regina was supposed to be an outdoor cat. To take care of the mice in the barn?"

"She does," Nonna insisted, pulling the gray-and-white mottled cat into her arms and cradling her like an infant. "She takes care of the mice and she runs the place too." Her grandmother rubbed noses with the cat, and Leila could hear the purring from where she sat. If the cat really ran the place, maybe they wouldn't be in this precarious situation right now. Regina was a stickler for routine and punctuality. Her grandparents on the other hand...they didn't worry. They didn't stick to a schedule. They rarely balanced the budget. They were both free-spirited and believed everything would work out.

For the most part, things had worked out in the past. They hadn't made a lot of extra money, but they'd made enough to be comfortable. They'd never had this much debt either.

And life had proven to Leila a long time ago that everything didn't always work out.

Once more, she thought about simply selling, paying off their debts, and making sure Nonna and Poppa would have enough for a comfortable retirement. That would be simpler. They would be taken care of, and she could find a job somewhere else, put her MBA to use.

Leila peeked at her grandmother, who was still fawning all over the cat. "You know, there's a buyer who's pretty interested in purchasing the winery." She anticipated the way her grandmother's face would fall at the prospect of selling, but she had to try. "Out in California. They've approached us before and—"

"No." Nonna set Regina back on the desk, and Leila quickly shut the laptop before the cat damaged her spreadsheets for good. "Absolutely not." Her grandmother wheeled her office chair to the other side of the desk and sat across from Leila. "This land belongs to us. To our family. Your poppa and I have poured our entire lives into it so you and your brother would always have a place. So we'd all have a place together." Her dark eyes got all glossy and sad, and Leila couldn't keep looking into them. "This land is our heart and soul. We can't sell. We both want to live the rest of our lives right here."

"Then I want that for you too." But she had no idea how to make it happen. "I just think we have to be practical about—"

An obnoxious ding from her computer announced she had a new e-mail. Leila lowered her eyes to the screen, ready to cling to any distraction that would save her from having to break her grandmother's heart.

From: August Harding

Everything around her dimmed as she stared at his name. Auggie. A fault line opened dead center in her chest, breaking her in half. He had sent her an e-mail?

"What's the matter?" Nonna started to lean gingerly over the desk, but Leila snapped her laptop shut before she could see the screen.

"Nothing." She blinked her grandmother back into focus and held her breath to ward off the stabbing pain.

"Something's wrong." Her grandmother's right eyebrow peaked. "When you looked at that e-mail, your whole face went white."

Yes, because at the sight of August Harding's name, all the blood in her body rushed straight to her still-fragile heart. God, her arms and legs felt like dead weight. Easing in a stabilizing breath, Leila forced a smile. "It's nothing to worry about, Nonna." The lie formed a lump in her throat. There was plenty to worry about. She hadn't even read the e-mail, but she already knew that much. August had to be contacting her on Forrest Kingston's behalf.

"I need to run out for a bit." She stood abruptly, snatching her laptop into her arms before wobbling her way across the room. "I forgot I had some errands to run."

"Are you sure everything's all right?" Her grandmother met her at the door. "You seem upset."

"No, no. I'm not upset." She forced a hollow laugh and slipped outside. "Just have a lot to do. But I'll be home in time for lunch!" Without a glance back, she dug her keys out of her pocket and hoofed it across the parking lot to her Jeep.

Once she was safely settled in the driver's seat, she opened her laptop again, her fingers shaking as she typed in her password. There was his name again, glowing on the screen. She shouldn't be surprised, but Forrest had mentioned that August had been busy with some other project in Oregon, so she had assumed she wouldn't have to interact with him at all.

Leila glanced around quickly to make sure the parking lot was deserted before clicking on the man's name. A short, to-the-point e-mail popped up.

Hey, I wanted to give you a heads up that I'm in town. Forrest sent me out to oversee things at the winery. I didn't want to show up without warning you first. I know this isn't the ideal situation, but I didn't have a choice. I'm staying at the ranch. Let me know when there's a good time for me to come up there so we can talk things through.

A good time? Not the ideal situation? August had clearly become the king of minimization in the years they'd been apart. There was no good time for August to come to Valentino Bellas. The minute he showed up, Nonna and Poppa would find out they were in trouble. She refused to let that happen.

Leila slammed her laptop shut and set it on the passenger's seat before jamming her key into the ignition to rev up the engine.

She was not about to let August Harding waltz in here to take over her family's legacy. By all the accounts she'd read, that was what he did. He took control of an operation and made it comply with the Kingston brand. Well, that wouldn't happen to Valentino Bellas on her watch.

Anger pulsed through her temples as she drove what had once been such a well-traveled route. When she used to turn onto the Harding Ranch's driveway, a sense of anticipation would always leave her breathless, but right now her lungs were as heaving mad as the rest of her.

Every part of this place still seemed so familiar to her—the aspens lining both sides of the road, the grand log lodge sitting at the center of the property in front of the twinkling blue lake. The sights dredged up the memories she'd managed to suppress with grad school and a failed marriage.

She pulled into the main parking lot in a spray of gravel and dirt, refusing to give in to the nostalgia that enveloped her senses.

Back when she and August were dating, she had loved being here. She'd loved sitting around the massive stone fireplace inside with Auggie and his family, or lying out in the sun on the lake's beautiful beach. But now, those memories were steeped in pain.

No. She wouldn't let him bring her more pain. She had to hold on to the anger now. Anger would make her stronger.

Climbing out of the Jeep made her stomach turn, but she marched herself toward the lodge's grand entrance anyway. Before she could reach the main door, she heard the distinct clomp of hooves beating the ground somewhere nearby.

Leila spun just in time to watch August and his brother Wes tear out of the woods and across the parking lot on two Appaloosas at a breakneck speed.

"Told you I could still kick your ass!" August yelled over his shoulder.

Wes ignored his brother as he slowed his horse to a trot and turned in Leila's direction. When he was few feet away, he slid out of the saddle "Leila, I thought that was you."

She didn't blame him for the shocked expression. She hadn't exactly visited the ranch since it had become apparent August wasn't coming back. In fact, she'd stayed as far away as possible. "Hey, Wes." She squared her jaw, hopefully serving up an unaffected smile. "Good to see you." She could not, however, say the same to his brother.

"Good to see you too." Wes gazed at her with open curiosity. "It's been a while. How are you?"

"I'm great." The small earthquakes in her joints begged to differ. Before she lost the nerve, she looked directly at August and found herself staring into the same blue eyes that had once held such power over her.

He'd finally come home.

At first, relief flooded her—every nook and cranny—but then a wave of sorrow crashed in and brought with it a renewed surge of anger. "We need to talk." Somehow, she managed to speak the words with authority.

"Yeah, I suspect we do." He dismounted and handed the horse's reins to Wes.

Unable to stand still, Leila wandered to the sidewalk that led around to the backside of the lodge, all too aware of August right behind her. Once she'd turned the corner where the lake came into view, she stopped and faced him.

August had come back, but he wasn't the same boy who'd walked away from her. That she could see. His face had filled out more—jaw broader and structured like stone. His dark hair looked different too—sun streaked and longer than he'd worn it in high school. Crinkles hemmed in the corners of his eyes, giving them a wise tint.

He looked good, but that didn't mean it was good to see him.

"What are you doing here?" *Don't look away.* She couldn't look away, or he'd know his very presence had gotten to her.

"Forrest sent me. I didn't have a choice in the matter." There'd been a time she could read this man's face with a simple glance, but now she couldn't detect what hid beneath his indifferent expression.

"Well, you have to go back to California," she informed him. "Nonna and Poppa can't know. They can't know about the partnership or that we might lose this place. It would *kill* them." He had no idea what they'd been through the last few months. The treatments her grandmother had endured, the sickness from the chemo. Not that she wanted to cry on his shoulder.

"I *have* to come to the winery." A familiar stubbornness reinforced his jaw. "My job is on the line here. Forrest has a stake in Valentino Bellas and he wants Kingston representation out here. Like it or not, I'm going to be involved in the winery's operations."

His tone gentled on that last sentence, and only irked her more. He did not get to look at her like some fragile girl he'd left behind. "Fine." She stared him down, unwilling to let go of control. If he had to stay, this arrangement would be on her terms. "But we're going to have to come up with a cover story for why you're here, because I refuse to tell my grandparents about Kingston." When their finances were more stable and she retained majority owner-ship for their family, she could tell them everything. But until then, she would protect them. "My grandparents have already been through too much this year. Nonna was diagnosed with breast cancer last spring—"

"Oh, Lei," he interrupted. "I had no idea. Is she okay?"

Don't call me that. He had lost the privilege to call her intimate nicknames, to pretend like he cared about her or her family. She held her chin up. "She's in remission." Nonna had walked through hell to get there, but for now, the cancer was gone. "But I don't want them to worry about the winery. Not right now."

"Okay." A sympathetic expression softened the rough edges of his face. "I get it. So, what's our cover story?"

She shrugged and took a few seconds to look out over the lake. The past seemed to close in on her again. They'd been so happy together once. They'd even skinny-dipped in that lake. Leila braced herself against the longing for those days. It wasn't August she longed for—not anymore. It was the girl she'd been then. Free to love someone. Unburdened and hopeful.

Someday, August will realize his mistake and he'll find his way back to you, her grandmother had told her right before Leila had moved away to go to grad school. *You'll see. True love will always find its way home.* Total baloney, in Leila's opinion, but as a hopeless romantic, that happy ending was exactly the story her grandmother would want to believe.

She peeked at August again. There was only one thing that would justify his constant presence in their lives. "We have to tell them we're back together." She almost choked on the words, but it was the only story that made sense. "We have to tell them we're engaged."

The proposal seemed to freeze the man right where he stood. It took him a few seconds to speak. "Uh, maybe we just tell them you hired me as a consultant."

"They'll never believe I willingly hired you. Not after—" What she'd gone through when he left her. As much as she'd tried to put on a good front, her grandparents knew her too well. They knew she'd never truly gotten over August. That was why they would fully believe she'd given him another chance. "Besides, we would never hire anyone from Kingston. They know we don't have the money for a consultant. And they'd be worried something was wrong."

August stared at the ground, his eyes shifting as though he were searching for an alternative.

Leila crossed her arms. "Don't look so concerned. You've already made it pretty clear how you feel about marrying me. I'll have absolutely no expectations this time."

His jaw tightened, but he said nothing.

Good. It would make things easier if they didn't argue. "Telling them we're together is the only way to explain you hanging around constantly." Leila walked to the bench at the edge of the lawn and sat to take the burden off her weakening knees. She'd always been a terrible liar, but this arrangement would only be temporary. "They're going back to Italy for the winter. After they leave, I'll tell them we broke it off because things didn't work out. Again." Except this time, she wouldn't wait around for years for him to come back. She'd know better.

August sat next to her, his posture still rigid.

"It doesn't have to be a big deal," she said, shrugging off every emotion seeing this man had dredged up in her. Emotion would not save her family's home. "There's a ton of work to do at the winery. Trust me." And she would make sure to give him all kinds of projects to keep him busy and out of her hair. If August thought he was the boss, he'd have to think again. "We'll hardly have to spend any time together at all. We'll divide and conquer." She would do this on her terms. Forrest might've sent August out to take control, but she wasn't going to give up so easily. As long as he was here, she would use him to help her grandparents. "As I understand it, I still have three months to improve things in order to maintain half ownership."

She didn't like the way August shifted his gaze from hers.

"That was my agreement with him. I made sure it was in our contract." Leila watched his face carefully, but August's pensive expression didn't change. "Well?" she demanded when he stayed quiet. "Isn't that what he told you?"

"Yes, technically, you have three months." The man clamped his mouth shut as though he wanted to say more but thought better of it.

"Great. Three months is plenty of time." She wouldn't give August or Forrest the satisfaction of failing.

Earlier that morning when she'd looked at the numbers again, her hope might have wavered. But who needed hope when she had determination?

Chapter Three

Are you sure this is a good idea?" August tugged on Leila's arm outside of the winery's office, but then quickly let go of her. He had no business touching her. He had no business feeling a distinct and long-abandoned stirring, a warmth kindling where a cold hollowness had been when he looked at her.

"I'm not thrilled about this arrangement either," she said, cocking her head to glare up at him. "But acting like we're a couple shouldn't be a problem, since our past is ancient history. We need to think of this like a business arrangement."

Right. It shouldn't be a problem to pretend—August pretended all the time—except seeing Leila again had already messed with him. She'd changed in the years since he'd stood with her at his father's funeral. The beauty of her silky olive skin, sleek dark hair, simmering brown eyes, and full soft lips had only grown more nuanced over the years, a lot like a fine wine. She also had a sharper edge these days...a different flavor about her. He'd seen a stiffness in her movements. He'd heard a rigidity in the same voice that had once been soft and velvety whenever she'd spoken to him.

There went that stirring again. The emotion must have come from the guilt he'd managed to bury beneath the passing years.

He should've come back to talk to her in person long before now. If he'd been a stronger man back then, he would have. Not that she wanted to hear any apologies from him. Leila made it clear he wasn't allowed to cross any personal boundaries, not even to express sympathy for her grandmother's illness. She'd shut down every attempt he'd made so far to connect with her, which would make their supposed engagement quite the challenge.

"So, here's the plan," Leila whispered. "We go in there and tell my grandmother that we reconnected a while ago and are planning to get married, so you're going to be around and part of the family business."

He nodded even though he wasn't at all prepared to walk into that room and pretend to be in love with Lei. He'd never had to pretend with her. "If that's what you want—"

The woman didn't give him a chance to finish before she opened the door and breezed into the office. "Nonna, I have a surprise!"

He trudged in behind her and took a hard punch to the gut when Leila's grandmother rose from her chair. She looked so much smaller than she used to, and her movements seemed guarded.

"August Harding! What on earth are you doing here?" Nonna lumbered around her desk to greet him.

"Hi, Mrs. Valentino." He hugged her gently, all too aware of her frail frame.

"He came to see me." August couldn't claim to know Leila anymore, but even he could detect the phony happiness ringing through her tone.

"What?" Nonna braced her palm against the desk when she pulled out of his hug.

Leila moved closer but stopped short of actually touching him. "We're back together." Only a slight waver came through. "In fact, we're planning to get married eventually."

All August could do was nod along while he wrestled out a smile. He got that Lei wanted to protect her grandparents, but they had a lot of work to do to make this facade convincing.

"That's why he's here," Leila rushed on before he could speak up and ruin everything. "As part of the *family,* he's going to be helping us out at the winery."

"I knew it!" Nonna hugged him again. "I always knew you two would find your way back to each other. I used to tell Leila that all the time. Oh, such happy news!"

"We have a whole lot to catch up on. I want to hear everything." Leila's grandmother prodded August and Leila to the small couch near the window, where she sat between them. "When did you two reconnect? How?"

"Earlier this summer," August said at the same time Leila said, "Last winter." He shot Lei a glance. *See?* They really should've gone over details before she rushed him over here to tell her grandparents.

"We've been talking since last winter," his pretend fiancée quickly corrected. "But we kind of made things official earlier this summer."

"Right. Kind of," August echoed.

Her grandmother sighed dreamily. "A modern-day love story."

Nonna had always been a hopeless romantic. Back when he and Lei were dating, her grandmother would always give him ideas about dates he could take her on and ways to surprise her.

"Anyway," Leila went on. "We started chatting and—"

"You finally both realized that you were meant for each other." Her grandmother squeezed their hands. "I always knew it, of course. Everyone did. Even at sixteen, you two were absolutely perfect for each other."

"I don't know about perfect," Leila muttered.

"I definitely wasn't perfect," August found himself saying before he could stop it. But Lei had been pretty damn close. And then he'd gone and left her.

"You don't have to be perfect to love someone." Her grandmother brought her hand to August's cheek, giving it a gentle pat. "Not when your souls were designed to be together. You can run all you want, but eventually, that love will win over time and

distance. And it has. Love has brought you back together. Oh!"
She struggled to stand, so August helped her to her feet. "I have
to run and tell Poppa the news! And Samuel too! Your brother is
going to be shocked!"

Leila's brother, Sam, would be shocked, all right. And not in a
good way. The man had never liked him—not even when August
been had in the rest of the family's good graces.

Leila stood too. "Can you let me tell Sam? Please, Nonna? I
don't want him to be upset that I left him out."

"Sure, sure. Yes, that would be best." Her grandmother shuffled
to the door. "But I will go find Poppa right now. I'm sure he's out
fussing over the chardonnays." She paused with another excited
gasp. "We must have a dinner tonight! With August as the guest
of honor."

"No, not tonight," Leila blurted before August could accept. "We
don't have to do that. He just got into town. He's tired and—"

"All the more reason to celebrate!" Her grandmother was practically singing now. "Six o'clock in the restaurant." She smiled
warmly at August. "Invite your family too, if you'd like. Call the
restaurant and tell them how many to expect." She turned and left
the office. "Goodness! An engagement! A wedding! This is so
exciting." Her voice faded until only an awkward silence lingered
between them.

He let himself study Lei for a few seconds, but she avoided
looking at him and sat behind her desk. "That went well."

Had it gone well? "I'm not sure we were very convincing." He
sat in the chair across from her.

"It was fine." Lei dismissed his concern with a wave of her
hand. "Now, as far as the winery goes, it's important you know
what you're walking into." She slid a large stack of binders across
the desk. "Here are the financial records."

August looked at the stack, his eyes wide. There had to be
thousands of printed pages in those things.

"You should read everything." A smugness snuck into her
smile. "It'll take you a while. You'll notice things aren't looking

very promising, but I have some ideas for how I can bring this place back. We'll have an official meeting on details tomorrow." She pushed out of her chair. "Right now, I have to go talk to Sam before Nonna finds him."

"That's probably a good idea." He suspected Leila's brother wouldn't take the news as well as Nonna had. August stood too, collecting the binders. "Do I need to worry about him?"

Lei shrugged. "I'll take care of him. It's not like he's going to beat you up or anything."

They stepped outside.

"That's good to know." But he was more concerned about Sam making his job harder. As the head winemaker, Sam would need to be on the same page with Kingston. But August would worry about that later. Right now, he had some "light" reading to do.

He headed for his truck, but then paused to watch Leila march herself down the cobblestone walkway toward the large, weathered barn where they housed their wine-making operation. She carried herself with an unmistakable confidence, her shoulders proud and straight, her hell-bent gaze focused directly in front of her.

His eyes followed her the whole way.

When she was out of sight, August opened the door to his truck and tossed the binders she'd given him onto the passenger's seat. Climbing into the truck, he tried to shrug off the reactions, the feelings, the whatever-the-hell all this was. He was here to do a job, bottom line. And yes, Forrest had told Leila she had three months to fix the mess at Valentino Bellas. But given the details Forrest had e-mailed him about winery's current financial state, she wouldn't be able to turn things around enough to convince his boss she should stay. He didn't have to read the binders to know this place was in trouble. Forrest would do what he could to get his way and completely take over Valentino Bellas. That August didn't doubt.

Taking it slow, he followed the curve of the road down the mountainside, switchbacking through the vineyards—their leaves lush and green, the nearly ripe varieties of grapes hanging heavy on the vines. Seeing the place where he'd spent so much time with Leila didn't help him outrun the memories.

This was a bad idea, them pretending. As if things weren't tangled enough. What was he supposed to tell his family when he got back to the ranch? As little as possible. That was the mantra he'd held on to for the last decade of his life. No connections, no feelings. Forrest was right—his lack of emotion was what made him good at his job.

The road gradually flattened, entering the valley floor. Here, the pine trees grew thicker, illuminated by swatches of light cast by the late afternoon sun.

Even years later, August could drive this route between the winery and the ranch with his eyes closed if he wanted. He knew every bend in the road, every bump. He must've driven it a thousand times in the years he'd dated Leila, but now, turning onto the ranch's winding driveway didn't feel like coming home.

His father had been his home; that had been the problem. That was why he'd gotten so lost after his death. Yes, he loved his mother and his sister, Jane...and his brother, Wes, most of the time. But his dad had been his hero, his anchor; without Charlie Harding here, the ranch had become an empty, sad place.

The parking lot sure as heck didn't look empty, though. August pulled into a parking spot outside the main lodge, squeezing between Wes's family SUV and Jane and her husband Toby's truck.

Before walking into the lodge, he heard the commotion of family fun happening all way down on the lake's beach, so he walked around the building and took in the sight from the lawn.

Wes and his stepson, Ryan, were out in a canoe fishing, while his wife, Thea, and stepdaughter, Olivia, watched from lounge chairs. Jane and Toby were splashing in the shallow water with their daughter, Charlee. God, was it possible his new niece had just turned one? The baby was toddling around while she squealed and giggled.

August started down the hill but then hesitated. He didn't exactly fit here. With them. When he'd arrived earlier that morning,

Wes had been the only one around. As usual, their quick horseback ride had turned into a competition. It was one thing to hang out with his brother, but being with everyone else only reminded him he no longer had a place at their family's ranch. It was his fault; he knew that. While he had gone and isolated himself, the rest of his family had stuck it out, building these close connections with one another. They probably got together this way at least once a month, even with Wes and Thea and their kids living in Texas.

"Uncle Auggie!" Ryan waved at him from the canoe.

Too late to make a quiet escape now. August waved back and joined everyone else on the beach, smiling like he would at a new wine release party and greeting Thea and Olivia before his sister beelined toward him.

"You're here!" Jane swooped her adorable daughter into her arms and then ambushed him with a hug, splashing him with the cold lake water.

He hugged her back as though it were the most natural thing in the world. But he didn't hug anyone except for when he came home, and they all tried to pretend he was one of them.

"Mom said she didn't know why you were coming home." His sister stepped back, peering up at him hopefully. "But she said you'll be here a while this time?"

"Yeah. A few months, more than likely." Unless things at Valentino Bellas completely imploded before that. He shook Toby's hand—thankfully, his brother-in-law didn't go in for an awkward hug—and then stole his sopping wet cherub of a niece out of his sister's arms.

He'd never been much of a baby person, but this little one had made quite the scary entrance into the world last summer—putting his sister in the hospital and arriving two months before she was due. Charlee was a little miracle baby. Quite the cutie too, with blond curls that stuck up all over her head.

"Aye ya bebop?" his niece asked, her jewel-like blue eyes wide.

"Yep." He had no idea what she'd just asked him in her baby language, but he'd pretty much give her anything or do whatever she wanted.

"This is going to be great!" Jane almost seemed as exuberant as her daughter. "We've hardly spent any time with you in years. Even for Wes's wedding, you were only here two days."

She likely hadn't meant the comment as a jab, but it still stung. "I came to the wedding to be the best man, didn't I?" He simply hadn't wanted to hang around. Every time he stepped foot on the ranch, grief haunted him, only reminding him of how he'd fallen apart, how he'd failed his mom and his siblings...

"The prodigal son returns," Wes teased from the canoe. He and Ryan paddled to the shore, and then August's young nephew hopped out and pulled the boat up onto the sand. "Look at me, Uncle Auggie! I can put the canoe away all by myself!"

He still wasn't used to anyone calling him uncle, but he had to admit the title had a nice ring to it. "Wow, I think you've grown a foot taller than you were when I saw you at the wedding." It was wild how much the kid had changed in only six months. He didn't know Ryan and Olivia well, but they'd always impressed him. They were good kids—thoughtful and respectful, even after losing their father when he'd been killed while serving in the military overseas.

"So, what did you and Leila have to talk about earlier?" Wes stepped out of the boat and looked him over.

All eyes focused on him as everyone waited for an answer. No surprise there. Wes had likely wasted no time telling them all that August's ex-girlfriend had shown up at the ranch. Before he'd arrived, August had been intentionally vague about his purpose for coming back to Silverado Lake. He hadn't wanted his family to know why he was there before Leila knew. "Well..." This was where he had to be careful and keep any information he offered as high level as he could. "Valentino Bellas is now a partner of Kingston."

"Seriously?" Wes frowned. "Yikes. That doesn't seem like a great fit. How does Leila feel about it?"

His brother had always been the master of twenty questions. "She's not thrilled." That was putting Leila's feelings mildly.

"So, you're like her boss now?" Jane's grimace made it clear what she thought about that arrangement.

"Kind of." *Aye, aye, aye.* He wasn't going to be able to keep their fake engagement a secret. If Nonna had her way, word would reach the town café by noon, and the owner was Jane's best friend. His family had best hear the details from him. "My assignment at the winery has turned out to be a little more complicated than being her boss, though."

"I would imagine so, seeing as how you and Leila never really had much closure," his sister said with a snicker.

"Who's Leila?" Ryan was looking back and forth between the adults as though trying his best to follow the conversation.

"She was the love of August's life once," Wes informed the boy with a smirk.

"Gross. Never mind." Ryan scampered off and snatched a shovel off the lounge chair before digging in the sand.

The kid had the right idea. Avoid and distract.

"So, you've talked to Leila, then?" Jane inched closer, her eyebrows raised with a blatant hopefulness. "Was she happy to see you?"

"Not exactly." He wasn't sure why he was bothering to beat around the bush. There was no way to hide their arrangement, especially because his family couldn't accidentally reveal anything about the partnership to Nonna and Poppa.

Charlee reached up to pat his cheek, babbling again, but her cuteness didn't distract Jane.

"Well? How'd the reunion go?" His sister nudged his shoulder. "Come on. You're holding out on us. I can tell."

Right. He'd forgotten his sister's uncanny intuition. "It was...unexpected." Jane posted her hands on her hips, silently demanding more of an explanation.

August sighed. Why was this so difficult to say? "She wanted to tell her grandparents we're engaged."

He paused for the impending reaction and was not disappointed.

Jane slapped a hand over her mouth.

Toby laughed.

And Wes—good old Wes—let out a few expletives before remembering his kids were right there.

"That's *two* quarters in the jar," Ryan informed him from the hole he was still working on a few feet away.

Thea laughed from her front-row seat in the lounge chair. "He's a stickler for language."

"Tell me about it." Wes winked at his wife. "I'm gonna go broke." His brother turned his grin back on August. "So how did you two lovebirds get engaged, anyway? Don't get me wrong, I'm thrilled for you, but this seems a little fast. I've heard of a shotgun wedding, but not a shotgun engagement." Cue the sarcasm in his brother's voice.

August shook his head, replaying the afternoon's events in his mind. He still wasn't sure what the hell had happened. "My boss assigned me to come out here to help manage the business, but Leila doesn't want her grandparents to know things have been going downhill, so that was the best story we could come up with for why I'd be around all the time."

"Whoa." Wes sat on the edge of Thea's chair, peering up at him. "So now you two have to pretend to be in love the whole time you're here? That won't backfire or anything."

August ignored the ribbing tone. "It can't backfire. I have a job to do." And he had to do his job well if he wanted to hold Forrest to his offer. Usually when he entered a new business venture, he took control. Something told him that wouldn't be happening this time. But maybe this would be like all the parties he attended back in Napa. He'd simply play a role and still be able to maintain a safe distance. "All I know is she asked me to keep the partnership quiet—"

"Look at all of my favorite people in one place," his mom sang behind him.

Snapping his mouth shut, August handed Charlee to her mom before turning to give his mother an obligatory hug. In some ways, Mara looked younger than she had in the years following his father's death. Back then, she'd taken on all the stress associated with trying to provide for the family. To make ends meet, she'd turned their dude ranch into a wedding venue so she could make enough to keep the place afloat. Now that Jane and Toby had taken over the family business, though, his mother seemed to glow. She traveled and met with friends and seemed to revel in her role as a new grandmother to Olivia, Ryan, and Charlee.

"What did I miss?" She parked herself on the edge of Olivia's lounge chair and added one more pair of eyes on him.

"Auggie and Leila are engaged," Jane announced, looking quite amused by the whole mess.

"We're not engaged," he corrected. "We're *pretending* to be engaged. There's a big difference." Mainly the involvement of real feelings. He couldn't get the cold look in Leila's eyes out of his head.

"Pretending?" Mara rose slowly from the seat she'd just taken. "Why? Why would you do that?"

He'd seen that same grim expression on his mother's face many times back in high school, and it still turned his gut to lead. "Because she asked me to." Sometimes, the truth was simpler than coming up with an excuse. "I know it sounds ridiculous, but Leila didn't want her grandparents to stress over how bad things are up there, that they needed Kingston to bail them out. So this is how she wanted to handle me working at the winery. I'm only trying to do what she wants." He already felt bad enough about being the one who would help Forrest take controlling ownership over the winery. He knew his boss. The man wouldn't let Valentino Bellas remain a mom-and-pop shop. August only hoped he could help Lei keep a job there at the end of the fall.

The explanation didn't seem to appease his mother. Her scowl deepened. "And just what am I supposed to tell my friends when they ask about you two? Everyone will know. Everyone will think you're getting married."

He shrugged, much like he had when he hadn't had an answer for her at eighteen years old. "Say you haven't heard much. Plans are still up in the air."

Mara shook her head, her lips pursed into a thin, rigid line. "I can't believe this. You know how I feel about lying."

"You're busted," Ryan informed him, trading out his shovel for a dump truck. "I bet you'll get grounded. That's what happens to me when I tell a lie."

"I wouldn't mind getting grounded right about now." Or being sent back to his home in California and away from all these complications. "I hate lying too." He rested his hands on his mother's shoulders and smiled at her so she would remember he was the good person she'd raised him to be. "But this is what Leila thinks is best for now. I'm not asking you to lie. Tell people you don't know what's going on and leave it at that." He dropped his arms to his sides and looked at both of his siblings. "The same goes for you two. Anyone asks you questions, blow the whole thing off." Given his past mistakes, people probably wouldn't believe he planned on sticking around anyway.

Chapter Four

Leila steered the ATV around the bend in the vineyard's eastern section of merlots, navigating the precarious path between the vines and a steep drop-off on the edge of the mountainside.

She'd always loved this view overlooking the valley, but she didn't dare take her eyes off the ruts in front of her. If she weren't in such a hurry to find Sam, she might have stopped to snap a couple of pictures for their social media posts to help draw in new customers with the allure of the ripe grapes hanging heavy on their vines, but photos would have to wait.

Sam had been out here somewhere all afternoon, and she had yet to find him to warn him about August, which should make their impending family celebration dinner a real fun time.

Slowing the ATV, she eyed the narrowing pathway and decided to continue on foot. It'd been a long time since she'd navigated these makeshift roads, and she didn't need to go for a tumble down the mountainside right now, tempting as it was to find a way out of sharing dinner with her fake fiancé.

Leila cut the engine and slipped off her helmet, setting it on the ATV's seat before wandering along the vines. She had to smile, remembering all the time she'd spent out here when she was growing up, roaming barefoot in the soft dirt and sampling the plump grapes when her nonna and poppa weren't paying attention.

The sweet scent of ripened fruit sharpened the memories, bringing more clarity. She'd once felt safe out here, happy and carefree. Now the countless issues the winery faced were piling up like rocks on her shoulders, pushing her down, and she wasn't sure how long she'd be able to keep her head above the water.

Her brother stepped out from the vines about fifteen feet in front of her, holding a bunch of grapes up as though inspecting them in the sunlight.

Finally.

Leila rushed to talk to him before she got lost in the memories forever. "Hey."

Her brother fumbled with the grapes, clearly startled. No surprise there. Her brother had always managed to tune out everything else when he was working in the vineyard. That was why he couldn't help on the business side of things. Before she'd moved home, Sam had tried—bless him—but he couldn't focus on details like sales and marketing when he was so obsessed with the chemistry behind pectolytic enzymes and pectins and tannins.

"Hi." He plucked a grape from the bunch and popped it into his mouth, chewing slowly.

"I've been looking everywhere for you." Leila approached him, taking a glance at her watch. August would likely show up anytime now for dinner. "We have to talk."

In response, Sam held up one finger in her direction, still savoring the grape with a thoughtful expression. Though he was three years younger than her, Sam was at least two heads taller and built like a linebacker, though he detested football. His strength came from working the earth, tending the vines, walking the vineyards, and repairing whatever needed to be fixed around here, which seemed to be more and more of a full-time job. Unlike her, though, he didn't seem to absorb the stress. His large, dark eyes and broad face still had boyish qualities, and his long, sun-lightened hair always lay over his ears unkempt.

Leila stared at him, resisting the temptation to rush him along. He'd never had her sense of urgency, and as much as it drove her up a wall, Sam would have to be eased into this conversation when he was good and ready.

"We'll have to harvest soon," he finally said after he finished chewing. "I would say another month or so."

"Okay." She hated that her first thought was how much they would have to pay a crew of seasonal workers to walk through and snip the grapes. Lately, everything came down to the money they didn't have. "I'm sure we can make that happen." Though once again, she had no idea how. "We can talk about harvesting later. Right now, there's something else we need to discuss." She paused, trying to figure out the best way to bring him up to speed on the August situation.

Her brother eyed her, like he was analyzing her the same way he had the grapes he'd been sampling. "What's wrong?" He let the rest of the bunch drop to the dirt and gave her his complete attention.

"Nothing's wrong, per se." She kept her tone light. God, why did her heart get all rattled and wild when she thought about August? "You haven't seen Nonna lately, have you?" Maybe she should've just let her grandmother break the news. At least in Nonna's presence, Sam would've been on his best behavior.

"No, I haven't seen her since early this morning." His pensive expression gave way to concern. "Why? Is she okay?"

"She's great." And Leila intended to keep their grandmother blissfully happy and unaware of the issues they were facing. "I have to tell you something, and you're not going to like it."

Heck, she didn't like August walking back into her life, but there was nothing she could do about his presence now except to retain control of this charade.

Sam's head tilted, a sign he was listening.

"It's um...well...it has to do with August." Ugh, why was it so hard to say the man's name?

A tic worked through her brother's jaw, so she rushed ahead.

"Remember how I told you about the partnership with Kingston?" From the very beginning, she'd kept Sam as informed as she could so she would have an ally.

"Yeeeaaahhh." He drew out the word with a menacing grumble.

"Well..." Leila shifted her weight from foot to foot, trying to manage the sudden weakness in her knees. "Forrest Kingston sent August out here to oversee our operations for the fall." She patiently waited for Sam's cursing to pass and then continued. "But the real problem is we had to tell Nonna we were engaged so she wouldn't find out the truth about the partnership."

"Engaged? To that *dito nel culo*?" The old Italian phrase had always been their poppa's favorite insult. "No. No way." Sam had a knack for cutting off entire conversations with that razor-sharp edge in his voice. "He had his chance and messed it up a long time ago." Sam looked around them. "Is he still here?" His hands pulled into fists at his sides.

Leila stared him down. "He's not here now but he's coming for dinner." The thought of sitting across from August for an entire meal made her stomach churn, but it was too late to back out of this arrangement now. She would simply have to power through. Much like when she'd been twenty years old and it had become clear that August wasn't coming back for her. She could still see the looks of sympathy on acquaintances' faces when she would run into them at the grocery store in town. *You doing okay, sweetie?* well-intentioned people would ask. *Of course!* she'd answered as though auditioning for a play. *I've moved on.*

She *had* moved on, which meant this whole situation didn't have to be a big deal. "This is the best way to deal with August," she insisted. "We have to keep our friends close and our enemies closer right now. Nonna and Poppa think we're engaged, so I need you to be nice to him." She wouldn't be able to pull off this charade without Sam's help.

"*Nice* to him?" Her brother's face flushed like it always did when he got indignant. "You want me to be *nice* to him?"

"You have to be supportive," Leila said firmly. "You have to treat him like a member of the family. For Nonna and Poppa." That was how they'd both get through this—by focusing on their grandparents. "August is our best chance to fix things here. I can use his knowledge and experience to our benefit." As much as she hated to admit it, she'd read up on him. She'd seen his accolades in those wine magazines. "He's good at his job, and we could use the help."

"I don't trust him." Sam crossed his arms tightly over his chest. "Not after what he did to you. I can't trust him."

"I don't trust him either." When she had looked at August, something in her iced over, freezing her heart. "But this arrangement is our only option right now." And she would be careful. She wouldn't be fooled by the man again.

"Fine," Sam mumbled as he walked past her. "But he'd better not get the wrong idea about you and him, or I'll have to set him straight."

"He won't get the wrong idea. Trust me." And neither would she. Leila hurried to catch up with her brother.

By the time she made it back to the ATV, Sam had put on the spare helmet and already had the engine running. She pulled on her helmet and climbed on the back, and he blitzed them up to the barn much faster than she would have dared.

When they crested the top of the hill, a very familiar truck came into view. It was a good thing she wasn't driving, or she might've swerved off the path.

How long would her heart take a dive every time she saw August?

Sam parked the ATV next to the barn, and August walked over to meet them as they climbed off.

"Nice to see you, Sam." To August's credit, he didn't cower, even though her brother must've had a good fifty pounds on him.

"I'm not a fan of this arrangement," he informed August as a greeting.

The man simply nodded as though he understood. "I would imagine you're not."

Sam moved in a step closer, but August still held his ground. "Don't screw it up, or I'll have to screw you up. Got it?"

August accepted the threat with another nod. "Got it."

Her brother walked away grumbling and left the two of them standing on the sidewalk in front of the barn alone.

"Nice to see he's still a people person," August said when Sam had made it out of earshot.

Leila shrugged. "He doesn't pretend." And sometimes, that was better.

Speaking of pretending... "Is your family coming?" She couldn't even imagine what Mara must think about this whole plan.

"No." August cast a quick glance around before his eyes met hers. "I told my family what's going on, though, so they won't mess anything up."

For some reason, the news didn't bring her any relief.

"But they'll probably steer clear of us for the most part." The words were borderline apologetic. "My mother is about as thrilled as Sam that I would lie to your grandparents."

"We can't think of it as lying." She'd never lied to Nonna and Poppa. She'd never had to. With her parents divorcing when she was young, and her mother and father too concerned with living their own lives to worry about children, her paternal grandparents had raised her and Sam. They'd always encouraged openness and honesty, and she rarely worried about telling them anything. Until now. "We have to think of it more like keeping a secret that would hurt them if it ever came out." Otherwise, she wouldn't be able to do this. "We're protecting them. If Nonna found out why you were really here, she would only get anxious. I can't risk my grandmother's health going downhill again."

Sympathy flashed in his eyes, and the familiarity of the look he gave her lifted her heart. It seemed he wasn't wearing the same mask of indifference he'd had on earlier. Leila inched backward. Where was her shield when she needed it the most?

August seemed to sense her unease and stepped back to give

her space. "So...we should probably talk about how we're going to do this..."

Across the parking lot, the office door opened, and Nonna bustled out. Without thinking, Leila grabbed August's hand and led him behind the barn to the edge of the vineyard so they couldn't be seen or heard. She quickly let go of him, but the touch had already made its impact, giving her heart a good jolt.

"It's like we're right back in high school sneaking around," August commented, raising an eyebrow as though he wouldn't mind revising some of the activities they'd enjoyed doing together back then. Sneaking out here behind the barn into the vineyards with a blanket had been at the top of the list.

Leila flinched internally, the way she always did when one of those buried memories worked its way up to the surface. "We need to run this fake engagement like a business arrangement." Which meant she couldn't dwell on their past together.

He crossed his arms, looking skeptical. "A business arrangement."

"Yes." She held up her chin, daring to stare right into August's eyes, letting her resolve take over. "That means no reminiscing, no charming, no flirting. We will focus only on getting the job done."

The man defied her with a one-sided smirk. "What if I do my best work when I'm flirting and charming?"

He was teasing her, but she refused to let her hard frown budge. "Charm may work with the women you're used to interacting with." Lord knew the man probably made a living off schmoozing the wealthy. "But I can assure you, charm won't work on me or on any of the other women in Silverado Lake, for that matter." He'd been gone too long. "This isn't Napa. People around here can see through a facade, so we're going to have to actually work for results."

"Okay." His grin fell. "What did you have in mind?"

"Let me do most of the talking and answering the questions." They didn't have time to go over all the details of their fake relationship before dinner. "That way, we won't contradict each other again."

"If we treat this relationship too much like business, your family isn't going to believe us." His voice dropped a note lower. "They've seen us together before."

He didn't need to go on. Theirs had been an intense relationship for two teenagers—deeper than most—which was why she now bore such damaging scars. Leila shored up her emotions, cutting them off. "They know we're both different people now."

August's eyes met hers, but then his gaze quickly diverted to the vines behind them. "I never got to tell you how sorry I was."

She refused to let her expression change. It was hard to apologize when not talking to someone.

"I never explained—"

"Don't worry about it," she interrupted. This line of conversation was exactly what they needed to avoid.

"No. Listen." He raised his hand between them. "I'm sorry I never came back. Things were hard for me after Dad died, and I—"

"Like I said, I don't want an explanation. Or an apology." She had to stop him. Stop this. She didn't want the subtle warmth curling through her at the sight of the concern in his eyes. She didn't want the feel of her heart fluttering in her chest. "I don't want to talk about the past, and I certainly don't need an apology from you." All she had now—all she could carry forward—was the lesson he'd taught her a long time ago. She couldn't rely on him. She couldn't rely on anyone. She stared into his eyes from behind the safety of her walls. "I'm not the same girl you left behind, and you'd best remember that."

Chapter Five

August stepped out the door behind Leila and once again had the sensation of finding himself in a different time and place. That dining table at the edge of the terrace—the one that had been set for their family dinner—was where he and Leila had sat together for countless candlelit meals.

Underneath the white globe lights that hung from trellises strewn around the stone patio, they would talk and laugh and sneak kisses when no one else was looking. In the months before he'd left for college, he'd told her that although he might be going off to school, he would never leave her. He'd told her he'd never love anyone else, which happened to be the only promise he'd kept.

When they'd sat out here together, when he'd said those things to her, he'd had no idea his future would change, that the very foundation of his life would be taken away from him, that everything would fall apart.

"Are you ready for this?" Leila had paused to wait for him so they could walk to the table together. Her grandmother and grandfather were already seated, and a server had started to pour the wine. "Because you don't look ready." She nudged him lightly in the ribs. "You look serious and...worried."

August smiled past the ache in his chest. "I'm not worried." But this whole assignment had already started to feel different from the roles he played back in California. These were people he'd cared about once. These were people he'd spent a fair amount of his life with. These were people who'd cared about him. They had known him more than anyone else ever had. How was he supposed to pretend in front of them?

"Remember, I'll do most of the talking." Leila grabbed his hand and prodded him onward, her grip too tight and desperate to be tender. "Follow my lead, and everything will be fine."

"There you are!" Nonna and Poppa both stood as they approached the table.

"Pleasure to have you back at Valentino Bellas." Poppa caught August's hand in a firm shake.

"Glad to be back." August leaned in to hug Nonna next. "Thank you for having me to dinner. Mom and Toby and Jane couldn't make it, I'm afraid."

Nonna waved off the apology. "That's understandable with this being so last minute." She settled back into her chair. "We'll simply have to plan another dinner as soon as it works with everyone's schedules."

"That would be nice." He focused on pulling a chair out for Leila so they wouldn't see the hesitation in his eyes. His hand grazed his pretend fiancée's bare shoulder, skimming the edge of the tank top, and he wasn't sure if it was her familiar citrus scent or being here where they'd shared so many intimate moments that had his equilibrium off.

He remembered how Leila's eyes sparkled when she'd look across the table into his, over the flickering candlelight. How the light had danced across her face while she'd smiled and held up her hand to admire the simple ring he'd given her as a promise. *I'll wait*, she'd told him. *I would wait forever to be with you.* He'd never forgotten those words, how she'd said them with such conviction.

August sat next to Leila, his eyes on her. How long had she

waited for him to come back? He didn't know, and she might never tell him.

"We found a bottle of sémillon from our first harvest that we'd hidden away." Nonna raised her glass. "We were saving it for a special occasion."

"We always knew you'd come back when you were ready." Poppa held his glass in the air. "And we couldn't be more thrilled for the two of you. Cheers to a long and happy future together."

"Cheers." Leila clinked her glass with her grandparents' and nudged August again. With the way his thinking stalled out in her presence, she might have to nudge him often over the next few months.

"Yes, cheers." He completed the ritual, fighting to hold on to his smile. "Thank you both. You have always been so hospitable."

Nonna set down her glass and shook out her cloth napkin before draping it over her lap. "We love this place, and we couldn't be happier that the two of you will build a life together here the same way we have."

Leila looked around, obviously deflecting the statement. "I thought Sam would join us?"

"He texted to tell me he has to make some preparations for harvest." Poppa shook his head with a grunt. "That boy lives and breathes wine."

Or, Leila's brother didn't want to sit across from August for a full evening. That was a definite possibility. According to Wes, Sam had had it out for him since Leila hadn't heard from him a few months after the funeral.

"He lives and breathes wine kind of like someone else I know," Nonna murmured with a good-natured chuckle. "That's our family curse," she told August, passing him the bread basket. "All of the Valentinos live and breathe their work. It's not only a job for us. It's a passion."

"Following your passion is really the only way to live." It seemed like the right thing to say, but he wasn't speaking from experience. August sipped the delicate white wine, which happened to hold impressive crisp flavors, considering how young their vines were.

"I'm glad you feel that way." Poppa shared a long, adoring look with Nonna. "Because now that you're planning to get married, we want to give up our house. For you two. Since we spend so much of the year in Italy anyway—"

"No!" Leila blurted, setting down her glass so abruptly that wine sloshed onto the table. "You don't need to give up your house. I'm fine in my cottage, and August is staying at the ranch for the next few months."

Nonna swirled a line of olive oil onto her appetizer plate and dipped in a piece of the fresh homemade bread August had always loved. "That's silly. We're not as old-fashioned as you might think. He doesn't have to stay at the ranch when you're engaged. You should be together."

This time, Leila kicked him under the table.

"I do have to stay at the ranch, actually," he said quickly. "I...um...have to stay at the ranch because..." He snuck a quick, stalling look at Leila. "My mom and Jane need help with—" *Damn.* What would they need his help with?

"With the barn," Leila finished. "They're re-siding it." She nodded in his direction as though prompting him to agree.

"Right The work on the barn." He eased out a breath and poured olive oil on his plate before dipping his bread. That was close. He'd best stick to eating and let her do the talking, like they'd agreed.

"Re-siding a barn won't take more than a few weeks," Nonna insisted, using a pair of silver tongs to give them each a helping of the restaurant's hearty Italian salad. It was still the best he'd ever tasted, with the salami and mozzarella and house-made Italian dressing. "Just know the house is yours to have together as soon as you're ready."

"Well, we're not going to get married for a long time." Leila wasn't eating much. She simply stirred the lettuce around on her plate. "A really long time. Like a year. That's what people are doing these days. They're having yearlong engagements because it takes so much time and effort to plan a wedding."

"That's ridiculous." Poppa dabbed at his mouth with a napkin. "There's no reason to wait a year when you've already waited so long to be together." He slipped his arm around his wife's shoulders, and the two of them looked into each other's eyes, sharing a smile that could only belong to people who had stuck it out for more than fifty years together.

"You don't want to waste one more minute." Nonna kissed her husband's cheek. "If these last several months have taught us anything, it's that life is too short to wait for what you truly desire."

August slid his gaze to Leila. A tear rolled down the curve of her cheek, and she stared at her plate as though she didn't know what to say.

Seeing her sad—at a loss for words—made instinct take over. "You're right. We don't want to waste one minute."

Leila peered at him with wide eyes, but he shot her a reassuring wink. He had this.

"We plan to savor every minute of our long engagement." He slipped his arm around her but made sure not to bring her in too close. "That's exactly why we don't want to rush down the aisle. That's why we don't want to move in together right now." He gave her shoulder a slight squeeze so she'd stop gaping at him like he'd grown another eyeball and smile instead. This was their best chance to buy some space.

"We want to take time to anticipate the wedding, to plan the ceremony and reception in a way that represents us and our journey." It was a relief to know he was still good with words, even when he was wading through so many reminders of the past. "We want to spend time looking forward to the day we'll stand in front of everyone and make that commitment. It's not something we're going to take lightly."

Leila blinked a few times before finally bobbing her head in a stuttering nod. "Mmm-hmm," she murmured. "Exactly."

"Glad to hear it, son." Poppa set down his fork. "Because I do have to admit... when Nonnie told me the news, I was more than a little shocked to hear you were suddenly back, after the way you left all those years ago."

"Poppa..." Leila's grandmother gave the man another coded look. "Let's not ruin our evening with talk about the past."

"No, it's okay." August removed his arm from Leila's shoulders and sat straighter. This conversation had to happen eventually. If Lei wouldn't let him explain things to her or apologize when they were alone, he would definitely take the opportunity now. "I don't mind answering for my mistakes." He held Poppa's stare but felt no judgment from the man.

"All I want to know is, why didn't you come back?"

"I don't want to talk about this," Leila murmured, slightly breathless. "It's not important anymore."

It was important, though. He couldn't expect to come back here—to sit with these people who'd once been such a big part of his life—and pretend he hadn't disappeared.

"I'm not trying to be rude." Leila's grandfather had always been too soft-spoken to ever sound rude. "I'm sure you two have talked about what happened, but Lei..." The man looked tenderly at his granddaughter. "You were devastated. For years. So I think we have a right to know what happened too."

Before answering the question, August took his time looking at the woman sitting next to him, his heart cracking in half. He hadn't meant to devastate her.

Leila stared straight ahead, her cheeks flushed.

"You do have a right to know what happened." This might be his only chance to explain himself to her—when other people were around. When she couldn't interrupt him or stop him from telling her what he should've told her a long time ago. It wouldn't change anything now, and it didn't excuse his abrupt departure from her life, but at least she would know why. "I was in a bad place after my father died." He spoke more to her than to her grandparents.

"Of course you were." Nonna reached across the table to pat his hand. "It's unimaginable what you went through."

"It was a tough loss," Poppa agreed. "For all of us. Your father was one hell of a man."

"He was." August couldn't seem to hold his glass steady. He sipped the wine, tempted to change the subject or speak the same meaningless words he'd used before when he'd talked about his grief in those days. *I'm fine. I made it through.* If those words were true, his hands wouldn't be shaking so hard now. "He was the person I looked up to the most." And yet, once August had left for school in California, he'd acted like his parents hadn't even existed. He'd been too busy partying and studying and enjoying his independence to use the phone much. If only he'd returned his father's call the night before he'd died. But there'd been a big football game. He'd missed his last chance to tell his father he loved him.

Leila and her grandparents waited patiently for him to continue.

"After I lost him, everything fell apart." This wasn't another script he was reading as some phony character. In fact, this might be the most honest he'd been with anyone in years. "I didn't know who I was anymore. Where I belonged. I only knew I couldn't come back here. Not without him around. It was selfish, I know that. I regret walking away. But I wasn't thinking straight." In those days after the funeral, he'd become someone he didn't recognize, someone he didn't even like.

"Then I met Forrest, and he offered me a job. He helped me finish my degree. He gave me a place to belong when I didn't feel strong enough to create a place for myself." He stopped there. That was enough. He couldn't tell them about the depression, about how long it had taken for him to feel some sense of purpose and hope. He couldn't tell them he feared that if he weren't careful, he could go back to that place again someday. "I'm sorry. I know that's not enough, but that's all I can say."

Leila still wouldn't look at him, but Nonna dabbed at the corners of her eyes with the red-and-white checkered napkin.

"We understand," she assured him. "It takes a while to work out the grief when you lose someone you love so suddenly." The woman's sad gray eyes seemed to spotlight Leila.

Before coming back, he'd never realized that Lei must have grieved for him, too, for what she'd lost when he disappeared from her life. Helplessness gripped him. There was nothing he could do about the past now. It was too late.

"Okay, since that's out of the way, we should eat." Leila briskly dished August a helping of lasagna and then took a much smaller one for herself. "We don't want Nonna's lasagna to get cold."

"Still the best lasagna in the world, even cold." Poppa took two pieces for himself, seeming to honor his granddaughter's request to let the earlier line of conversation drop.

"I would agree with that." August tried to shake off the heaviness of his past transgressions to bring levity back to the table. Leila clearly wasn't comfortable with his honesty, so he changed the subject, entertaining them all with anecdotes about his early days of learning how to tend the vines.

"You two should go walking in the vineyards before dessert," Nonna said when their plates were cleaned and the conversation lulled. "Like you used to."

Memories simmered again, brimming over. Back then, they hadn't done much walking in the vineyards. There'd been kissing and laughing and talking late into the night. And when they'd gotten older...more. Desire shivered through him. The moments were still vivid, almost like they'd happened last week.

"I don't know about walking." Leila started to stack the plates. "I'm pretty tired."

"Nonsense." Nonna snatched the plates out of her hands. "You're savoring every moment, remember? The sun has just set, and the love of your life is here. You two should go enjoy the evening."

August caught his pretend fiancée's audible sigh, but Nonna and Poppa apparently missed it.

"Take an hour or so," her grandmother prodded. "By the time you get back, the tiramisu should be set up perfectly."

"Sounds great." August pushed out of his chair and offered his arm to Leila. She glared at him for a few seconds before taking it.

"Have a wonderful time," Nonna called as they walked away. Luckily, Leila's grandmother couldn't see the tight frown on her granddaughter's face.

They cleared the patio and stepped into the soft grass that grew between the vines. The low-sitting sun softened the sharpness in her eyes.

"That was a great performance at dinner," she said after a moment.

"It wasn't a performance. It was true. Every word." He'd already decided he wouldn't lie more than was necessary. Maybe his explanation hadn't been the whole truth, but it was as much of the truth as he could offer her.

Leila stopped walking and faced him. "Why did you come back here?" Anger laced the words.

"I had to," he said simply. He wasn't standing here to bring her pain or to stir up the past for either one of them. "Forrest didn't give me a choice." This was supposed to have been an assignment like any other his employer had given him. But it wouldn't be. He already knew that.

The outline of her dark eyes seemed even more distinct in the dusky light. "And if he had given you a choice, you wouldn't be here?"

"I don't know." That was the most honest answer he could give her. He would've been tempted to come back if Forrest had offered him the option, but he might not have had the courage. "There's a lot riding on this assignment for me," he admitted. "But I want to help you too." If they could improve operations and profitability, he'd be able to convince Forrest to let Leila manage the place. Maybe it was the guilt driving him. Maybe he was trying to make up for the past. Or maybe his intentions had more to do with the desire she still stirred in him.

Though he wanted to, he didn't dare move a step closer. "This is what I do, Lei. I fix wineries that are broken. I make them profitable, and I can help you do that here. I know I can."

He couldn't guarantee what he did would be enough for Forrest to leave her alone, but he would buy them as much time as he could. "You don't have to trust me." He'd never expected to win her trust back. He knew better. She'd been hurt enough by people she'd loved. Not long after they'd started dating, she'd told him how abandoned she felt by her parents, who were so busy traveling the world and doing their own thing that they only bothered to visit her and Sam a few times a year. And then he'd gone and abandoned her too, returning to California right after his dad's funeral and ignoring her calls and texts for months afterward. Now Leila would never trust him, not when he'd wounded her so deeply.

He looked directly into her eyes. "I want this place to succeed. I want you to succeed. That's the goal."

For once, he wasn't as focused on the bottom line as Forrest was.

Leila regarded him for a few seconds, the low light shining in her eyes. "I'm glad I don't have to trust you, because I can't," she finally said. Then she turned and walked away.

August kept his eyes on her until she disappeared around the corner. He'd never get used to that—watching her walk away from him. He'd never get used to battling the rush of longing he couldn't act on. If only things were different. If only he could give her a reason to stay.

Chapter Six

August had never been a procrastinator, but ever since he'd arrived at the ranch a week ago, he'd found plenty of diversions to keep him away from the winery.

This morning, his mother had asked him to turn out the trail horses to the pasture for the day, giving him yet another excuse to avoid the Valentinos. But now that he stood outside the red barn, he found it difficult to go in.

The building itself had gotten a facelift in the time he'd been gone—new siding, new windows, a new coat of paint. But it was still the same place he'd spent countless hours with his father, tending to the horses, learning how to be a cowboy.

See? This was why he hadn't made it home much. It made him too sentimental. Focusing on the past wasn't going to help him move into the future Forrest had promised him. Shaking off the memories, he pushed the door open and stepped inside the dim light, immediately struck by the familiar scent of hay and manure. That smell, more than anything else, reminded him of his father. They'd spent hours here mucking out the stables, joking around the whole time. He'd learned to tack up and groom a horse. But more than that, he'd developed a love for the animals.

August walked down the line of stalls, looking over the new additions his mother had acquired over the years. All of them were beautiful and strong, but he wanted to find one in particular.

There. At the end of the line. Knievel had been his father's favorite horse and sidekick while August had been in high school. The two of them had been nearly inseparable.

He approached the stall and reached out his hand, beckoning the horse to the half wall. "Hey, boy." He'd caught a glimpse of the old chestnut quarter horse earlier that week when he and Wes had tacked up for their ride, but then Leila had shown up at the ranch, and he'd been too distracted to make it back to the stable since then.

Knievel raised his head, his ears perked.

"You remember me?" August continued to hold out his hand. "It's been a long time." Too long. The horse now had an arthritic hunch to his shoulders, and gray whiskers sprouted at the end of his muzzle. A pang lodged itself under August's ribs. Knievel had been so strong once, robust and healthy, just like his father. According to his mom, the horse had taken his dad's death hard and had never been the same. It seemed Knievel had become wary of people.

"I can relate." August clicked his tongue, trying to lure the animal closer. "I still miss him too."

The horse regarded him with his large pair of wise, watery eyes and then plodded forward a couple of steps, stopping just out of reach.

"You need some oats, don't you?" August walked swiftly to the tack room and dumped the treat into a bucket. Knievel had never been able to resist oats. He carted the bribe back to the horse's stall and held it over the gate.

After a few suspicious sniffs in his direction, Knievel shuffled the rest of the way over and put his muzzle right into the bucket.

"I thought so." Still holding the bucket with one hand, he managed to give the horse's withers a good pat. "See? People aren't all bad." Complicated and messy, maybe. Which was why he'd avoided deeper relationships too.

"Looks like you've still got it." Wes strode down the corridor between the stalls. "I haven't been able to get Knievel to eat much at all lately. Mom's been worried about him. She said he's going downhill."

"Hard to believe he's almost eighteen." August set the now-empty bucket aside, but the horse didn't move away. Instead, Knievel nuzzled his shoulder.

"That's more affection than I've ever gotten from him." His brother watched from a few feet away. "When I try to get near him, he turns his head."

"He and I always had a connection." Likely because August had been the one to help his dad in here. "He's definitely aged, but I think he's still got some life in him." Looking into the horse's eyes, August saw a spark.

"Well, this is the most he's perked up in a long time." His brother ambled to a shelf and found a brush. "He could probably use a grooming. Who knows how long it's been?"

"Sure. I'd be happy to." August took the brush from his brother and then slipped into the horse's stall. Knievel stood taller, as though giving him permission to come close.

August brushed the horse the way his dad had taught him. He missed this more than anything else at the ranch—tending to the horses. A few times over the years, he'd considered purchasing his own stock, but he'd never been home for a long enough stretch to make it happen.

"So, I've noticed you haven't been spending much time with your fiancée." Wes leaned his arms over the stall gate. "I thought you were supposed to be working at Valentino Bellas."

Working there would be easy. Pretending to be engaged to Leila, however, made this his toughest assignment ever. "I've been giving Lei space." And catching up on the reading assignment she'd given him. He'd finally finished poring through the binders last night.

"Is that because she wants space, or because you do?"

August shrugged, still working the brush. His brother had

gotten nosy in his old age. "Both, I guess." Being at Valentino Bellas brought up memories he'd rather forget. Kind of like being in this barn.

"Is it tough seeing her after all these years?" Wes pressed.

The question made him pause. He let the brush fall to his side in his hand. "Seeing Lei again brings a whole new meaning to the word *regret*." Now that he had to face what he'd walked away from, how he'd changed the trajectory of their lives, he'd taken on a whole new burden. "But she's been better off without me. I don't doubt that."

Knievel whinnied and nudged August's shoulder, so he started to brush the horse again.

"How do you figure she's better off?" Wes opened the stall's gate and stepped inside next to him.

August avoided his brother's gaze. "I've never been good at keeping connections with people." He hadn't even stayed connected to his parents when he'd left for school. Shortly before his father's death, his mother had even written him a letter telling him how much his dad missed him. *It would help so much if you could call and talk to him a little more*, she'd said.

"Knievel here hasn't been good at connections either." Wes gave the horse's muzzle a good scrub. "But it looks like that might be changing." His brother walked out and started to open the stalls for the other horses so they could lead them to the pasture. "Sometimes opening up just takes the right person."

* * *

Leila stumbled to the coffeepot in the office and poured herself another cup, filling the travel-size mug all the way up to the very top. There wasn't enough coffee in the world to remedy a full week of sleepless nights.

. So far, she'd downed a whole mug of the dark Italian roast her grandmother received every month from her cousin in Trieste, and it hadn't made a dent in the exhaustion. She usually didn't have trouble sleeping. Growing up at a winery and restaurant, she'd learned how to tune out noise, but she still didn't know how to shut off her thoughts.

And she happened to have a few things on her mind at the moment.

Regina meowed and jumped up onto the counter where they kept the coffeepot plugged in, swaying her back end importantly as she sniffed the rim of Leila's mug with obvious distaste.

"Don't judge me." She rubbed behind the cat's ears. "You don't know what it's like lying to Nonna and Poppa, having August in town." She likely wouldn't sleep for the entire fall season. "Things are a mess, kitty." She lifted Regina into her arms. "But you already know that. Why else would I have come in here before six o'clock this morning?" Typically, she preferred to ease into her day—maybe take a quick run around the vineyard before schlepping herself into work—but this morning, she didn't have the energy to exercise.

Mercifully, she hadn't seen August since she'd managed to make it through dessert with him, Nonna, and Poppa. But that didn't mean their little ruse hadn't consumed her thoughts. It would be bad enough if she were only keeping the truth from her grandparents, but having to pretend with August—having to sit and listen to him explain why he'd never come back—had proven to be outright torture. It had taken her a long time to close that chapter on her dreams with August, and now he was back trying to rewrite the past.

"Why does it still hurt so much?" she asked the cat, setting Regina down on the counter. It shouldn't. It had been years since August had walked away from her without a word, and yet one look at him was all it had taken to reopen the wound. Not that she would admit those feelings to anyone other than the cat.

Leila took her coffee back to her desk and returned her attention to the database she'd created for their wine club members— their *rapidly diminishing* wine club members. They'd lost more than twenty-two in the last six months alone, and they hadn't had many to start. This was exactly the kind of problem she needed to focus on right now to tune out the many others plaguing her thoughts.

"We have to grow the club." Yes, she was talking to the cat, but right now, Regina happened to be her only true coworker. "What would you think about—?"

Across the room, the door handle jiggled and then clicked. Leila braced herself as the door opened and August stepped through carrying two coffee cups.

"Good morning." Damn those dark fitted jeans of his, that buttoned Henley that stretched across his broad shoulders. Damn that appealing grin, which hadn't dimmed since high school.

As always, her first instinct was to look away from him. "Morning," she said halfheartedly, refocusing on the computer screen in front of her.

"I brought you a cappuccino from the café." He set down the cup on the corner of her desk like a peace offering.

"Thanks." She'd have pure caffeine running though her blood by noon, but she wasn't one to turn down a good cappuccino.

"No problem." The man backed away from her desk and immediately Regina approached him.

"Hey, kitty." August knelt to pet her.

Leila snuck a sip of the cappuccino, which was the perfect balance of bitter and creamy. "The cat doesn't really like other people—"

Right as she spoke the words, Regina proceeded to weave herself in between August's legs, rubbing up against him like the man was made of catnip.

Seriously? Why did cats have to be such traitors?

"Huh." August picked up the cat, and Regina settled into his arms, gazing admiringly at his face while she purred him a love song. "She seems pretty friendly to me."

"Well, she's not," Leila muttered. "Most of the time, anyway." She hadn't realized her cat had a thing for cowboys-turned-wine-aficionados.

"So, what're you working on?" August wheeled over a chair and sat on the other side of her desk, still a few feet away but too close for her liking nonetheless.

"I'm looking at the wine club." She pretended to study the information on the screen even though she knew the numbers by heart.

"Ah, yes. I read about the wine club in the binders." The teasing tone drew her gaze to his. "I see you have the same information on your computer."

He was onto her plan to keep him occupied with "light" reading. Leila held her expression in check. "I just finished creating the database. Before this, all of our records were done by hand."

"Yeah, I caught that." He leaned back and had the nerve to look casual. In contrast, every muscle in her neck had turned to steel.

"You read through every binder already?" Great. Now how would she keep him busy?

"It took me most of the week, but yes." August drank from his coffee cup.

So he hadn't slept either. Well, good. That made her feel a little better.

"You could've just e-mailed me the documents." It seemed those endearing crinkles still formed in the corners of his eyes when something amused him. "Instead of sending me home with fifty pounds of binders to read through."

"I'm not completely finished with the electronic copies yet." She hadn't had the time to go back and proofread them. "Besides, it was important for you to see where we're coming from here. How far we have to go to run this place like a real business."

"You're off to a good start." He stood and leaned around the monitor to look at her computer screen.

Too close. Leila inhaled the subtle scent of his cologne—oaky, like the wine barrels they used—familiar and delicious. "Um." She scooted her chair back. "Anyway, about the wine club."

"That's going be our biggest tool for growing business." August shifted back into his chair, taking that alluring scent with him.

"Those are your loyalists, your partners. Not only in purchasing your wines, but also in getting their friends to purchase."

"Right." She blinked at the screen, trying to bring her fuzzy thoughts into clarity. "We've never been proactive about our wine club. It's been more of an afterthought than anything." Her grandparents were far too humble to continually promote themselves, even to their regular customers.

"You have quite a few contacts with people who have visited or come to a tasting." August picked up the cat, who had been meowing at his feet, again. "So, here's what I'm thinking..." His eyes had always lit with a certain energy when he had a good idea, and they still had the power to draw her into his plans. "We'll have a big event for the wine club members in October. We'll make a whole weekend of it, with free tastings and a banquet." He rose from the chair and paced, still cradling the cat in his strong arms. Once upon a time, that had been her favorite place to be— wrapped up against him, so close she could hear his heartbeat.

"My mom said the ranch is free that weekend, no weddings, so we can offer a package deal that includes lodging, if they're interested. We can also partner with some of the other bed-and-breakfasts and hotels in nearby towns for a special rate."

Her exhaustion set in again. Leila picked up her cappuccino to ward off the fatigue. Forget her plain coffee. The cup August had brought happened to be exactly what she needed right now. Not that she'd tell him that. "An event sounds great, but we don't have the budget or the manpower to pull off something like that." August had been in Napa too long. The money probably grew on trees there—or vines. "As you saw in the binders, we're hardly scraping by right now, so—"

"I have my own Kingston budget for things like this." He let Regina jump out of his arms onto the desk and dug his phone out of his back pocket. "We have plenty. Trust me. Whenever we do events like this for Kingston, we get a huge response, a very nice bump in our numbers."

Leila watched him continue to move around the room as he

worked on his phone, his magnetic energy on full display. As much as she would like to be, she wasn't immune to his intensity. August had been passionate when he was younger. It seemed he still was.

"Forrest shouldn't pay for this event." She was supposed to prove she could manage this business on her own. Her best-case scenario was that she would improve their bottom line so Forrest would leave her alone and let her continue running the winery the way her family wanted.

August halted with an abrupt pause. "Kingston is now a partner of Valentino Bellas," he said slowly. "You signed the paperwork. That means you can use all the resources at your disposal."

Except for the fact that she never wanted to be dependent on this man again. Leila stood. "That doesn't mean you can come in here and take over." This was exactly what she'd been worried about— why she'd had her lawyer spell out the agreement in the contract she'd signed. "If I increase the profit margins by thirty percent, we retain majority ownership, which means we make the decisions. We keep our brand." And hopefully, she would eventually be able to buy out Kingston's share and send them packing.

"Lei . . ." His shoulders slumped. "Thirty percent is a lot—"

"It doesn't matter," she interrupted before he could tell her how absurd this agreement was. "I will make this work. I will increase the profits and I will save this place for my grandparents." She didn't give him a chance to argue. "I won't rely on some big budget to do an event. Everyone loves my grandparents. I'm sure the town will help me pull this together." And she would do it with or without August's help.

"Fine." August's eyes had dulled. "Then what do you want me to do?"

"You can call around to some rental companies and get some large canopy tents donated. Tell them we'll advertise their business so it's a win-win." As much as it killed her to be with him— to spend time alone with him—he'd promised to help, and she had to let him. "I'll work on an e-mail to our wine club members.

We'll have to get that out ASAP. And then I'll meet with Sam and our chef about a menu." The one good thing about this event was that they'd likely both be so busy no one would wonder why they weren't going on dates and spending late mornings together in her cottage. That would make it much easier to hide their secret.

"Sounds like a plan. If you'll focus on the food and the communication, I can work out lodging specials with businesses in town too." He typed something into his phone before looking up at her.

Her heart swelled. That look right there. He'd given it to her before. Anytime he'd been proud of her or impressed by her.

"You're right, Lei," he murmured. "This town loves your family. I'm sure everyone will pull together to help."

For the first time in months, hope lifted her heart. This was what she'd been missing. A big enough base of support. But if this event worked, she could prove to Forrest they had a strong enough backing to survive. "I'll start on the invitation." She sat down at her desk and clicked around on the computer to run a merge of e-mail addresses for anyone who'd joined their mailing list or stopped in for a tasting. "What should our theme be?"

When August didn't answer right away, she looked up and found him sitting in the chair near her desk again. Another memorable expression on his face stilled her hands.

This was how he used to look at her right before he'd kiss her—eyes darkened and slightly narrowed, lips parted with a hint of a smile that made her tingle with anticipation. God, when he'd kissed her back then, it had been like the whole world had faded around them.

"Reunion. That should be the theme." His smile grew. "Do you remember that project we did together for our marketing class your junior year?"

She hadn't meant to look into his eyes, to lean forward slightly, but now it was too late to protect her heart from the inevitable free fall.

"We had to think up a product and come up with a marketing

plan," he went on as though he really believed she might've forgotten. "You convinced me to help you design a new and improved bra."

"Hey, that was the best idea in the class." She had to laugh too. For their product, they'd taken one of her regular bras and one of her sports bras and patched them together to create the ultimate Hybrid Deluxe 2000 Bra. "You know why we won the contest, don't you?" she asked. "Because you modeled the bra for the whole school." After his modeling debut, every girl in their school said she would buy the bra. "It was a brilliant marketing strategy."

August shrugged off the praise. "We made a good team."

"I still can't believe you wore that bra on the outside of your shirt all day." She laughed again, remembering how he'd even kept it on during their gym class. He'd had the whole school talking about their product within an hour. "That was a gutsy move."

"I would've done anything for you, Leila."

The sincerity in his tone immediately changed the air between them, chasing away her levity, her smile. This was dangerous territory—remembering their best moments, staring into each other's eyes, sitting close enough that the chemistry crackled between them. "Um...we should...I need to work on the e-mail," she stammered, gluing her gaze back to the laptop. "There really isn't much time to make plans, and we need a good turnout. We should let people know about the event as soon as—"

The door opened, mercifully cutting off her stumbling words.

"Nonna!" Leila popped out of her chair. "Good morning." She realized she sounded overly happy to see her grandmother, but she couldn't help it. Alone time with August had proven to be a problem. "How are you?" She hurried to the coffee pot to pour her grandmother a cup. When she turned around to present the coffee to her, Nonna shot her a quizzical look.

"I'm fine. Is everything all right with you?"

"Wonderful." Leila handed her the mug. "Never been better. August and I are working on a big event to grow the wine club."

She rushed back to her desk and managed to get settled again without looking at the man once.

"That's a marvelous idea." Her grandmother sat in a chair next to August. "I can't wait to hear more about it. But first, I was hoping you two could come with me to the AppleFest in town today. We signed up to host a booth for a few hours."

"The what fest?" Instead of simmering like they had been moments before, August's eyes were full of confusion.

Leila laughed. She couldn't keep all the small-town celebrations straight either. There was always some festival going on around Silverado Lake.

"The AppleFest." Her grandmother laid a pamphlet on the desk. "It's a pre-harvest celebration for the orchards, and it's such a wonderful time. We like to go support them and chat with anyone who might be interested in the winery. I'm sure I mentioned it to you, Leila."

She probably had, but Leila had been preoccupied with other things lately.

"Oh, right. I did hear something about the AppleFest," August said. "My brother and Thea are taking the kids."

Yet another reason she and August should stay far away. The whole town would be there. Nonna would make sure to spread news of the wedding like a wildfire. "Isn't Poppa going to help you?" She made sure to tap her fingers across her keyboard and look very busy. "This event is going to take a lot of planning—"

Her grandmother scoffed. "Poppa and Sam are busy obsessing over when to start the harvest. But I would love to attend with both of you." She smiled sweetly. "Nothing would make me happier. It would be the perfect chance for you two to do some networking for the winery anyway."

"I don't know..." The last thing she wanted to do right now was make a public appearance with her fake fiancé. But she'd always hated disappointing her grandmother. "We have a lot of work to do here."

"You'll always have a lot of work to do here," Nonna said

sternly. "That's something you two are going to have to balance when you run this place together. There will always be work, but sometimes you have to put it aside to focus on each other. You have to go looking for the fun moments. The moments of togetherness and reprieve. You have to protect your love at all costs, or you will lose it."

Their love had already been lost, but she couldn't tell her grandmother that.

August gazed at her, obviously putting the final decision in her hands.

"We'll only be gone a few hours." Nonna rose from her chair as though they'd already agreed. "And besides, it might be a good chance to start getting the word out about this event you two are planning."

Still, August held off on responding, letting her decide.

What choice did she have? "Okay. Sure. We'll go." But if August looked at her the way he had five minutes ago, she would have to find a way to escape.

Chapter Seven

August loaded the folding table and small portable canopy into the back of his truck and shut the tailgate.

Eyeing the office door, he checked the time on his phone. They were already running late. Nonna said setup for the booths was supposed to be done by eight thirty, but Leila seemed to be stalling. He couldn't tell what she dreaded more—spending time with him or making their first public appearance in town as a couple.

Damn, he kept messing things up. He hadn't meant to bring up the past again, but when he let himself think back to the time they'd shared, his guard came down, and he started confessing things like *I would've done anything for you.*

The statement couldn't have been more honest. Back then, he'd lived to make her smile, to make her happy, to cheer her up, to be her best friend. But that didn't mean Leila wanted to hear those words from him now. They had lost all credibility around her, and the last thing he wanted to do was make her uncomfortable. That meant he had to get a handle on those unguarded moments and stop getting swept into the past.

Leila and Nonna finally emerged from the office, each carrying a small box.

"Look at what my talented granddaughter came up with for the invitation." Nonna held out the box for him to see. "We were only able to print a hundred before we ran out of ink, but I think it's a good start."

"It looks amazing." Especially for less than a half hour of work. But then, Leila had always had that unique blend of practical business smarts and creativity. He studied the card's intricate scrolled design.

You're invited to a family reunion, the invitation began before going into more details about the event.

"I love it. That's the perfect message to send."

"It was your idea," she muttered before stepping past him and climbing into the truck's passenger's seat.

Chuckling, Nonna leaned in and whispered, "Did you two get enough sleep last night? She seems a little cranky today."

Back in the day, he'd definitely been the reason Leila missed out on a full night's sleep. One of their favorite things had been sneaking out to camp under the stars. But Leila had never been cranky the next morning—at least not with him. She'd been sleepy and smiley and content. These days, though, he did seem to make her cranky.

"She's probably stressed about the event." He opened the back door of his extended cab and helped her climb in.

"Being stressed is all the more reason for you two to take a break this morning," Nonna said when he got into the truck. "Whenever I feel the stress of running this place, I always go into town so I can remember why I'm here. To be part of a community. To bring joy to people. There's more to running a business than managing the details."

"Very true." August started the engine and drove them down the winding road, turning up the radio to take the edge off his pretend fiancée's silence.

The music didn't stop Nonna. "It must be such a treat for you two to be back in Silverado Lake together. Reliving all the memories you two made here."

"Mmm-hmm," August murmured. The memories they were

both trying so hard to avoid. He turned the music up and hummed along to Alan Jackson, with Nonna joining him for a few bars. But the reprieve didn't last long. Once on the outskirts of town, she started in again.

"I still remember that incredible date you took Leila on your senior year." Nonna leaned over the seat. "Remember, sweetie? You told me all about how he took you on that hike to the waterfall and made you a picnic?"

Leila didn't turn around. "Yep. I remember."

"You told me it was the best night of your life," her grandmother said wistfully. "And now here you are with so many best nights ahead of you."

August snuck a peek at Leila's face. Her jaw had gone rigid.

"There won't be much time for extravagant dates in the next few months," she said, her gaze directed out the window. "There's too much work to be done."

"We'll see about that." Nonna harrumphed with a nudge into August's shoulder. "Auggie is too much of a romantic to let you become a workaholic."

"Wow, what do you know. We're already at the park." He pulled the truck into a spot near the grassy area where people were setting up their canopies and booths. "You two show me where you want to set up, and I'll get everything unloaded."

He quickly got out of the truck and opened Nonna's door for her, giving her a hand to climb out. Before he could make it to Leila's side, she'd already hopped down herself. "We should set up near the pavilion." She walked past him. "I can help you unload."

"Sounds good." He pulled down the tailgate.

While Nonna directed, he and Leila unloaded the table and then the tent, their supplies, and the handouts. The work kept them both busy, maneuvering around each other, maintaining a healthy distance. When they were finishing the setup, his sister's friend Beth came running over.

"August! Leila! Congratulations, you two!" She gave them

both hugs. "I heard about your engagement at the café, but Jane won't say a word about the details."

"Well, you know... we're taking things slowly." Leila started to smooth a white cloth over the table.

"*Slowly*?" Beth laughed. "No one even knew you were back together, and now you're engaged! Don't get me wrong. I couldn't be happier for you. Married life is amazing. Such an adventure!"

"I'm sure it is." August moved to the other side of the table and helped Leila straighten the winery's branded poster on an easel.

Beth had gotten married almost two years ago. Her wedding was what had brought Jane and Toby together. He still envied both of his siblings for how they'd seemed to have gotten past their issues to find happiness with the ones they loved.

"When's the big day?" Beth asked, still hanging around.

"Oh, we're not sure." His pretend fiancée unpacked a stack of the invitations and arranged them on the table. "There's no hurry."

August wondered if Beth knew Leila well enough to read her the way he could. Right now, Lei's shoulders were tense, her eyes were downcast, and her movements stiff. She didn't like lying any more than he did. Especially to friends and family.

"Well, be sure to let me know." Clearly, the woman hadn't picked up on Leila's discomfort. "The café would be happy to help cater if you're planning the wedding here, which I assume you are."

"Actually, we might elope." August stepped in between the two women to give Leila a reprieve.

"Seriously?" Beth gasped. "How romantic! If I had it to do over again, I would elope too. Weddings are great and all, but there's a lot of stress."

"Exactly." August glanced at his fiancée—pretend fiancée—who had stopped organizing things to watch him. "Why go through all of that planning and ritual when you could just sneak away to a beach together? Isn't that the best part about getting married anyway? Being together?"

"It totally is," Beth agreed solemnly. "Oops...I'd better get back to my booth. See you two later!"

As the woman jogged away, Leila approached him. "You would want to elope if we were really getting married?"

"Heck, yeah. It shouldn't be some big performance." He could admit, Jane and Toby's wedding was fun, but putting on a big show was mainly for everyone else. "I'd invite my siblings and Mom, of course. But I wouldn't be interested in orchestrating some big spectacle for an audience." For once, he couldn't tell what she was thinking. "I mean, I would be open to doing whatever my fiancée wanted, but the most important thing to me would be time together to focus on the marriage."

She said nothing, but her lips curved in a small smile.

"Uncle Auggie!" Ryan bolted to the table, the rest of his family following at a much slower pace. "Did you see the bumper cars set up over there?" The boy pointed to the sport courts on the opposite end of the park. "My mom and dad said I can go later! Maybe you can go with me! I'm a really great driver!"

"I'd love to." He reached around the kid to shake his brother's hand and greet Thea and Olivia. "Good to see you guys."

"You too." Wes looked back and forth between him and Leila. "How are things going?"

That was a loaded question if August had ever heard one.

"Things are great." Leila unpacked another box full of Valentino Bellas swag. "We have a lot of good things coming up at the winery. In fact, I have the perfect job for you, Ryan." She handed him a stack of invitations. "I need you to help me hand these out to everyone who'll take one. Think you can do that?"

"You bet!" Ryan read the card out loud. "Oh, you're having a party! I'm super good at inviting people to parties!"

"I'm happy to help too." Olivia took a stack as well.

"I'll walk with you." Thea followed Leila and the kids out of the tent and the four of them hurried away chatting.

"Are things really going great?" his brother asked, hands posted to his hips.

August was too busy watching Leila to answer. She'd stopped at a booth across the way and was talking with a man he'd never seen before. The guy said something to make her laugh—her real laugh—the one he'd only heard fleeting glimpses of earlier that morning when they were reminiscing. "Who is that guy?"

Wes turned his head in the direction August was staring. "Oh. That's Blake Riordian. He's the dentist in town. Moved here a few years ago."

"Interesting." August continued to watch the two of them interact. The man kept touching Leila's arm. "Do they know each other?"

"Yeah, I've seen them hang out." Wes turned back to him. "There were rumors they dated for a while, but I don't know details." His brother was sporting an amused grin. "Is that a problem?"

"No. Not for me." The heat churning through his gut begged to differ. "But she's supposed to be engaged and she's over there flirting with that guy in front of the whole town." Okay, that was overkill. He knew that even without having to witness his brother's *Are you serious right now?* glare. The whole town wasn't here *yet,* but they would be eventually.

"What're you doing, Auggie?" Wes's question held a familiar challenge. His brother was about to call him out.

"I'm doing my job." He started to unpack the box of stemless wineglasses they'd brought to give away so he wouldn't have to watch Leila laugh with a man she clearly enjoyed *or* look at his brother's knowing expression.

"You sure that's all this is? A job?" Wes shut the lid on the box, stopping his busywork.

"What do you want me to say?" His voice lowered to a growl. "I screwed everything up." He'd never had to face how badly he'd screwed up because he hadn't been home long enough to see the collateral damage his decisions had left behind. Now he had no choice but to face the pain he'd caused her. Not to mention his own family. "All I want to do now is help her. I want to help her family hold onto Valentino Bellas. I owe this to her."

Wes cocked his head to the side. "So, if it's only guilt from the past driving you, why do you care if she's flirting with some other guy?"

"I *don't* care." That was what he'd keep telling himself and everyone else. He'd lost the right to care. August turned his back and opened another box. "It doesn't look good, that's all."

"Well, you might want to stop focusing so much on how things look and start thinking about how you want things to be."

He deflected his brother's pitying look with a glare.

"Speaking as someone who somehow got lucky enough to get a second chance after royally screwing things up...you can't make the same mistake twice. If you're lucky enough to get a second chance with the person you love, you make the most of it."

Wes didn't get it. There wouldn't be a second chance for him. He wouldn't go there, no matter how he felt about Leila. He'd already learned that loving someone and losing them hurt too much.

"Whatever ship Leila and I were on at one time has sailed. Trust me." He had to stay focused on his mission here—make the winery profitable so he'd get his promotion, and also help Leila stay involved in the operation. Once he'd accomplished that, he could go back to California and stop traveling wherever his boss wanted to send him on a whim. He could actually put down roots, hang some pictures on the walls of his house. Maybe he would even build a stable and purchase some horses.

"Hey, Uncle Auggie!" Ryan waved him in the direction of the bumper cars. "I'm done handing out my invitations! Can we ride now?"

"I don't know, buddy. I should probably stay here and help with the booth." He dug the last stack of pamphlets out of the box and set them on the table.

"Nonsense." Nonna rushed over from where she'd been chatting with her friend. "I'd like the first shift at the table. You and Leila should take Ryan to the bumper cars. Have a little fun."

"Yes!" The boy grabbed August's hand and dragged him to the

booth, where Leila stood telling someone about the event. "Nonna says we have to have some fun," Ryan informed her, taking her free hand too.

"Oh." Lei held out the stack of invitations she still had in her other hand. "I haven't given all mine away yet—"

"I'll take care of those." Wes swiped them from her with a grin. "You three have fun."

"We will!" Ryan promised, pulling on both his and Leila's hands.

"I can't remember the last time I rode bumper cars." Leila eyed the contraptions warily. "Maybe I'll watch."

"Watching's no fun." Ryan dug in his pocket and handed them each a ticket. He'd come prepared.

"He has a point," August offered. Riding bumper cars together was the perfect way to lighten things up. Maybe it would remind them how to act as friends. "But you'd better watch out for Lei here." He made a scared face at Ryan. "She's quite the fast, reckless driver when it comes to bumper cars."

"That's right." Her eyes narrowed, but she smiled too. "I think I beat you pretty bad in the bumper cars one time."

"At the Independence Day carnival," he confirmed. "I couldn't even keep up with you."

"Well, you're not going to beat me!" Ryan handed his ticket to the attendant and raced in through the gate, selecting a blue car as his weapon of choice.

Still smiling, Leila followed him. "This silver one looks pretty fast."

"And I'll take the orange one." August climbed into the car next to her. He couldn't get enough of that smile on her face. It made her eyes come alive. "Go easy on me. It's been a while since I've driven one of these."

The sound of her laughter made his heart pound.

"All right, everyone. Start your engines!" The attendant moved to the other side of the gate.

August turned the key, and next to him Lei revved her engine.

"Come on, Ryan. Let's get him!" Leila crashed into August's left side while Ryan came from the right, giving him a good jolt.

"Yes! We got him!" The boy bumped him again.

"Oh, yeah?" August cranked the wheel left and hit the gas, making them think he was going to retreat. Just when they started the chase, he flipped a U and got them both.

"Ah!" Leila squealed and steered away, crashing into three other people before she came at him again. They collided, right as Ryan hit his bumper.

"We got him again!" The boy leaned over his steering wheel to high-five Lei.

August couldn't help but laugh, and all three of them did so the entire time, getting jolted by the relentless crashes. He couldn't even drive three feet without those two smashing into him. When the attendant told them to turn off their engines, August parked by Lei and helped her out of her car.

"I think I have whiplash," she said with a happy smile.

"You're the best driver ever," Ryan declared, leading them out of the fenced area. "She got you good," he told August.

"She sure did." And it had been worth every jolt to see her laugh like that. He'd never had more fun with anyone than he'd had with Lei.

"Can we get some ice cream now?" the boy begged. "All that crashing made me hungry."

"Why not?" He glanced at Lei. Her eyes sure seemed brighter.

"I'm game." She led them to the ice cream truck parked near the playground.

"I'll have a rocky road cone," Ryan told the woman behind the counter.

"And we'll take a mint chocolate chip and cookies and cream cone too," August added. "Oh, wait." He shouldn't have ordered for Lei. "I mean cookies and cream and whatever she wants."

"You had it right." She gazed up at him almost shyly. "Mint chocolate chip is still my favorite."

"Coming right up." The woman went to work preparing their

ice cream, but August couldn't take his eyes off Lei. He couldn't stop remembering how they'd shared plenty of mint chocolate chip kisses while they'd enjoyed their ice cream.

She stared back at him as though she felt a stirring too.

"Um, Uncle Auggie..." Ryan tapped his shoulder. "You have to pay for the ice cream."

"Right. Yes. Of course." He turned back to the counter and handed over some cash. Probably too much, but he hadn't paid attention when the woman had told him the total. "Keep the change."

"Thank you very much." She handed their cones to him one by one and the three of them walked away together.

"This is deee-licious." Ryan already had an ice cream mustache. "Oh, look! There's Toby. He's roping that pretend steer. I gotta go see!" The boy bounded off, leaving him and Lei alone.

August couldn't resist indulging in the memory of sharing a mint chocolate chip ice cream cone with her in his truck after a football game his senior year. The ice cream had been melting fast, and some had dripped down Leila's chin and neck. He'd licked the sticky sweetness from her skin while she'd moaned with pleasure.

"I remember that night," Lei murmured, holding his gaze as she licked her ice cream.

/ Busted. She knew exactly what he'd been thinking. "That was a good night." Thanks to the melting mint chocolate chip ice cream, they'd ended up making out in his truck for an hour.

"We had a lot of good nights."

Was he imagining things, or had her voice dropped lower?

"We did." What he wouldn't give to spend one more night with her. As much as he tried to deny his feelings, he couldn't ignore the yearning simmering low in his belly. Only one woman had ever made him this hot.

Leila's shoulders rose and fell with her breaths. "We should get back to the table to help Nonna," she half whispered.

"Yes. That would be best." Before he gave in to temptation and licked that drip of ice cream off her chin.

Chapter Eight

See? I told you the AppleFest would be a great place to network." Nonna watched the group of tourists walk away from their table with a delighted smile. "That's six more people we've managed to sign up for our event." She checked the list she'd scrawled out on the clipboard notepad she'd brought to collect sign-ups for their newsletter list.

Her grandmother had always loved to write lists.

"We're up to thirty-five people who've already RSVP'd today alone!" She showed her the clipboard, sporting a *told you so* grin.

Leila had to admit, that was about twenty more people than she'd thought they'd be able to sign up in two hours of standing at an event. "I've already gotten six responses back from the invitation I e-mailed out earlier too." She checked her phone again, still shaky from the encounter she'd had with August an hour ago. "Make that seven. So that brings our total guests up to forty-eight." They had a lot of good momentum going. This event might actually work. "I also talked to Blake. His cousin is a country-western singer, and he's happy to donate a few hours of his time for the cause."

"Wonderful! Wouldn't you know it? August has only been

here for a week, and things are already looking up." Her grandmother gazed across the park to where her fake fiancé was
playing a carnival game with Ryan while Thea snapped pictures
on her phone.

"That man is something else," Nonna murmured.

"Yes, he is." As much as she wanted to avoid looking at August,
Leila let her gaze drift back to him again. She'd had a difficult
time looking anywhere else all morning. After reminiscing about
mint chocolate chip ice cream, they'd worked side by side, chatting with AppleFest patrons about the winery and their upcoming
event. August had likely secured 99 percent of the sign-ups for
their event with his charm and charisma. The only people she'd
signed up were Nonna and Poppa's dearest friends, who lived in
Denver but had a summer house in Silverado Lake and would've
come anyway.

"August has such a way with people," her grandmother mused.

Yes, especially with children. Leila watched the man laugh
with Ryan while they fished small toys out of a baby pool. The
boy obviously loved spending time with his uncle Auggie. It was
a side of him she'd never gotten to see before. "I didn't know
he was good with kids." In high school, he had been good with
everyone, but they hadn't exactly spent a lot of time with young
children.

"He'll make a wonderful father someday." Nonna slipped her
arm around Leila's waist with an excited squeal. "You two have
had a rough road, but you already know the most important part
of any relationship."

Leila stared at her grandmother, mind racing. She didn't. She
didn't know anything about building a solid relationship.

"Forgiveness," Nonna said gently. "Learning how to forgive the
one you love is all you need." She squeezed Leila's waist in her
loving way. "If you can forgive, you can be together forever."

Leila stared at August and Ryan again, a darkness descending
over her heart. She hadn't forgiven the man for walking away,
no matter how sad his circumstances had been back then. If he'd

talked to her—if he would've let her in—she would've been there for him.

"You will both make many mistakes," her grandmother went on. "Just like Poppa and I have. But with forgiveness, you can overcome anything."

But how do you forgive someone for breaking your heart? she wanted to ask. How could she forgive him for taking away her belief in love?

Across the park, Ryan and August's turn at the baby pool ended. They high-fived and raced each other to another game set up near the parking lot.

"Oh, look!" Nonna hurried away. "It's Jenny Spokes. She hasn't heard about your engagement yet!"

That was surprising because her grandmother had told pretty much everyone who had walked past the booth about the up-coming wedding that wasn't to be. Leila hung back while Nonna greeted yet another friend with the happy news. Just when she thought her heart couldn't get any heavier. This whole facade had been a mistake. She never should've—

"Hey, Leila."

She turned her head toward the familiar voice. "Jane." August's sister walked under the tent, pushing her daughter in a stroller. "Hi." Leila cleared her throat so her voice wouldn't sound so awkward. She'd been close to August's sister back when they were dating, but the women had lost touch since then. She'd only run into her a couple of times in town since moving back, but not since getting fake-engaged to her brother. "How are you?"

"We've been good." Jane knelt and lifted Charlee out of the stroller, setting her on the ground so she could toddle around.

Geez, the girl was a cutie—a halo of blond curls and round, expressive blue eyes.

"How about you?" Jane's gaze followed her daughter everywhere she went.

Leila wasn't sure how to answer that question. August's sister knew about their arrangement, so it wasn't like she had to pretend.

Nevertheless, she also didn't need to burden the woman with the long list of her current predicaments, so it was time to change the subject. "Wow, Charlee is getting big."

"I know." Jane snatched the winery's brochure out of Charlee's hand just before the girl took a bite out of it. "She's walking all over the place. And she's into *everything*."

"I can imagine." Leila had to smile, watching the girl glance at all the swag on their table with wide-eyed curiosity. "Here." She picked up one of the foam cup cozies with their logo and handed it to Charlee. "Totally toddler proof."

The girl happily took it, babbling her thanks before she stuck it right into her mouth.

"Perfect." Jane laughed. "That ought to keep her busy for a while." She swung Charlee up into her arms and held her on her hip. "So, you didn't answer my question. You doing okay?"

"Sure." Leila focused on the toddler so she didn't have look into Jane's eyes. August's sister had initially been there in the aftermath of her brother's abandonment. She'd even apologized on his behalf once, telling Leila she knew her brother would eventually get it together and come back. Neither one of them had thought it might happen more than a decade later.

After a quick glance around, the woman leaned closer. "Auggie told me about your arrangement. It has to be hard pretending, after everything that happened with you two."

The woman didn't know the half of it. "Yeah." She finally raised her eyes to Jane's. "I obviously didn't think this whole thing through." They hadn't even made it a full week without her falling into the past. If she had spent five more minutes with him and her mint chocolate chip ice cream cone, she might very well have kissed him right in front of Ryan. Every time she saw a glimpse of who he used to be—of how they used to be together— she was tempted to forget the way he'd abandoned her. How was she supposed to keep this up for a few more months?

"Maybe it'll be good." The woman switched Charlee to her other hip. "I know things ended badly between you, but August has

changed a lot since back then. I mean, look at him." She gestured
to where Auggie and Ryan stood at the archery display, shooting
arrows at a target. "I never thought of him as a family type of guy,
but he's seriously the best uncle. The kids love him."

Nope. This was exactly what would get her into trouble with
August—focusing on his good qualities, watching him have fun
with Ryan. Eating ice cream with him. "I thought I was over what
happened all those years ago." It had taken a long time, but she'd
managed to stop thinking about August altogether. And then he'd
come back. "I should be over it." She shouldn't have such a hard
time looking at him, spending time with him.

"I'm not sure how you ever get over someone you truly love."
Jane's tone held both sympathy and understanding.

"I did love him." She might have only been in high school, but
she had given her whole heart to Auggie. And she'd never quite
recovered it.

"I know you did." Jane lowered Charlee back into her stroller.
The girl still seemed content to sit and gnaw on the cup cozy. "I
know this might not help, but I really believe he loved you too,"
the woman said quietly. "In his way, he's trying to make up for
how things went."

Was he? Or was he here only for the benefit of his career?
"Thanks." She didn't know what else to say.

"I'm here if you ever need to talk or anything." Jane's smile
turned snarky. "Or if you want me to put him in his place. You let
me know."

A laugh lightened her mood. "I might have to take you up
on that."

"Anytime. I'm happy to get in his face." Jane waved at Toby,
who was now talking to August and Ryan near the games. "I'd
better go find Miss Charlee some real food before she has a melt-
down. But let's get together soon."

"I'd like that." Leila hadn't had a lot of time to do anything other
than work and take care of Nonna over the last several months.

"Give me a call," Jane said as she walked away.

"I will." Maybe after the event. It would be nice to rekindle some of her connections in town, to put down roots again. She could use a friend to help her get through these next few months. Especially a friend as nonjudgmental as Jane.

"Looks like you could use some fun." Blake approached from the table he'd set up to promote his dental office a few booths down. He didn't appear to be a typical dentist—at least not the dentists she'd experienced. The man had a friendly white smile, naturally, but he was also casual, usually wearing jeans and a T-shirt when he wasn't dressed in his scrubs. He wore his black hair longer and had an overall rock-and-roll vibe about him. Or maybe she simply thought of him as a rock-and-roll guy because he played the classic rock station in his office.

"I meant to ask you this earlier. How'd you manage to get the whole morning off?" she asked, returning his friendly smile. His practice was always completely booked. She'd had an appointment with him not long after moving back, and he'd immediately put her phobia of dentists to rest with his humor and approachable smile. When he'd asked her out the next day, calling the winery, she'd accepted, wondering if maybe she could finally manage to fall in love with someone else after August. But after a few dates, she'd told him she only wanted to be friends. And he had been a friend, namely texting her to check in after her grandmother's treatments and dropping off meals when they came back from appointments in Denver.

"Don't tell anyone I'm still here." His eyes scanned the crowds. "I really should get back to the office, but I was thinking about trying out some of the carnival games over there first. Care to join me?"

"I don't know..." There weren't as many people milling around the promotional booths now. Everyone either seemed to be playing games or enjoying the treats from the various food trucks and stands. Besides, if Leila wanted to find more people to invite to the event, her best bet would be to head over to where the fun was happening. "I guess I could take another break. For a few minutes, anyway."

She checked on Nonna, who was now surrounded by a cluster of Silverado Lake's quilting club members a few feet away from their booth—most likely discussing what Leila and August's wedding quilt should look like. "Let's go." Right now, before they started asking her about patterns and fabrics. "I would love to play some games."

"Maybe I'll win you one of those stuffed unicorns." Blake held out an arm like a true gentleman. He might be a rock-and-roll guy, but he also had this chivalrous quality about him. Like when he offered his hand to help her up out of the dreaded dental chair, and always stepped aside to let her go into the hallway first. He would make a great partner for someone. If only she had been more attracted to him.

"Where should we start?" he asked as they passed by the bottle ring toss. "I used to be a pitcher in high school, but throwing is about my only skill."

"What about the balloon dart game?" She led him across the grassy corridor to a small tent with no line. "If you're good at throwing, you can win me the unicorn." Then she could go give the stuffed animal to little Charlee.

"Darts." Blake nodded and grinned. "Sure. I like your style." Together, they approached the small wall of balloons that the local newspaper staff had secured to a board.

"Here you go." The young girl working the game handed Blake six darts. "If you get six in a row you get the grand prize." She stepped back out of the way.

"We want the unicorn." Blake stood behind the line they'd marked off in the grass and closed one eye, holding up the dart as though aiming. "Here goes nothing." He let the dart fly and it struck a red balloon with a loud pop.

"That's one," the girl called.

"Five more to go." Leila gave him an encouraging pat on the shoulder. "You've got this."

"I hope I've got this." He seemed to set his aim again, and then one after another he popped five more balloons in a row.

"Woo-hoo!" She cheered him on from the sidelines while the girl pulled the unicorn down from a shelf behind her.

"Here you go, my lady." Blake handed it to Leila with a bow. "One stuffed unicorn."

"Thank you. Charlee will love—"

"Hey." August marched between her and Blake, eyeing the unicorn. "I've been looking for you."

"Oh." Really? He had? Not ten minutes ago, the man had been completely occupied with Ryan. "What do you need?"

Instead of offering her an answer, August faced Blake. "I'm August Harding. Leila's fiancé."

For a second, she was too stunned to speak. What the hell was he doing? He'd come all the way over here just to let the man know he had some claim on her? That wasn't like August at all. At least, not the August she used to know. She'd had a lot of male friends and even hung out with them when they'd been dating, and he'd never acted jealous.

"Fiancé?" Blake looked to her for an explanation. "Wow. I saw you two hanging out earlier, but I had no idea you were even dating anyone."

"Oh. Yeah." She hadn't been, she wanted to tell him. Not until a week ago when she'd suddenly gotten herself engaged. "Uh . . . sorry. I guess it never came up." Suddenly, she noticed the stares starting to come from all around them.

"Right." Blake started to back away, as though he didn't want August to get the wrong idea about them. "Well, congratulations, you two. I should get back to my booth."

Leila's face burned. "Blake, wait. I'm sorry I never said anything." He probably wondered why she'd held out on him when he was constantly entertaining her with stories about the women he dated.

"No worries." He waved her off. "We should get together for coffee soon, though." His raised eyebrows told her she had a lot of explaining to do.

"Right. For sure." Why did her voice suddenly waver? She hadn't thought twice about playing a game with the man, and yet here August stood, his shoulders as rigid as the expression on his face.

The few people who'd stopped to watch them shuffled on past, but for some reason, it still felt like all eyes were on her and her fake fiancé.

Mortification transformed into anger, and Leila quickly turned on her heel and marched away from the balloon dart game, her feet blazing a trail toward the parking lot. She wasn't about to make a scene in front of everyone like August had.

"Where are you going?" he demanded behind her.

She kept walking. "I'm going to put my unicorn into the truck so I don't have to carry it around." She needed another break, a second to hide from the eyes, the excited squeals from her grandmother's friends. She would have to give Charlee her present later. Right now, she had to get away from the man who was currently following her so she didn't yell at him in front of the whole town.

Thankfully, no one had congregated in the parking lot. Leila made it to the truck and tossed the unicorn into the back, barely acknowledging the beeps as August used his key fob to unlock the vehicle's doors. When she turned around, he stood directly in front of her.

"What the hell was that about?" Forget not making a scene. He'd totally embarrassed her in front of Blake and whoever else had been watching. "That man happens to be my friend, thank you very much. Which is more than I can say for you."

"You almost blew our cover," August shot back. "What if your grandmother saw you flirting with that guy? What would she think?"

"Flirting?" Leila laughed. If that was flirting, she was in big trouble. "We weren't flirting. We were talking." August had no clue about her relationship with Blake. "I was watching him play a game so he could win me a unicorn that I could give to your niece. Last time I checked, it wasn't against anyone's vows to have a conversation with a *friend*." But August's shoulders remained rigid, and anger flashed in his eyes. "It's not like I was cheating on you," she whispered loudly. "We're not really engaged."

"I know." He blew out a sigh and seemed to wilt right in front of her. "You're right. Sorry. I didn't mean to embarrass you." August planted his hand against the top of his extended cab and stared at the ground. "We're not together. Not really."

"Then why?" She watched him carefully. "Why did seeing me have fun with Blake bother you?"

"God, Lei." He dragged his tortured gaze up to hers and stole the breath from her lungs with a single look. "Being with you, I forget. I forget that I screwed everything up. I forget things aren't the way they used to be. I take one look at you and—" His jaw seemed to lock.

"And what?" she croaked, unable to look away.

It felt like it took him a year to answer. Maybe longer. Her heart beat mercilessly against her ribs, punishing her with a growing ache.

"And I remember why I loved you so damn much," he finally uttered.

She remembered too. Not *why* he'd loved her, but *how*. As much as she wanted to forget, she remembered how he'd always looked deeply into her eyes for so long before he would kiss her. She remembered how his hand would always find hers and hold on—no matter if they were sitting in their art class or walking in the vineyard together. She remembered how he would sing the perfect song to her, whether she was happy or sad or in need of cheering up. In those moments, she'd never felt more loved by anyone ever.

"I have no right to want you." He said the words almost to himself, as though trying to make them sink in.

He did, though. He wanted her. She could read the want in his eyes, and that tormented look made tenderness bloom in her heart again.

Leila had no idea when she'd ended up so close to him, but as she clutched a fistful of his shirt in her hand, she didn't know if she wanted to push him away or pull him closer. Her heart was flying away from her now, bringing her outside of herself. Only one man had ever made it beat like this—frantically, out of control.

"I have no right to want you." August spoke the words with more force this time, but that tone only made her blood rush faster. She could no longer make a sound decision, so she pulled on his shirt, bringing him close, standing on her tiptoes so she could touch her lips to his.

The shock of that small brush of a kiss nearly knocked her back. But August's arms came around her, steady and sure. He eased her back against his truck and caressed her lips with his, luring her into the same rhythm they'd perfected long ago.

Leila inhaled him, the spice and pine, as she tasted the mint on his tongue from the wintergreen gum he'd always liked, so familiar and yet somehow all new too. Every kiss they'd shared was still branded into her heart, but this was not a boyish August. There was an urgency behind the kiss that hadn't been there when they'd been kids messing around.

These were a man's lips, firm against hers, insistent and teasing too.

Leila locked her hands at the small of his back, bringing him closer than she dared, and melted into him. Kissing August was like walking into a warm, cozy room after being out in the bitter cold for too long. Relief enveloped her, somehow grounding her and making her float at the same time.

"Ahem."

The sound of a hearty throat-clearing tore them apart. Leila opened her eyes, but it took forever for the world come back into focus. When she could finally see past the blinding rush, she noticed Jane standing a few feet away with Toby and Charlee.

"Sorry for interrupting," August's sister said with more than hint of amusement. "We're heading home, and Charlee wanted to say good-bye to her uncle."

August didn't even turn his head toward his sister's voice. Instead, he continued to stare into Leila's eyes. "Good-bye, Charlee. See you later."

Jane laughed. "Ha. You don't see her at all right now. But that's more than fine. You two carry on."

Leila heard the stroller moving, the wheels scraping the asphalt, but she would have to give Charlee the unicorn another time. Right now, she couldn't step away. She couldn't think. She couldn't breathe.

The only thing she could do was kiss August one more time.

Chapter Nine

This shouldn't be happening.

August suppressed the thought with a moan against Leila's sensual mouth. It was only a kiss. One kiss. He usually wasn't a selfish man, but he'd wanted this moment with her. One moment when he could touch her the way he used to, the way he'd craved touching her since he'd walked back into her life.

One more minute. That was all he would take.

He slowed the kiss so he could savor her, so he could remember how she felt against him—curves and softness and strength—before they both came to their senses and pulled away again.

Leila tasted sweet, like the ice cream they'd had earlier. August breathed her in, every sense triggered into a heightened awareness. The rush inside of him intensified, unleashing things he hadn't felt since the last time he'd kissed her. Before his heart had gone dark.

Passion. That was what had been missing from his life. One touch of her lips to his was all it had taken to bring the desires he'd denied roaring back to life.

But kissing Leila was a door he shouldn't have opened. Because he refused to go where this would lead them.

An icy dread spread over him, dousing the fire.

It felt good to kiss her, to hold her against him, but beyond this physical connection, he had nothing to offer her. He couldn't make her think otherwise.

August forced himself back, putting space between them. They stared at each other, both breathing heavily, but he couldn't tell what she was thinking.

"We should probably start packing up the booth." Gravel stuck in his throat. They should go back to the park before he kissed her again and lost the will to stop.

Leila blinked at him. "Yes." She awkwardly dodged around him and darted away without another word or a look back.

August gave her space, clumsily following her at a distance all the way back to the winery's booth.

"There you are!" Nonna greeted them with a beaming smile. "August, I wanted to introduce you to some of my dearest friends." She gestured to a cluster of women standing near the table. "This is Jenny and Bess and Veronica and Glenda and Tasha." She pointed out each woman and he dutifully shook their hands.

"Nice to meet you all." He tried to get a look at Leila's face, but she had turned her back to him.

"It's nice to meet you too." Veronica? Bess? said. "We were talking about your wedding quilt. We have tons of ideas. Maybe you two can come to our next meeting to discuss what you'd like?"

"Oh." A wedding quilt? What the hell was a wedding quilt? "Um—"

"We'll see if we can make it." Leila bumped his shoulder in the direction of the table. "Right now, we need to pack up. It looks like the festival is over, and we have a ton of work to do back at the winery."

"Good idea." August smiled at Nonna's friends and moved to the other side of the table, gathering up the various brochures and swag scattered around and packing it in the boxes. He and Leila moved quickly and efficiently, steering clear of each other, breaking down the folding table and then the tent in record time.

"Is everything okay?" Nonna asked after their second trip back to the truck. "You two were awfully quiet during the cleanup."

"Everything's fine," Leila assured her grandmother, shifting the box in her hands. "There's just a lot going on. Things are a little overwhelming."

And he'd only added to the chaos when he'd gone and spoken his true feelings.

"Well, sure. There is a lot going on," her grandmother agreed. "I understand." She slipped an arm around Leila's waist. "The stress is starting to get to you, sweetie. I can see that. You two need to have a little more fun." After a few more steps, Nonna gasped. "I have the best idea! Why don't you two take the day off together tomorrow? You've been working nonstop ever since you moved home, sweetie."

While Leila started throwing out excuses for why they couldn't take tomorrow off together, August loaded the tent, table, and boxes into the back of his truck, purposely not looking at either of them. He needed to spend less time with Leila, not more. But they were supposed to be engaged. What engaged couple wouldn't take every opportunity they could to steal a day alone together?

"I know the event is coming up soon." When he turned back around, Leila's grandmother gave him a look that clearly begged for his help. "But you can work a few hours in the morning and at least take the afternoon off. Maybe you could go for a trail ride or something. You two used to love doing that."

Nonna sure was persistent; he'd give her that.

"We simply can't take the time." Leila hurried around to the passenger's door and quickly escaped into the truck before Nonna could argue.

That left him standing there, and he'd never been able to tell the woman no to anything. She'd always treated him like a member of their family. How was he supposed to argue with her now? August helped the woman climb into the backseat while Leila settled herself in the front.

"You need to sweep her off her feet on a date tomorrow after-noon, Auggie," Nonna whispered before he shut the door. "She's taken too much on herself these last several months. She deserves to have a break."

What could he say to that? "Sure. Okay." Though he had a feeling going on a date with him was the last thing Leila would want to do after the way he'd ended that kiss so abruptly. She hadn't made eye contact with him since.

He climbed in next to his pretend fiancée, but he might as well have been invisible. Leila kept her gaze glued to her phone screen the whole way back to the winery. When he parked the truck outside the office, she finally looked up, released her seat belt, and quickly climbed out.

"What's her hurry?" Nonna muttered.

"Not sure." August got out of the truck and helped her out of the backseat, and then they met Leila at the tailgate.

"After we unload, I need to meet with our chef about the event," she said briskly. "We'll have to put in an order for the food right away."

August simply nodded at her. She wanted to run from him, and he couldn't blame her. He should've left well enough alone and kept his mouth shut earlier. Then she never would've kissed him, he never would've kissed her back, and he wouldn't have had to stop before things got out of control.

"It's fine," he told her. "You go ahead and meet with the chef. I can unload everything myself." He lowered the tailgate and slid out the canopy.

"Great." Leila had already started across the parking lot to the restaurant. "You can put everything in the office closet."

Yet again, August watched her walk away, and yet again he resisted going after her, pulling her into his arms the way he had earlier.

"I can't figure out what has gotten into her." Nonna raised a single eyebrow and stared at him with that knowing look. "Does it have anything to do with that Blake fella?"

"Oh. Uh. Well…" *Damn.* She must've seen their exchange after he'd confronted Blake.

"Because you know she doesn't have feelings for anyone else, Auggie." Tears misted her lovely gray eyes. "Those two are friends, but she has never had feelings for anyone else, I'm afraid. So, if you're worried—"

"I'm not," he interrupted. He couldn't listen to how much Leila had loved him, how crushed she'd been when he'd failed her. "I'm not worried." He swallowed a tangle of shame. "I've never had feelings for anyone else either." His biggest worry right now was how easily he forgot reality when he spent time with Leila.

"I know you haven't." Leila's grandmother watched her granddaughter disappear in the restaurant. "That's how I know you two will be together forever. You're soul mates."

He wanted to tell her he was too messed up to be anyone's soul mate, but he held his tongue.

Nonna looked at the pile of boxes still in the back of his truck. "If you're sure you can handle this mess, I think I'll go sit in on Leila's meeting. She might need my help with Simon."

"I'm more than sure." He could use a few minutes alone to clear his head too. Kissing Leila had messed with him. Worse yet, it made him want to sweep her away from everything else and kiss her again. And again.

Instead, he hauled the tent into the office and secured it in the closet before going back for the table and then the box of brochures. After everything had been put away, he stepped outside. What was he supposed to do with himself now? He didn't exactly have an official workspace here, though he'd likely have to set one up soon. Today might not be the day, however. He'd already created enough turmoil for Leila. Maybe he should go work at ho—

"August." Poppa waved at him from courtyard in front of the barn. "Just the man I wanted to see." He lumbered over with his arthritic gait.

August met him by the truck. "What can I do for you?"

"Walk with me. In the vineyards." Poppa nodded in the direction of the chardonnays.

Tension hiked up his shoulders. Did he know? Could Poppa know he and Leila were lying to the world? He didn't have the guts to ask. "Uh, sure."

They walked along the edge of the parking lot until he stepped in the dirt, August dragging his feet like a teenager who was about to get busted.

"Crop's finally coming back after those early freezes we had a few years back." Poppa stopped to examine a cluster of the plump green grapes and then plucked one and popped it into his mouth. "We're making plans for the harvest."

So, this was a talk about the grapes? Relaxing, August took a grape and broke it open in his mouth, judging the sweetness and sourness. "I'd say that's about right, from my perspective." The taste was there, though he wasn't an expert on growing grapes in Colorado's unique climate. "I'll help in any way I can."

Poppa nodded, continuing on his way along the vines, shoulders bowed slightly and hands clasped behind his back. He had aged since August had left home. The man moved more slowly and stiffly than he used to, but his eyes still held a spark.

They walked in silence until Poppa paused at the edge of the terrace overlooking the valley. "Look at that." The man shook his head slowly, as though still marveling at the view after all this time. "When we bought this land, I never dreamed this was what it would someday become."

"It's incredible." In his opinion, Valentino Bellas sat on the most beautiful plots of land in Silverado Lake. The acres of vineyards were tucked into the mountainside in terraced rows with wide paths between them. "You've accomplished a lot here." Poppa and Nonna has been on the forefront of wine making in Colorado and could be listed among the industry's pioneers. If they cared to claim that honor. They'd neither cared nor fought for any recognition. For them, wine making, building this business, had been about love. That was a stark contrast to Forrest Kingston.

"We always dreamed this place would be our legacy." Poppa rested a sun-weathered hand on his shoulder. "Not only for our family, but for Silverado Lake. This is a special place, son—the community, the kinship. We've never cared about being fancy. We've only tried to welcome everyone who walked through our doors. I know you and Leila will continue to be part of that when you take over for good."

The permanent knot of guilt sitting in his stomach tripled in size. They would never take over this land together. And he feared Forrest would be the one to eventually change the legacy of Valentino Bellas into something that fit with his brand instead. "Have you thought about selling the winery?" He had to ask the question. If they simply sold to Kingston without being forced to, they could likely retire comfortably. Sam and Leila would have to find other employment, but August could help them both with his connections in the industry.

"Selling?" Poppa turned to face him fully, his forehead furrowed. "We can't sell. We built this place, Nonna and I. We poured our souls into tending these vines, into making the wine." He pointed up at August. "And it's far better wine than you'll find in most of Napa, I can tell you that much."

Poppa had always had an inner fire. It was one of the things August had admired most about him. "It's very good wine." And he didn't say that lightly.

"This place is part of us." The man turned back to the vista before them. "Like the ranch will always be part of you. These acres are full of memories, and there's a deep connection, even if you try to ignore it."

Yes, that connection to the land was partly why he'd stayed away. Coming back had been too painful.

"Nothing brings us more joy than knowing you and Leila will build your lives here the same way we did." Poppa dug in his pocket and pulled out a small square box. "That's why Nonna and I wanted to give you something."

August braced himself, but the guilt continued to roil hot and fast inside of him. He couldn't take anything from them when this wasn't real.

Poppa opened the box and revealed an intricate diamond and sapphire ring. "This was Nonna's engagement ring. She hasn't taken it off her finger for fifty years, but we noticed you and Leila hadn't picked one out yet."

"No, we haven't." Because they weren't engaged. They weren't getting married. They weren't going to continue the Valentino legacy on this land.

August stared at the ring in disbelief. He and Leila should've thought of the ring sooner. They should've found a fake one to put on her finger so this wouldn't happen.

"I know it's probably not as impressive as what you could afford to buy for her." Poppa studied the ring with a fond smile. "But it's a part of our history, and it would sure mean a lot to see it on our girl's finger."

"It's a beautiful ring," he choked out. The stones weren't big, but they didn't need to be. Not with the band's unique engraved detailing design. "But we can't take it." He took a step back. "You two should hold on to the ring. I'm sure Nonna still loves it." He racked his brain for a sounder argument, but nothing came. Offering the ring was a beautiful gesture. How was he supposed to tell the man no?

"Nonnie does still love the ring." Poppa placed the box into his hand and closed August's fingers around it. "That's why she wants Leila to have it. That's why we want you to give it to her. Whenever the time is right. There's no rush. You've both had a lot going on." That spark returned to his eyes. "I have no doubt you'll create the perfect moment to give her such a special gift."

August slipped the box into his pocket, his heart a deadweight in the center of his chest. "I'll do my best."

Chapter Ten

Leila braved a stare into Simon's sharp green eyes. "I'm thinking tapas."

Their head chef deplored appetizers, but in this case, she wasn't sure they had much of a choice. Serving a full sit-down meal would require a lot more resources than they currently had at their disposal, and she didn't intend on asking August to use his spending account. Taking money from Kingston wouldn't do much to prove that Valentino Bellas could survive on its own.

"Tapas is *not* a meal." Simon's chin rose with stubborn disdain. They were seated in the kitchen—she, Nonna, and Simon—surrounded by stainless steel and cooks doing their prep work for the dinner rush.

Back when she'd been a kid, Leila had loved to spend time in here, following Simon around in her apron, ready to jump in and help wash up the vegetables or clean dishes. She'd loved the hustle and bustle of the kitchen—the chaos, the constant noise with pots clanging and steam whooshing around her. Back then, it had felt like an exciting place to be. Now the kitchen was one more thing she had to manage and worry about.

"What about serving our prime rib dinner instead?" The chef

flipped through his famous handwritten notebook. Simon had come to work at Valentino Bellas before computers were a thing, and he still preferred to scrawl all his secret recipes in the book. Likely so no one else would ever be able to decode them.

"Ah. Here we go." He stopped on a page midway through the book. "We could make my roasted garlic parsnip puree and roasted tender-stem broccolini with blue cheese, and a shaved brussels sprouts salad and—"

"Whoa. I think we're getting carried away." After all those years of following Simon around and having him scold her, she still found it difficult to act as the authority figure. "We need something simple. I'm picturing a stand-up mingling reception on the terrace with some hors d'oeuvres…" Which sounded much fancier than tapas. "And a selection of wines specially paired with the flavors."

"That sounds wonderful," Nonna agreed. "People love wine pairings, and I know with your talent, you can come up with the perfect combination of unique and delicious flavors to challenge their palates." Leila's grandmother had always known exactly the right things to say to Simon.

The rigidity in the man's spine immediately dissolved. "I suppose I can prepare some specialty hors d'oeuvres to complement our most popular wines." The man flipped through his book. "Ah. Nut and cheese gougères are always a delight. Oh, and robiola-stuffed figs with pomegranate and—"

"Maybe we should pick four really good appetizers," Leila said before he could get carried away.

"Four?" Simon hopped off his stool in outrage. "No one has an hors d'oeuvres party with only four selections! What if someone is allergic to nuts and can't eat the gougères? Then they would only have three to pick from." Simon crossed his arms and glared at her the way he used to when she would help by "taste-testing" the desserts. He still saw her as a five-year-old who stuck her finger in the frosting.

"We can't have people going away from Valentino Bellas hungry."

And they couldn't afford to feed all these people a full menu. Leila silently begged for Nonna's help.

"Very well." Her grandmother rose regally from her stool. "You can select *five* of your very best hors d'oeuvres for the party."

Simon shot Leila a satisfied smirk, even though that was only one more appetizer than she'd suggested. "Sounds like a good compromise to me. I'll e-mail you a food budget for the event."

Before he could argue about having to follow a budget to order the supplies, Leila walked out of the kitchen and into the restaurant's main dining room.

"You're worried about money." Her grandmother emerged behind her. "How bad are things?"

Rather than turning to face the woman, she gazed out the wall of windows that overlooked the valley. The late-afternoon glow gently caressing the vineyards was almost enough to take the edge off her stress. "Things are pretty tight," she said through a defeated sigh. She hadn't wanted to burden Nonna with any of this, but the challenges they were facing were getting harder to hide. "The restaurant is keeping us afloat, but only barely. I think we're going to have to raise our prices."

"Mimma…" Her grandmother came alongside her and wrapped an arm around her, drawing her close. "Things will work out. You'll see. I know you've taken too much on since you've come home, but we're here to help you. August is here to help now too. Things will be fine."

If only she knew the truth. August could be the person who helped Kingston take everything away from them. Sure, he *said* he was on their side, but Sam was right. He'd been working for Forrest Kingston for years. He was the man's right-hand guy, not to mention a shrewd businessman on his own, from everything she'd read about him.

"We need this event to be a success." A robust wine club meant consistent income—money they could count on. "That's where August said we need to focus."

"Well, then, we'll make sure it's a success." Nonna tugged on her hand until Leila turned around. "All of us together. You're not in this alone. I know you felt the need to become independent and your own woman after losing August the way you did, but you're going to have to let him back in now." Her expression brightened. "You two are getting married. That means you'll share everything, even the burdens you carry."

Leila's heart buckled, causing her determination to waver. She should tell her. Everything. Now. What a relief it would be to—

"Hey, sis." Sam blitzed into the dining room from the kitchen. "I've been looking for you. We have a problem."

"Is it one you can solve yourself?" Because she was maxed out on problems right now.

"Sure, I can solve it myself." Her brother pushed his dark hair out of his eyes. "But not without roughly seven grand."

A real honest-to-goodness giggle slipped out. She was definitely losing it. Did he realize how absurd that request was right now? "We don't have seven grand. There is no seven grand." The high-pitched ring in her voice made the words crack.

Sam disregarded their lack of unlimited funds with a shrug. "Well, our crusher is broken. The motor went out. I've tried fixing it, but we've already been babying the thing along for the last few years, and now it's kaput."

Leila froze where she stood. She couldn't open her mouth, couldn't breathe. Maybe if she stared at him long enough, she would simply melt into the floor.

"Now, now. Nothing to worry about," Nonna insisted. "I'm sure Poppa can fix the crusher. He's fixed that thing at least ten times before."

"We both worked on the motor all morning." Sam still spoke nonchalantly, as though this new issue didn't have the power to break them. "Poppa said he thinks it might be time to replace it."

"Replace it?" The giggle escaped again. It was better than crying. "We. Don't. Have. Seven. Thousand. Dollars." It was simply not there, not even within reach.

Sam shrugged again—easy to do when he wasn't carrying the burdens on his shoulders. "Maybe we should get a loan."

Leila widened her eyes, silently reminding him they couldn't get a loan. With their current financial situation, they wouldn't qualify, and she couldn't take the money from Kingston. Letting Forrest bail them out would only give him ammunition to use against her.

"Have Poppa take a look at the books." Nonna began straightening the settings on a table that had been readied for the dinner hour. "I'm sure he can move some funds around and find the money we need."

Leila watched the woman move a fork to the right angle, and then a spoon, and then a knife. She didn't know. Her grandmother had no idea what they were dealing with because Leila had hidden everything. But a woman in her seventies who'd only recently gotten her life back after cancer treatments shouldn't have to deal with financial woes. Nonna might have gotten clearance on the cancer, but the chemo had taken a toll. She'd become frailer than she used to be, seeming tired all the time. The reason Leila had moved back to Silverado Lake in the first place was so she could make sure her grandparents could enjoy their lives more.

"Sure. Maybe I'll have Poppa look over the books." She managed to put on a smile. "Or I can go over everything again." But she already knew what she would find. "I'll take a look at the crusher too. Maybe there's something I can do to fix it." She'd pretty much performed every role around here at some point, from food server to dishwasher to harvester to payroll clerk. She might as well add mechanic to the job description.

"You're going to fix it?" Sam laughed, but abruptly stopped when her expression darkened.

"If we can't fix it, we'll figure out something," Nonna assured her. If her grandmother had seen the books, she wouldn't have that ring of optimism in her voice.

"I know we will." Leila hugged the woman tightly and reminded herself to count her blessings. After Nonna had been diagnosed with cancer, she hadn't been sure how much longer she would have the woman who'd raised her in her life. That was why she was doing this—that was why she had to save this place. For Nonna. "Come on." She waved her brother out of the dining room. "Let's go have a look at the crusher."

"You can't fix the thing, and we're not going to be able to get by without a crusher." Sam had never learned the art of subtlety. "We actually have a decent crop this year. We can't lose the next few months because of no crusher."

"Then we have no choice but to fix the machine." Leila marched up the hill that led to the wine-making barn, outstriding her longer-legged brother. "There's no money in the budget."

"Poppa has gotten loans before," Sam argued, hurrying to catch up. "I don't see what the big deal is—"

Leila came to a dead stop. "The big deal is no one will give us a loan. I applied for two before contacting Forrest Kingston and both applications were rejected." She tried to strike a tone between stern and patient. It wasn't Sam's fault he had no idea what was happening with their finances. Her brother had been doing his job. He made the best wine in the valley—some might say in all of Colorado—but when it came to crunching the numbers, well, he simply didn't.

Her brother held open the barn door for her. "Like I said, Poppa and I worked on this thing all morning and got nowhere."

The wine-making barn had never been her favorite place at the winery. It was in a perpetual state of disarray. There were mismatched shelves and plastic folding tables with gadgets stashed all over the place—things she had no idea what to do with or what they did. The machinery for crushing, de-stemming, and filtering took up what was left of the space. Overhead, fluorescent lights buzzed and flickered, creating a prison-like hue. And, unlike the wonderful savory scents of garlic and basil that permeated the restaurant, this room had that sour smell of fermenting grapes, which she loved when she opened a bottle of cab, but not when it constantly floated in the air.

"We cleaned the whole thing out, tightened every screw, greased the wheels," her brother said, leading her to the crusher. "Those are the things Poppa said worked in the past."

"Then we'll have to find what will work this time." Leila approached the large stainless-steel machine. "Did you try plugging it in?" she joked.

Sam shook his head at her. "If you ask Poppa, we need to go back to a manual crusher instead of these newfangled motorized machines. 'They sure don't build 'em like they used to,'" he said, doing his best Poppa impression.

Leila examined the various buttons and levers next to a small screen. "Are the manual crushers cheaper?"

"Way cheaper." Her brother flipped a lever to turn on the machine. "But you also have far less output. We can make a lot more wine with a motorized crusher."

"And we need a lot more wine." Especially if they grew their wine club.

"Exactly." Sam hit another button, and the contraption made a loud grinding sound, but nothing moved. "It's like the drum is stuck or something." He turned the crusher off.

"Right. The drum." She had no idea what the drum was. Leila knelt to unplug the machine and then pulled over a stepladder to peer into the large, rectangular opening at the top. She couldn't see much from that vantage point. "What about those wires and stuff?" She climbed down the ladder and went around to the back of the contraption where cords coiled around.

"Neither Poppa nor I are electricians," Sam reminded her. "If the wires are messed up, we'll have to get someone from the company to come out here to fix it."

Which would likely cost nearly as much as getting a new machine. This thing was so old, they'd probably have to special order the parts. "I don't understand how it could break down. I thought this was a top-of-the-line crusher." At least that was what her grandparents had said when they bought it years ago.

"Sure, it was the best. Way back when." Her brother walked to the long, stainless-steel counter where he had a bunch of glass containers lined up. Likely his unfiltered taste-testing station. "The fact is, these machines don't last forever, and there aren't any mechanics around these parts who know a damn thing about them."

"Maybe we should look up a how-to video online." Surely someone had filmed themselves fixing their grape crusher and posted it on social media. Leila messed with some of the metal wheels at the mouth of the machine and proceeded to get her hands all greasy. "Can you bring me a paper tow—?"

The barn door creaked open with an obnoxious squawk, and August strode in. One look at his face transported her back to the park, and her heart dropped like it had when she'd kissed him.

"Hey." Her voice floated away from her. She awkwardly held her dirty hands in front of her waist. "What're you doing here?"

August hung out by the door, obviously not any more eager to get close to her than she was to him.

Because she'd lost her mind and had gone and kissed him, and then he'd pushed her away.

"Your grandmother found me and told me there's something wrong with the crusher?" He seemed to be waiting for permission to come fully into the room.

Sam's shoulders seemed to grow broader. "We've got it under control."

While she appreciated her brother's protectiveness, who was he trying to kid? They currently had nothing under control around this place.

"You sure?" August focused on her greasy hands. "I've worked on a lot of crushers over the years."

Oh, for the love of God. Leila stuffed her pride down deep where it belonged. So he'd pushed her away after she'd kissed him. He'd done her a favor. She didn't need him to make out with her in the park, she needed him to fix the damn crusher. "We don't even know how to take the thing apart." She wiped her hands on a towel she spotted on the counter. "The motor quit. Sam and Poppa haven't been able to fix it, and we don't have seven thousand dollars to buy a new one right now." She might as well be completely honest.

August didn't ask any questions. He simply rolled up his sleeves. "Do you have a toolbox?"

Leila raised her eyebrows at her brother.

"I put them all away but, sure, I'll go find them." Sam stomped out of the room in obvious disgust.

August walked over and plugged in the machine again. "Nice to see he's warming up to me."

"He'll come around." Heck, if Auggie fixed this machine, she might even come around and forget all about the humiliation that had pricked her skin when he'd backed away from, wide-eyed and repulsed.

"I'm sure I deserve every bit of your brother's dislike." His eyes barely grazed hers, but the quick look was enough to soften her knees. Why, oh why, had she kissed him? It had been too easy to find herself in his arms again, opening to each other the way they used to.

A tentative silence stretched out between them a beat too long while August examined the crusher's control panel.

He didn't know what to say either. Luckily, she didn't have a problem making small talk. "So, have you fixed a lot of crushers during your career?" Whatever she did, she had to steer clear of discussing the kiss. She had to pretend like it never happened, like it didn't affect her.

"A few." The man took a knee and looked at the underside of the machine. "I've pretty much done everything there is to do at a vineyard. Had to work my way up over the years."

Leila watched while he stood and turned on the machine, taking a few seconds to listen to the horrible grinding before turning it off again.

"Do you like what you're doing now for Kingston the best out of all the jobs you've done?" She couldn't help but be curious about him. Back when they'd been dating, she never would've assumed he'd be an executive, spending much of his time on the business end of things. He'd always loved the outdoors, the hands-on work he'd done with his father at the ranch.

"I wouldn't say that I like what I'm doing now the best." August seemed as intent on avoiding her gaze as she was on avoiding his. "I like being in the vineyards. Planting, tending, harvesting. And I recently made some of my own wine too."

"You made wine?" Sam appeared in the open doorway again. "We don't need any help making wine around here." Her brother shoved a large toolbox into August's hands. "You might have some fancy job and make a lot more money than us, but we have our own way of doing things, and that's not going to change."

Leila almost chastised Sam for being so rude, but she couldn't blame him for feeling threatened. August's very presence here was a reminder of the deal she'd made. He might not mean to be, but the man was a threat to all of them.

"I don't plan on taking over," August said easily. He set the toolbox on the ground and dug around until he found a screwdriver. "Making wine is more of a hobby for me. You have nothing to worry about."

Her brother grunted something inaudible and then said more loudly, "I have to go meet a group of harvest volunteers at the café in town. If you'll excuse me." He made it out the door in a few long strides.

"Sorry." Leila moved in closer to August. "He's the only one here besides us who knows the real situation. I think he's worried." She knew how often she woke up at night with her heart racing. Maybe Sam was better at hiding the stress than she was.

"I get it." August unscrewed a few bolts on the machine and then pulled a stainless-steel panel off it to reveal more gears and wires. "Neither of you have any reason to trust me."

"We don't have any choice but to trust you." That was what she had to come to terms with. She didn't have to trust him with her heart; she had to trust him with her mind, with her business.

"I hope to prove myself trustworthy." He stepped away from the machine and pulled off his Henley.

"Whoa." She hadn't meant to react, but she hadn't been prepared for him to lose his clothes. "What're you doing?"

"There's a lot of grease here. Don't want to ruin my shirt." He tossed the shirt onto the table and selected a wrench from the toolbox. At least she was pretty sure he had a wrench. It had gotten difficult to focus on anything besides the rippling muscles in his back. Auggie had always had a well-defined physique, but his shoulders had grown broader, and his skin had a rugged quality. He must spend at least some hours outside.

"Hey." August glanced over his shoulder. "Can you find me a pair of pliers?"

"What? Huh? Oh. Pliers." She managed to rip her gaze off his body. "Yes. Pliers. No problem." Her quaking hands fumbled with the tools in the toolbox. "Pliers. Here we go." She thrust the tool into his hands and then backed away so quickly she tripped on a box Sam had left on the floor. "Oopsies." Leila steadied herself before she fell on her butt. What was wrong with her?

He offered her his hand. "You okay?"

"Yep! I'm good." She laughed awkwardly. "Still a klutz." And still a sucker for August's body.

"All right, then." August went back to work on the machine.

Leila watched his hands work. Those same large hands had held her face tenderly while he'd kissed her only a few hours ago. The memory sent her stomach gently rolling all over again.

The man tinkered with wires and the gears, tapping things, tightening parts with a wrench. It shocked her how much he resembled the old August, especially when he focused on something. His left eye still narrowed slightly, and he continued to set his jaw with determination. He gave the task all his attention, stepping back a few times as though to bring the whole picture into view.

"Some of the parts are wearing down," he said after at least fifteen minutes of tinkering and working. "But I think we can make it last another season or so." He set down the wrench, separating and examining the wires. "I know a guy. We can order new parts, and I can rewire the motor. I've replaced the guts on one of these things before. I'm sure that'll take care of the problem for now."

August finally pulled back on his shirt, thank the good Lord.

"Let me worry about this." He closed up the toolbox. "Don't give it another thought."

Before she could cut off the rise of emotion, tears burned in her eyes. Relief. Pure, utter relief. "Thank you." God, it was awful to have him here, to be reminded of what she'd lost every day. But it helped too. She'd been on her own for a long time.

Now, like it or not, August was here to share her burdens. But she couldn't let herself get used to having him around.

Chapter Eleven

It took everything in him not to wrap his arms around Leila.

Keeping his distance when those tears made her eyes glow required every shred of discipline and rapidly fraying self-control August could muster. But if he pulled her in close, his lips would inevitably find hers again. His hands would settle on her hips to draw her to him. He'd inhale her—that Leila scent he'd always loved. And this time, he wouldn't stop himself from exploring where a single kiss might take them, now that they didn't have to sneak around behind the grown-ups' backs.

Hunger growled through him. He could still taste her. He might never stop tasting her...

"I'm sorry. I have no idea why I'm getting emotional." The woman who currently had his pulse stuttering grunted with frustration and dabbed at her eyes with her shirtsleeve. "So, you'll order the new parts for the crusher?"

"Yeah." August looked away so his gaze wouldn't keep falling to her mouth, so he could think of something else to say that would distract him from that slow, swelling ache she made him feel.

"Okay, then. That's settled." She stalked away from him and started to straighten up the mess of measuring cups and stemless wineglasses and scattered notes of paper on a nearby table as though she couldn't stand the mess her brother had left. She'd always liked order—even back in high school. She used to tidy up everything.

"Do you remember when you did an intervention and cleaned my room?" The memory hit with razor-sharp clarity. He must've been a junior that year, which would've made her a sophomore.

Leila peered over her shoulder with one eyebrow cocked. "Your room was always a complete mess. Someone had to do something before the mess resulted in a natural disaster."

He grinned at her quick rebuttal. The woman was never at a loss for words. It was one of the things he'd loved most about her. She had a response for everything. "You showed up with a whole bucket of cleaning supplies and kicked me out." He'd tried to distract her with a slow-simmering kiss that afternoon, but Leila had always been the kind of woman who couldn't be diverted when she had a mission.

"Someone had to do an intervention." Leila gathered up a few crumpled paper towels and tossed them into the trash can. "I found an old banana peel under your bed that day. And don't get me started on the dirty dish collection in your closet." Playfulness sparked in her eyes the same way it used to when she'd tease him with a wink from across the dinner table when he dined with her family. "I don't know how Jane lived with you and Wes all those years."

"Yeah. She had it pretty tough." And his sister never let them forget the way they'd tortured her with their very presence. "You might be surprised to learn that I'm actually kind of a neat freak these days."

Leila's eyes dulled suddenly. "Yes, well, neither of us is the same person we were back then." She sidestepped him and started to stack empty canisters on a shelf.

Maybe her avoidance should've made it easier for him to keep his distance from her, but he couldn't seem to tear himself away, to take his eyes off her. "No. We're not the same people." She had grown more beautiful, stronger. Sure of herself. And yet even with all her strength and capability, she still had this warmth about her smile, this authenticity he'd never encountered in anyone else. "But that's a good thing." He hadn't meant for his voice to drop. "We've both grown up." But that didn't stop him from feeling the same way he had when he'd been sixteen years old and had taken her hand for the first time.

Leila stilled, her back turned to him.

He had her attention. He might not get this opportunity again. "If things were different..." No, that wasn't quite right. "If *I* were different, I wouldn't have stopped kissing you this afternoon." His heart clanged against his ribs like a warning bell, but he needed to say this to her. "I can't pretend I don't want you, Lei. But I also can't pretend I deserve you." He had never let himself ask the *what if* question, but being here with her, he couldn't avoid wondering. What if his father hadn't died? What if he hadn't gone adrift in life? Would he and Leila be standing here stealing kisses away from the watchful eyes of the kids they'd talked about having?

Slowly, Leila turned to him, not fully but enough that he could see the flush on her face. "I should go. Call Sam." She made a sudden movement in the direction of the door. "I need to tell him you're going to fix the crusher."

He'd said too much. Again. But she had to know he hadn't walked away from kissing her because he'd wanted to. "I'll talk to Sam." August made it to the door first and opened it for her.

Leila paused on her way outside. "*You're* going to talk to him?"

"Yeah. I'll go find him at the café." He and Sam needed to clear the disgruntled air between them if he was going to be able to help the winery. And he'd best steer clear of Leila for the rest of the day anyway. He wasn't doing either of them any favors bringing up the kiss that couldn't happen again.

"Ohhhhkay, if you're sure you want to talk to Sam." She walked with him to the edge of the parking lot. "Let me know how that goes." Her scrunched forehead made it clear how she thought a meeting between her brother and him would go.

"I will." He gave her a wave and settled in his truck, cursing himself for getting distracted during a business mission. He'd never had a problem keeping things professional until he'd come back to Valentino Bellas. It was the memories, the constant reminders of how good they'd been together once.

He navigated the switchback where he and Leila had slid off the road not long after she'd gotten her license. He inhaled deeply, as though he could breathe in the memory. He'd let her drive his truck for the first time. Maybe not the best idea he'd ever had, since it had snowed the night before. She'd taken the turn too fast, and they'd done a donut right into the edge of the vineyard. Three seconds had seemed like five years while the wheels spun, and when they'd come to a stop—still on the mountain and not plunged off the cliff—he'd released his seat belt to make sure she was okay. Then he'd kissed her with all the fear and desperation that had churned in him, and they'd stayed there in the cab of his truck kissing for a good thirty minutes before finally digging out of the snow.

And there he went again, wandering back into the past.

No more thoughts, no more memories. The rest of the way to the café he kept his mind clear and parked in front of Silverado Lake's most popular hangout.

At least he shouldn't run into any memories here. Jane's friend Beth and her husband had completely renovated the old diner, keeping some of the charm, but making it look like a whole new establishment—whitewashing the brick, adding lacquered black shutters to the windows. The inside had completely changed too, with new flooring, new tables, and a new counter that ran nearly the whole length of the restaurant.

August entered the establishment, scanning the crowd.

"Auggie!" Beth waved from behind the espresso machine. "Hey. Good to see you. Anything new on the wedding planning front?" she called loudly. "Are you going to elope?"

Was it just him, or did the entire place quiet in anticipation of his answer?

"No news yet." He approached the counter so the everyone in the restaurant wouldn't get in on this conversation.

"I don't mean to nag you. I love weddings, is all." Beth flicked some levers on the machine, releasing a hiss of steam into the air. "But you two are totally right; you should enjoy being engaged too." She sprayed some whipped cream on some elaborate coffee drink and slid it to a customer he didn't recognize a few seats away. Then she leaned over the counter across from him. "Speaking of engagements, how did you propose, anyway? No one seems to know anything."

There was a good reason for that. He and Leila hadn't even thought to go over a proposal story. "Oh. Well. It was great." He had always thought he would officially propose to Leila in the vineyards, just the two of them. No public gestures, no pomp and circumstance. Just a simple intimate moment they could share together. Kind of like when he'd given her the promise ring. But was that what she would want? He had no idea. "You know what?" he finally said. "I should let her tell you the story."

The prospect of hearing the details from Leila seemed to thrill the woman. "I'd love to hear the story from Leila! Maybe I'll ask her and Jane to meet me for coffee. I need some girl time anyway."

"That'd be perfect." Then he'd be able to warn his pretend fiancée ahead of time so she could come up with something to say. "Leila needs some time away from work too." Or maybe she needed time away from him.

"I'm sure she won't enjoy time with me half as much as she enjoys her time with you," Beth said with a wink.

That was debatable. "I'll let her know to expect your call." He glanced around. "I'm really here to see Sam, though."

"Sure. He's in the back booth around that corner." She pointed to the other side of the restaurant. "They just finished up their harvest meeting."

"Great. Thanks."

August made his way around the tables and turned the corner.

Sam watched him walk all the way across the room but said nothing when he got there. August wasn't sure how the man had perfected that ominous stare growing up with Poppa and Nonna, two of the friendliest people he'd ever met.

"Can I sit?" he asked when it became clear Sam wasn't going to speak.

"Sure." Leila's brother started to scoot out of the booth. "I was just leaving."

"You should stay for a few minutes." August sat across from him. "We need to talk."

Sam sat taller and gazed down at him with an unreadable expression. Though they'd gotten along okay back when he'd been dating Leila, August wouldn't say they'd been friends.

"I can fix the crusher." August met the man's dark eyes. "I'll put a rush order on the parts and can hopefully have it up and running by next week."

"Great." He started to slide out of the booth again.

"Hold up." This wasn't working. As the winemaker, Sam was one of the most important employees at Valentino Bellas, and yet August hadn't even had a full conversation with him since arriving. They had to get past the personal issues for the good of the winery. "I know you hate me for leaving all those years ago. And I don't blame you, but we have to be on the same team right now. I'm trying to help Leila save the winery. We're all going to have to work together."

"I don't hate you because you left." Sam shook his head, a silent lament of August's idiocy. "Hell, I don't even hate *you*. I hate what you did to my sister. I hate that she waited so long for you, and you didn't even have the decency to call her. I hate how many times she cried over you."

Each statement wrenched his heart, sinking his hopes for ever redeeming himself.

"I hate that she still loves you," the man mumbled.

"No." August stopped him right there. "She doesn't love me. She can't." Years had passed. He wasn't worthy of her love.

"If you really believe that, you don't know Leila's heart." Sam continued to glare at him. "She's the most loyal person walking this earth. I swear she's more like Nonna than she is like our own mom."

Yes. Leila resembled Nonna. Nonna who never gave up on anyone. Nonna who'd been in love with the same man since she'd been fifteen years old.

He almost opened his mouth to deny Leila could still feel anything for him, but his jaw locked. Was that the connection he felt to her? Did it come from feelings that had never fully dissolved? It didn't matter. "I don't deserve her love."

"Finally, something we can agree on," Sam muttered. "Unfortunately, deserving her love doesn't matter. If she didn't love you anymore, this wouldn't be so hard on her. Having you here. She wouldn't care."

How hard was this for her? He hadn't bothered to ask. A heaviness pressed against his ribs, tempting him to run away from this conversation.

After a lengthy silence, Sam spoke again. "You want to know the worst part about what you did? She really believed you would come back. She had faith in you. And now she doesn't have faith in anyone."

August clenched his fists but he couldn't fault the man for telling the truth. He couldn't fault the man for trying to protect his sister from more pain. Sam cared about Leila, and August had to respect that. Coming here had been a mistake. He should've fought Forrest harder. He should've turned down the potential promotion. Staying away would have been better for Lei. On some level, though, he'd wanted to see her. He hadn't admitted that truth to himself, but there it was.

"I only have one question for you. Are you gonna stick around this time?" Sam eyed him as though he already knew the answer.

August couldn't bring himself to utter a no. But he couldn't stay. He couldn't open his heart to that kind of intimacy. Not when he might lose her someday. He couldn't go through that kind of pain again.

Sam slid out of the booth and stood. "Because if you're only going to leave her again, you need to back off and make sure she knows where you stand. Don't you dare mess with her, August. It's not fair."

Chapter Twelve

Leila tried to focus on her computer screen so she could finish up the inventory, but her gaze kept wandering to the door.

Yet again, August hadn't shown up to the office. When she'd first learned Kingston had sent Auggie out, she'd thought she would have to give him assignments to keep him away from her, but he was pretty good at staying away all on his own. Since fixing the crusher, he hadn't graced them with his presence once in the last three weeks. Sure, he'd sent her plenty of e-mails detailing his work for the upcoming event, but she was starting to wonder if he would ever come back.

"August sure has made himself scarce," her grandmother mused innocently across the room. "I feel like I haven't seen him in weeks."

You and me both. Leila held off a scowl. "He's been super busy. We both have." The excuse sounded lame even to her. What man wouldn't want to spend time with his fiancée? Not one she would marry, that was for damn sure.

"See, there you go again with the busyness." An exasperated sigh puffed from her grandmother's lips. "You two are young and in love. There is no reason in the world you shouldn't be spending time together."

Tell that to August. Or . . . maybe she should tell that to August before her grandparents got suspicious. "Actually, we're having breakfast together." Leila shut her laptop. "At the ranch. I'm supposed to meet him there."

"Oh, good." Her grandmother shook her head. "I was beginning to worry."

"No need to worry." Leila snatched her purse out of the drawer and hurried to the door. "Everything's great!" Or at least things would be great when she gave August a piece of her mind. He'd agreed to this whole scenario, and now he wasn't holding up his end of the bargain.

"I'll be back in a few hours," she called as she stepped outside.

"Or hopefully longer," Nonna muttered.

Leila pretended not to hear. She got into her Jeep and drove to the ranch, her anger building the whole time. Instead of parking at the lodge, she drove around to the back where the cabins were located and parked in an empty dirt lot.

Across the road, August's mother sat on her front porch reading a book. "Leila. It's nice to see you." The woman stood and ambled down the porch steps.

Heat clouded Leila's cheeks. "Hey, Mara." She couldn't face this woman right now. Who knew what Mara thought about her arrangement with August? "Is Auggie around?"

"He was down in the pasture with the horses last I checked." She tucked her book under her arm. "That's where he's spent practically all of his time since he came home."

That explained a lot. He was too busy being a cowboy to show up at the winery. "Thank you." Leila pulled off her best smile. "I'll see you later."

"Hold on." Mara stepped into stride with her. "I want you to know that I don't judge you for pretending to be engaged. I understand how tough things have been for your family and I know how much you've had to take on." She gave Leila's shoulder a squeeze of solidarity. "I support you, sweetie. No matter what."

Sudden tears stung her eyes. "Thank you. That means a lot to me."

"Of course." Mara hugged her. "You let me know if there's

anything I can do to help with the event too. We'll have a lodging special for people who are attending that weekend, but I'm happy to volunteer for whatever you need."

Speaking again might've let out a sob, so instead Leila nodded.

After one more pat, Mara walked away, leaving her to stumble along the path to the pasture alone.

When she'd passed the boat shed, Leila spotted August in the center of the enclosure. He had his back to her while he directed a chestnut-colored horse to trot in a circle. Quietly, Leila crept closer until she'd made it to the outside of the fence.

"'Atta boy." August strode to the horse and fed him a carrot. "See there? You're already moving better."

The horse nosed his shoulder as though sniffing for another carrot.

August laughed, and Leila didn't want to interrupt. He sounded happy.

"All right. One more carrot." He held out the treat, letting the horse gobble it from his hand.

Leila followed the fence, walking around into his line of sight. That horse... "Is that Knievel?" The animal sure resembled Charlie Harding's old sidekick.

August turned his head to her, his expression neutral. He didn't seem surprised she'd shown up. "Yeah. I've been working out here with him a lot." He led the animal to the fence where Leila stood. "At first when I got here, he didn't want to come near me, but we've made a lot of progress since then."

"That's great." The lecture she'd prepared about avoiding her suddenly didn't seem so important. Not with the energy in August's eyes. He loved being out here with this horse. She could tell. "Uh, I've been wondering what you were up to since I haven't seen you around much."

The man adjusted something on the horse's bridle. "I've been around. I fixed the crusher, and I e-mailed you everything I've done for the event." He seemed hell-bent on not looking at her.

"I know." Something was off. He'd never flat out refused

to glance at her before. "But my grandparents are wondering why we're not spending time together. They've noticed. Just this morning, Nonna made a comment."

"Yeah. Sorry." August's shoulders slouched. "I guess I got distracted with this guy." He patted the horse's withers. "He changed after my dad died. Wouldn't let anyone ride him. Since then, he's hardly interacted with anyone at all."

"He's interacting with you." Leila raised her hand to the horse's muzzle, and Knievel allowed her a few pats.

August finally let his gaze graze hers. "He responds to me. I'm not sure why."

She had a pretty good idea why this horse would latch on to August. "Maybe he knows you miss your dad too." Horses were brilliant. They could sense emotions. She wondered if Knievel could sense her urge to reach for August. To hold his hand or find some way to comfort him. He hid it well, but his father's death had changed him too.

"Yeah, I guess he and I have something in common." Auggie stared at the horse. "I was thinking about trying to ride him."

Yes. A ride. This would be the perfect time to go for a horseback ride. She had to kill at least two hours anyway. "I haven't been riding in years," she hinted. Not since she and August used to go together.

"Huh." He clearly didn't want to give her an invitation, but whatever awkwardness had come between them, they needed to fix it fast.

"What the hell is wrong with you?" she demanded. The last time she'd seen him he'd kissed her and spilled his guts, and now he'd disappeared for the better part of three weeks, right after he'd talked to her brother. Ah. Yes. She should've put this together sooner.

"Nothing's wrong." August's hand kneaded the back of his neck. "But I don't want to make this harder for either of us than it has to be. I figure we should keep some space between us whenever possible."

He thought so, or Sam thought so? "Listen, I have no idea what my brother said to you when you two met at the café, but the more space we put between us, the more suspicious my grandparents will be. So we need to figure this out now. I think we should try being friends." Simple as that. They had to get through these next few months together.

"I'm not sure being friends is possible." Auggie went back to messing with the reins as though he needed something to keep his hands busy. "Things between us have always been intense, Lei. We never could do casual."

"We've both come a long way. We're adults." What, did he think she wouldn't be able to resist his magnetism? Now she was determined to do just that. "When you came out here, you agreed to do things my way. So we're going to give the friends thing a shot. We're going to go for a nice, casual horseback ride together." No kissing, no ogling, and definitely no mint chocolate chip ice cream.

After a pause, August nudged Knievel in the barn's direction. "All right. I'll get the horses tacked up."

"Good. Thank you." She crossed her arms to convey a strength that didn't quite materialize. Seeing him with the horse, hearing him say he missed his father, had turned her heart to mush. She wanted to stay angry with him for abandoning her. But she also had to acknowledge the emotional aftermath of what he'd gone through. He'd hurt her because he'd been hurting. He was still hurting, and it was hard to watch.

Leila wandered to the barn and met him as he finished buckling Knievel's saddle.

"I suited up Bonnie for you. She's a gentle old soul." August handed her the reins.

"Perfect." She ran her hand down the horse's soft muzzle. "You'll go easy on me, won't you, Bonnie?"

August came alongside her. "You want a boost?"

"Sure. Thanks." Leila stepped into his hand and swung her other leg over the horse, settling herself in the saddle.

"You good?" He checked the saddle strap again.

"I'm great." She'd forgotten how it felt to sit in a saddle—all tall and proud and untouchable.

After handing her the reins, August approached Knievel. "Whoa, boy. I'm not sure how he's going to feel about this. It's been years since anyone tried to climb on his back."

Leila studied the horse. Knievel stood at attention, his head lifted as though ready. "That horse trusts you. I can tell."

"I hope you're right." August lodged one boot into the stirrup. "Nice and easy, Knievel. We're gonna go for a ride."

She realized his deep, gentled voice wasn't meant to soothe her, but her heart settled anyhow.

August pulled himself onto the horse's back and took the reins, his shoulders appearing even broader, his strength on display.

Friends. They were only going to be friends, no matter what that shiver of desire tried to tell her.

"Good boy, Knievel." He ran his hand down the horse's shoulder. "I can't believe it. He didn't even react."

"Maybe he's just been waiting for you to come back." Leila snapped her mouth shut. She hadn't meant to say something that could've conveyed her own feelings. "I mean, not waiting, necessarily, but—"

"Why don't we stick to the flat path around the lake," August offered.

"Great idea." Maybe she would keep her mouth shut and focus on the scenery. Her gaze gravitated toward his biceps. Wait, not *that* scenery. The lake. She enjoyed the view of the lake.

August gestured for her to go first out of the gate. Thankfully, good old Bonnie didn't need much direction from her. These trail horses likely had this path memorized.

"I'm sorry I haven't been around." Auggie fell in line behind her. "I'd forgotten how much I missed being with the horses."

"It's okay." Leila peered over her shoulder but lost her balance and nearly fell off the horse. "Whoa." She'd better look straight ahead. "But I kind of need you around more." As much as she hated to admit it.

"Then I'll be around more." It almost sounded like he was talking to his horse again.

She held more tightly to the reins and eased out a slow breath to quiet the sudden trill in her heart. "I'd forgotten how beautiful this path is." They'd ambled through a stand of aspen trees and had now come out into a clearing that opened up onto a view of the lake, with its stunning, glacial tint. Leila pulled Bonnie to a stop.

"Yeah. I'd almost forgotten too." August paused Knievel next to her and petted the horse while he looked out on the water. "I missed everything around here more than I realized. I'm actually really happy to be back."

"That's great." Leila found it easier to smile at him out here. "I'm sure your family is happy you're back too."

August grinned. "My mom tried to do my laundry this morning. It's like we've regressed fifteen years."

She laughed. It was good to laugh with him, to talk with no one watching, with no expectations. See? They could do this. They could be friends. As long as he didn't take his shirt off again, she'd be fine.

* * *

"Woo-hoo!" Leila pressed send on an e-mail confirming the supplies order for their big wine club event. "That was the last to-do item on my list. We are officially ready for the party." She pulled Regina into her lap and scratched at the cat's jaw the way the queen liked.

"See? You're almost done with the planning already." Nonna finally looked up from her computer, where she was e-mailing answers to questions they'd gotten about wine club options. Since announcing the event, they'd received many inquiries about their memberships. "There's nothing to stress about. Maybe you can finally allow yourself a little fun now." Her grandmother gave her a pointed frown. "Speaking of fun, where is August this morning?"

She hemmed and hawed. "Uh, well, hmm." It had been a few days since their horseback ride, but so far, he hadn't made good on his promise to be around more. "Don't know." The warmth brought on by the simple mention of his name curled its way into her limbs, her knees, the tips of her ears. "I'm sure he'll be here soon."

"Wonderful." Nonna closed her laptop. "I have something to talk to you two about."

The unmistakable sparkle in her grandmother's eyes set her on edge. Nonna always had that sparkle when she'd cooked up a surprise.

"It's not something having to do with the wedding, is it?" She wouldn't put it past her grandmother to plan a surprise wedding, and that was the last thing they needed right now.

"No, but we could chat about the wedding too." Her grandmother rose and poured herself another cup of coffee at the counter.

"Let's not talk about the wedding today." Leila joined Nonna on the other side of the room. "August and I want to ease into wedding plans. We have plenty of time. I don't think we should start planning anything until after we get through this fall." She stopped there lest it sound like she was begging her grandmother to forget about what was supposed to be the best day of Leila's life. The day that wasn't going to happen.

"But Poppa and I will be gone by the end of the fall." Her grandmother resorted to a sad, guilt-inducing frown. "I know August said you two want to enjoy the engagement, but we're not coming back until April. Surely you're planning to have an early-summer wedding next year? I still can't understand why in the world you would want to wait any longer than that when you've loved August since you were fifteen years old."

A valid point. Leila concentrated on filling her own coffee mug. "We haven't settled on a date yet." They hadn't settled on much of anything. Even though they'd given the being friends thing a good shot while riding horses, she might have woken up in the middle of the night thinking about him taking off his shirt when he'd looked at the crusher weeks before. "But we'll figure things out for the wedding soon." Hopefully when August showed up, they could go somewhere private and discuss some good stalling techniques. Earlier that morning, she'd gotten a voice mail from Beth asking when she could meet her for coffee to tell her all about how August had proposed. Yet another question she couldn't answer. She had no clue how the man would propose.

"I don't want to rush you." Nonna shuffled back to her desk, nursing her coffee. "It's only that—"

The door opened, and August walked into the room. Impeccable timing as usual.

"Good morning!" Nonna abandoned her mug on her desk and shuffled across the room to greet him with a hug.

Leila watched the way August hugged Nonna back, carefully but tenderly with a gentle pat on her back. The sight shook the walls around her heart again. She stood and walked over to join them. "Hey."

"*Hey?* Is that any way to greet your fiancé?" Nonna all but nudged Leila into August's arms.

"Whoa." He caught her awkwardly but quickly released her. Still, the quick touch had been enough to accelerate her pulse.

August stuck his hands in his pockets. "So, uh, what have you two been up to this morning?" Was he nervous?

"We've been working hard, as usual." If her grandmother noticed any awkwardness between them, she didn't let on. "Which is exactly what I wanted to talk with you both about."

Great. Her grandmother was going to bring up the whole date thing again. "We haven't been working *that* hard—"

"Since you two can't seem to make your own plans for a date, Poppa and I made plans for the four of us. We're going on a double date next week!" Her hands rose in a silent *ta da!*

Leila swallowed a groan. A whole evening with her grandparents? She wasn't sure she and August would make it through when they couldn't even greet each other properly. "Wow." Her voice got all breathy, but she tried to disguise the panic as excitement. "A double date, huh?" She snuck a peek at August's face, but couldn't read his expression. "What, um, did you have in mind?"

"It's already planned." Nonna pulled them both to the couch they'd all sat on when this lie had started. Thankfully, her grandmother sat between her and August. "We'll drive to Denver together. We have reservations for dinner, and then we're going to see *The Phantom of the Opera* at the performing arts center!"

"*Phantom*?" She did her best not to grimace. Those tickets had to have cost her grandparents way too much money and they were likely nonrefundable.

"Yes, isn't that amazing?" Nonna didn't wait for an answer. "I'm so excited. We found last-minute tickets. And it will be too late to drive all the way home after that, so we booked two rooms at the Brown Palace Hotel. It's our treat."

August visibly stiffened.

An overnight double date? Leila couldn't swallow right. "Nonna, we can't accept this. *The Phantom of the Opera*? Not to mention the Brown Palace Hotel. It's too expensive." And too much. Too much time with August. Too much time being forced to pretend in front of her grandparents.

"Your grandfather and I have always been very careful with money. We have plenty." Her grandmother waved away her concerns. "Besides, my darling, you have done so much for us over the last few months."

Leila diverted her gaze to the floor. What had she done for them? She'd made a deal with a shark, and now Forrest might take over their life's work. If that hadn't been bad enough, she'd lied to them about being engaged. "I haven't done much." She'd done what she thought she had to do, but now everything was such a mess.

"That's not true at all." Nonna turned to August. "Leila drove Poppa and I to Denver for every doctor's appointment, every chemo treatment. She made me tea and read to me and took over all of the housework and cleaning while I was recovering from surgery." Her grandmother's eyes teared up. "All while taking such good care of the business for us."

The words drove a spear through her. "You and Poppa have done a lot for me. Everything." And if she couldn't save this place, none of what she'd done for them over the last few months would matter.

Nonna turned Leila's face to hers. "Please let us do this for you. For both of you. Nothing would make your poppa and me happier than celebrating your engagement properly. This is our gift to you."

"Of course, we'll go." Her voice squeaked. "Thank you for doing all of this, for the tickets, the hotel." God, the hotel. She would be stuck with August in a romantic room all night long.

Her grandmother glanced at August next, her eyebrows disappearing beneath her white, feathery bangs.

"Can't wait." He smiled warmly at her grandmother, but Leila could detect every hesitation that lived underneath it. Probably because she harbored the same doubts. Being friends on a horseback ride was one thing—but all night in a hotel? August had been right when he'd said there'd always been an intensity between them.

"Wonderful!" Nonna stood and gathered her purse from the coatrack by the door. "Oh, what fun we'll have! Poppa will be thrilled you've agreed. I'll go tell him right away." She left the room, humming to herself.

After the door closed, silence thumped in Leila's eardrums. She found the courage to angle her body toward August, though she couldn't look into his eyes. "I guess we're going on a date."

"Guess so."

Their eyes connected, and her heart bloomed. God, he was gorgeous, especially with the stubble on his jaw.

"How're we going to do this?" He ran a hand through his hair. "I'm trying to think of you as a friend but—" He cut himself off.

He didn't have to explain. They could be simple friends for

an hour here and there. Overnight would be an entirely different situation. "Maybe we need to forget the labels." Her forehead got all feverish. "At least for those forty-eight hours." She started to pace. There were dangers to this plan, of course. Potential risks. Feelings. But the alternative was the awkwardness, the wondering, the worry over missteps—all which would be easily noticeable by the biggest romantics in the Northern Rockies. Yes. This was what they had to do. "We go to Denver with Nonna and Poppa and forget everything else. Forget the rules, forget boundaries. Just have fun and enjoy the date, enjoy the time with them, and convince them we're happy so they lay off the wedding talk a little."

A frown pulled at his mouth. "I don't want to confuse things."

It was a little late for that. Things had been confused the moment he'd walked into the office and back into her life. "Too late. Things are already pretty damn confused," she reminded him.

A smile flickered on his lips. "Yeah, you're right."

"But they don't have to be." She pressed a hand to her chest, trying to slow her galloping heart. "We both know this is temporary. There are no expectations. We need to focus on the goal—making sure Poppa and Nonna get to keep their legacy in the family." She would do absolutely anything to make that happen, even if it meant she had to let August back in.

Chapter Thirteen

Leila dawdled on the sidewalk in front of Beth's adorable café—a hotspot for not only old-fashioned cinnamon rolls, strong coffee, and the best shakes and malts in the region, but also for all the best gossip running through Silverado Lake.

Even with the hint of fall's briskness in the air, perspiration clung to her forehead and sweat slicked her palms. She'd always been a terrible liar. Once, when she'd been twelve years old, a group of her supposed friends from school had convinced her to sneak them into Nonna and Poppa's wine cellar so they could steal a bottle and try a sip of real alcohol.

Wanting to be considered cool, Leila had done it. She'd snuck six other girls into that cellar while her grandparents were sleeping, and they'd huddled around taking drinks of a particularly dry chardonnay, coughing and choking on the wine's strong finish. Before they'd even downed half the bottle, they'd heard a distinct creaking on the old staircase. Her friends had scattered, and Leila had dropped the bottle on the floor where it'd immediately shattered. When Poppa had rushed into the room, she'd fabricated a story about playing hide-and-seek and accidentally knocking the wine off a shelf. All it had taken was one raise of his eyebrows for her to break and admit what they'd really been up to.

Right now, the prospect of sitting across the table from Beth and making up stories had her as sick to her stomach as that lie she'd told to Poppa, and she wasn't even doing anything illegal like underage drinking.

She rounded the corner to the restaurant's main entrance, attempting to steal glances through the windows to see if Beth and Jane were already seated. Being that it was 9:59 a.m., she had exactly one minute to concoct a creative, convincing proposal story that would satisfy Beth and also prevent her from asking a hundred more questions Leila couldn't answer.

"Hey!" Jane hurried across the street, followed by Toby pushing Charlee in a stroller. "Glad you're just getting here. I thought I was going to be late."

"Nope, I was just going in." She took a quick second to fawn over the blond toddler cherub. "Are you joining us too?" Leila asked Toby hopefully. Nothing provided a better distraction than a sweet, babbling toddler.

"Nah. Charlee and I are going on a date at the library." Toby ruffled his daughter's wispy hair. "We're gonna read some books, aren't we, peaches?"

Charlee kicked her chubby little legs. "'Ooks!"

"Have fun, princess." Jane bent and planted a kiss on her daughter's head and then stood to kiss Toby.

The display of affection forced Leila to look away. When she was younger, she'd always thought she would be where Jane was now before the age of thirty. She'd thought she would be married to August. She'd thought they would have a cherub toddler. She'd pictured them walking around town together pushing their own stroller.

Why was it so hard to let go of a dream?

"See ya around, Leila." Toby waved good-bye and continued past them on the sidewalk, chatting with his baby girl.

"Oh, I'm so glad we're doing this." Jane linked their arms

together. "I could use some girl time. Not to worry, though. I'll let you take the lead in the conversation and everything since I have no clue what's going on between you and my brother."

"Join the club," Leila muttered, hesitating outside the door again.

"It sure looked like something was going on at the AppleFest," Jane said in a singsong tone.

"Yes, well, we've talked about it, and we agreed we're going to keep things simple and be friends." At least for the most part. She decided not to mention they'd be going to Denver together.

"Right. Friends." Jane nodded encouragingly, her wide eyes hinting at a healthy skepticism.

If they were going to get through this conversation with Beth, Jane needed to be more convincing. "Listen, I'm planning to keep this conversation high level." If only she could do the same with her feelings—keep them high level and generic. The fluttery warmth igniting at the very center of her chest defied her. There had never been any such thing as high-level feelings when it came to her and August.

"Sounds good to me. Like I said, I'll follow your lead." Jane opened the door. "Just remember, Beth can be a little pushy when she's on the hunt for information. She loves details."

"Right. Details." Tension tightened the back of her neck. Why had she agreed to this again?

"Hey, you two!" Beth skirted the counter and flew at them, catching them both in a hug at the same time. "I have a booth all ready. Blake wanted to join us too!"

Perfect. Leila waved at Blake with a plastic smile. He raised his coffee mug in her direction like a toast.

"Beth invited me to hang out. Hope that's okay," he said as they approached the table.

"Of course." She scooted in next to him. "I've been meaning to call you." She still owed him an explanation for her fast engagement. Not that she had a good one.

"No worries. You've apparently been busy." He nudged her shoulder. "Don't feel bad on my account. I'm happy for you."

"So are we." Beth returned from a brief trip to the counter and set down two mugs before sliding into the booth across from them, along with Jane. "There's a cappuccino for you." She pointed at Leila. "And a crème brûlée latte for you." She nodded toward Jane. "Plus, an assortment of baked goods for the four of us, of course." She pointed to a platter that was already in the middle of the table.

"This is fun." Jane selected a mini chocolate muffin from the platter of goodies sitting between them. "I'm glad we could find a time to hang out."

"For sure." Leila plucked one of the glazed lemon biscotti from the platter and set it on her plate. Maybe she would make herself too busy eating to talk.

"I've been dying to hear all about you and August. I remember how in love you two were in high school, and this one won't tell me a thing." Beth waved a hand in Jane's direction as though dismissing August's sister.

Blake set down his mug. "Meanwhile, I've never heard one word about August."

Jane simply smiled. "It's hard to tell anything when I don't know anything either."

Leila's stomach knotted up. "No one really knows anything." Least of all her. "August and I have kept things pretty quiet." She broke off a piece of the Italian cookie and popped it into her mouth to buy some time.

"I figured." Beth shot her a conspiratorial grin. "But you two can't hide anymore. When did you and August reconnect, anyway?"

Leila finished chewing, but she might as well have been swallowing rocks. "Over the last year. We've been in touch on social media." She cleared her throat, her eyes watering.

"So you two dated in high school?" Blake prompted.

"*Dated*?" Jane laughed. "They were practically married."

"But that's all in the past," Beth said impatiently. "I want to hear about the present."

All eyes focused on her again. "Oh, uh, well, we talked on the phone a lot after we got back in touch." God, that sounded so lame. She was horrible at making things up on the fly. "We kind of got reacquainted, and then we saw each other and...bam. We were engaged." That was the truth of it. Neither one of them had had any time to consider the potential consequences—how many lies they would have to tell, how much time they would have to spend together, the potential for old, dormant feelings to stir back to life.

"I guess when you have such a history together you just know," Beth said through a dreamy sigh.

"Well, it sure explains a lot about why I only got to take you out on a few dates," Blake teased. "You've always had a thing for this guy."

"I guess I have." She'd had a few relationships in grad school, but none of them had gone anywhere.

"That's why I'm so excited for you and Auggie." Beth wiped her mouth with a napkin. "You two were *the* couple in Silverado Lake for all those years. I mean, all the girls envied you. Even back then, August seemed like such a romantic." She paused as though waiting for her to agree.

"He was." She had to force herself to go back to who they'd been in high school, to search beyond the protective layers she'd built up since then. "He was always surprising me." With dates and gifts and thoughtful gestures.

"So, it must've been a romantic proposal, then?" Beth asked. "I mean, I remember you two were always going on the most amazing dates for a couple in high school."

"Yeah, tell us about the proposal," Blake added. "Maybe I'll get some good ideas."

Memories were flooding her now—scenes of her and August, young and in love. "The proposal was beautiful," she heard herself say. For years, she'd kept this specific memory locked away, but now she could see every detail clearly. Shortly before August had left for college, he'd made her a promise, a proposal of sorts. "He set up a picnic in the vineyard, at that spot right on the southern edge where the vines are terraced into the mountainside." That had always been her favorite place on her grandparents' property.

"That night looked like something out of a magazine. There were flickering candles everywhere, and a soft white blanket sat near the vines." They'd rode there on horses he'd trailered over from the ranch, and when he'd led her to that place, she'd known. She'd been sure that night would change her life. "August made a charcuterie board with all of my favorite snacks—black grapes and brie and almonds and Italian prosciutto." All presented on her grandmother's hand-painted platter from Sicily. "We watched the sunset and drank wine. The small-batch sémillon, Poppa's specialty." They might've both been underage, but growing up at a winery meant her grandparents trusted her to drink responsibly.

"It sounds beautiful," Jane murmured, her eyes clouded with empathy.

"It sounds incredible." Beth popped her chin on her fist, gazing across the table as though completely entranced.

"Truly magical." Blake mocked them in his good-natured way.

Leila found herself smiling. It was too late to stop the memory now, even though it brought pain boiling back up to the surface. "For dessert, he'd made the most amazing chocolate mousse." They'd eaten the whole batch, and after, they'd shared a long, chocolatey kiss. "Then we lay down to gaze up at the stars, and he took my hand."

Beth squealed and leaned closer.

Emotion pressurized her throat, but she kept going. "I wasn't expecting the ring. But he raised my hand above us and then pulled the ring out of his pocket and slipped it onto my finger." She still had that ring. The promise ring. A simple, narrow gold band. A placeholder, August had called it. "It's at the jeweler."

"He put the ring on your finger before he even asked you to marry him?" Jane demanded.

Leila had to laugh at her irritation. If someone was telling her this story, she might've had the same reaction. "Yes. But somehow, it was perfect. He put the ring on my finger and told me that, whether or not I said yes, the ring would always belong to me the same way his heart always belonged to me."

"I can see why you said you'd marry the guy." Blake winked at her. "Trust me, I'm taking mental notes."

"Oh, dear God." Beth snatched a napkin from the dispenser at the edge of the table and dabbed at her eyes. "I had no idea August was so good with words."

"He was. *Is*," she quickly corrected. That had been the first lie she'd told in a good five minutes. Back then, he had been good with words—honest and open and even eloquent in telling her how he felt. But he wasn't like that anymore. There were still glimpses—like when he'd told her he wanted her, but then his own words seemed to spook him, and he'd pull away, shut down, avoid her again. "August is...really something."

"Well, I propose a toast." Blake raised his coffee mug in the air. "To Leila and August and a long happy life together."

"Cheers," Jane and Beth said as they clinked their mugs.

"Yes, cheers." She did her best to beam with the glow of a woman in love, hoping she pulled it off. Forget a long and happy life. She hoped they could make it through the next month.

Chapter Fourteen

August stepped out onto his cabin's front porch, rolling his carry-on suitcase behind him. Damn, he was bringing a suitcase. On a date with Leila.

When Sam said not to mess with his sister, spending the night in a hotel with her likely wasn't what he had in mind.

Once again, he marveled at how quickly this charade had spiraled out of control. He was about to spend a whole twenty-four hours with the woman sans rules. Talk about dangerous.

He'd always been one of those strange breeds of kids who liked rules. In fact, he'd thrived on them. Yes, there were times he broke them—what good was a rule if one didn't test it?—but rules were concrete. Rules provided a road map: Don't do this. Don't go there. Maybe that was the reason he'd had such a hard time after his father died. There were no common rules for getting through grief. There was no emotional outline to follow. One day, he would think he had everything handled, and then the next he would find himself unable to get out of bed.

Without rules, he got lost, and he couldn't afford to go off course with his mission in Silverado Lake.

He lifted his suitcase and tromped down the steps to where he'd parked his truck near the lodge's expansive back deck.

"Where are you off to?" His mom set down the spade she was using to plant a batch of bright yellow mums in a large barrel near the doors.

"I'm headed to Denver." He stashed his suitcase in the back seat of his extended cab before climbing the steps to give her a hug.

"Denver, huh?" His mother gave him a good long look. "Here I thought with you being home for a few months I'd get to spend some time with you. I've hardly seen you at all."

Guilt put him in a chokehold. "Sorry. Between Knievel and things at the winery, I've been busy." Or, rather, trying to keep his head on straight while he worked with Leila. "This'll be a quick trip, though. Maybe we can have dinner together tomorrow night?"

"I was hoping you would join us for dinner tonight." His mother went back to her mum planting. "Wes and Thea and the kids are leaving for Texas tomorrow."

"Right," he said through a sigh. "Sorry. I forgot." All he could think about right now was what he should be doing—or not doing—with his fake fiancée. "I'd stay if I could, but Nonna and Poppa have this whole date night planned for Leila and me in Denver." Saying the words out loud tightened the guilt's hold on his throat. Man, this was so messed up.

"I see." His mother patted the fresh soil around a clump of the plant's roots. "How are things going with Leila, anyway?" The innocent rise of her eyebrows didn't disguise her knowing expression very well.

Being the wise woman that she was, he couldn't hide the truth. "Things are...complicated."

"Well, of course they are." She carefully pulled another clump of soil and mums from a plastic container and placed the roots in the small hole she'd dug in the dirt. "Lies have a way of getting very complicated."

"Yeah, I'm realizing that." Maybe it wouldn't be so hard if he didn't have a history with Leila. He found it much easier to pretend with people he didn't know well. But she'd known him better than he'd ever let anyone else know him. Being away for so long, he hadn't ever been forced to face what he'd walked away from. Not only a life with Leila, but also with his family. His mom, specifically. She must've felt as heartbroken as Leila had when he didn't come home.

August watched her go back to work for a few minutes, planting and humming to herself. She'd never been the pushy sort. His mother had believed more in natural consequences than in long lectures. Now he could finally understand why.

"Hey, Mom. I'm sorry. I never apologized to you for not coming home," he finally said. "After Dad died. I should've been here. I should've moved back." Instead, he'd disappeared from her life too.

A smile plumped his mother's cheeks. She stood upright and pulled off her gardening gloves. "I didn't expect you to move home, Auggie." She had aged, though her green eyes still sparkled with a magnetic radiance. "Your father wouldn't have wanted you to come home. You needed to be out in the world, finding yourself."

He wasn't so sure his father wouldn't be disappointed in him for staying away, especially because he hadn't exactly found himself. He was still searching.

August gazed out over the lake, the sun shimmering across the surface. For the life of him, he couldn't figure out how his mother had stuck it out here so long with the daily reminders of what she'd lost. "Did you ever think about selling the ranch and moving on after Dad passed away?"

She inhaled deeply with her gaze fixed on the lodge she and his father had built together. "Sure, I thought about it. But during that time, I needed to feel grounded. I needed Jane to feel grounded." She tilted her head and glanced up at his face. "Different people react differently to grief. I know you probably can't understand this, but holding on to this place allowed me to hold on to your father in a way I couldn't have if I'd left. And that's what I needed. It's what I still need to feel close to him."

"I wish I could feel close to him." That was the first time he'd admitted the longing out loud. "But instead, there's just a hole there." He angled his body toward the lodge, needing to escape the sun's heat on his face. "I was in rough shape after the funeral."

"I know," his mom said quietly beside him. "A mother knows when her child is suffering. Even if he's away from home." She took his hand, squeezing it in hers. "I understand why you weren't able to be here. I know it's difficult for you even now. You don't need to apologize or feel guilty, honey. All I want is for you to continue your journey toward healing. However that works for you."

"I'm not sure there's anything to continue," he admitted, watching the canoe that Wes and Ryan were paddling come into focus from the other side of the lake. He wasn't even sure where to start with a journey toward healing.

His mother let go of his hand. "Maybe this is only the beginning of that journey for you, then. We all have to start somewhere."

"Maybe—"

"Grammy!" Ryan hopped out of the canoe in waist-deep water and sprinted for them in a frenzy of splashes. "I caught a fish! It's a nice one too! A cutthroat trout! He's in the bucket! Come see before we let him go!"

"A fish. Wow." August's mother jogged down the steps and across the grass to meet her grandson. He followed behind at a much slower pace, caught in a memory of him leaping out of that same canoe after he'd caught a cutthroat with his dad.

He stopped and closed his eyes for a brief second. If only memories like that brought him happiness instead of grief.

"Hey." His brother's voice forced his eyes open. "You gonna join us for a family dinner tonight?"

August shook off memories, but the melancholy lingered, enveloping his heart. "Nah, I can't. Leila and I are going on a date to Denver with Nonna and Poppa."

"Really." Amusement turned up the wattage on his brother's grin. "Overnight?"

"Yeah." He watched their mother gush over Ryan's fish rather than meeting his brother's eyes.

"Well, that should be interesting." Wes paused as though waiting for more information, but August kept his mouth shut. He couldn't bring himself to pretend that spending the night with Leila in a hotel wouldn't be difficult for him.

After a few seconds of silence, Wes let him off the hook. "Since you won't be here for dinner, I guess I should let you in on our little announcement now." His brother's voice was hushed as though he didn't want Ryan or their mom to hear.

He gave Wes his full attention. "Announcement?"

"Thea and I are having a baby," his brother whispered. "She's due in early April."

His heart stalled, paralyzing him with a sense of envy for only a quick second before genuine happiness flooded him. "That's amazing." August embraced his little brother. "I'm thrilled for you, Wes. You're a great dad. Just like ours was."

"We had the best example." His brother watched Ryan and their mother as they waded out with the bucket and released the fish back into the wild. "I still miss him. I wish he were here to see us now. I wish he could know the kids. They'd've loved having him as a grandpa."

The yearning expanded, deepening an ache that went all the way into his bones. "He would've made an incredible grandfather." August wrestled out the words past a sting of emotion. "And he'd be proud of you."

Wes clapped him on the shoulder. "He'd be proud of you too."

There wasn't much for his father to be proud of. Charlie Harding had made his whole life about his family, about building relationships with the people who came to stay at their guest ranch year after year, and August had walked away from nearly every relationship he'd ever had.

His brother studied him. "So, after spending all this time with Leila, you think anything could ever happen between you two again?"

This line of conversation wasn't any easier than talking about his father. "I don't think so." Not after the damage he'd done.

"Let me rephrase that question." His brother waited until he looked at him. "Do you want something to happen with her?"

What he wanted and what he could give were two different things. "It's too late." That was the simplest answer. He couldn't tell his brother how he felt too broken to love anyone, how he feared he'd get lost again if he really let himself go there with Leila, and things didn't work out.

"Come on, Auggie." Wes nudged his shoulder. "I know you love her."

But there were a lot of other things he didn't know. "Dad's death changed me." His gaze drifted to Ryan again. "I can't have what you have. I can't make room for those kinds of attachments." He didn't know how to develop deep connections anymore. "Life is easier for me when I'm on my own. I'm constantly traveling with my job. Half the time, I only have a few days' notice on a new takeover project. I can't really be tied down right now." The excuses flowed out easily.

Wes nodded, his lips pressed into a firm line as though considering his response. "It's terrifying," he said slowly. "Having a wife. Kids. Jesus, it's absolutely terrifying."

The admission shocked August into complete stillness.

"But building this family—being there for my family," Wes went on. "That's the most important thing I've ever done." His brother shook his head as if in awe. "I don't even know how to describe it, but all of these random moments, like when Ryan catches a fish and I help him take it off the line, or when Olivia asks me to help her with her homework, or when Thea comes home upset after a tough day at work. Every single one of those moments gives me the deepest sense of purpose I've ever felt." His face broke into a smile. "And the absolute joy I find in being there for them outweighs the fear."

That bubble of envy expanded in August's chest again. Wes had found whatever it was their father had. August used to think he himself was the one most like their father, but his younger brother had gone and proven him wrong.

"I understand it now," Wes said. "Why dad was always so big on family dinners and family hikes and creating a place where families could connect." His brother's voice dropped. "Having a family is scary and hard and messy. I didn't think I was capable of being a dad or a husband, but those connections are what brought me back." His brother started to walk away but then stopped abruptly and faced him.

"Maybe they would bring you back too."

Chapter Fifteen

August walked to the window overlooking the rush-hour traffic that was inching down Seventeenth Street and loosened the tie he'd knotted a half hour ago when he'd gotten dressed for dinner and the theater.

Torture. This whole afternoon had been torture, being next to Leila for the three-hour drive to Denver while they pretended to be the happy couple.

He couldn't cage the attraction that hit when Leila smiled or touched his arm, or hell, even when her eyes held his. Desire swelled hot and fast inside of him. The reactions he couldn't control put him at war with himself. He wanted her more every time he was with her, and yet Sam's words continued to haunt his thoughts.

Don't mess with her.

When they'd arrived at the hotel, Nonna had worked her magic and gotten them a free upgrade to a romantic suite, complete with a canopy king-sized bed and a Roman soaking tub. Not even thirty seconds after he and Leila had walked through the door, Leila had disappeared into the palatial bathroom, saying she had to get ready for dinner. He hadn't seen her since.

He'd thought about her, though. He couldn't stop thinking about her. He'd likely worn a path in this plush carpet with all the pacing he'd done while Leila had been in the shower. Hearing the spray of water, thinking about her in there—naked and dripping wet—had made him prowl the perimeter of the room.

And on that note...August checked his watch before he let himself wander too far into the fantasy of getting into the shower with her. Five minutes. They had to meet her grandparents in the lobby in five minutes.

Good. Logistics were the perfect distraction. He crossed the room and knocked lightly on the bathroom door. "You about ready? Don't want to keep Nonna and Poppa waiting."

"Yep, coming." The words were slightly harried and muffled.

He turned to grab his keys off the dresser, hearing the door open behind him. "Do you think we should walk to the restaurant or—" A peripheral glimpse of the woman walking toward him was all it took to shut him up.

August lifted his head to get a better view of her, of the way her dark hair rolled softly down to her shoulders, of the way her red lips bowed together with a hint of uncertainty, of the way her strapless black dress dipped into a slight V at the center of her chest and then cinched at her waist before flaring to hug the curves of her hips.

"Jesus." He let his gaze wander down her body once more. So much for avoiding any fantasies.

"What?" She looked down and examined her dress like she thought something might be wrong.

He was powerless to offer her anything other than the truth. "You're beautiful. More than beautiful." Elegant and graceful. Captivating.

Leila's gaze dropped to the floor, but she smiled. "You look nice too." She peeked up at him from underneath her long, dark eyelashes like she'd done so often before they'd started dating. Almost shyly. "It's been a while since I dressed up. I'm just glad this thing still fits."

Fits? "That dress was made for you." He fought the urge to move closer. Her no-rules stipulation only made him even more wary of touching her. Once he crossed that line, it would be impossible to stop.

Don't mess with her.

He was trying. Damn it, he was really trying to be a good man. "We should go." Once again, he felt like the room was closing in on him. "Do you want me to drive to the restaurant?" He quickly opened the door for her, ready to escape the confined space.

"No. Nonna said she wanted to walk." Leila grabbed her wrap off the dresser before she slipped out into the hallway, and he tried not to notice the sway in her hips. After making sure he had his keys, August followed her down the corridor.

"Things seem to be going okay so far." She paused to wait for him. "I mean, the drive down went fine."

"Yeah." He hit the button for the elevator. "Your grandparents are still a trip." He'd always enjoyed spending time with Nonna and Poppa. They told the best stories. "How long have they been married, anyway?"

"Fifty-five years this summer." Leila's face sobered. "After Nonna got diagnosed with stage III cancer, I wasn't sure they'd make it to that milestone."

The elevator doors rolled open, and August gestured for her to go first. "I can't imagine how hard that must've been for you. To take care of everything at the winery while helping them get through her treatments."

"It was awful." Leila watched the numbers above the doors as they ticked down to the first floor. "She was so sick for a while, thanks to the chemo treatments. But it meant a lot that I got to be there for them. They've always taken care of me. If I hadn't come home, I would've missed the chance to take care of them."

Who took care of Leila, though?

The elevator stopped on the first floor, and the doors opened. Leila went to step out, but her heel caught on a tile and made her stumble. August managed to get his arms around her in time to steady her, and then they swiftly moved out into the lobby all tangled up.

"Look at you lovebirds," Nonna called from a few feet away.

"That's us." Leila hugged him like they'd planned to end up in each other's arms all along.

"It sure is." Ignoring the hunger growling inside, August released her but kept a hand at the small of her back in case she stumbled again. "I hope you two haven't been waiting long."

"No, no." Poppa waved off the statement. "Nonnie wanted to have a look around this fancy lobby."

"It's so glamorous, isn't it?" Leila's grandmother tipped her head back, staring up. "All that marble and the cathedral ceilings?"

"Not nearly as glamorous as you, my love." Poppa took his wife's hand and kissed it, and August marveled at the affectionate gesture. Fifty-fifty years of marriage, and those two still acted like newlyweds. They were a golden couple—Nonna clad in an emerald-green dress and Poppa in a dapper gray suit.

"Leila, darling, you look radiant." Nonna admired her grand-daughter's dress. "Isn't she lovely, August?"

"She's stunning." He didn't even try to hide his admiration. If he hadn't been admiring her so intently, he might've missed the faint blush on her cheeks.

"We should get going." Leila linked her arm through her grandmother's. "Are you sure you want to walk? We can always take a cab to the show."

"I'd love a walk." Nonna beamed her smile in August's direction. "That will give us plenty of time to catch up."

They paraded outside with the lovely ladies leading, and then the four of them fell into stride on the sidewalk.

"How is the rest of your family, August?" Nonna asked. "It's strange; I haven't run into your mother for ages. We usually get to say hello at least once in a while."

"Everyone's good." As far as he knew, anyway. He hadn't exactly made himself available to hang out with them. "Wes and

Thea are visiting a lot. They're splitting their time between Texas and Colorado, so Mom's been busy." Right about now, his brother would likely be sharing the news about the baby with the rest of his family. He dammed back another surge of jealousy. *Maybe those connections could bring you back too.* Could they? What if it were possible? What if he could someday have the kind of love Wes had for Thea, for his kids? Would love be enough to change him?

August found himself staring at Leila. For the first time in what seemed like forever, hope breathed new life into his heart.

"I'm sure Mara has been thrilled to have all of her kids home together," Nonna said when they paused at a stoplight. "How many grandchildren does your mom have now?"

"Three." And Olivia, Ryan, and Charlee had become the lights of his mother's life. If he were being honest, he'd admit they'd become lights in his life too. No, he didn't get to see them much, but when he did, Ryan acted like they were best friends. And sometimes, the boy texted him pictures he drew for him, telling him he couldn't wait to see him again with about fifty exclamation points punctuating the words. And don't get him started on Charlee. One look at her melted his heart into a puddle. "There's also another baby on the way."

"How exciting!" Nonna held on to her husband's arm as they walked through the crosswalk to the other side of the busy street.

Leila glanced up at August, her eyes wide. "I didn't know Jane was expecting again."

"Actually, it's Thea and Wes." The jealousy still stalked his happiness for his brother, but he wouldn't let it take over. "He told me today before I came to pick you up. He was going to make the big announcement tonight."

"That's great news." His pretend fiancée slipped her hand into his. "Congrats on being an uncle again."

"Thanks." He held on to her, not caring if this was part of the act. He wasn't sure what was real and what was pretend anymore, but he wouldn't let go.

"That also makes you an auntie too, you know," Nonna reminded her happily.

August didn't have to look too closely to see Leila's smile tighten. She kept her eyes focused in front of them and moved more quickly down the block. "Oh, would you look at that? We're already here."

He released her hand, but the warmth of her skin still lingered in his palm. Maybe that was the hope working its way all through him.

Thankfully, the restaurant wasn't like one of the Michelin-star places Forrest was always taking him to in Napa. He'd never understood fancy food and tiny portions. Instead of a sleek entrance, this place had a mismatched brick facade and small windows.

"Buona Nottes is owned by our friend Rafael," Poppa explained, hurrying to get the door for them. "It's real Italian food. His minestrone is almost as good as mine."

"No way." August hadn't had Poppa's minestrone in years, but he could still taste it. That had been their Sunday appetizer at the restaurant before the man had agreed to promote Simon so he could spend more time with his family. "I always get minestrone when I go out for Italian food, and I always end up disappointed."

The man slung an arm around August as they stepped inside. "I knew I liked you."

There was nothing special about the restaurant's interior either, but something about the simplicity of the scuffed wood floors and old plaster walls felt welcoming. People packed the small dining room, all of them enjoying family-style portions of Italian classics. A perfect hint of garlic wafted in the air.

"Mr. and Mrs. Valentino." A young hostess waved at them from a small desk. "My dad said to bring you right back when you got here."

"Thank you, Mari." Nonna hugged the girl. "It's been so long since I've seen you. What a beautiful young lady you've turned into." She waved Leila and August over. "This is my grand-daughter, Leila, and her fiancé, August."

Her fiancé. It might only be a title—a part he had to play—but he didn't mind being introduced as Leila's fiancé. The title had started to take on a different meaning for him. When he'd introduced himself to Blake that way in the park, he'd been making a point, but now it felt like he was stepping into the role.

After the necessary handshakes and polite greetings, they paraded all the way to the back of the restaurant and through the double doors into the kitchen. The space reminded August a lot of Valentino Bellas's kitchen, with chaos erupting in front of stoves, and line cooks and food runners maneuvering around each other to get the meals to the tables while they were hot.

"Angelo!" An older man in a white chef's coat left his post in front of a stove and hurried to greet Poppa. "And Frannie!" He peppered Nonna's cheeks with kisses. "How wonderful to have you here. It has been much too long." His accent came across much thicker than Leila's grandparents'.

"Leila? Can that be you?" The man didn't wait for an answer before capturing her in bear hug. "When did you grow up? I remember your nonna holding your hand so you wouldn't get near the stoves."

"I remember that too." She straightened and reached for August's hand, tugging him over. "Rafael, I'd like you to meet August Harding. My...fiancé," she added after only a slight hesitation.

The man's gasp conveyed true delight. "You're getting married?" He sternly signaled a server who happened to be walking by. "We need a bottle of our finest champagne. *Proprio adesso!*"

The young man nodded and rushed away.

"We can't tell you how thrilled we are to be here." Nonna inhaled deeply. "It smells like heaven in this kitchen. I can't wait to try everything."

"And you will." The man ushered them past the cooks and the stainless-steel counters to a corner where a large farmhouse table sat. "You have the seats of honor tonight." He pulled out chairs for them. "Sit, sit. We will bring you that champagne and some of our best appetizers."

"The burrata with marinated tomatoes?" Poppa asked hopefully.

"Of course." The man clapped him on the back. "You enjoy yourselves and celebrate. Let us take care of everything else."

"We do have a lot to celebrate," Nonna said after Rafael had walked away. Her gaze settled on August and Leila.

"We do," August agreed. It had been a long time since he'd enjoyed an evening this much. It had been a long time since he'd been this unburdened. "It's not only our engagement we should celebrate either. You two have been together for over fifty years." Five decades and they still had this intense fire burning between them. "So, please share. What's the secret to a long, happy relationship?" What did he have to do if he wanted to have the kind of marriage they had someday?

They stared into each other's eyes, seeming to speak without words.

"You have to guard each other's dreams," Nonna finally said with a definitive nod.

"And you treat those dreams like your own," Poppa added. "We haven't always agreed on everything, but we've always wanted the best for each other above everything else."

August found himself gazing at Leila again. A smile softened her lips as she stared back. Something about the way her mouth curved seemed genuine, not part of their fabrication.

"I'll remember that advice." He did want the best for Lei, and he could still guard her dreams, even if they weren't together.

Chapter Sixteen

The standing ovation practically shook the theater while the cast onstage continually bowed. Leila clapped and whistled, still caught up in the emotion and the drama of the performance.

August clapped next to her, looking dangerously sexy in his suit. He had been the perfect date all evening: attentive, funny, and a fantastic conversationalist with her and her grandparents. She couldn't help but wonder if her life could've looked like this if she hadn't lost him. Would they have still gone on extravagant dates together? Maybe they would be too busy with a family by now.

The house lights came on and dimmed the applause into appreciative chatter.

Nonna gathered her purse and started to shuffle out of their row and into the aisle. "Wasn't that incredible?"

Poppa followed with a supportive hand at her back. "I'm not much of a theater man, but I have to admit I was impressed."

"I told you," his wife teased, holding onto his elbow. "I love the theater."

"That had to be one of the best *Phantom* performances I've ever seen." August helped Leila put on her wrap.

Yet another thoughtful gesture that seemed completely natural for him. "Have you seen many performances?" She scooted into the aisle behind her grandparents, and they slowly made their way to the exit with the masses. It was strange to think she had known August so well once upon a time—and in some ways still did—but she didn't know much *about* his life.

"I've seen a few performances in California."

Leila became hyperaware of him behind her, close and warm, his deep voice bringing goose bumps to her neck. Even with her toes being pinched in the heels that had seemed like a good idea when she'd packed them this morning, she focused on walking tall and straight, making sure her knees didn't wobble and trip her up again.

They streamed out of the theater with everyone else and then huddled on the sidewalk. The city lights had come on, dressing up the streets and giving the downtown scene a vibrance it hadn't had when they'd walked to the theater from the restaurant.

"Maybe we should take a cab back to the hotel," Nonna said through a yawn. "We haven't been out this late in years."

"Exactly what I was thinking." Poppa moved closer to the curb and signaled a passing taxi.

Leila hung back. Her feet were killing her, but the quicker they got back to the hotel, the sooner she and August would have to navigate sharing one of the most romantic hotel rooms in Denver. Nerve set her stomach abuzz. Would something happen between them? Did she want something to happen? She had no idea, which meant it was a beautiful night to procrastinate. "I think we'll walk back, if that okay."

"I like that idea." August positioned himself beside her, his arm brushing hers.

If her heart thumped any louder, he would certainly hear it.

"All right, then. It is a beautiful night for a romantic walk." Nonna hugged them both, seeming thrilled they were going to spend some time alone. "We'll meet you in the lobby for breakfast."

"Sounds good." August escorted Leila's grandmother to the

waiting taxi and shook her grandfather's hand. "Thank you both. For the dinner, the show, the hotel. This has been the best night I've had in a long time." His genuine tone warmed Leila's heart. The man had been amazing with her grandparents all night, truly interested in their lives, truly appreciative.

Poppa opened the door for Nonna. "It was our pleasure."

"We're beyond happy to see you two back together." Leila's grandma climbed into the car. "Enjoy your night."

"We will." August slipped his arm around Leila's waist and they both waved as the taxi pulled away. She let herself lean into him, only slightly. What harm could it do? This date had only served to remind her what a gentleman August had always been. How easy he was to be with. This had been the best night she'd had in a long time too.

After the taxi made it out of sight, August let his arm drop to his side and they started down the block. Within only steps, her poor, crunched toes were protesting the decision to walk.

Ow, oh geez. It had to have been nearly a year since she'd worn heels. Enough time to forget how much she hated them.

"It's a ways back to the hotel." August watched her closely while they crossed the street. "You sure you don't want to take a cab?"

"I'm sure." She tried to smile past the fiery pain. It was too late to change her mind now. All the taxis that had been lined up outside the theater were gone. "I like to walk." Maybe not when her toes were likely bleeding, but she would simply have to soldier on.

"I like to walk too." August shoved his hands into his pockets. "I feel like things went well tonight."

"Things did go well." She gritted her teeth against the pain in her feet. Think about something else. She had to think about something else.

The man studied her again. "You don't sound convinced."

Leila didn't meet his eyes so he wouldn't see how bad she was hurting. "It's not that I don't think the date went well." It scared her how easy it was to pretend when she was with him. "I mean, this—being with you is easier than it probably should be." They paused at an intersection, waiting for the light to turn. "But back at the winery, it's getting exhausting to pretend like things are fine. Business-wise. It's hard to keep the truth from my grandparents."

She shifted her weight from one foot to the other to alleviate the misery in her toes. How much farther did they have to go?

August held his hand under her elbow while they crossed the street. She must be teetering in the heels more than she thought.

"Hopefully, all of our work pays off and you won't have to worry about keeping the truth from them for too much longer," he said, guiding her in front of him so she could step up onto the sidewalk.

Dear God, did she have to? Pain seemed to rip through her toes now with each step.

A whimper slipped out. *Oh, God.* She could feel the blisters forming.

August slid his arm around her waist and drew her close. "Are you crying?"

"Nope," she murmured. "Not crying." At least not externally. She stepped away from him and staggered on. What was it, five more blocks to the hotel? Now real tears pricked her eyes.

"Hey." August tugged her to a stop. "Something's wrong. You didn't even cry when we watched that horrible *Stepmom* movie my senior year."

Despite her throbbing toes, she laughed. "You were bawling."

"I had something in my eyes." He corrected her with a grin. "Anyway, I know something is wrong, so you might as well spill it."

Leila shifted again, weighing her options. She could risk doing major damage to her feet over the next five blocks or she could tell the man the truth.

"It's the shoes," she moaned. "They're the worst, and it's been so long since I've walked in them. I think my toes are full of blisters."

August looked down at the red stilettos with an appreciative smirk. "They're nice shoes."

"Sure, they're nice. And evil." At this point, she would happily walk over to a trash can and toss them in if it didn't mean she'd have to walk back to the hotel barefoot. "I never should've worn them." She groaned. "Whatever. I'll just have to suffer."

"No, you don't." August pulled out his phone. "We'll use a ride share service." He tapped his phone a few times before frowning at the screen. "Must be a busy night. A driver could be here in thirty minutes."

"I'm not waiting thirty minutes to ride five blocks." Leila took a step and swallowed a groan.

"All right, then." August turned his back to her and knelt in front of her. "Climb on."

"What?" Leila glanced at the people walking past them. So many people.

"Climb on," August repeated. "I'll give you a piggyback ride back to the hotel."

A nervous laugh bubbled out. This was ridiculous. "All the way to the hotel?"

"Sure," he said, as though he offered women piggyback rides every day. "It's only a few more blocks."

"A few like five." But at this point, pain trumped pride. "If you say so." She hiked up her dress above her knees and put her arms around August's neck. He effortlessly stood, his large hands holding her thighs against the sides of his waist while he strode down the block.

"Whoa." She clung to his broad shoulders, doing her best to not strangle the poor man. "Everyone is staring at us."

"So?" August turned his head and peered up at her. "You've never cared much what people thought. You're fearless."

Maybe she had been, at one time in her life. Back in high school, she'd been bold, full of opinions, adventurous. That was before she realized how much life could hurt. Nowadays, she couldn't remember the last risk she'd taken.

August paused at another crosswalk. "Doing okay up there?"

"Mmm-hmm," she lied. She'd been okay. Maybe not great, but before August had shown up, she'd been fine. And now, here he was making her want to go back in time, making her want to be the girl she used to be, making her want him.

She did. She wanted him with an intensity that was getting harder to fight. She wanted him to touch her the way he used to, to make her feel free-spirited and alive.

She ducked her head slightly, avoiding people's stares as they walked the blocks to the hotel, but also bringing her lips closer to his neck. The scent of his shampoo made it seem like she was inhaling an ocean breeze. She stayed that way for a while, content and warm. Somehow, August hardly jostled her at all.

"Honey, we're home." He said the words jokingly, but her stomach still did flips.

Leila peeked up as August approached the hotel and entered the lobby.

"Hey. What's up? Hi, there." The man seemed to greet everyone they passed as though thoroughly enjoying the stares. He moved swiftly to the elevators and hit the button for the eighth floor.

"You can put me down now." Not that she was looking forward to standing in the shoes, but the poor man had to be dying after carrying an adult human being for five blocks.

"We're not back to our room yet." August held her right where she was while the elevator zipped up to their floor.

The closer they got to the room, the more Leila's heart skipped. What would happen when they got there? Would they sleep in the same bed? Would she be able to sleep in the same bed without touching him?

August didn't appear to feel the nerves—or was it anticipation?—coursing through her. He blitzed down the hallway at his normal, quick pace and withdrew the keycard from his wallet. Once inside the room, he still didn't set her feet back on the floor. Instead, he walked into the bathroom and carefully lowered her to the ledge of the soaking tub. He turned on the water, plugged the drain, and tested the temperature with his fore-arm. Then, without a word, he lifted her feet into his hands, gently removing her shoes, and then placed her aching toes in the warm, soothing water.

"You should soak them for a while." He stood and laid out a towel next to her before walking out of the room.

Leila sat on the tub's ledge, breathing hard, heart beating wildly, while the warmth took the sting out of her raw toes. August hadn't changed like she'd thought. He hadn't grown colder or become arrogant in his success. He had a different life, a different job, but he still had the same heart she'd fallen in love with.

Driven by the newfound rhythm in her own heart, Leila shut off the water, dried her feet, and quickly walked into the bathroom's closet to take off her dress. After stashing it in her suitcase, she put on the safe, practical sweats she'd brought in her suitcase. Anticipation simmered low and deep and hot, softening her knees as she opened the door and walked into the bedroom.

August lay on the edge of the bed staring up at the ceiling, his feet planted firmly on the floor. He'd shed his suit coat and tie; the collar of his white button-down shirt was rumpled.

Leila padded across the plush carpet and lay next to him with her legs hanging over the side of the mattress. There were so many things she wanted to say to him, to hear from him, but first, she had to know something. "I always wondered if I didn't do enough to help you get through your loss after your dad died. Or if I could've done more for you—"

"No." August turned his head and waited for her to look at him. "I shut you out. I shut everyone out. You were best thing in my life, Lei. But I was in such a dark place that I couldn't see anything good."

"I wish I could've found my way through the darkness to bring you out of it," she murmured, the longing for how things used to be straining her voice.

"You did a lot for me." August smoothed a lock of her hair away from her face and tucked it behind her ear. "It scares me how easily I walked away. How I let pain and grief take over everything."

She held her palm against his cheek. "You loved your dad."

"I loved you too." He moved his body closer, gaze dropping to her lips. "I loved you and then I messed everything up."

Leila propped herself up on her elbow, hovering over him. "Let's not talk about the past. Not tonight." She was tired of thinking about their history, tired of trying to sort it all out while the minutes passed them by. "Maybe it's better to live in the present." All she knew was right now, her heart had started to beat to that wild cadence again. Desire flickered, a blue-hot flame at her very center, and that was all she chose to feel. Not guilt or uncertainty, only want. "Maybe now is all that matters. Not the past. Not the future." In the present, she could hold him and touch him; she could feel him against her again.

She brought her shaky hand to the first button at the collar of his shirt and watched his eyes darken while she worked it open. August stared up at her, his broad chest expanding with each breath. Leila moved down to the next button, finding it even easier to undo.

"We're supposed to keep this professional," he uttered, closing his eyes.

She pressed her finger to his lips. "No rules. Remember?"

August opened his eyes and kissed her finger, and then clasped her wrist and moved her hand so he could kiss her knuckles, and then her palm.

When had her palm become an erogenous zone? Leila pulled her hand out of his grasp and went to work on the buttons again, getting the third, fourth, and fifth undone in record time. That only left one more.

"You make following any rule one hundred percent impossible." August sat up and pulled her into a kiss, distracting her from her mission to get that shirt off him.

Oh, yes. His lips provided quite the distraction, hot and wet and moving against hers with an urgency that matched her own.

Without breaking the kiss, Leila moved to her knees, inching closer to straddle his lap while she slipped her hands inside his shirt to push it off his shoulders.

August took care of the undershirt, swiftly pulling it up and over his head before he kissed her again.

She couldn't make herself break away from his mouth, from the way his tongue stroked hers. Instead of looking at his chest, she moved her hands across it, feeling the firm contours and bends. This kind of muscle wasn't built inside a gym. Her hands moved lower, climbing down the rungs of his abs until they ran into that one stubborn button at the bottom of his shirt. Just as she went to unbutton it, August put his arms around her and stood, lifting her off the bed.

She wrapped her legs around his waist. "Hey."

He gave her a sly smile while he whipped the comforter back to reveal the crisp, white sheets. Then he carefully laid her back on the bed.

"That damn button." Leila reached her hands up to his shirt and finally undid the last barrier to getting a full look at the man's brawn. The shirt fell all the way off, displaying his tanned skin and toned build.

"What are you going to take off?" He eased onto the bed, watching her.

Leila smirked. "How about this frumpy sweatshirt?"

He took a good look at the tattered University of Denver hoodie. "Trust me. Nothing could ever look frumpy on you." He leaned in and kissed her neck, his warm breath awakening her skin. "You could make a snowsuit look sexy."

"Mmm-hmm." Leila let her head tilt to the side, giving him more access.

August took advantage, kissing and nipping and sliding his tongue up to her ear. "What do you want?"

She closed her eyes. When was the last time she'd thought about what she *wanted*? For months, life had been more about what she had to do.

He stopped kissing her and waited for an answer. Leila opened her eyes and turned her face to his. Seeing him there, so close, shirtless, and staring at her with such a focused intensity made the answer simple. "I want to remember." How he'd made her feel, how he'd touched her, how he'd seemed to know her in a way no one else ever had. She moved her hand to his jaw and guided his lips back to hers. The kiss brought her memories back into focus. She'd forgotten the happiness he'd once brought into her life. She'd wanted to forget after he was gone, but now that same elation unfurled in her heart again.

August slowed the kiss, his hands finding hers while he tenderly wove their fingers together. Why had she kept him away? His mouth knew hers, searching, exploring, teasing until she sputtered to find a breath. He could give her so much more.

Leila withdrew her hands from his and let her head fall back to the mattress. August shifted to his side next to her, gazing into her eyes. "Are you sure about this, Lei?"

She answered by inching the hem of her sweatshirt up painstakingly slowly, pausing before she revealed her bra. "Quick side note here... I wasn't planning to get undressed in front of you." If she had been more prepared, she would've chosen her best undergarments instead of a plain old boring black bra and underwear combo with zero lace.

"You're beautiful and sexy and seductive." August lowered his lips to her belly and deposited a few kisses that made certain parts clench. "You. Not your clothes or your lingerie. You, just you, exactly as you are." Her lowered his mouth back to her skin, kissing his way up her belly and then ribs before moving her sweatshirt up higher and gently pulling it over her head. "I've never wanted you more than I do right now." He gazed into her eyes as his hand slipped beneath her back and unclasped the sensible bra.

"You want me more now than you did when I wore that corset thing to surprise you before you left for school?" She raised her eyebrows, searching his face for any hesitation.

"That was pretty incredible, but yes." He pulled the bra away from her chest. "I want you more now than I did then because now I know. I know what it's like to be without you. I know what it's like to miss you." He lowered his mouth to her breast, leaving a trail of fire along her skin with his tongue. "God, I missed you, Lei," he breathed against her skin.

"I missed you too." The words came out winded and needy and desperate, but she didn't care. She'd been fooling herself to think she could resist this man. She never could resist him. Not back then. Not now.

August continued his exploration of her chest, electrifying her with his mouth and tongue, murmuring how good she tasted, how he wanted to taste more of her.

More.

Yes.

Yes, more. Leila smoothed her hands into his hair, urging his head up, guiding his lips to hers. He tasted good too. Like spice and the mint gum he'd chewed earlier during the show.

His lips parted, and her tongue frantically searched for his, all her synapses firing. The pressure building between her legs intensified into a throb.

As if feeling her urgency, August started to stand, still kissing her, pulling her up with him. Once on her feet, she wobbled, her legs boneless and weak, but August held her up.

Breaking the kiss, Leila went to work on his belt, somehow managing to unbuckle the complicated contraption so she could unbutton his suit pants.

"Fair warning, I didn't wear my best boxers," August said with a smirk.

"Whatever." She pushed his pants off his hips and then went right for the underwear. "It's not the boxers I'm interested in." There were still too many clothes, too many barriers between them. She managed to slide the elastic waistband off his hips and then he took care of the rest, stepping out of the underwear while snatching his wallet off the dresser.

The sight of him putting on a condom captivated her. Auggie

had always had a nice body, but he'd filled out more, the muscles stronger and defined. "Well?" he asked, giving her a full frontal.

"You're perfect." She pushed her pants and underwear both down in one fell swoop—no need for him to see her boring panties—and then walked to him with an extra sway in her hips. "I've never wanted you more than I do right now." The heat rising all through her body proved it.

Pressing her palms against his shoulders, Leila backed him to the bed and prodded him to sit on the edge.

The levity disappeared from his expression, and his eyes turned greedy as she eased her knees onto the mattress, straddling his waist. "In fact, I want you so much that I'm not going to wait anymore," she murmured into his ear. She couldn't wait. Her body cried out for a release.

With a shift of her hips, she slid onto him, taking all of him into her. Her breath caught and her body stilled.

"Look at me," August said quietly.

She raised her eyes to his.

"I want to see you. All of you." August kissed her again, moaning against her lips, echoing her ecstasy.

Leila started to move against him. She couldn't help it, couldn't be still. They fit together, every part of them all through the past into the present.

"That's it, Lei." August rested his hands on her hips but didn't move her. "Show me what you want."

Everything. She wanted to feel every sensation and hope and desire she'd desperately tried to submerge since he'd shown up. She inched up higher on her knees and came down on him again, arching her back. August lifted his hips to meet her thrusts, holding her in his arms.

The titillating pressure built low in her belly, swelling through her. "Kiss me." She needed his mouth against hers, needed to feel him breathe as heavily as she was.

Somewhere in the blind rush of sensations and emotions, his

lips found hers. The kiss was wet and hot and stuttering between their collective gasps and moans.

Leila dug her fingers into his shoulders and tightened her legs around him, moving the way her body begged her to until she finally had to let go, convulsing under the powerful climax that radiated through every part of her.

August held his lips to hers as he shivered, pulling her in closer, moaning her name when his entire body tensed. He fell back to the mattress with a contended sigh, and she collapsed next to him, her head nestled in the crook of his neck.

For a long time, he simply stared at her and she stared back, losing herself in his gaze.

"I thought I'd lost you forever," he finally said, skimming his thumb across her cheek.

"Well, you know what Nonna always says." Leila captured his hand and pressed it to her lips. "Nothing can be lost when it's already a part of you." And August had always been a part of her heart.

Chapter Seventeen

August." Someone shook his shoulder. "Come on. We have to get up."

He shifted his body and managed to get his head halfway off the pillow. Leila. It was Leila. In bed with him. Still naked. Thank God the whole night hadn't been a dream.

"Come on." She shook him again. "We're supposed to meet Nonna and Poppa for breakfast in the lobby in fifteen minutes."

Fully awake now, he put his arms around her and pulled her back to him. "How about we stay right here and order room service?"

He kissed her neck. Her body relaxed, melting into his, and a smile graced her face. "We can't ditch my grandparents. No matter how much I might want to."

He didn't want to ditch Nonna and Poppa either, but if they left this room, the spell would be broken. They'd have to get back to the planning and the orchestrating and the pretending for everyone else that they loved each other while pretending to themselves they didn't. Or did they?

He rested his head on her shoulder and closed his eyes. "But if we go to breakfast, we'll have to put on clothes."

Leila laughed, still snuggled up against him. Clearly, she wasn't in any hurry to get out of here either.

"And you wouldn't put on clothes when room service delivered our food?" she asked, tracing her fingers up his arm.

"Nah." What would be the point when he'd only be taking them off again? He brought his lips to her shoulder, kissing his way down. "Come on, let's text your grandparents and tell them we're still in bed."

"No!" She propped herself up on her elbow and gaped at him. "Then they'll know we had sex. Or that we're having sex again, which is worse."

"Umm." August stole a kiss from her incredulous lips. "They got us a hotel room," he said when he pulled away. "I'm pretty sure they knew we were going to have sex before we did."

When they'd left Silverado Lake, he'd been hell-bent on this exact thing not happening, thanks to Sam's lecture, but Leila's brother had been wrong. August wasn't messing with her. His feelings were real. He simply didn't know what to do with them outside of this room.

All the more reason to stay right here.

"I don't want my grandparents thinking about our sex life at all." Leila stared up at the ceiling with a grimace. "That's so weird."

"It's not weird." He caressed her shoulder while he still had the chance. "Your grandmother has always been a hopeless romantic. She'd be all for us making love." He was all for it now too, and Leila still wasn't trying to get out of bed. "I like being with you." That was all he needed her to know. "Alone. Like this." When they could both simply be real.

"I like being with you too." She turned fully on her side to face him and wrapped her leg over his. "And last night *was* pretty great."

"See, now that kind of talk is not going to make me want to get out of this bed." He could do better than great. He had no doubt he could achieve mind-blowing and amazing, given the opportunity.

August moved his hands up the sides of her body and then over her breasts, knowing exactly how she liked to be touched, what turned her on.

"Oh, God," she moaned, but then started to wriggle away from him. "Wait. We can't. We just can't. I want to." She leaned over and kissed his lips. "I *soooo* want to, but we have five minutes to throw on our clothes and get down to the lobby. They're probably already sitting at a table waiting. You know how Poppa doesn't like waiting to eat."

"All right. You win. We'll go get some breakfast." He pulled her in close once more so he could leave her with a long, heady, tempting kiss that would stay with her a while.

Leila kissed him back, arching into him slightly, her hands wandering from his shoulders down to his abs. She leaned back, breathing heavily. "Maybe we can steal an hour or two in my cottage when we get back to the winery."

"Really?" She was going to take a few hours off work in the middle of the day? He shot her a skeptical smirk. "What happened to being a workaholic?"

"You're broadening my horizons." She squeezed his butt and then threw off the covers and started to get dressed.

"I'm happy to keep broadening your horizons." He forced himself to get up too, admiring her while he walked to the dresser where his suitcase sat next to it. "You want broader horizons, I'm your man."

"I'll keep that in mind." With a flip of her hair, Leila disappeared into the bathroom.

August gave her some time and then followed so he could quickly wash up and brush his teeth. While Lei fussed with her hair in the mirror, he pulled on the change of clothes he brought and then went back into the bedroom and repacked his suitcase. Unfortunately. Rushing to meet her grandparents wasn't exactly how he'd like to end this date.

Leila walked back out, her hair smoothed into a ponytail, her face and eyes both bright. "If an hour or two during the day isn't enough, you could always stay at my place tonight." She gave a casual shrug. "Only if you want. Everyone expects us to be staying together anyway."

He didn't like the ring of uncertainty in her voice. Did she really think he wouldn't want to stay with her? August crossed the room and took her shoulders in his hands, making sure his gaze stayed with hers. "I know things are complicated. I know our lives are very different and the future isn't exactly clear. But I don't want you to think this was some casual hookup for me, Lei."

She peered up at him, her expression soft and open. "It wasn't for me either."

"So we'll take it day by day." He might not be able to commit to her, but he cared about her. "And enjoy the time we have."

"Yes." She rested her hands on his chest. "I need more of that in my life—enjoying the moment. I've been too worried about the future since I got home."

"I need to enjoy the moment more too." The future hadn't been his problem, but rather the past. The loss, the guilt whenever he let his thoughts drift to this woman. There were no guarantees in life—he knew that better than anyone—but these next few months were a gift, and he intended to treat them that way.

With that in mind, he snuck an arm around her waist and pulled her in for a kiss. No, not only a kiss. With Lei, there was no such thing as *only* a kiss. Their lips spoke for them—connecting and knowing and understanding and expressing things they couldn't say.

"Is it tonight yet?" Leila asked, her lips still pressed to his.

"This is going to be the slowest day of my life," he groaned.

Grinning, she broke away from him. "Anticipation isn't a bad thing."

"Right. Anticipation." August trudged to the dresser and unplugged his phone. The screen lit up with a whole list of notifications. "Huh. That's weird." He studied the numbers.

Leila zipped up her suitcase. "What's weird?"

"I missed three calls from Forrest already this morning." Those notifications were all he needed to see to bring reality slamming back down. He wasn't here to be spending nights with Leila. He was supposed to be doing his job. Forrest rarely called him when he was away. August always kept his boss informed on what was happening, but the man usually left him alone.

Leila rolled her suitcase to where he stood. "What does he want?"

"I don't know. I haven't talked to him much since I came out here." He shoved the phone into the back pocket of his jeans and pulled his suitcase off the stand. "I'll call him when we get back to Silverado Lake. I'm sure it's not a big deal."

If only he felt as confident as he sounded.

* * *

"I would say this trip was exactly what we all needed." Nonna sat in the backseat of August's truck looking quite pleased with herself. He could detect the triumph in her eyes even with her quick gaze into the rearview mirror.

And, really, who was he to argue? "You were right, as usual." He glanced sideways at Leila, who was sitting a lot closer to him on the truck's bench seat than she had been on the way down the mountain yesterday.

A secretive smile softened her mouth, making him want to kiss her again. In fact, during the hours they'd been on the road, all he'd thought about was kissing her again.

Taking his right hand off the wheel, he eased his arm around Leila the way he used to when they drove around in his father's old truck.

"You two seem different somehow. Lighter," Nonna observed. "Didn't I tell you a break would do wonders for your stress level?"

"You sure did." Leila rested her hand on his thigh, giving him a jolting reminder of how her hands had felt on his body last night. Ten more minutes. They had already driven through Silverado

Lake and would arrive back at the winery—and Leila's cottage—in only ten more minutes. And once they got there, he planned to get exactly no work done for the rest of the day.

"Thank you for convincing us to get away, Nonna and Poppa." He glanced at her grandparents, who were sitting as close as two people could possibly get with seat belts on. "I can't tell you how much we needed this time together." One night had changed everything. Leila had always been the only woman who'd managed to spark hope in him, and somehow, she'd worked her magic again. He felt lighter with her now, unburdened and free.

"You are so welcome." Leila's grandmother squeezed his shoulder.

"Make sure you remember this feeling," Poppa added. "Life isn't easy. Marriage isn't easy. But it's the times like these—the moments of happiness—that'll hold you together no matter what comes your way. Sometimes, you have to go out and make those moments happen."

August watched in the rearview mirror as Nonna laid her head on Poppa's shoulder and the man pressed a tender kiss on her forehead. They were speaking from experience. Nonna's illness couldn't have been easy for either one of them, but they were the picture of strength, devotion, and affection. What would it be like to have that with someone? Someone to share burdens and pains with instead of isolating and carrying those things alone?

"I was actually surprised you two made it to breakfast on time." Leila's grandmother giggled. "If we were forty years younger, we might've wanted to stay in bed and take advantage of that romantic hotel suite."

"Nonna!" Leila turned her head to gape at her grandmother, but August simply raised his eyebrows at his fiancée. See? They could've skipped breakfast, and her grandparents would've been totally cool about it.

"What?" Her grandmother smiled sweetly. "There's nothing

wrong with the physical expression of love, my dear. It's every bit
as important as words. You'd best remember that."

"Oh, we'll remember," August assured the woman with a wink
at Leila. He would have no problem remembering to keep her
physically satisfied. At least, as long as he had the opportunity.

August turned the truck onto the winery's driveway and
navigated the first switchback.

"So, what do you two have planned for the rest of the day?"
Nonna asked, gathering up her purse.

He caught Leila's eyes and fought a grin.

Her perfect lips pursed as though she could read his thoughts.
"I need August's help with some work in my cottage this afternoon. The kitchen sink is leaking."

"Leaking?" Poppa leaned forward. "I fixed the sink last month.
It can't be leaking again already."

"I'll check it out," August offered. Man, it was hard not to laugh.

"I can help you," Poppa said gruffly. "I don't do shoddy work."

"Of course not." Leila turned around. "I think it's something
I did. I probably cranked the faucet too hard. Nothing to worry
about. August will take care of it."

"I sure will." He cast a glance back at Poppa. "But I'll let you
know if I need help." Hopefully, the comment would keep the
man from barging in on them at an inopportune time.

He guided the truck around the last switchback. "Do you two
want me to drop you off at your house?"

"Nope. We're going straight to the restaurant," Nonna said.
"After that long drive, I could use a light lunch."

"Sounds great." Leila's tone lightened. She likely felt the
same relief he did that her grandparents would be occupied for
a while.

August turned the truck into the main parking lot and eased
a foot onto the brake while he took a second to check out the
Hummer parked a few spots away. His heart dropped. A Hummer
was Forrest's signature rental car choice.

"Who's that?" Leila had noticed the vehicle too.

"It might be a friend of mine." He drove the truck to the far side of the parking lot near the restaurant and parked along the sidewalk to put plenty of space between them and the Hummer.

Leila jerked her head, staring at him with wide eyes. According to the panic there, she'd figured out exactly whom he'd meant when he said "friend."

August wished he could reassure her, but he had no doubt his boss was here. Right now, the important question was where had the man gone?

"I didn't know you had a friend visiting." Nonna opened her door and he quickly got out to help her step down to the curb.

"Uh, yeah. I wasn't sure if he'd come, but it looks like he's here." Somewhere. And right now, he had to keep Forrest away from Leila's grandparents.

"We'd love to meet him." Poppa eased himself down from the truck and scanned the parking lot.

"I'm sure August will introduce us later." Leila rushed to her grandparents and ushered them along the sidewalk. "But I'm starving too, actually, so why don't we go sit down for lunch and then they can come find us after a while?" Her eyes narrowed, telling him he'd better not let Forrest find them.

"Great plan." Since his boss's car was parked at the other end of the lot, he hoped Forrest hadn't made it near the restaurant yet. "We'll come on by soon." Or rather, he'd send his boss packing.

With one last desperate glance over her shoulder, Leila led her grandparents into the restaurant.

August waved and then trotted to the Hummer, trying to determine in which direction Forrest would've headed first. There weren't many choices. He'd likely either gone to the wine barn or right into the vineyard. Damn. He really should've called his boss long before now.

Veering to the left, he ducked into a row of vines and followed the worn dirt path. It seemed he'd chosen correctly. Forrest stood at the edge of the cliff, looking out onto the valley.

"Hey," August called, speeding up. "What're you doing here?"

He couldn't help the accusatory tone. Forrest's arrival was not a welcome surprise. He and Leila should be holed up in her cottage right about now.

"What am I doing here?" His boss strode to meet him. "I'm here for an update. Other than the vague financials you sent, I've hardly heard from you since you left."

"I didn't realize you would be babysitting me on this assignment." His words held a sharp edge. Forrest typically didn't worry about what he was doing when he was on-site. "What do you want to know?" He had to get rid of his boss fast. This would be a problem for Leila—Forrest showing up whenever he wanted when her grandparents had no idea what was really going on. And if it was a problem for Leila, it was a problem for him.

"For starters, what steps has Ms. Valentino taken to increase revenue?" Forrest glared at him, a belligerent slant to his eyes. "Her time's almost up. I think it's best if you start working on a transition plan to bring this place fully under the Kingston brand."

"She still has a month." He'd been hoping they wouldn't need a transition plan.

"Maybe I didn't make myself clear when I sent you out here." His stepped closer. "I don't want Ms. Valentino or her family staying. That's not the goal, August. In order to do what needs to be done here, we need them out of the way."

August took a long pause before responding so he didn't come across as overly defensive. "Why? Leila could be a valuable asset to Kingston. She's sharp and educated. And she's got a good plan to move this place forward." She might not be using conventional business practices, but she'd rallied the community for the event. She'd generated excitement and interest.

"We don't need her." Forrest shrugged like he didn't understand why August would think they did. "She'll only be in our way."

"I see." He let a few seconds pass until he could be sure he'd control his tone. Why had Forrest's shrewd, merciless business practices never bothered him before now? "You never intended to let her stay either way." From the very beginning, this deal Leila made doomed her to fail.

"I warned her it would be an uphill battle. But she needed the partnership." And Forrest needed a new challenge.

"This is her family's place." His poker face started to slip. "You can't kick them out."

"I'm not kicking them out," Forrest shot back. "We have an agreement, and when the terms aren't met, they'll have to leave. They'll still come out with a nice retirement."

"They don't care about retirement." Poppa would never want to retire. He'd want to wander this land for the rest of his life.

"Let me be very clear this time." His boss had a way of looking right through a person. "Your job is to make sure Ms. Valentino doesn't succeed in reaching that thirty percent profit increase. That's what I want you to do."

August quickly weighed his options. He'd never been emotionally invested in a job. In fact, some probably would say he'd always been as shrewd as Forrest. The Valentinos' fate mattered to him, but he couldn't let Forrest know or his boss would send him packing right now. If he wanted to help Lei, he had to play along.

"That shouldn't be a problem," he lied. He made sure to hold eye contact. "I'm already heavily involved in everything the family is doing. In fact, Leila and I were together a long time ago, and she didn't tell her grandparents about the partnership with Kingston. So when I showed up unannounced, she told them I had come to visit because we're getting married."

Forrest threw back his head and let out a good cackle. "*Married*? And they actually believed her?"

Right. It was hilarious because he wasn't marriage material. "Listen, if you want me to make sure to sabotage their efforts to reach that thirty percent increase, you're going to have to go along with this ruse too." This was the only way to protect Nonna and Poppa. "If you stick around, you're staying as my friend and colleague. And you'll need to keep out of my way."

He braced himself for pushback, but the man nodded. "All right. Fine. You can use Ms. Valentino's deception to our advantage. You need to be involved in their plans. We need to know what they're doing."

"Right." August eased out a breath. Forrest had made one thing clear. If August chose to be with Leila, he would have to give up everything else.

Chapter Eighteen

Leila really had to quit guzzling wine.

She kept her eyes trained on the windows and forced herself to eat a butter-basted breadstick to soak up the pinot noir. It had been at least a half hour since they'd gotten back, and August had yet to come and reassure her that he'd gotten rid of Forrest. Was the man still around? Would he come in and announce their partnership?

She picked up her wineglass again.

"Is everything okay?" Poppa squinted in the direction of the windows. "Are you worried about the leak in your sink? Because we can go fix—"

"No!" She nearly spilled her wine. "I mean, I'm not worried," she quickly amended, forcing a smile. They were staying put until she knew for sure the threat to her secret had been neutralized. "I'm sure August will join us any minute now." Without Forrest, because that man had better be on his way back to California. Yes, August would join them for lunch and tell her he'd gotten rid of his boss for good, and then they could go back to her cottage and pick up where they'd left off that morning.

She'd always been a dreamer.

"Hopefully, we'll get to meet Auggie's friend," Nonna said cheerfully. Her grandmother had always loved making new friends. "Where's he from?"

"Oh. Um." Leila set down her wineglass before she really did drop it. "California, I think?" She shoved in a bite of salad so Nonna wouldn't ask any more questions.

"Did you know his friend was coming for a visit?" her grandmother pressed. "Because we could've set up a special lunch to greet him properly."

Greet him properly? She silently harrumphed. A special lunch would do little to impress Mr. Kingston. "I think he's only passing through." He couldn't stay or he'd ruin everything. "Kind of a last-minute thing. No big deal. I bet he only wanted to say a quick hello to August."

"Well, make sure Auggie sends him off with a bottle of wine." Nonna blotted her mouth politely with a napkin. "Maybe he'll join the wine club."

If it hadn't been for another bite of lettuce in her mouth, Leila might have busted out a laugh. "I don't think—"

"We can give him a bottle ourselves." Poppa gestured to the windows. "It looks like he and Auggie will join us for lunch, after all."

A bit of radish stuck in Leila's throat as she watched August lead—*lead!*—the enemy into the restaurant. An involuntary gasp lodged that piece of radish right into her windpipe, blocking her inhalation. She slammed both hands down onto the table, choking and coughing.

"Oh dear!" Nonna rose from her chair. "Are you okay? Poppa, do something!"

Her grandfather rushed to her side, knocking over his chair in the process. "I know the Heimlich!" He started to put his arms around her, but Leila gagged, and the radish came flying out of her mouth, landing in her wineglass.

Sweet air! She pulled a long breath into her lungs, the burning in her throat sending tears to her eyes.

"What happened?" August now stood next to her with Forrest only steps behind.

Leila continued to breathe. This was it. Their plan was over. Four hours ago, she'd been blissfully happy, in bed with August, and now she was about to break everyone's hearts.

"She was choking." Nonna patted her back. "Are you all right now? Goodness, that scared me."

"I'm fine." The words scraped her throat. She couldn't look into her grandmother's eyes. Any second now, Forrest would out her, and they would know she'd risked their family legacy for a financial buyout.

August knelt beside her, studying her face. "You sure you're okay?"

How could he look so calm? How could he have brought Forrest right to her grandparents?

"I'm fine." Her voice shook with a blend of anger and sadness. They'd been so close to rekindling a connection, and now she was on the verge of watching everything fall apart. Instead of standing, August stared steadily into her eyes.

Everything's going to be fine, his seemed to say.

Despite her better judgment, she settled her nerves. He'd always had the magic touch when it came to calming her down.

Placing his hand over hers, Auggie stood back up. "Since everyone is okay, I want to introduce you all to my friend Forrest."

"Forrest?" Poppa's eyes seemed to sharpen as he gave the man a long appraisal. "Forrest Kingston?"

"*Really?*" Nonna peered up at the man. "I thought you'd be much older."

"I'm old enough, I assure you." Forrest stepped to the table wearing that million-dollar smile Leila had seen in many magazine articles. "You must be August's fiancée. Wonderful to meet you." He extended his hand with a sparkle in his eyes, but she couldn't move.

August helped her stand. "I told him all about our engagement."

"That's great." Just great. August had really invited this man into their already very complicated arrangement?

"And I couldn't be more thrilled for the two of you." Though the words sounded genuine enough to the untrained ear, she detected the amusement in Forrest's tone. "I have to admit, I never thought August would settle down, but here we are."

Yes, here they were. "It's nice to meet you," Leila choked out, finally shaking his outstretched hand. In reality, this would be the second time she'd met him. The first had been when she'd flown out to California months ago to sign a deal with the devil.

"It's an honor and a privilege to welcome you to Valentino Bellas." Poppa offered the man a hearty handshake. "I've tried a few Kingston bottles in my day. It's good." Her grandfather pointed at the man. "Not as good as Valentino Bellas, but good."

Forrest laughed. "I have to admit, I haven't had the pleasure of tasting a Valentino Bellas blend yet. But I'm looking forward to sampling one."

The man's jovial tone started Leila's internal fire. "You can take a bottle with you when you leave." He wasn't supposed to be here. He'd agreed she would have the fall to turn this place around, and then he showed up unannounced?

"You're not leaving already, I hope?" Nonna pushed out the chair next to hers. "Why don't you join us? You could try our red flight."

"I would love to." Forrest plopped down into the seat like he'd been dying for an invitation. "I was hoping to stick around, at least for a few days." He winked at Leila. "See the sights while I'm here."

Oh, God. He was here to torture her. To look over her shoulder and remind her she was only a month from complete failure. She almost walked away from the table. Almost. But she couldn't leave Forrest alone with her grandparents for a whole red flight. Who knew what the man would tell them?

"I'll go put in the order, and we can add some appetizers while we're at it." Poppa turned away from the table.

"Wait!" Leila bolted in front of him. "I'll go put in the order." She needed a couple of seconds away to get herself together, to walk off the nervous energy buzzing inside of her.

"I'll come with you." August slipped his arm around her and led her away. When they turned the corner out of sight, Leila stopped abruptly.

"What are you thinking?" She leaned against the wall to take some of the pressure off her legs. "How could you let him stay? How could you bring him to my grandparents? You know what's at stake here!"

"I couldn't force him to leave." August eased closer to her. "But you don't have to worry. He won't give up our secret. He knows your grandparents aren't aware of the partnership."

Was that supposed to reassure her? "Why is he here?" All the anger and the panic that had been churning inside of her came out, directed at August. "What does he want?"

"He wants to..." August hesitated. "See how thing are going." He rested his hands on her hips and nudged her closer. "I'm sorry, Lei. I know this puts all kinds of pressure on you, but you have nothing to worry about. I promise. I'm here to take that pressure away. I'll keep tabs on him. I won't let him step out of line. I've spent years managing Forrest. This'll be no different. Things will be fine."

She wanted to melt into him and say okay. She wanted to let him hold her until she believed everything would be fine—that she would be able to save this place, that there might be a future for the two of them together.

But she'd stood at a crossroads with August once before, and she couldn't put her heart and her future into his hands again. So she pushed him away. August could give her no guarantees on anything. Not on the winery, not on them.

"I'm going to put the order in." Leila ducked into the kitchen before he could get a glimpse of the tears in her eyes.

August didn't try to come after her, which was just as well. Tears wouldn't help her now. Neither would feelings. She had to refocus and go back to simply playing a part. Pretending was much safer territory than where she and August had gone last night. Her sole priority and focus had to be her family.

After putting in their appetizers and Forrest's flight orders with their server, Leila rejoined the table, sitting between August and Forrest with steel in her spine. This man might believe he could come out here and intimidate her, but she was about to show him she was tougher than he thought.

She smoothed her napkin over her lap and masked her worry with a bright smile. "The food and wine will be right out."

"Wonderful." Nonna happily dipped a breadstick into the olive oil. "Forrest was just telling us how many wineries he's acquired on the West Coast."

And yet, the impressive number still wasn't enough for the man. "Yes, I've heard you've grown your operation quite large." She held eye contact with him, steeling her gaze. "I'm sure you'll see how different Valentino Bellas is during your visit. Instead of a cold, corporate operation, we're offering our customers a welcoming, unpretentious experience that allows them to actually be part of a community."

Forrest's eyes gleamed at the challenge. "Yes, I can already see it's quite homey here. Rustic. I'm sure there's a certain clientele that is drawn to the simplicity." *But not enough of a clientele to make any money*, his smirk seemed to add.

"Our focus has always been on people." Poppa gestured to the rows of photographs hanging on the opposite wall. The pictures depicted laughter and fun—groups of people visiting the tasting room and enjoying a meal at the restaurant and helping with the harvest. "We like to think of everyone who visits as family. With such a large base, do you get to know many of your customers?" he asked Forrest.

Only the ones with the deepest pockets; Leila had no doubt about that.

"Sure, I get to know some of them." The man looked like he might say something else, but their server appeared with his wine flight.

"Valentino Bellas makes the best wine in this whole region," August informed Forrest after the server had introduced each glass and stepped away.

"The blend is handcrafted from the vine to the glass," Nonna added proudly. "We do everything right here ourselves."

"I can't wait to try a sip." Forrest lifted the first glass, swirling and sniffing like a true wine snob.

It broke Leila's heart to see how eager her grandparents looked—how hopeful—that a man like Forrest Kingston would enjoy their wine. That was what they had always cared about more than the bottom line: making people happy. Little did they know, Mr. Kingston didn't care about them or their labor of love.

The man let the first sip sit for a bit on his tongue, and both Nonna and Poppa leaned in, waiting for his approval.

"Delicious," he said after a lengthy deliberation. "There's such a nuanced flavor."

"That's the grapes," Poppa insisted with a grin that stretched from one ear to the other. "I swear this mountain air gives them a unique flavor all their own."

"Is that so?" Forrest practically salivated at the news. "And would you say you're consistently able to bring in a good crop?"

Poppa threw up his hands. "Depends on the year. No offense, but growing grapes out here is a lot more challenging than what you're used to." Pride puffed his chest. "I mean, we're battling early and late freezes and constant temperature swings. It makes the grapes heartier."

"Interesting." Kingston took his time trying out the pinot noir, which Leila believed was one of their best. "I'm impressed." He set down the glass. "This is high-quality wine you're producing here."

Leila didn't buy the man's compliments for one second. Yes, it was some of the best wine in the entire region, but he didn't care about their wine. He was intrigued by prospect of taking over.

For the next half hour, he proceeded to charmingly interrogate her grandparents—asking them all kinds of questions about their processes, and they were all too happy to answer. He was probably taking mental notes for when he ran the place.

Finally, Leila couldn't take it anymore. During a lull in the conversation, she pushed her chair back. "Well, I'm sure we'd all love to stay and talk longer, but there's a lot of work to do around here."

Nonna and Poppa stared at her blankly.

"Remember?" she prompted politely. "The harvest is starting tomorrow?" She'd gotten the official text from Sam last night.

"That's right!" Poppa stood too. Harvest had always been one of his favorite times of the year. "I have to go sort the supplies for our volunteers."

"And I have to see to the morning breakfast preparations." Nonna reached for her husband's hand, and he helped her to her feet. "I hope you'll join us for the harvest," she said to Forrest. "We always provide a huge free breakfast for our many volunteers."

"*Free* breakfast?" The man cast a glance at Leila as though it were her fault they were throwing money away.

"It's a tradition." She made sure to put a razor-sharp edge in her tone. "Everyone looks forward to gathering for breakfast before the harvest each year. It's part of that important community thing I was talking about earlier." Their events brought people together. Those were things she couldn't change. Those were things she wouldn't change, no matter how ridiculous he thought they were.

"The harvest is seriously a highlight for the whole town." August slipped his arm around her, and Leila immediately stiffened. Hopefully, no one else noticed.

"Well, it sounds like I'll see you in the morning for breakfast, then." Forrest finished off the last pour of wine and then stood too. "In the meantime, I was hoping August could give me a tour of the vineyards. Leila, you're welcome to join us, of course."

"I'm afraid I have too much work to do." She'd likely be up all night brainstorming additional ways to increase revenue so this man would never take over her family's land. "But I'll look forward to seeing you all in the morning." Without waiting for a response, she crossed the room with her most confident gait and slipped outside before finally letting her shoulders wilt. Forrest clearly wasn't here only to visit and check in. That greedy jerk couldn't wait to take this place away from her. From Nonna and Poppa. And she couldn't let him. She had to do everything she could to fight back.

"Hey." August hurried to her side. "I wanted to make sure you're okay."

"Okay?" She half laughed. "No, I'm not okay." Every time she looked in his eyes, her entire body softened, so she avoided his gaze altogether. Now was not the time to go soft. "You know as well as I do the odds are against me." Not *them. Her.* She stood to lose everything, and August would lose nothing. "Forrest wants this place. Even if I could increase our profit margin—which is highly unlikely—he'll still find a way to take it." And August would help him. That was his job.

"That's not going to happen. Come here." He started to pull her into his arms again, but she held him off. "This will all be easier if we go back to the original plan." She stared past him. "Last night was..." Well, she couldn't even find a word to describe how wonderful it had felt to be with him those few, brief hours. "But this whole situation is going to end in failure for one of us." It was too easy to forget they were on opposite sides. "And I can't be the one to lose."

Leila walked away.

"Wait!" he called behind her, but she didn't even turn around. She couldn't wait again. She had to save Valentino Bellas, even if it meant leaving him for good.

Chapter Nineteen

Are you sure you want to come?"

August peered at his mother's grim frown as he navigated the truck over the washed-out potholes in the ranch's driveway. "Because I can turn around and take you back to your house if you'd like." No sense in ruining her day by forcing her to lie for him.

"I haven't missed one harvest at the vineyard in thirteen years." His mother gave him the same stern look she used to wear when he and his siblings would come up with some elaborate story after they'd broken a vase or a window back in the day.

"And I won't miss one because of this harebrained charade you and Leila have going on either." Her brows pinched tightly together. "How do you think it would look if I didn't show up? Nonna has already left me two messages about scheduling a dinner so we can celebrate your engagement. I can't keep avoiding her."

"I know." She'd mentioned that a couple of times already this morning, and he deserved every bit of her irritation. "I'll tell her we need to wait to have the dinner until things slow down a little. Or maybe until Wes can come back out." He couldn't stomach the thought of a faking his way through an engagement celebration right now anyway.

All he'd wanted to do last night was drive to Leila's cottage and hold her in his arms the way he had the night before, but she'd shut him out. It was the right thing for both of them—he knew that in his head. Having any kind of real relationship with her wasn't practical or logical or even smart right now. No matter what happened, he had to help her increase the revenue, even if it cost him his job. So far, he'd managed to call a few Denver news stations to tip them off to a heartwarming story about a local family that was trying to save their winery. With any luck, the stations would put the word out, and Valentino Bellas would get some free publicity.

"How is the ruse going, anyway?" his mother asked, crossing her arms—another maneuver meant to incite guilt.

"It got a lot more complicated when Forrest showed up." Sure, his boss had agreed to keep things quiet and go along with their supposed engagement, but now he would be here keeping an eye on them, which would put a lot more pressure on them both.

At least he'd managed to convince Forrest to stay at the ranch for the time being. Then he could babysit him as much as possible.

"Does this mean I'll finally get to meet your boss?" his mother asked.

"Yep." Not that he wanted his mom anywhere near Forrest's charm. "He was on a conference call this morning, but he said he'll meet us up at the winery later."

"That should be interesting." She buzzed her window down. "So Forrest has no problem with you pretending to be engaged to the woman he's trying to fire?"

"Nope." Especially because he fully believed August was only pretending so he could ensure a Kingston takeover. He focused on the road and decided not to tell his mom that his boss also thought he was too emotionally stunted to have a real relationship with anyone.

"He obviously trusts you," she pressed. "Does he know about your history with her?"

"Yeah. He's aware." He'd never been one for interrogations. Especially when the interrogator had such freakishly good intuition.

"Auggie, I know this is none of my business, but—"

"Forrest isn't worried about the fake engagement because he knows where I stand on relationships." That admission would be better than telling her he was now pretending with both Forrest and Leila.

His mother angled her body to face him. "And just where do you stand?"

Seeing the turn for the winery's driveway up ahead, he pulled the truck off the road and onto the shoulder. This wasn't something he wanted to discuss while navigating the switchbacks.

"Relationships aren't for me." He probably should've told her this a long time ago, but they hadn't had many heart-to-hearts since he'd moved to California. "I like being on my own. I like not having to worry about anyone else."

His mother let out a humorless laugh. "No. You like not having to *share* yourself with anyone else. And I'll tell you right now, you're missing out."

Spending last night with Leila was all he needed to see exactly how much he was missing out on. "My work is all I need." At least it had been before he'd made the mistake of coming back here.

His mother sighed, the exasperation on her face softening to empathy. "I know I can't tell you what to do anymore, Auggie, but let me say one thing."

Unless he missed his guess, his mother had more than one thing to say.

"Leila is a woman who is worth worrying about. And I think you know that."

Yes, he knew how incredible she was. He also knew he didn't have much to give her. Except this one success. "I'm going to help her save the winery." That was the best thing he could do for her. "And then I'm going to go back to my life and let her live hers."

The finality of that statement didn't seem to shake his mother the way it shook him. "You know, back in our early days at the ranch, there were a few times your dad and I thought we might lose the place." Her eyes misted as she traveled into a memory. "Money was tight; we were in the process of building the cabins, and there were a few months we couldn't make the mortgage payments on time. I was so stressed out, of course. But your dad...he saw things differently."

A mention of his father never failed to knot up his throat.

"Your dad told me the bank could take our land, but they couldn't take what we had," his mom went on. "He said that even if we lost everything else, we'd always have each other."

"But you didn't always have each other." He hadn't meant to say the words, but now it was too late to take them back. "You don't have him anymore." Neither did he. They'd lost their rock. "So in reality, having each other wasn't enough." Sorrow stung his throat. This was pointless, talking about the past. He should've changed the subject like he always did when someone brought up his father.

Mara inhaled deeply, the green hue in her eyes brightening. "I do still have him," she said with her jaw set. "I still have him with me—in every part of me. In every laugh and in every tear and in every moment, I choose to acknowledge his presence in my life." His mother stared at him with a conviction he wasn't sure he'd ever seen on her face. "And you have him too, Auggie. Whether you can see that or not."

He couldn't see his father in his life. There was only a big, gaping hole left, an emptiness. "We should get up there before they assign groups." August shifted the truck back into drive and guided it onto the road. "I'm really sorry you have to be stuck in the middle of this mess."

"At least I'm in the middle of it with you," Mara said softly. "I've missed you. And I'm glad you're home."

All he could muster in response was a nod. In some ways, he was glad to be home too. In other ways, well, it would've been easier to stay away.

Silence settled between them, and he let it sit all the way up to the parking lot.

"It looks like the whole town is here," his mom observed as they drove past row after row of full spots.

"That's a good sign." This place might not have multimillionaire customers, but they had a lot of support in Silverado Lake. That had to count for something.

His mom pointed across the lot. "Who's that with Leila?"

August slowed the truck. "That's Forrest." He did a double take. Were Leila and Forrest actually laughing together?

"Wow, she sure doesn't seem too upset with him." Mara pulled a pair of sunglasses out of her purse and slipped them on.

"No. She doesn't." In fact, the two of them almost looked like...friends. He had to remind himself to step on the gas to keep going to find a parking spot.

After driving down three more completely full rows of cars, he finally found a spot at the far corner. He got out and hurried around to open the door for his mom.

"That's something your father always did," she said pointedly. "He taught you boys to be gentlemen."

"Yeah, I remember." His dad had ingrained in him to make those thoughtful gestures—not only for family, but for strangers in town too. *Opening the door for someone can go a long way in making them feel important*, his old man used to say. Oddly enough, that memory didn't hurt.

Together, he and his mom made their way through the gathering crowd and joined Forrest and Leila near the entrance to the restaurant.

"Good morning, honey." The Leila who greeted him looked nothing like the woman who'd walked away from him yesterday. In addition to the phony smile, her eyes were too wide and overly expressive. "I was just telling Forrest about the winery's history."

"Entertaining me is more like it." His boss shook his head. "I love the story about Nonna and Poppa chasing away the birds with remote control airplanes."

"Yeah, that's a good one." He couldn't smile nearly as big as Leila. What was she doing? She didn't like Forrest.

"Mara, thanks for coming." Leila gave his mother a hug, momentarily pausing her theatrical expression. "It's good to see you."

"It's good to see you, too, Lei," his mother said warmly.

"Mara?" Forrest swooped in. "So, you're the famous Mara Harding? August has told me a lot about you."

"Has he?" His mother lifted her sunglasses away from her eyes. "I'm afraid he hasn't said much about you to me, Mr. Kingston."

"Forrest," his boss corrected with a schmoozing grin that worked so well at all of their parties.

Except August didn't want that grin anywhere near his mother.

"We should find Nonna and Poppa to see what group we're in." He tugged on his mom's sleeve. Every year, the Valentinos split the volunteers into groups to spread out in the vineyard. With any luck, his mother would be a mile away from Forrest.

"Oh, we're all in a group together." Leila revved up that fake smile again. "It's the four of us along with Jane and Toby and Nonna and Poppa."

"Mmmkay." He didn't have any phony smile talent whatsoever. He didn't have much to smile about. All of his worlds were colliding right now. He would spend the whole afternoon with his family, his boss, and his pretend fiancée's family. What could possibly go wrong?

"This should be fun." There was nothing fake about his mother's demeanor. She genuinely seemed to be looking forward to what would surely turn into a shit show.

"I agree." Forrest looked awfully closely at Mara for August's liking.

"Are you sure we shouldn't split up?" He tried to make the suggestion casual, but this was getting out of hand. Forrest was a known womanizer. "Maybe it's better for those of us who are familiar with the vineyards to be in different groups."

"Don't be so worried." Leila winkled her nose at him like she was talking to a puppy. "Each group has a team lead who's done the harvest before. Everything'll be fine." She was reiterating the same words he'd spoken to her yesterday, and now he realized how trite they sounded.

It was pretty clear everything would not be fine.

* * *

"So, Mom and Forrest seem to be getting along well."

Jane snipped a bunch of the chardonnays and dropped them into the wheeled cart they were pushing along with them.

"Don't remind me." August had stopped looking at his mother and Forrest a long time ago after he realized he wouldn't be able to keep distance between them. Within the first ten minutes after the harvest's start, everyone had spread out, and somehow Mara had ended up at the front of the pack, while he'd been relegated to the back, his sister insisting he had to show her exactly how to snip the grapes so she didn't do anything wrong.

It wasn't so bad hanging out with Jane, though. And Charlee, though currently his niece was having a nap in the child carrier backpack Toby wore. Spending the afternoon with Jane and Toby was a lot better than navigating the awkwardness that had descended upon him and Leila.

The woman could win an Academy Award for how much acting she'd done today, especially with Forrest. Leila had spent nearly every moment with his mother and his boss, chatting about their wine selection, pointing out certain vistas while they worked their way down the rows of vines, telling stories about the early days of the vineyard. She was obviously trying to sell the man on what a great place the winery was. The problem was sentimentality didn't appeal to Forrest, and no amount of history would change his mind.

August clipped another bunch of grapes, popping one into his mouth before he stashed them in the cart.

"Is there a reason you're avoiding Leila?" his sister asked with fabricated naïveté. "How'd the big date go?"

The big date seemed like a month ago now. "It went great, but then Forrest showed up." Carrying their different realities on his shoulders. "He's never visited a job site when I've been in charge."

Jane devoted all of her focus to clipping another bunch of grapes. "You could always quit."

"I'm sorry?" Did she really suggest he quit his job when it was all he had in his life?

"You could totally quit." She dropped the grapes into the cart and turned to him. "I'm sure you have savings from all these years of working and having absolutely no responsibility, right?" Her casual shrug nearly made him laugh.

"Yeah. I have plenty of savings." But that wasn't the point. "You have no idea what Forrest did for me. This job is my stability, my purpose." It had carried him through the darkest time in his life. Besides, if he left right now, he wouldn't be able to protect Valentino Bellas. Forrest would take control himself.

"Sure, but does your work have to be your whole life?" Without waiting for an answer, Jane traipsed to Toby and Charlee.

Apparently, she had meant the question to be rhetorical, but he refused to consider the possibility. If Forrest fired him for failing in his assignment, that would be one thing. But he couldn't walk away now.

August went back to work, clipping and tossing, but the grapes on this section seemed different—smaller, not quite as plump. After stashing his shears in the cart, he started to examine the vines, lifting their leaves, studying the stems.

His sister walked back to him and peered over his shoulder. "What're you doing?"

August continued pulling up the leaves, analyzing the stems all the way to the ground. "Look at this yellowing on the vines." The coloring was subtle, but he'd seen it before at a vineyard in Oregon.

"Yeah?" She didn't seem to understand the significance.

"It's phylloxera. It has to be." The pest had taken out large swathes of vineyards all over the world before they'd introduced resistant varieties. "There must be an infestation in this section."

"What does that mean?" Jane looked at him like he was speaking a different language.

Right. Not everyone had spent the last decade living in a vineyard.

"It means these vines are doomed." He grabbed his shears and snipped off a whole stem, holding it out for her. "See how they're yellowing? In a few more years, they won't even be producing."

"Yikes." She inspected another stem nearby. "Can you fix it?"

There were no quick fixes for growing grapes and tending vines. "It's a lengthy process. You have to graft new phylloxera-resistant vines on with the old." He scanned the area in front of them. "It's hard to tell how many acres would be affected. But this might be good news."

Once again, Jane looked at him like he'd started speaking gibberish. "How do you figure?"

"When I tell Forrest about the phylloxera, there's a chance he'll walk away." His boss knew full well what it would take to bring the vines back to health. "I can use this to try and convince him to back out of the partnership. He wanted a new challenge expanding to Colorado, but dealing with phylloxera is more than he bargained for."

When they'd detected the problem at an operation in Oregon, Forrest had put on the brakes and had backed out of the deal to purchase the property. "He might not want the headache, which means the Valentinos could keep the property and I can help consult on how to graft on the new vines. It'll take a while, but it can be done."

Jane studied him for a few seconds with an unreadable expression. "You really care about Leila, don't you?"

He didn't see how that mattered. "Sure. I care about her family too. They were an important part of my life."

"Were?" His sister had always enjoyed teasing him.

"I'm going to talk to Forrest." If he could pry him from his mother's side, that was.

"Good luck," Jane called behind him.

"Thanks." Convincing Forrest to walk away might be a long shot, but he had to try. August swiftly moved past Nonna and Poppa until he'd caught up with his mother, Leila, and Forrest. "Can I talk to you for a second?"

He prodded Kingston off to the side of the path. Leila shot him a questioning look.

"There's something going on back in California," he said. "We'll catch up in a few minutes." There was no use getting Leila's hopes up if this plan didn't work.

His fake fiancée narrowed her eyes, but at least she kept walking.

Forrest stopped to face him and shaded his eyes from the sun. "What's the crisis?"

"I found evidence of phylloxera in the vines." August put a grave tone in his voice. "I'm not sure how widespread it is, but it's definitely a problem that will need to be addressed as soon as possible."

Forrest pulled on a vine close to them and studied the stem. "You're sure?"

"Pretty sure." August pointed out the yellowing underneath the leaves. "You may not have noticed, but the grapes on this section are smaller, so the damage is already starting. If we do nothing, it'll only take a few more years for these vines to die out."

His boss nodded. "That makes my decision easy, then."

"Yes, it does." He kept a burgeoning smile in check. "I know for a fact Leila would be happy to terminate the contract you two signed, since they weren't aware of the problem at the time."

"Terminate?" Forrest let go of the vine. "I'm not terminating anything."

Damn. August hid his disappointment. "I didn't think you'd want to put the time and money into replanting. It could take years to bring back this section of the vineyard."

"Exactly. I don't want to put the time and money into replanting, but look at this place." He gestured in the direction of the
mountain peaks in the distance. "The scenery alone is a gold
mine. I have no reason to grow the grapes here."

"But the vineyards are part of the charm," he argued. No, they
didn't have to grow anything here. They had plenty of grapes
back in California. "Most people want to experience the vineyard,
especially with those vistas."

"We'll keep the healthy parts of the vineyard for aesthetics
and sell only Kingston brand wine," Forrest went on, pacing with
a new energy. "We'll simplify the operation. I'll ship the grapes
out so people can still watch the wine-making process. But it will
be all Kingston—the wine and the grapes." He whacked August's
shoulder. "This is great. We'll have to take the damage into
consideration when looking at the profit margins, but I think this
means we can speed up the whole acquisition process."

Speed it up? *Shit.* August closed his eyes. "No, that's not what
I was—"

"Good catch, August," Forrest interrupted. "See? That's why I
sent you out here. That's why you're my second in command. I
can always count on you to get the job done."

Chapter Twenty

August couldn't hold Knievel back anymore.

The horse strained against the reins, begging to be set free. While he'd once worried about Knievel's age, their daily rides had brought back the animal's strength and drive, and now all he wanted to do was run.

"All right, boy. Let her rip." He loosened his grip on the reins, giving the horse more power, more control. Knievel's energy swept August up too. He crouched low in the saddle, leaning forward as they galloped across the meadow, the crisp wind chilling his face.

The faster Knievel went, the more August's shoulders lightened. For the first time in two weeks—since he'd spent the night with Lei— the stress he'd been carrying released into the wind around him. All he could feel was the power and the movement and the sun's waning warmth on his skin. He'd almost forgotten how riding like this made him feel untouchable. From the time he'd been three years old, his father had told him he belonged in a saddle. Now he remembered why.

The rush didn't last, though. Knievel's pounding hooves eventually slowed to a trot, and the burdens August carried settled back on his shoulders, heavy and real and confining.

"Good boy, Knievel." August patted the horse while they took a cooldown loop. The brief escape from reality hadn't been long enough to make him forget what the Valentinos were facing. For the past two weeks, he'd been trying to work out a solution for them, even while he and Forrest developed the acquisition plan to transfer ownership of Valentino Bellas to Kingston.

Knowing his boss would create the plan with or without him, August had played along, stalling things as long as he could. But he was running out of time.

Thankfully, Forrest had traveled back to California after the harvest, but he video-called every day—going over details on the plan, running through the numbers, discussing what staff they would need to run the new operation. Between those phone calls, working with Knievel, and obsessing over how he could stop what had already been put in motion, August had managed to avoid pretty much everyone. Most of all Leila.

God, how was he going to tell her about this mess?

He steered Knievel back toward the barn. He couldn't tell her. He had to fix this first. He had to find a way to stop Forrest before the man ruined Leila's life.

"Hey."

August jerked his head and looked over his shoulder. Electricity zinged through him when he caught sight of Lei standing near the fence in fitted jeans and a red flowy top that set off her dark hair, but the regrets quickly killed his desire. Breaking her heart would kill him.

"Hey." He guided the horse toward her, but kept his distance so she couldn't pick up on the dread slowly filling him.

"I haven't seen you much lately." She climbed up onto the first fence rail and leaned over the top. Last time they'd talked, she'd pushed him away, but now her smile seemed to invite him closer.

August stayed where he was. She'd be better off pushing him away. "Forrest has me working on some projects." A takeover plan. He couldn't meet her eyes.

Leila turned her attention to the horse. "Knievel seems to be doing well. I swear, he doesn't look a day over five years old."

"He's really come back to life." Meanwhile, August was dying. His heart had never hurt this bad. Not even when he'd lost his father. The thought of taking away the place Leila loved nearly forced him to his knees.

She watched him carefully for a few seconds before speaking again. "Since I haven't seen you, I wanted to come by and tell you the good news." Her smile grew brighter, shining in her eyes. "I've been working on the numbers. With the event coming up next week and our increased communication with our wine club, we've already seen a twenty percent increase in sales."

The utter joy in her demeanor knocked the wind out of him. "That's great," he managed to say, though the words had a hollow ring.

"I think we're going to make it, Auggie." She hopped off the fence and hurried through the gate. "For the first time, I really believe we can be at thirty percent after the event."

He found himself nodding along while the rest of his body tried to hold his composure together. He couldn't tell her he'd failed her. There had to be another way out of this mess he'd created.

"Not only that, but a Denver news station came up to interview me the morning." Her lips quirked. "They said an anonymous source tipped them off on our story." She raised her eyebrows, silently calling him out.

August said nothing. His stomach roiled. He couldn't smile back at her. He couldn't speak.

"Anyway," she went on. "The reporter said this story has come at the perfect time because they were already doing a story on how hard the Colorado wine community has been hit by the weather these last few years. They were headed out the Western Slope to talk to a pretty big operation that's facing foreclosure."

Foreclosure. A winery on the Western Slope was facing fore-closure? "Do you know the name of the place?" The words came out with desperation, all running together. This was exactly what they needed.

"Sure." Her head cocked as though she were trying to read him. "It's called Spark Winery and Vineyards. They're actually pretty well known, but with everything they've been battling the last few years, it sounds like they're giving up."

August finally managed to inhale a full breath without a stabbing pain in his chest. All he had to do was go out there and broker a better deal, and then he could present this other option to Forrest. As long as it created a better financial picture for Kingston, Forrest would be all over it. "Spark Winery and Vineyards? You're sure?" He dismounted the horse.

"I'm sure." Lei gazed at him with open curiosity. "But why does it matter?"

He didn't have to time to explain everything to her. Not right now. But this was their solution. Forrest only cared about the bottom line. If he did this right, if he showed Kingston how profitable this other winery would be, maybe the man would leave Valentino Bellas alone. "I have to go away." He led Knievel along the fence. "There's some business I need to take care of."

Lei followed behind him. "But the wine club event is next week."

"I know." He started to jog. "I'll be back before that. I promise. If you need anything from me, shoot me a text. This can't wait. I have to take care of something."

He had to do what he hadn't done years ago—fight for the woman he loved.

* * *

Days later, August parked the truck outside of the Valentino Bellas' office and got out to stretch his back. Even though he'd left the Western Slope well before dawn, he was still running late. He should've been here over an hour ago to help Leila set up for the event. He scanned the far end of the parking lot where the white canopy tents stood. The rental company had come out last night to put them up, but it seemed the rest of the setup had already been completed. Someone had hung the white lights and arranged the tables, though none of them were set yet. It must've taken her all morning to get this put together. But hopefully all would be forgiven when he told her the news.

The wind had picked up some, and a line of clouds formed over the peaks. That was all they needed before the shindig tonight—a rainstorm. Still, even the gloomy weather couldn't ruin his mood. It had taken the better part of a week, but he'd worked out a deal to acquire Spark Vineyards on behalf of Kingston. Now all Forrest had to do was sign the paperwork later tonight when the man showed up at the party.

He pushed through the office door and found Leila sitting at her desk. "Am I too late?"

"No." She didn't look up from her computer screen. Man, he missed that brief, twelve-hour window when she'd actually looked into his eyes. Those moments were ancient history now. The glance she gave him now was especially cold.

"I tried to get back in time to help set up." He sat in the chair across from her desk. "But it seems the work has already been done."

Regina the cat hopped into his lap and brushed her head against his thigh before rolling over onto her back so he could give her a belly scratch.

"I woke up before five and couldn't go back to sleep." Leila gave the cat an annoyed look. "So I figured I might as well get as much done as I could."

He wondered if she woke up thinking about him the way he'd woken up thinking about her. In fact, he'd thought of her the whole drive back. "You could've called me. I was up pretty early too."

"I was fine setting up on my own," she muttered. "Sam helped some."

Right. They'd each gone back to their corners and were no longer a team. She likely didn't appreciate him running out on her the week before the event. "Aren't you going to ask me where

I was?" He gave the cat another scratch while the woman across from him danced her fingertips across the keyboard, ignoring him again.

She didn't look up. "Nope."

"Trust me," he said, trying again. "You'll want to hear all about—"

A low rumbling rattled the office.

Leila sat up straighter. "Was that thunder?"

"Yeah." August took the cat in his arms and walked to the window. "The clouds were building when I came in. Looks like it's gonna rain anytime now." The wind had started to blow harder too.

"No! It can't rain!" Leila pushed out of her chair and headed straight for the door, opening it right as a louder crack of thunder ripped the sky apart.

Regina leapt out of August's arms and dove underneath the desk.

"This isn't good," Leila said as he followed her outside. "What about the tents? I've already put all the tablecloths on."

"The tents should be okay. They're sturdy." But already, some of those tablecloths were flapping around. "We can put everything away until it passes." He started to jog across the parking lot right as a gust of wind picked up two of the tablecloths and sent them parachuting through the air.

"Oh, no!" Leila raced ahead of him, chasing the white linens into the edge of the vineyard. August veered to the left in pursuit of another rogue tablecloth that had wrapped around a tent pole. He unraveled the material quickly and bunched it up into his arms before running to help Leila with the other two.

Lightning streaked across the sky overhead, followed by another thunderous roar. Rain started to pelt his face, making it hard to see. He and Leila followed the flashes of white tablecloths while they drifted across the ground, but every time they got close, the wind took them farther into the vineyard.

The rain drove harder now, soaking them both to the bone. "Let's forget these for the moment," he called over another clap of thunder. They were too muddy to use anyway. "We can come back for them later. We need to get the rest of them off the tables before they're all ruined."

"Okay!" Leila pushed the strands of rain-slicked hair out of her face. Together, they slogged back through the mud and under the canopy. Most of the tablecloths were now strewn around the parking lot. August collected the two left on the tables, and then he and Leila ran around picking up the rest.

"We can bring them to my cottage!" Leila waved him out of the tent. On the way, he picked up the bundle of tablecloths, and they both ran down the cobblestone sidewalk that led to her cottage.

"Whew." Leila closed the door behind him and leaned against it. "That was intense. We're soaked." She laughed.

Despite his wet boots and jeans and shirt, August laughed too.

"Oh, my God, you should see yourself." Leila flopped down on the couch and started taking off her shoes. "I know, I know. I don't look much better." She smoothed her hands over her drenched hair, laughing even harder. "You know what this reminds me of?"

August dropped the soggy tablecloths in a pile by the door and opted to sit on the stone hearth so he didn't get her chair wet. He hadn't been in this cottage since he and Leila used to sneak in here when it was an unused caretaker's apartment, and yet everything about the space seemed familiar.

The cottage was small and simple, with a tiny kitchen in one corner and a cozy living room oriented around this stone fireplace. She'd put her fingerprints all over the space too—from the dozens of plants crammed onto every windowsill to the inviting, comfortable furniture arranged around the fireplace to the bright, colorful abstract paintings in oranges and yellows and turquoises.

He stopped looking around and noticed that Lei seemed to be waiting for something. Right. She'd asked him a question. "What could this situation possibly remind you of?"

"Your graduation party." Her smile had a genuine slant to it. "When that freak storm came out of nowhere and sent that canopy your parents had rented flying into the lake."

They both laughed again.

"That was wild. And somehow the best party ever." The scene had been very similar to him and Leila running around gathering the tablecloths, except after they'd managed to canoe out and pull the tent back to shore, his family and friends had started a volleyball game in the driving rain.

"I'll never forget how much fun your dad had that day. Even in the storm." Leila's grin softened. "He was running around cleaning things up, stashing them in the shed, laughing and joking around the whole time."

"Yeah." He waited for the sharp, searing grief the memories usually brought, but it didn't come this time. Maybe because it had been Leila sharing the memory with him. "Nothing fazed Dad. 'It's all part of the adventure,' he always said."

Leila stood and walked to a closet behind the couch, pulling out two fluffy towels. She handed one to him. "I see a lot of your dad in you, Auggie. Even more now than I did back when we were kids."

"I wish I could see." All he saw were his own weaknesses, his own failures. He dried off his hair, but his clothes were hopeless.

Leila wrapped the towel around her shoulders and sat on the couch again.

"I saw your dad the day before he passed away." Her head ducked slightly, as though she was afraid to look at him.

"You did?" He held his breath, bracing for the onslaught of grief, but once again, it didn't come.

"Yeah." She pulled the towel tighter around her shoulders. "I was in town running some errands and saw him outside of the café." She lifted her head. "You had recently aced your college chemistry test, and he was raving about how proud he was."

That chemistry test. August had been sure it was going to kill him. The second he'd seen his perfect score, he'd called his dad. *I knew you'd ace it. I've always believed in you, son, and I always will. I love you.* That had been their last conversation, and it had taken place weeks before his father had passed away.

"He, uh, also told me how much he and your mom cared about me," Leila went on. "He said he and your mom had always considered me part of the family, and I could come by to visit them anytime I wanted, even though you were away."

The lump that formed in his throat now wasn't grief. It was cold, hard regret. "Family was everything to him. He'd always wanted his to grow bigger and bigger." Shortly before he'd left for school, August had told his dad he intended to marry Leila, and the man had been ecstatic.

"It's funny; I always thought I would make peace with his death eventually." Why was it so easy to talk about this with her when he usually avoided even thinking about the past?

"But you haven't made peace with losing him." It wasn't a question.

"No." He'd never truly faced his father's death because he'd stayed away. "When I'm not here, I don't have to deal with the grief. I can move on and ignore it, but that's not the same as making peace with it."

Lei nodded with understanding in her eyes. "I'm not sure how anyone ever makes peace with losing a part of themselves. I don't know if that's even possible. It's more likely that you learn to live the grief, that you learn to live with the pain, but also with the joy that person left for you."

"I think I'm starting to understand how to accept all of those things." The grief and the sadness but also the comfort and the happiness in the memories. "My dad gave me so much. He taught me how love." For years, he'd used his loss to push everyone away, and that was why he'd been so empty. But now, he'd seen only a glimpse of the happiness he could have with Leila, and he was finally ready to embrace the life he wanted.

Chapter Twenty-One

Sitting with August alone in her cottage was asking for trouble.

This was exactly the situation Leila had tried to avoid since they'd arrived back at the winery after their date and Forrest had burst their fairy-tale bubble.

Rain still beat against the windows, a romantic serenade, and the occasional flash of lightning lit up her dim living room. The cold from her wet clothes had started to seep in, even with the towel pulled around her shoulders. Yet she couldn't move. August needed to talk about his dad. She could see his internal battle playing out—his smile while they reminisced but also his jaw tightening with an unexpressed pain. Working through the memories, talking about them, going back in time, seemed to unburden him, and she wanted him to be free.

"I can't talk about him with anyone else," August said, drawing her attention back to his face. "But I feel like I can tell you anything."

There'd been a time when they *had* told each other everything. She'd never had a relationship like that with anyone else before or after August. No one had ever known her the way he once had.

"It's probably because we used to be close." She downplayed

the sudden uptick in her pulse with a shrug. Their connection was much more than simple history.

They'd always had this current running between them. Even while she'd been telling herself to keep her distance emotionally, she couldn't deny her energy would change whenever August was close. She didn't even have to look up to know he was nearby.

"I think it's more than the fact that we used to be close." August scooted forward on the hearth. "It's you, Lei. It's your compassion. Your understanding. You get me. You've always gotten me in a way no one else ever has."

She could say the same. Auggie had known what she needed, what to say, when to make her laugh. Pretending to be together simply didn't work with the two of them. Maybe because her feelings for him weren't make-believe.

But feelings wouldn't get them very far in their current situation. "Being with you has been wonderful," she admitted. "But now with Forrest making things difficult—"

"I found a different vineyard for him to buy." August moved to his knees on the floor and inched his way to her. "There's a place on the Western Slope. It's perfect. Fifty acres with mountain views and a full wine-making operation."

Hope swept up her heart, carrying it away. "Really?"

"Really." He stayed where he was, on his knees in front of her, close but not touching her. "That's why I left last week. When you told me what the reporter said, I knew this was our chance to save Valentino Bellas."

Tears slipped down her cheeks. And here she'd thought he'd run away from her again.

"I spent the last week brokering an acquisition deal with them," Auggie went on, sweeping the tears from her cheeks with his thumbs. "I haven't talked to Forrest about the possibility yet, but I think I can convince him that the other property is a better investment. He's walked away from vineyards he's wanted to acquire before. I'm hoping I can convince him to do it again."

"I don't even know what to say." God, the relief brought light back to every part of her. "This is amazing, Auggie. You're amazing." She drew his lips to hers, and paused, just feeling him there, close and warm and still so much a part of her. Shivers ran through her, maybe more from the intensity of her feelings for him than the cold.

August pulled back and gazed into her eyes. "You're shivering. You must be freezing."

"I'm a little cold." At least she had been before he'd touched her…

He stood and pulled her to her feet. "You should get out of those wet clothes."

"What about you?" Her heart had slipped into that different rhythm again—the one that played when August came close. She toyed with the first button of his shirt. "You must be cold too."

"I'm not," he assured her in a low growl.

Hearing the want in his voice brought Leila a step closer to him. "I'm actually warming up too."

His arms came around her waist and drew her closer to his body. "Yeah?"

"Oh, yeah." She touched her lips to his skin and kissed her way up his neck. "We should probably both get out of these wet clothes, though," she whispered in his ear.

"Yes, that would be best." He pulled her long-sleeved T-shirt up and over her head, dropping it onto the floor next to them.

"And maybe we should take a shower to warm up more." Leila undid the buttons on his shirt and shoved it off his shoulders.

"A shower is a great idea," he agreed, moving her bra strap out of the way and lowering his mouth to her shoulder.

Leila let her head fall back with a moan as he kissed her collarbone and unclasped her bra. Forget everything she'd said about how impractical it was to be with August. What did logic matter when he made her feel this way?

"You're going to have to stop wearing these complicated belt buckles," she informed him, going to work on the metal clasp.

"Gladly." He took over for her, opening the buckle and then shoving his jeans and boxers down to the floor.

Growing more impatient, Leila stepped out of her pants, too, kicking them aside. "I have an amazing shower," she told him, pulling on his hand to direct him to the bathroom. "It's the one thing in this cottage I had professionally renovated."

"I can't wait to see—"

"Leila!" Nonna's frantic voice outside her door froze them both. "Are you in there?" Her grandmother pounded on the wood. "You wouldn't believe the mess out here after that gully washer! The event staff just arrived, and the tablecloths are all gone."

"Crap!" Leila tore away from August and found the towel she'd discarded earlier, wrapping it around her body. "Get down behind the couch!" she instructed him.

He stood in the middle of the room in his full naked glory. "Seriously?"

"Yes!" She tossed him a towel. "Get down. I have to let her in."

"So let her in." He secured the towel around his waist. "She won't care that I'm here. We're not sixteen anymore, thank God."

But they were both naked! "She's my grandmother and she doesn't need to know what we were doing in here."

The knocking started again. "I hear you in there, Leila! Is everything all right?"

"I'm fine, Nonna! Be right there!" She tugged August behind the couch and pushed on his shoulder until he lowered himself to the floor and out of sight.

"I'll make it up to you later," she whispered.

The promise toned down his scowl.

Leila smoothed her wet hair and rewrapped the towel securely around her on her way to the door. She pulled it open with a smile. "Hey. Sorry. I was in the shower."

"Oh, that's why it took you so long to answer the door." Her grandmother stepped inside, but Leila held her position so the woman wouldn't move toward the couch.

"I didn't mean to make such a fuss, but there's still a lot to be done." She noticed the pile of tablecloths by the door. "There they are! Thank goodness. I thought all the linens had blown away."

"No, we—I mean *I*—wanted to get them somewhere dry." She cleared her throat to drown out the rustling and shuffling behind the couch.

"We have no time to lose. Not with the mess." Her grandmother stooped to pick up the bundle of linens. "I asked Sam to find some new tablecloths from the restaurant. We'd better get back to work. Is August here?"

"Oh…um…no." She'd always been the worst liar. Her eyes were probably bugging out of her head right now. "He's definitely not here. I haven't seen him all morning." An image of his naked body flashed through her mind.

"His truck's in the parking lot." Nonna glanced over her shoulder. "But he wasn't outside, and he wasn't in the office."

"Huh." Her voice went so high it squeaked. "That's weird. Maybe he's in the bathroom somewhere." She heard the man snort but covered up the sound with a cough. "I'll throw on some clothes real quick." She started to dart down the hall, but stopped in her tracks when she caught sight of August lying on his side sans towel, fully displaying all the goods.

He grinned at her and bounced his eyebrows.

Leila did her best to disguise her laugh as another cough. "Just wait right there, Nonna," she called. Her grandmother would have a heart attack if she walked over and saw Auggie like that. "I'll be fast." She stumbled into her room and pulled on some of her nicer undergarments—in case she and August could sneak away later—and then threw on shorts and a dry T-shirt. As she rushed past August again, he flexed his biceps.

Another laugh slipped out, but she quickly recovered. "I'm sure August will join us shortly," she said, rejoining her grandmother at the door. "He knows how much we need his help out there."

"Let's hope so." Still holding the bundle of tablecloths, Nonna stepped onto the sidewalk, and Leila closed the door securely behind them.

Whew. That had been a close call.

The sun had come out again, which was par for the course with

fast-moving mountain thunderstorms. "At least the rain stopped."
And it had made every color seem brighter. Or maybe that half
hour with August had brought more vibrancy to her world. "We'll
get everything set up again in no time."

She took the bundle of tablecloths from her grandmother and
walked back to the tent with a bounce in her step. For the first
time since she'd signed that partnership with Forrest, the heavy
stone of worry that had sat in her stomach had disappeared. Of
course August could convince the man to buy a different vineyard.
Why had she been questioning him? Auggie made it clear he was
fully on her side. He wanted her family to stay, and he would do
everything he could to help her.

"Hey, ladies." The man in question crossed the parking lot,
fully dressed in his still-damp clothes, unfortunately.

Leila smirked at him. He must've slipped out her back door.

"There you are." Nonna hurried to meet him. "Where've you
been? We were looking all over for you."

"Let's just say I was lying around." August's eyes found
hers, and Leila fought off another giggle. He'd sure looked good
lying around.

"But I'm here now. Ready to help out. Put me to work."

"Poppa is trying to fix all those globe lights the wind blew
down." Nonna pointed to the tent where the rental company had
set up a dance floor. "I don't want him on the ladder."

"No problem. I'm on it." He paused, holding Leila's gaze, and
then leaned in to brush a kiss across her lips.

Her heart responded with a desirous shudder.

"I'll be back," he murmured as though they were the only two
standing there.

Leila watched him walk away. God, she loved those jeans
on him.

"That man," Nonna mused with a shake of her head. "You sure
caught a good one, my dear."

"I did." And without the takeover hanging between them,
maybe they really could build a future together.

"All right, I'm here." Sam lumbered down the sidewalk in his slow, carefree gait, with an armload of new tablecloths. "I found plenty of clean linens in the storage room."

"Great." Leila dumped the soiled clothes in a heap on the ground. "Let's get these tables set up so the event staff can put out the dishes." In keeping with their Italian heritage, they'd agreed to serve the hors d'oeuvres family style from the tables, so everyone wouldn't have to walk around while they ate.

"You want me to help put on the tablecloths?" Her brother looked at them in disbelief. "I was experimenting with a new red blend."

"You'll have plenty of time to experiment later." Their grand-mother took one of the linens and shook it out. "We only have a few hours to finish up here." She smoothed the cloth over one of the round tables. "You two start over there, and we'll meet in the middle."

"Roger that." Leila snatched half of the tablecloths and beck-oned her brother to the other side of the tent. "Don't worry. We'll get this done fast, and then you can go spend more time with your beloved grapes." She flung one of the tablecloths out, and he caught the other side.

"I still don't see why we have to have this event." Sam spent way too much time pulling the material to exactly the right angle on his side.

"Come on. It'll be fun." She was surprised to be looking forward to the mingling and the dancing and the celebrating with old and new friends. But, then again, Auggie had managed to wipe out her worries. Now she could simply enjoy the evening. Hopefully with him.

They moved to the next table, but Leila kept getting distracted. August had climbed up on the ladder and was reaching a strand of lights higher. His shirt rose slightly, revealing a nice sliver of his very firm abs.

"Hello?" Sam held out his hands. "We're not going to get through this fast if you keep ogling the enemy."

"I'm not ogling him." Leila flung one end of the next tablecloth in his direction. "And besides, he's not the enemy. He's doing everything he can to help us."

"Sure he is." Her brother pulled the material so it was perfectly symmetrical over the table. "Please tell me you're not getting wrapped up in this fake relationship."

Leila moved onto the next table, peeking over at August again. He and Poppa were laughing about something together. "I don't know that our relationship is all that fake anymore." August had said he could open up to her in a way he couldn't with anyone else, and she felt the same way.

"You can't trust him." Sam came around the table. "He had no problem walking away from you before."

"Right. When he was nineteen, after his father died." Seeing Auggie's perspective had allowed her some space to look past her own hurt and acknowledge his. The time she'd spent with him had revealed the other side of the story. She understood why Sam was trying to protect her, but that was a completely different time. "He was lost and upset. I really think he's finally dealing with the past. He wants to move on." And so did she. "He told me he found another place for Forrest to buy on the Western Slope. He's going to convince him to walk away from Valentino Bellas."

"And you believe him?" Sam shook his head. "His promises have meant nothing before. Why would they mean anything now?"

"I know him." They might have been apart for years, they might have led completely different lives, but she and August were finding their way back to each other. They'd both grown up, and now she believed with her whole heart that they could build something real.

Her brother uttered an exasperated sigh. "And what if he can't convince Forrest to buy that other property, Lei? What then?"

Leila watched August again as he and Poppa laughed together. Then getting her heart broken again was a real possibility.

Chapter Twenty-Two

August tied the stems of his carefully curated bouquet together with some twine he'd found in the shed, doing his best to form a decent version of a bow.

No, no, no. He unraveled the whole thing and started over again. Tying a bow had never been part of his skill set, but he wanted this bunch of wildflowers he'd picked from the meadow to be perfect.

They were all Leila's favorites—bluebells and fireweeds and blanketflowers and lupines. He'd spent an hour out there selecting the perfect flowers to make the bouquet look similar to the one as he'd made her for her on his senior prom night.

The same anticipation he'd felt then heated his blood. This could be the night everything changed. For him. For them. If he could convince Forrest to purchase the vineyard on the Western Slope, then August wouldn't be far away from Leila. He could manage that place during the week and still spend all his weekends here with her. Though he'd told his mother he wasn't built for relationships, maybe that wasn't exactly true. He'd simply been built for a relationship only with Leila. It didn't matter how much he tried to reason with himself. His heart was drawn to hers, and he couldn't keep fighting the pull.

Jane walked up his porch steps and eyed the mass of flowers on the rattan table. "What're you up to?" Before he could answer, her smile morphed into a full-on smirk. "You made a bouquet."

"Yeah." He tried tying the bow again, but the ends pulled all the way through.

Oh, forget it. There was nothing wrong with a plain old knot.

"I'm assuming this lovely arrangement isn't for your favorite sister." Jane's sing-song tone mocked him.

"It might be. If I had a favorite sister."

"Hey!" She whapped his arm. "After all the teasing I endured for *years* from both you and Wes, now it's my turn."

"I suppose you're entitled." He picked up the bouquet and pulled off a few wilted leaves. "But I don't have time to indulge your teasing right now. I have to get up to the winery." If he played his cards right, he and Leila would have a little time alone before they had to show up at the grand soiree. Maybe they'd be able to pick up where they'd left things off earlier that day.

"Well, you can't show up with the flowers looking like that." Shaking her head, Jane swiped the bouquet out of his hands and undid the twine, laying the flowers out on the table. "Let's see." She examined the varieties, and then started putting stems together. "Am I to assume that this special bouquet means you and Leila have finally acknowledged you have *real* feelings for each other?"

"Yes, we've acknowledged." It was impossible not to acknowledge his feelings when he was with her. He'd tried keeping his distance, and that had backfired on him.

"So what did you say? What did she say? How were those real feelings acknowledged?" His sister continued matching the flowers' stems together with painstaking slowness.

"I don't know." He glanced at his watch. This would seriously cut into his time with Leila. "Things were said." None of which he needed to repeat to his meddling sister.

"You and Wes." Jane rolled her eyes. "You two are terrible with the details when it comes to juicy gossip."

"Now, see, that's why we're terrible with the details," he informed her. "Because you're so good at spreading the juicy gossip."

A proud smile perked up his sister's mouth. "Well, maybe I'm just happy for you. Really, Auggie. I've always thought you and Leila were meant to be. But what about Forrest? What about the situation with the winery? How's this all going to work?"

"I'm figuring it out." He didn't have time for this conversation right now. "I'm going to convince him to buy a different Colorado property, and then the Valentinos can keep the vineyard." And he could keep his job and still spend time with Leila. Maybe he'd even be giving her that ring Poppa had given him one day.

"That's great." His sister handed him the nicely arranged bouquet, complete with a perfect bow. "Seriously. I'm happy for you both." She gave him a hug, nearly smashing the flowers in the process.

"Easy." August stepped away from her, and they both walked down the porch steps. "Will I see you up there tonight?"

"We wouldn't miss it." Her eyes sparkled. "Mom said she's dying to babysit Charlee for us, so we'll have a whole kid-free evening."

It was more likely their mother didn't want to face Nonna and Poppa with all the lies still going around, but with any luck, soon they wouldn't be lying anymore. "Nice. I'll see you there." He rushed to his truck and carefully set the flowers on the passenger's seat.

"Tell Leila I said hello," his sister called as he sped past her.

He waved and grinned like a fool all the way to the winery. Before rounding the last switchback, August parked his truck in the dirt near the edge of the vineyard and got out. They'd need as many parking spots as possible in the main lot up top, and this would allow him to cut through the vines and stop by Leila's cottage before he could run into anyone else who might want to talk to him.

After collecting the bouquet, August secured his truck and

took off on the dirt path, making his way up the hill. Thank God he didn't have to wear a tux to this shindig. The whole party would have a completely different vibe than the Kingston parties back in California. Instead of a bow tie and vest underneath his tailored suit coat, he wore a gray button-up shirt along with black pants and his black Stetson.

By the time he'd made it to Leila's front door and knocked, he was nearly out of breath. But it wasn't from the walk. Damn, he'd missed the spike of adrenaline that shot straight to the heart of him. He used to experience the same rush every time he'd stood outside Leila's front door, and the feeling was as strong now as it had been when he was a kid.

"Coming." Her voice floated out to him, airy and light and happy.

The door opened, and he held the flowers out in front of him. He started to say something, but the sight of her wiped out all coherence. She'd pinned her dark hair up, letting a few waves spill down to caress her neck. The strapless teal dress she wore hugged her curves before flaring out above her knees. And she had on the sexiest pair of western boots he'd ever seen.

"Wow," was all he could eventually manage.

Real smooth.

"A wildflower bouquet." Her smile brightened her eyes. "It's exactly like the one you gave me before prom. All of my favorites." She stepped aside so he could walk in.

Right. He had to move. He had to talk. "I swear to God you're more beautiful every time I see you."

"You're not looking so bad yourself, cowboy." Leila took his hand and pulled him to her, kicking the door shut with her boot. She set the flowers on the kitchen counter and tipped up his cowboy hat before touching her lips to his. "Sorry about earlier," she murmured. "I really hated to leave you lying naked on my living room floor."

"It's okay." He pulled her into his arms. "We always have tonight."

"Mmm-hmm," she hummed, the sound drowning in their kiss. He was drowning too. In the scent of her, in the feel of her, in the way their lips moved together, so in tune. "Maybe we should call in sick," he suggested, dragging his lips along her jaw. "Then we could go to bed early."

"I wish." Her breath stuttered. "We only have to make it through a couple of hours and then we'll have all night." She rested her hands on his chest. "And maybe most of the day tomorrow too?"

"I'll take as much time with you as you're willing to give me." August kissed her lips again, knowing they'd have to walk out the door any second.

"I think we both deserve tomorrow off." Leila stepped away and quickly put the flowers in a vase before grabbing a white sweater off the hook by the door. "We've been working hard, so we can do whatever we want."

August opened the door for her. "I know what I'd like to do."

"Go to the library?" she teased as they stepped out into the dusk.

"Sure, I'm good with the library." He slipped his arm around her waist. "There are plenty of quiet, secluded corners there."

Leila laughed, elbowing him lightly in the ribs. "How about we start with breakfast in bed and go from there?"

"Sounds like the perfect plan." They walked up the sidewalk side by side, serenaded by the sounds of the band warming up. "No matter how busy things get tonight, promise you'll save me a dance."

"I promise." Leila paused and turned to face him. "Were you able to talk to Forrest yet?"

"Not yet." He rubbed his hands up and down her arms. "He should be here tonight though. I told him we had something important to discuss."

She nodded, but her smile dimmed. "I hope this works."

"I'll do everything I can to convince him." It would be enough. It had to be enough. Now that he had Lei back in his life, he couldn't lose her again.

"I know you will." She wrapped her arm around his and continued to walk toward the tents.

"Leila! Yoo-hoo! Over here!" Nonna waved them to the food tent. "Were we planning to set six places or eight at each table?"

Leila squeezed August's hand and then hurried in front of him. "Eight."

"Oh, good. For a moment there, I thought we'd have to redo the place settings." Her grandmother released a relieved sigh and hugged her. "You look lovely, my dear."

"You both look lovely." August gave the woman a hug too. "Where do you need me to help out?" As much as he'd assisted with the details, he wanted this to be the Valentinos' event. They should be the ones to shine tonight; he would simply be there to support.

"Everything is all set." Poppa walked under the tent to join them, clearly having overheard the question. "I saw the first cars starting to come up the hill."

"Oh, wow." Leila smoothed down the sides of her dress. "Why am I nervous?"

"This is only the biggest event we've ever done." Nonna looked around them. "But it's come together beautifully. You have absolutely nothing to be nervous about. You two have done a marvelous job. You make a wonderful team."

"We do," August agreed, holding his gaze on Leila. "But I can't take much credit. Your granddaughter is the one who really fought to make this happen." She'd been fighting for this place—for her grandparents—for months. And in a way, she'd fought for him too. Encouraging him to open up about his father, sharing her own fears and struggles. Without knowing it, Lei had helped him find his way again. "She's incredible."

Leila's eyes met his and, for a few seconds, it seemed like only the two of them were standing there. Sounds swirled around them, but everything seemed muted, secondary to this woman standing across from him.

"I hate to break up whatever this is, but people are showing up," Sam called from a few feet away. His scowl seemed especially dark when he looked at August, but he could fix that too. He could prove to Sam he wasn't the same kid who'd walked out on his sister.

"What a wonderful evening this will be." Nonna joined their hands together. "You two deserve to enjoy every minute."

"We'll try." Leila turned to watch their first guests arriving, and August let her take the lead. For the next hour, he stayed by her side while they greeted the masses—old acquaintances, good friends from town, and the few loyal wine club members. August did what he could to support her—playing the charming fiancé, getting her a glass of wine, talking up the different assortment of reds and whites they offered at the tasting bar. All in all, the event got off to a successful start. The wine flowed, people sat and ate together, and a few brave souls even broke in the dance floor.

When the number of newcomers started to dwindle, Leila hooked his shoulder. "Hey, I promised you a dance."

"You did." He held out his hand. "Is now a good time?"

"Now's a perfect time." She led him from where they'd been stationed at the tasting bar to the dance floor, which was still only half full with a few couples who seemed happy to be in their own worlds.

The slow country song the band played gave him the perfect excuse to pull Leila close and hold her while they swayed to the music.

"Are you having fun?" he asked, pulling her into a turn.

"I am." She rested her cheek on his shoulder. "It's exhausting, but it's also encouraging to see how many people came, how many people love this place as much as we do."

"It's you," he murmured against her hair. "You draw people in. You're a light that attracts everyone."

Leila raised her head and kissed him, still dancing, still moving against him. His whole body responded to her, to her closeness, to the intimacy between them even while surrounded by people.

He closed his eyes and let the moment sink in while everything else faded into—

"August, can I borrow you?"

It took a few seconds for Forrest's voice to break him out of the trance Leila had put him in.

When had he arrived?

"Uh, yeah." He didn't let go of Leila. "Is it okay if I step away for a minute?"

"Of course." She moved back, offering a hopeful smile. "Go, go. I'll be fine. I need to eat something anyway."

"Be right back." He tried to force his brain into business mode and followed Forrest to the outskirts of the tent, preparing the monologue he'd scripted last night.

"I need you to go to New Mexico," Kingston announced before he had a chance to bring up the Western Slope.

"New Mexico?" What the hell was in New Mexico?

"I got a lead on a new place down there." The man sipped from the wineglass he held in his hand. "Sounds like they're about to enter bankruptcy. I want you to leave tomorrow and check it out for me."

"Wait. Hold on." Just hold on. Tension locked up his neck. He wasn't going to New Mexico. "Listen, there's this place out on the Western Slope, only a few hours from here." He rushed the words, not giving Forrest the chance to respond. "Spark Winery and Vineyards. It's a much larger operation than Valentino Bellas with even more room to expand. They're on the verge of bankruptcy, so I drove out there last week and worked out an acquisition deal." He waited a beat before adding the real draw. "Trust me, the price is right. We can get it for 10 percent less than what you'll pay for Valentino Bellas."

Genuine confusion pulled at Forrest's mouth. "What the hell are you talking about? Why would you travel to some other vineyard without talking to me first?"

"Come on. You can't be serious about taking over here." He pulled out his phone and pulled up the numbers he'd worked out.

"Take a look at the projections. I think you stand to lose money here, even if you only sell Kingston wine. It's not worth it. This other place is capable of producing twice the amount of product." Given Forrest's history with going after the profits, this should be an easy decision. "Most of Colorado's vineyards are on the Western Slope anyway."

"I don't want to be on the Western Slope." Forrest sharpened his gaze and pushed August's phone away. "I want to be in Silverado Lake. It's closer to Denver, an easy drive from the airport. And it's mountain country. We can expand our brand. The scenery alone will draw people here."

Since when did his boss care more about the scenery than the money? "This partnership is a bad idea." Even with a rising desperation, August kept a handle on his tone. "It's not a good business decision." He never challenged Forrest's decisions. He always offered his professional opinion without overstepping, but he couldn't stand by and watch the man take this place away from the Valentinos.

Kingston studied him. "You're obviously biased, so I don't trust your opinion this time."

Yes, he was biased. He wouldn't deny the truth.

"I've already set everything in motion," Forrest went on. "I've met with lawyers. The contract Leila Valentino signed is airtight. She's not going to get out of it, especially with her vineyards in trouble."

Anger burned through his chest. "But her family—"

"I can't believe I'm saying this, but bringing you out here was a mistake. This facade has gone on long enough." Forrest laid a hand on his shoulder. "It's over, August. I won't talk about this project with you anymore. You need to get your head back on straight before you do something you'll regret." He'd resorted to using the same fatherly tone he'd used when August had first started working for him. "You're leaving for New Mexico tomorrow, and I'll oversee things here. This place all but belongs to Kingston now. You need to let it go."

Chapter Twenty-Three

Oh, my God, this is the best sauvignon blanc I've ever tasted." Beth held up the wineglass as though inspecting the contents. "It's like magic in a glass."

Jane sipped from her glass, closing her eyes with obvious rapture. "My favorite is the new rosé Sam made." She took another lusty sip. "But I can't decide if I'm having so much fun because of the wine or because this is my first night out with Toby in forever."

"It's probably both," Leila said with a smile at her friends, but her gaze started wandering again. August had been gone too long for her liking. She'd lost sight of him when he and Forrest had left the tent, and she had no idea what was happening.

Her nerves fluttered. Was he talking to Forrest about the other property? What was taking them so long?

"This looks like a great turnout," Beth said, holding her glass over the bar so the bartender could give her another pour. "Will you and August stay at Valentino Bellas after you get married?"

"We haven't made a final decision yet." But she couldn't help the hope that swelled beneath her ribs. Would they build a life here together if Auggie could convince Forrest to move on? She couldn't imagine being anywhere else.

Jane scoffed. "Of course they'll stay here." She set her glass aside. "You two will want to be close to family, right?" August's sister nudged her playfully. "I'm happy to offer free babysitting services."

Leila pictured August riding Knievel across the pasture. "I do think Silverado Lake is where we both want to be." He'd never looked happier. "I think your brother has missed the ranch more than he's let on."

"That makes me so happy!" Jane gave her a sidearm hug. "Think of all the fun we'll have!" She started to list all of the things their families could do together.

Leila nodded along but she wasn't listening. She was watching two shadowy figures march across the parking lot. It was Forrest and August, moving toward the tents quickly, and neither one of them looked happy.

"Excuse me." Leila started to push her way through the crowd, but before she could get far enough to meet Auggie, he followed Forrest to the edge of the stage where the band was finishing up a song.

The two men were talking intensely, glaring at each other while their words flew back and forth.

"What's that about?" Jane murmured behind her.

Leila hadn't even realized Auggie's sister had followed. "I don't know, but it doesn't look good."

"No, it doesn't." Her friend moved in front of her, trying to clear a path for them. But before they'd gotten five steps, the song stopped and Forrest walked across the stage, waving to the crowd.

A surge of panic stopped Leila cold. "What is he *doing*?"

A polite applause broke out, even though the man was not supposed to be on that stage.

Leila shared a desperate look with Jane. *What the hell was going on?*

"Thank you, everyone." Forrest took the mic and waved, clearly trying to dazzle with his embellished smile. "I'm Forrest

Kingston. On behalf of Valentino Bellas and Kingston Family Vineyards, we want to welcome you to the party."

No. An electric current stopped her heart. He hadn't just said that in front of everyone. He couldn't have outed her secret in front of five hundred people.

She held on to Jane's arm for support.

"What's happening?" her friend whispered.

She couldn't answer. She couldn't even breathe.

"You might be surprised to see me up here," Forrest went on, plunging her deeper into a nightmare. "But we wanted to wait until tonight to make our exciting announcement." He let silence fall in a dramatic pause before continuing. "We are thrilled to tell you all that Kingston Family Vineyards has joined forces with Valentino Bellas."

Murmurs went through the crowd, but Leila couldn't hear them clearly. Everything slowed except for her heart. No, actually, her heart was trying to leap out of her chest. She frantically scanned the area for her Nonna and Poppa. Maybe they'd already left. Maybe—

"We'll be taking this fine establishment under the Kingston brand," Forrest said cheerfully into the mic. "Starting in November, we'll offer Kingston wines and an unparalleled tasting experience right here at the winery." He raised one hand and waited for the crowd noise to die down. "And for all you wine club members here, you have nothing to worry about. You'll be grandfathered into the Kingston Club program at the rates you're currently paying."

Jane gasped. "That jerk!" She started plowing forward, shoving her way through the crowd. Leila managed to follow at a slower stumble, looking to her left and right, trying to spot her grandparents. Oh, her sweet grandparents. They shouldn't have found out like this.

Forrest brought the mic to his mouth again. "In the coming weeks, we'll be sending out more information on the changes, but in the meantime, we invite you all to celebrate this exciting new development in Silverado Lake. Enjoy the food, enjoy the dancing, but most of all, enjoy the wine!" He raised his glass to the crowd as he cradled the mic.

Instead of applause, a stunned silence sat heavily over the crowd. Most of the people around Leila were looking at her with wide, questioning eyes.

"I can't believe he did that!" Jane took Leila's arm and marched her the rest of the way to the stage, meeting Forrest just as he came down the last step.

"What do you think you're doing?" her friend demanded. "You had no right to make a public announcement like that without clearing it with Leila first."

The people around them dispersed, like they weren't quite sure what to do with the scene unfolding in front of them.

"I told you that wasn't the best way to do this," Auggie growled from the edge of the stage.

Leila turned her head to stare at the man.

His eyes were wide, pleading with her. "I didn't know he was going to do that. You have to believe me." Auggie approached her, his arms held out in front of him.

Not Auggie. She kept getting confused. This was August. August Harding, Executive Director of Acquisitions for Kingston Family Vineyards.

Her heart steeled itself against him, and she backed away. If she even tried to open her mouth right now, a sob would burst out, and she wouldn't give him the satisfaction.

"Leila did what she had to do." Jane seemed intent on speaking for her. "This event is proof. She increased the profits, so you can't say Kingston is taking over. You can't just go tell all of their loyal customers that!"

Forrest belittled her with an irritated sigh. "August found phylloxera in the vineyards. We have to take that into account when looking at the financials."

"Phylloxera?" Leila's voice gained strength. August had found a problem with the vines and he hadn't even bothered to tell her about it? "Auggie?" His nickname slipped out again, damn it. From now on, she'd be calling him Mr. Harding.

He closed his eyes and heaved in a deep breath. "I saw it when we were harvesting, but I thought I could—"

"That's why he's my right-hand man," Forrest interrupted. "He knew that little problem would change things for our agreement. We've spent the last three weeks working on an acquisition plan."

"An acquisition plan?" This whole time August had been working with Forrest behind her back? Leila snapped her mouth shut before she choked on a sob.

August came at her again. "No. It wasn't like that. Lei, I'm on your side. I swear. I thought I could fix everything if I pretended to help Kingston."

"Fix everything?" Her throat burned. He'd kept things from her. No, he'd flat-out lied to her face. She jolted back and ran right into her grandfather. His arms came around her.

"Poppa." She struggled to get away. She couldn't do this. She couldn't face them right now.

"What's all this about?" Her grandfather demanded, releasing her to Nonna's care. Her grandfather stood toe-to-toe with Forrest. "What the hell do you think you're doing, getting up on that stage and spouting off a bunch of lies?"

Everyone's gazes locked on her. They were waiting for a response. Forrest and August and Jane, and all the people who'd lingered on the outskirts of their conversation, including Beth. The faces blurred in front of her, all around her.

"I can't believe I trusted you!" she shouted at August. "You told me everything would be fine."

"I know." He reached for her. "I'm sorry."

"No. Don't you dare touch me." Leila pushed him away. "You should've told me the truth. Because of you, my family's going to lose their home. You helped Kingston take it away from us."

"What?" Her grandmother gasped, and her grandparents closed in on her, the hurt and utter fear showing in their heartbroken expressions.

"I'm sorry." People still stood around them, listening in, and now everyone would know. Everyone would know how she'd lied. How she'd failed. But she didn't care. She was tired. God, she was so tired. "I signed a partnership with Kingston. I didn't know what else to do." Leila stared back at her grandparents, shutting out everyone else. They were the only two who really mattered, and she'd let them down. "I knew we couldn't say afloat much longer, so I contacted Kingston."

"Oh, Leila." Nonna took her hands. "Why didn't you tell us?"

"You already had enough to worry about." She closed her eyes, willing the tears to stop so she could explain without falling apart. "You were sick. I thought...I thought I could work everything out so we would hold on to majority ownership." But keeping the agreement from them wasn't even the worst thing she'd done.

She shifted her gaze to the man she would've given everything to not ten minutes ago. He had managed to reach her heart again, and now she was paying the price. "August...he acquires wineries for Kingston. That's why he showed up." She steadied her jaw. "Not because we're getting married. Not because he cares about me or because we reconnected." *Don't break.* She couldn't break in front of him. "The whole engagement was a lie." She'd even been lying to herself.

That was it—the truth in its ugly entirety. "I'm sorry," she said again. Then she turned away from them all and walked as quickly as she could, her heart finally shattering.

"Leila, wait—!" August called.

"I think you'd better let her go, son," Poppa said a ways behind her. "Let her be."

Leila didn't pause to see if August listened. She walked as fast as she could, blindly maneuvering around people and tables and chairs until she found the darkness of night to hide her. She made her way down the sidewalk to her cottage, choking on the sobs she couldn't hold back anymore. She'd lost everything in one night. Absolutely everything. Her family and her job and her love—all gone.

She fell against her front door, unable to find the strength to push it open.

After some moments, Nonna came alongside of her. "There now." She hugged Leila tightly as though trying to shelter her from the pain. "It's okay."

"Come here, princess." Poppa took her in his arms and managed to get the door open, the three of them stumbling into her living room.

"I'm sorry." Leila dropped to the couch, her face in her hands. "Oh, my God, I'm so sorry. I never meant to lie to you two, of all people." Uneven breaths stuttered through the words. "I didn't know what to do. I was trying to fix everything, and instead things got worse and worse." Her throat ached from crying, from the long, deep fissure in her heart.

"Shhh." Nonna sat beside her, enveloping Leila in the scent of lavender, offering immediate comfort. "Things aren't as bad as they seem, dear one. I promise."

"Things are awful," she sobbed. "Worse than awful. This place is your entire life. It's you're legacy, and I lost it." Forrest was right. They were already too deep in the hole. They couldn't take one more setback, especially in the form of phylloxera.

"Come on now, Lei." Poppa sat on the other side of her. "We never should've put all that burden on you. You were on your own. We share plenty of the responsibility for the state things were in when you took over."

"This is not your fault," Nonna added. "We've done our best, but the truth is, times are changing. It's harder to keep a business afloat these days. We probably should've agreed to that buyout from Kingston last year."

Their compassion only made her cry harder. She didn't deserve this. She didn't deserve their forgiveness. "This place means everything to you two."

"No." Nonna lifted Leila's chin. "You and your brother mean everything to us. A place is only a place. Our family is our life." She brushed an affectionate kiss on her cheek. "*You*, my dear, are our legacy."

"And we're proud of you," Poppa said gruffly. "You did your best. Especially after the mess we left things in." He smoothed his worn hand over her hair like he'd done often when she had been a little girl sitting on his knee. "Maybe this was meant to be. Maybe it's time for all of us to move on and find a new adventure."

What if she didn't want a new adventure? What if she still longed for the one she'd thought she and August would go on together?

"I'm sorry there won't be a wedding," she murmured, setting off a fresh round of tears.

Her grandmother directed Leila's head to her shoulder. "Are you sure what you and August had wasn't real?"

"It felt real." At least to her. "We talked about making it real." She had to fight her way out of the dream again. "But I don't know how to pick up the pieces this time." Because of what he'd done, she was about to lose everything.

Chapter Twenty-Four

August stood outside of Leila's door, trying to clean himself up.

He re-buttoned the top buttons on his shirt and straightened his sport coat before combing out his hair with his fingers. After watching her walk away from him in tears last night, he hadn't been able to drive home.

Instead, he'd gone down and sat in his truck, dissecting every wrong move he'd made, turning the mistakes over and over in his mind until he'd watched the sun come up an hour ago, and then he hadn't been able to take it anymore.

He knew Poppa had told him to let her be, but he had to explain everything. He had to see her.

Raising his hand to the door, he knocked quietly, holding his breath to stave off a shout. He was desperate to get in, but he also knew he couldn't force her to listen. He might have lost her for good this time.

"Lei?" he called softly, knocking again. "Please talk to me. Please let me explain."

Silence met his request, so he sat down on the red bench underneath the living room window. The shades were drawn, and the house sat eerily quiet. Maybe she was still asleep. It didn't matter. He'd wait as long as it took to see her.

August closed his eyes. He couldn't get Leila's heartbroken expression out of his head. That was all he saw—her eyes red and swollen, her mouth twisted with pain. The image would haunt him forever.

Opening his eyes, he tried to focus on the mountain vista in the distance. What could he do? What would his father do? He couldn't even ask the question. His dad never would've put himself in this situation.

After a while, Poppa came lumbering out of the vineyard on the other side of the cottage, his shoulders bent slightly. "She's not there."

August waited to speak until he came closer. "Is she okay?"

The man stared at him a long time, the breeze ruffling a tuft of his white hair. "She's not okay right now," he finally said. "But she will be." He took a seat next to August as though settling in for a long conversation, but Leila was the only person August wanted to talk to right now.

"I'd like to see her." He started to stand, but the man grabbed his arm and prompted him to sit back down.

"Now's not the best time." He said the words with a blend of kindness and sternness. "She needs some space. We had her spend the night at our house, and she was still sleeping when I left."

"Right." August let his shoulder slump. Fatigue had started to set in, making his eyes itch, but he wouldn't sleep until he'd explained himself. "None of this was supposed to happen." He kneaded his forehead. "I thought I could convince Forrest to buy another place, out on the Western Slope. I was so sure he'd go for it."

It was a hell of a time for Kingston to decide he cared more about aesthetics and location that he did about making money on this place. "I wanted to help Leila find a way out. Things just got so messed up." The harder he'd tried, the worse this situation had gotten.

"I understand." The man didn't seem to be looking at him any differently than he had yesterday. "Leila knows it too, deep down." The man's expression hinted at a smile. "I suspect you two found it a little too easy to pretend to be in love."

"I do love her." But it had taken him too long to figure out his feelings. August reached into the inside pocket of his sport coat, where he'd stashed Nonna's ring. He'd made a habit of carrying the small box with him, maybe to let it bring him hope, but he wouldn't need to hold on to the box anymore. "I wanted to give this back to you."

He placed the ring box into the man's hand. "I know Leila said it was all a lie, but I never lied about how much I care for her." He stood. "Forrest is sending me to New Mexico. I'm leaving later today."

Poppa pushed off the bench with a groan and stashed the ring box in his pocket. "You're sure that's what you want to do? Run off to New Mexico?"

"Forrest didn't exactly give me a choice." After Leila had walked away, Kingston had told him either he went to New Mexico or he lost his job, his stock options, his ability to work in the wine industry. They might've been empty threats, but he'd made his point.

"Seems to me this is not Forrest Kingston's choice to make." Leila's grandfather shuffled past him with a clap on his shoulder. "He's not the one living your life, Auggie. That's up to you." Poppa continued down the sidewalk, but then paused and walked back to him. "You should keep this." He pulled the ring box out of his pocket and handed it back to him. "Hold on to it a little longer." The man moseyed away, whistling as he disappeared back into the vineyard.

Poppa's words sat heavy long after he'd walked away. August ran them over and over in his mind as he tucked the ring into his pocket and hiked back to his truck. *He's not the one living your life.* That wasn't exactly true. Forrest Kingston had been running his life for almost a decade. Only August hadn't had much reason to care until now.

He climbed into his truck and drove down the switchbacks,

thinking through every assignment his boss had sent him on. He'd never questioned, never pushed back. He'd never had a reason to. The constant traveling, the endless assignments, had kept him content. But they weren't enough anymore.

Driving faster, he turned onto the ranch's driveway, but instead of heading for his cabin, he went straight to his mom's house.

She was sitting in her favorite Adirondack chair, reading and enjoying her cup of coffee like she did most mornings.

After parking behind her car, he got out and dragged himself to the chair next to hers.

"Looks like you had a rough night." She slipped off her glasses and set them on the table between them as though she knew they'd be here for a while.

"I screwed everything up," he told her as if she didn't already know. He had no doubt his sister had relayed every painful detail of the scene with Forrest. "I lost her, Mom. I should've been honest with her. I should've told her everything instead of trying to fix the problems on my own."

He let his head rest against the chair and stared up at the swirls of clouds in the royal blue sky. "The look on Leila's face..." A soul-crushing despair weighed him down. That had been the worst part, seeing her lose all faith in him. "The Valentinos are being pushed out because of me. And Lei? She'll never forgive me."

His mother had always been a good listener—something he'd forgotten. She often sat quietly, letting another person's words have the space they deserved. It hit him now how much he'd missed talking to her, how big a mistake it had been to keep her on the fringes of his life all these years. He added that to his growing list of regrets.

After a lengthy quiet between them, she sighed and angled her body to his. "I think it's past time I told you something, Auggie." The gravity in her tone mirrored the solemnity in her eyes. "Your father left me once."

"What?" He bolted upright, immediately defensive of the man

who'd been his biggest hero. His father had left? No. Impossible. He hadn't heard right. "What did you say?"

"We'd only been married for three years." Her eyes went blank, like she'd traveled back to a place she didn't want to go. "We'd just bought this land and had barely finished staining the logs on the house here." Her hand absentmindedly touched one of the log beams behind them. "I'd started talking about wanting to have a baby. He was getting ready to turn thirty, after all. But...I think it was too much for him—the house and the baby talk and the fact that he had a milestone birthday coming up."

August fought to keep listening, fought to keep his denials to himself, to keep his mouth shut so she could continue.

"I noticed him distancing himself from me for a couple of weeks." Her inhale sharpened, as though the memory still hurt. "And then one day, I came home from the grocery store, and he was packing up his car. He said he couldn't be tied down, that he wasn't ready for everything I wanted."

"Jesus, Mom." His stomach buckled, making him nauseous. His father—the man he'd idolized—had walked out on his wife because he hadn't wanted to be tied down? He didn't even know how to process that. "What did you say to him?"

"What could I say?" She blinked a few times, likely to keep tears at bay. "I loved him. I saw how conflicted he was, how he was struggling." She sat up taller and leaned closer. "But, honey...if I had forced him to stay, I would've lost him. Love doesn't force. Love offers freedom. So I let him go, and I told him that I would be here, that he could come back. I told him I would always keep a place for him in my heart."

How had she offered his dad the option to come back after watching him walk away from her? August scrolled back through all of his memories of his father, the man who had held his family close. The man who had always put his wife and kids first—above everything else. "I can't believe he left. I can't believe you let him come back."

She smiled now, as though the weight of the memory had

been lifted. "He didn't even last three months before he drove back into this driveway." For all the pain her smile held, it still showed a glimpse of joy. "I heard a car coming and somehow I knew. I walked out the door just as he turned off the engine and I simply opened my arms. He walked into them and we never looked back."

"It was that easy?" Emotion tightened his throat. It sure as hell didn't seem that easy to right past wrongs, to make up for mistakes.

"It wasn't easy, but we worked at it. And we made it." She rose from her chair and walked to the porch rail, looking out over the lake. "I think maybe—because of the way we lost him—we put him on this pedestal." His mother turned to face him again. "He was a good man, a strong man, a family man, an honest man. But Auggie, he wasn't perfect. And he wasn't *always* the man you remember him to be. He had his struggles and his failures. He made mistakes sometimes."

"I can't seem to remember any of them." He'd been a lucky enough kid to have a father whom he could look up to. In his eyes, in his memories, his father had been perfect. He was the man August had always compared himself to, and he knew he would never measure up. "I wanted to be like him, and then after he died, I failed. I failed to be strong. I failed to help you."

His mother simply held his stare, listening again in her wise way.

"I've made a lot of mistakes." Not only recently with Leila and her family, but over the years with his own. "I'm sorry I disappeared. I'm sorry I was too much of a coward to come back."

"You weren't a coward." His mother pulled her chair closer to him and sat back down. "You have so much of your father in you, Auggie. You feel things as deeply as he did. You are every bit as loyal and devoted as he was."

How could she think he was loyal and devoted when he hadn't let people into his life? "I wish I could see the similarities." Then maybe he'd know what to do, how to make things right with Leila.

His mom took his hand. "One thing about your father, he never let his mistakes dictate how he lived his life. He overcame them. He owned them and he allowed each of them to make him into a better man."

That was why August remembered him as being perfect. "After he came back to you, he made his family the most important thing in his life."

"Exactly. He promised me he would never turn his back on me again, and he never did." His mom wiped away a tear. "Your father left us far too soon, honey, but I know for a fact if I would've had the chance to look into his eyes before he took his last breath, I wouldn't have seen one single regret there. He lived a big, beautiful life full of joy because those mistakes he'd made taught him how to love people well." She waited until his eyes met hers. "And you can use yours to make sure you don't have any regrets either."

"Thank you for telling me about Dad." Hearing his parents' story had given him a new perspective. "I don't know if Lei can forgive me for how things have gone. But even if she doesn't, I'll make this right." He didn't have any doubts. There was no way he was leaving for New Mexico later. Instead, he would go back to California and take on Forrest.

Chapter Twenty-Five

Leila pulled the covers up to her chin. How much longer could she get away with avoiding the world? Bright sunlight filtered in through the small window in her grandparent's guestroom, but she couldn't get out of bed.

Hours had passed since the worst night of her life, but the scenes wouldn't stop playing in her head—Forrest up on that stage, the humiliating whispers and stares. August gazing at her helplessly.

A nightmare.

And yet those things had really happened. She couldn't live in denial and avoid the repercussions.

Leila threw off the comforter. While she'd love to stay in bed and wallow all day, she had to get out there and do some damage control. Forrest had stolen her opportunity to manage the message about this new partnership, but she wouldn't let him have the satisfaction of driving her away now. She still had a few weeks here, damn it, and she would make those weeks the very best that Valentino Bellas had ever seen. Then she would throw her grandparents the retirement party of the century right before they all headed off to Italy—and she wouldn't bother cleaning up afterward.

So there.

A new energy carried her out of the bed and over to the small duffel bag she'd packed when sweet Nonna had insisted she sleep at their house. She pulled on a pair of jeans and a sweatshirt, tying up her hair before she slipped out into the hallway. Pots and pans banged around in the kitchen, and now she could smell the sweet scent of maple syrup mixed in with the salty aroma of bacon.

Sugar and grease—her favorite combination.

Her stomach growled as she walked into the kitchen. Nonna stood at the stove flipping pancakes, wearing her favorite apron, exactly like she had when Leila had been in high school.

"Good morning," her grandmother sang, handing her a plate. "How did you sleep?"

"I'm not sure how to answer that." Leila carried her plate to the table, already comforted by the familiarity of the smells and warmth in her grandparents' kitchen. Oh, to be in high school again when she didn't have to worry about much except getting her homework done or what to wear on a date with Auggie.

And there he was again, breaking into her thoughts the same way he'd broken into her dreams last night.

"I made your favorite." Nonna brought a whole stack of pancakes to the table. "Cinnamon swirl pancakes and extra-crispy bacon." She leaned over and poured her a glass of freshly squeezed orange juice.

"Wow." Leila smoothed a cloth napkin across her lap. "I should be humiliated more often. It's been a while since I've had a breakfast that looked and smelled this good."

"You know what I always say." Nonna brought over the plate of bacon and joined her at the table. "There's nothing a good, hearty breakfast can't fix."

Leila couldn't help but smile surrounded by her grandmother's cheerfulness. She took a couple of bites of food, the comfort wrapping around her more. "Yes, I remember hearing that after a couple of botched math tests back in the day."

A barrage of emotion came on suddenly, choking her up. "I

can't believe we won't be having any more breakfasts together in this kitchen." The wave of sadness wiped out her appetite.

"Now, now." Her grandmother wiggled the plate of pancakes in front of her. "Chin up. There are some beautiful kitchens in Italy. Maybe we'll like them better anyway."

"But they won't be *this* kitchen." The one she'd been raised in. The one they'd shared laughter and meals in. Grief buried her heart. "Nonna, I'm going to miss this place so much. This is where some of my best memories are."

"We do have many memories." Her grandmother took over and put two more pancakes on her plate. "But we can take those with us wherever we go." She nodded toward the food and aimed a stern frown directly at her until Leila took another bite of the pancake.

The flavors melted in her mouth and reignited her hunger. "Thank you for breakfast." She stifled the sadness with gratitude. "You really shouldn't have gone to all this trouble."

"It makes me happy to take care of you for once." He grandmother dished up her own plate. "Besides, it's been far too long since I made these pancakes. I almost forgot how."

"I doubt that." Leila helped herself to a few pieces of bacon. "Do you—?"

The back door opened, and Poppa came in, stomping the mud off his boots on the rug.

"You're just in time for breakfast, tesoro." Nonna hurried to grab another plate from the cabinet.

"I sure know how to time things." He winked at Leila and sat across from her, helping himself to four pancakes. "Tromping around in that mud makes a man hungry." He removed his old, weathered cowboy hat and hung it on the back of his chair. "Auggie was right. There's phylloxera in a whole section of those vines out there. Hard to see in the early stages, but it's still there."

The mention of the man's name gave her heart a good punch. "He should've told us right away. He should've been honest with me." Instead, he'd told Forrest, only giving the man more ammunition to use against them.

"Well, he wasn't the only one being dishonest," her grand-mother murmured, her tone as gentle as her nonjudgmental gaze. "Why did you lie to us about the engagement?"

"Because I wanted to protect you—"

Oh.

"Yes. You wanted to protect us." Nonna smoothed her hand over Leila's hair. "Maybe that can help you understand why Auggie did what he did."

"He likely thought the news about the vines would send Forrest running in another direction." Poppa dug into his food like he would've any other morning, eating a few bites and then wiping his mouth with a napkin. "I saw him out there, by the way."

"August? Out there?" Leila almost bolted from the table to look through the window. Was he still outside?

"He was standing outside your door knocking when I went past," her grandfather said. He'd never been overly forthcoming with details.

"Well, did you talk to him?" Why did her heart have to race every time she thought about August?

"A little." Poppa shrugged. "He was worried about you. Looked like hell too. I don't think he ever went home last night. Must've slept in his truck."

"What did he say?" Leila did her best to rein in her impatience. Her grandparents had made their point. Maybe Auggie had only wanted to protect her the way she'd tried to protect them.

"He said he never meant for this to happen." Poppa poured himself a large glass of orange juice. "And then he said Forrest is sending him to New Mexico today."

"Today?" Nonna's fork hovered in front of her mouth. "That seems mighty hasty, doesn't it?"

"It's for the best." The words would've sounded more convinc-ing if her voice hadn't shaken. Auggie was actually leaving? He was walking away from her again.

"He sure didn't seem happy about it." Her grandfather took

another bite of food. "I told him he shouldn't live his life for Forrest, but what do I know?"

"He does live for that company." She shouldn't have forgotten that. Humiliation burned through her all over again. If he cared about her, he'd fight for her this time. He'd fight for them. Instead he was leaving for New Mexico. That hurt worse than any lie. "I'm going to see Sam." She pushed away from the table, leaving most of her food untouched.

"But your pancakes." Nonna stood too. "Don't you want to finish at least one of them?"

"Can you save them for me?" Leila was already putting her shoes on by the door. "I'll eat them later. Promise. I'm not hungry right now."

"Oh, all right." Her grandmother relented but hurried over with her travel mug. She'd filled it with her orange juice. "At least take this with you."

"Thank you." Leila took the juice in one hand and wrapped the other arm around her grandmother. "I don't know what I would do without you two. Seriously. You're the best grandparents in the world."

She left them there before she started bawling again and walked out into the sunshine, following the path around the back of the house and up the hill to the barn.

As usual, her brother was too engrossed in whatever he was testing to even notice she'd come in. At least he didn't seem to be wallowing.

"Hey." She walked to his table, which was every bit as messy as it had been before she'd tidied it up the other day.

Sam set down the glass beaker he'd been holding up. "Hey. I stopped by your cottage this morning. Thought I would see if you wanted to go get a coffee."

"Really?" She tried to think of the last time she and Sam had gone to get coffee together but came up blank.

"Yeah." Her brother turned his attention back to the beaker. "You okay?"

"No." He'd see through a lie anyway. "I should've listened to you."

He poured some clear liquid into what she assumed was red wine. "I didn't want to be right."

"I know." For all his eccentricities, Sam had a heart of gold. "But you were. I should've listened. I'm sorry. I know you love your job." And she'd lost it for him

"You don't have to be sorry on my account." Her brother graced her with his full attention again. "I've already had three job offers this morning. All out on the Western Slope, of course. But I'll be fine, Lei. Like I said, I'm worried about you."

"I'll be fine too." It would take time, but she would find a way to move on from this. "We're going to make these last few weeks the best in Valentino Bellas' history." She would need the distraction to get her mind off August. She wouldn't wait for him this time. Wouldn't hope.

Her brother's dark eyes narrowed. "And what about you and Auggie?"

"There is no me and Auggie." Miraculously, she got the words out with only a slight wobble in her voice. That was something.

Her brother called her out with a knowing glare. "I saw you two together. There was something between you and Auggie. You should've seen the guy after you ran off last night. He was frantic, arguing with Forrest. He obviously cares about you."

This kind of talk was not helping her Forget-about-August campaign. "You hate the guy." Was he or was he not the one who'd been pointing out all of August's shortcomings?

"I don't hate him," Sam corrected. "I feel kinda bad for him, actually. He seems pretty broken up about what happened last night."

"So I've heard." She let herself picture August sitting in his truck all night. She knew exactly how his face would look stewing over what had happened. His mouth would be pinched; his jaw would be rigid. Her heart softened.

Voices outside cut her off and launched her heart into her throat. Was August out there?

"Hello?" Jane's voice floated through the open window. "Leila, are you in there?"

She darted to the wall and peeked out through the opening in the curtain, making sure August hadn't come with his sister. Nope. Only Beth and Jane lingered outside the door. *Great.* She wasn't exactly ready to face anyone after last night, but she couldn't hide now.

Leila let them in. "Hey." She couldn't look either one of them directly in the eyes. Jane hadn't been shocked about the engagement revelation, but she'd lied right to Beth's face on more than one occasion.

"Forrest Kingston is going down." Beth stomped into the barn, fuming. "That man is unbelievable! If he thinks for one minute that he can just move in here and take over with this town's support, he has another think coming."

Leila had to laugh. The cavalry had arrived.

Jane hushed Beth with a look. "We don't mean to overstep, but this whole Kingston thing is all anyone has been talking about all morning at the café."

"There's already an online petition and an online fund-raising page started," Beth added. "Your family has been a fixture in our community forever, and we're all going to stand behind you to fight for this place."

The conviction behind their words brought tears to her eyes. "Really?"

Jane gave her a hug. "Really."

Beth pulled her phone out of her purse. "Look at this. So far, we have over two thousand signatures on the petition." She showed Leila the screen. "Everyone in town is on board with this fight. Now we just need to put some pressure on Mr. Kingston."

Leila wished it would be that easy. "I'm not sure it's going to matter."

"How does he think he'll sell any wine when it's not tourist season?" Jane demanded. "This town will be important for his success. Trust me. If we don't want him here, he won't want to be here."

Their confidence pulled her in. "You're right. Kingston knows nothing about Silverado Lake, about how we all pull together and take care of each other." With the town behind her, she could face the man. She could tell him exactly why he should let her family keep the winery. She had nothing to lose. "I'm going to California."

Jane gasped. "Yes! Maybe you'll see Auggie while you're there!"

Leila's breath got caught in the conflicting emotions—longing, anger, fear. But the strongest response to his name was always love. She loved him. She always had. Yes, he'd made mistakes, but so had she.

"I thought he was going to New Mexico. Poppa said Forrest put him on some new assignment down there."

"He told my mom he's not going," Jane said hopefully. "He left for California a while ago."

Her pulse picked up, finding the same rhythm that'd swept her up whenever August had pulled her close. "I need to talk to Auggie too." He'd walked away from her once, and she'd let him, but mistakes could be forgiven. This time, she was going after him.

Chapter Twenty-Six

August drove into the driveway of his house, which was set against the backdrop of vineyards terraced into thousands of rolling acres.

The sun hovered low over the eastern horizon, shining a pinkish light into the dawn. He parked in front of the expansive three-car garage—still empty though he'd lived here for five years—and got out to stretch his back. He'd only made three quick stops during the fifteen-hour drive, continuing through the night so he could get here. So he could set about righting his mistakes as soon as possible.

In those lonely, dark hours on the road, he'd actually felt his father with him for the first time since his death. He'd let himself feel the loss, no longer afraid of what the grief would do to him.

Maybe his mom taking the man off the pedestal to show he'd been flawed had helped. Human. A lot like him. Maybe in idolizing a dead man, August had been hiding from a standard he feared he could never live up to.

The only thing he knew for certain right now was that he actually did have a chance to be like his father—to let the mistakes he'd made change him and help him become the kind of man Charlie Harding would be proud of.

August walked up the porch steps and unlocked the door of the sleek, modern, clean-lined home Forrest had let him live in rent free, but there were so many other strings attached. This place didn't belong to him. This life didn't belong to him.

Everything he had came from an unspoken understanding that he would give his life to this company, and he had.

Feeling like a stranger, he walked across the dyed concrete floors in the foyer before the space opened into a great room with the contemporary grayscale kitchen on one side and the staunch colorless living room on the other. The house's stark bleakness had never bothered him before, likely because he'd lived a colorless life. He'd kept everything in his life as clean and as bare as this house. But now it was time to add some color.

He glanced at the clock. Being that it was so early, Forrest likely wouldn't even be awake yet, but August couldn't wait. He walked back outside and decided to cut through the vineyard to get to Kingston's house rather than taking his truck.

The air still held the crisp coolness of night, though the sun warmed his skin. He followed the worn path between the vines, the plump cabernet sauvignon grapes hanging low. Back when he'd first started working here, the harvest had been his favorite time of year. He'd spent every hour—sunup to sundown—walking these paths, holding the result of his hard work from the rest of the year in his hands. He might have been hiding from relationships, true, but working here had taught him a lot too. It hadn't been wasted time. He'd learned loyalty and devotion and perseverance and diligence. Each of those things would serve him well moving forward. Those were the traits he had to take into his relationships. This next act was the first step toward bringing those traits into a relationship with Leila.

He started up the slope to Forrest's house—the castle on the hill. For all the wealth he'd amassed and the success he'd had, Kingston's place wasn't any more inviting or warm or personal than August's. It was beautiful for sure, with some of the best views in the valley, but what were views if you had no one to share them with?

After only the slightest hesitation to sigh out the sudden pressure in his chest, August rang the video doorbell. No doubt Forrest would check his phone to see who would dare darken his doorstep before seven o'clock in the morning. Hopefully, when he saw August, he wouldn't ignore him.

The minutes seemed to stretch longer and longer as they passed, but he stood his ground. This was one door he had to walk through—the only barrier between him and what he'd learned he wanted most. A life with Leila. The life they'd dreamed about together. The one he'd delayed.

A beeping sound on the other side of the door indicated that the alarm had been turned off. The door opened, and his boss appeared in his bathrobe and pajama pants. His normally slicked, silver hair was sticking up in tufts around his head, a reminder that Forrest was only a man too.

Flawed. Human.

The biggest difference between Forrest and August's father was that Kingston didn't value relationships. He didn't want to get loving someone right. And August didn't want to find himself standing in the man's shoes someday.

"You didn't go to New Mexico." Forrest's voice was flat, but the tinge of surprise on his face gave him away.

"No, I didn't." For the first time since he'd started working for the man, he hadn't followed a directive. "Can I come in?" He didn't want to have this conversation on the front porch.

Forrest gave him a good, long glare but finally stepped aside so he could walk through the door.

The man's house was remarkably similar to the one he'd given August, modern and grayscale and too clean to have any personality. He wandered through the cavernous great room to the kitchen, where he pulled out a chair at the reclaimed-wood table.

Forrest opted to sit across from him. "You can't do this," the man said before he could speak. "Do I have to remind you how much you have to lose? Your house, your car, future prospects in this business, your financial security. It all belongs to me."

And that was why he had to walk away. "I'm quitting. Consider this my official notice." He'd thought those words would be harder to say, but they came easily. "And I'm happy to give up the house and the car and all of my financial security. I'll even voluntarily give up my stock options. Under one condition."

His boss didn't move or speak, but obvious anger turned the man's face red.

"I want to buy out your part of the partnership with Valentino Bellas." It might very well cost him everything he had, but this would be the most important purchase of his life. "In all these years I've worked for you, I've never asked you for anything. I'll pay you what that other vineyard on the Western Slope is worth. You can purchase that place and have your Kingston presence in Colorado."

August would cash in his more lucrative investments to make this happen. Forrest wouldn't be able to turn down that kind of deal. Yes, he wanted August to stay with the company, but his life had been about the bottom line. "You know that's far above what this deal was originally worth to you."

"You've lost your mind." Forrest laughed incredulously. "Do you realize how ridiculous you sound? All of this for some woman from your past?"

"Leila isn't some woman from my past." She was everything. And he would do this for her even if she didn't forgive him. "I've loved her since I was sixteen years old. She's the one I want to build my life around. Not some job. Not status and wealth." Especially after seeing how those things had worked out for Forrest.

"Fine," his boss grumbled. "Forget New Mexico. You can manage the Valentino Bellas property under the Kingston name. But I still want only Kingston-branded wine sold there. We can—"

"No." Once again Forrest was trying to get his way. "I won't work for Kingston. I want to buy you out so I can release the Valentinos from any obligations." He would help them work those vines. He would help replant and graft on new vines over time. They wouldn't make much, but they could find ways to get through.

The man held on to his typical, stubborn frown, but August could tell he was thinking things through.

"If you want to throw your life away, I won't stop you." Forrest rose from the table and left August sitting there. "I'll have my lawyers start on the paperwork." The man paused and glanced over his shoulder. "But don't ever come to me for anything again. I saved you. I did everything for you. And this is the thanks I get?"

August stood. "I appreciate everything you did for me, Forrest. And I'll never forget it. But it's past time I saved myself."

* * *

Leila drove the rental car in through Kingston Family Vineyards' wrought-iron gate, slowing to admire the intricacies of the design cut into the metal.

She'd known this place would be impressive, but the stunning landscape and the stone buildings dotting the hillside went far beyond what she'd pictured in her head. When she'd previously traveled to California to negotiate with Forrest, she'd purposely avoided his empire. Instead, she'd met him at a small, unassuming restaurant in town. Neutral ground. Or so she'd thought. With Forrest, there was no such thing as neutral ground.

Leila followed the road as it wound between the lush rows of vines, their stems and leaves heavy with ripe grapes. The vines here were robust compared to the ones at Valentino Bellas—taller and fuller and apparently much healthier.

She rolled passed a few workers who were tending the ground with their tools, and she thought about August again. He'd likely started out like those men, tending the ground until he'd worked his way up to being Forrest's right-hand man.

Leila couldn't help looking for his truck when she drove into the parking lot in front of the massive stone-and-concrete building that housed Kingston's main tasting room and operations, but there were too many vehicles to sort through. It didn't matter where he was. She would find him after she met with Forrest.

She couldn't wait for this conversation to happen. With the support of Silverado Lake behind her, she had to make her case for retaining ownership of her family's winery.

Even though it was only midmorning, she had to park near the back of the lot. She climbed out of the rental car and followed the stamped concrete sidewalk along the edge of a hill that looked down over the symmetrical rows of vines on an acreage at least fifty times the size of Valentino Bellas'. With all of this, why in the world would Forrest care about her family's modest winery?

She wandered into the tasting room through a pair of heavy glass doors and stopped to gawk at the fountain running all the way down the wall, filling the space with a calming swooshing sound.

She was anything but calm.

The open space housed heavy wooden tables of all sizes. Strewn around the outlying corners were more casual seating options with colorful leather chairs and couches. The bar sat in a white concrete square at the very center of the room, where nicely dressed sales reps were talking up the wines with wealthy constituents.

What was she thinking showing up here unannounced? She was way out of her league with Forrest. Even in her best pantsuit—which she'd scored from the Nordstrom sale rack—she still didn't fit in. This was pointless.

Leila turned to walk out the door.

"Welcome to Kingston Family Vineyards," a man said behind her.

For a few seconds she debated bolting out the door, but instead, she steeled her spine and turned to face him. This was her last chance to make her case with Forrest. She owed this to her grandparents.

"Hi."

"Can I get you started on a tasting?" the man—Liam, according to his name tag—asked.

"Oh. Uh. Well..." It probably wouldn't hurt to have a couple sips of wine before facing Forrest. "Sure. I'd love that." Business school had taught her how to procrastinate well. She had all day to find the man. She might as well enjoy some of her time here.

Liam grabbed a menu. "Would you like to sit inside or out?"

"Outside would be lovely." Kingston had obviously spent a fortune on this space, but the sleek, contemporary vibe seemed stifling compared to her family's rustic, homey tasting room.

"Follow me." Liam waved her along past a few tables of groups enjoying flights together, and then out through a wall of windows at the back. The stamped concrete patio ran the whole length of the building, showcasing those lovely views again.

"Have you visited the Kingston tasting room before?" Liam asked, gesturing to a small bistro table for two. He was so polished and polite, dressed in that fancy suit.

"Uh, no." Leila sat down under the shade of an umbrella. "This will be my first time."

"Well, we're glad to have you." He set a leather-backed menu down in front of her. "All the wines on the menu have won many accolades and awards over the years. The best way to get a full taste of Kingston is to do a flight. We have a fabulous red flight on special today." He pointed out the list at the top of the menu. "Or you can opt for one of our white flights or combo flights. Do you have a favorite type of wine?"

"Not really." Her favorite type was whatever Valentino Bellas made. "I think I'll do the combo flight to start."

"Wonderful choice." Liam's practiced smile held the perfect blend of professionalism and charm. "I'll put that in and leave the menu so you can read more about our wines while you wait."

"Thank you." Leila turned her attention to the views after the man walked away. She wasn't sure she'd seen a more romantic spot. The patio had fountains too, along with towering flowerpots brightening everything with splashes of color.

A small part of her hoped August would appear in front of her. Okay, not a small part, a big part of her. Every moment they'd shared over the last several months seemed to crowd into her heart. Yes, the scene at the party had been humiliating, but she couldn't put all the blame on him. If she hadn't lied to her grandparents, none of this would've happened. She was the one who'd set this whole debacle in motion. August's biggest mistake had been trying to fix the problems himself instead of being up front with her.

"Here we are." Liam reappeared, carrying her flight on a custom tray. He set the arrangement in front of her and went on to give a lengthy spiel on each wine.

Leila listened intently and then picked up her glass of the unoaked chardonnay at his direction. "Mmm." She gave the expected nod of approval, though she swore her brother's version was smoother.

"That's a very popular wine for us," Liam told her. "We sell it by the case, especially through the summer."

"I'm sure." Leila enjoyed another sip, letting the flavors rest on her palate. "It almost has a caramel undertone." A little too strong of an undertone, if one asked her.

"Yes." Liam grinned. "You obviously know wine."

She swirled her glass around, inhaling. "I know a little."

"So what brings you to Kingston today?" Liam was on to her. He seemed to detect she wasn't a simple tourist. No surprise there, considering she'd dressed like a businesswoman and had come alone. "Actually, I'm an acquaintance of Forrest's."

She swore the man stood up two inches taller. "Forrest?" Poor Liam looked a little flustered. "Wow. Okay. That's wonderful. Is he expecting you?"

"No. I'm only passing through." Leila finished off the mediocre chardonnay and moved on to the sauvignon blanc. "But I would love to find out if he's available to see me, if you wouldn't mind checking?" She smiled sweetly.

"No. Of course not. No problem." Liam hurried away, but then dashed back to the table. "Can I tell him who's asking for him?"

"Leila Valentino." She projected all the confidence she could muster. There was a real possibility Forrest would hear her name and refuse to come see her.

"Wonderful. I'll call over to the offices to see if Mr. Kingston is available." Liam walked away at a more controlled pace, and Leila let her shoulders relax. Like Beth and Jane had said, she had nothing to lose. The worst Forrest could do was laugh at her and send her on her way. But at least she'd tried.

While she waited, Leila worked her way through the pinot noir and the cabernet sauvignon, which she enjoyed more than the whites. She was about to start on the merlot when Forrest walked out through the glass doors, commanding all of the attention on the patio. He headed directly for her table, seemingly oblivious to the stares and whispers he'd stirred up.

"Ms. Valentino. I wish I could say I was surprised."

She didn't invite him to sit, but he did anyway, right across from her, eyes sharpened into an intimidating glare.

She refused to look away. "But you're not surprised to see me."

"No. I figured you would want to have a conversation with me eventually." He seemed to try to read her mind. "So what brings you all the way out to California?"

During her flight and the ensuing drive, she'd rehearsed for this very moment, and yet somehow, words eluded her. She wasn't scared of the man, but there were so many things she wanted to say, so many emotions, after the way he'd humiliated her at the party. Though she knew her feelings wouldn't matter to him. She had to go after his business sense. "I thought you should know there is quite a bit of local opposition to Kingston moving into Silverado Lake."

His head tilted, conveying more amusement than irritation. "Is that so?"

"Yes. An online petition has garnered over two thousand signa-tures, and the people in town are vowing to boycott all Kingston products." She showed him her phone so he knew she wasn't bluffing. "I'm sure I don't have to tell you how much Valentino Bellas has relied on the town's support during the off-season."

The man leaned over the table with a snide smile. "Kingston doesn't need the town's support. We ship wine all over the world, Ms. Valentino. The money we would make off the people in that town would only be a drop in the bucket."

Leila's resolve started to crumble. What could she say to that? How could she convince him to walk away when he obviously didn't need more wealth?

"This whole conversation is irrelevant anyway," Forrest said as though already bored. "I've started the paperwork to sell off my percentage of ownership in Valentino Bellas."

"Sell it off?" She jumped to her feet, ready to turn the table over. "You can't do that. You can't just sell it off to some other corporate outfit. I want to buy it. I want to buy you out."

His laugh belittled her. "Trust me. You couldn't afford what the other party offered."

"Who?" she asked feebly. Who would be holding the future of Valentino Bellas in their hands?

He stared at her for a long moment, so long she was afraid he wouldn't say, but then pulled a business card and pen out of his pocket and wrote an address. "You'll find the new owner here. I'm quite sure he'll be open to speaking with you." He stood. "Now if you'll excuse me, I have some important business to take care of."

"Thank you," Leila called to the man's retreating back. She rose on shaky legs. Was Forrest messing with her or would the new owner truly be willing to work with her family? She couldn't wait another minute to find out.

She stashed the business card in her pocket and rifled through her purse to find a fifty-dollar bill, hastily securing it under a water glass so it wouldn't blow away. Then, she rushed through the restaurant and out to the parking lot, practically jogging to her rental car.

Once she'd settled herself in the driver's seat, she typed the address on the business card into the GPS and followed the directions that led her out of Kingston's gate and back into the rolling vineyards.

This doesn't look right. She turned into the driveway of a boxy, contemporary home and eased the car to a stop so she could check the business card again. Forrest had sent her to the new owner's house?

Whatever. House, office—it didn't matter. She had to talk to the man before she lost the nerve.

Leila got out of the car and smoothed her wrinkled clothes, straightening her posture and aiming for a professional stride as she made her way to the front door. Before she could get there, it opened. August stepped outside carrying a box in his hands.

"Auggie." The sight of him made her breathless.

"Lei." The sound of her name on his lips held such tenderness, such incredible hope.

She rushed the rest of the way to him in a blind whirl of emotion. He dropped the box and caught her in his arms.

"I talked to Forrest." She had to pause and catch her breath. "He sent me here to talk to the new owner. It's you? You bought him out? You—"

"Would do anything for you." His hands held her face close to his. "I would do anything for you, Leila Valentino."

Unable to stop herself, she closed her eyes and touched her lips to his, holding them there so she could be sure this was happening. He was really here. This kiss was better than all the others they'd shared, small and simple but encompassing a future she'd only hoped for.

August pulled back too soon. "I'm sorry you had to wait so long for me to figure things out." He smoothed her hair away from her face. "I know I don't deserve another chance, but I promise you I won't leave you again. Ever."

"I know you won't." On some level, she'd known he wouldn't leave her since he'd kissed her at AppleFest. "This is our time. Our future. Starting right now." She backed him up against the porch's column so she could kiss him again. "And I promise I won't ever look back."

Chapter Twenty-Seven

August lay perfectly still so he wouldn't disturb the beautiful woman asleep in his arms.

Five more minutes had turned into ten and then twenty, and now he was inching ever closer to being twenty-five minutes late for his meeting with Poppa in the vineyard.

Over the last month, they'd been pruning and preparing the vines for grafting. The project would likely take months, but Leila made it very difficult for him to find the motivation to get out of bed.

After coming back to Valentino Bellas, this had become his favorite time of day, when they were tucked into Leila's cozy cottage. When he could hold her and simply admire her while she slept.

Most of their hours had been filled with seriously hard work—with him out in the vineyards with Sam and Poppa and the many volunteers from town who'd stepped up to help them regenerate the vines while Leila and Nonna managed the growing wine club orders. It had been years since he'd worked so hard with so few resources, and yet this last month had been the happiest he'd ever been.

Leila stirred and let out a contented sigh, burrowing her cheek against his chest. "Are you late again?"

"Yep." But he didn't move.

"Sorry. I was going to get up and make you breakfast before you went out." She lifted her head to peek at him, some of her dark hair spilling down over her eyes. "But I guess I'm not getting enough sleep at night." Her wry smile made it clear that was his fault.

"I'm sorry too." August cleared the strands of hair away so he could fully look at her face. "But sleeping is the last thing I want to do when I get in bed with you." Mainly because he couldn't seem to get enough of her. August weaved his fingers through hers and brought her hand to his mouth, kissing her skin.

Her expression brightened, bringing light to her eyes. "I'm not complaining."

He loved when she smiled like that—big enough to put a tiny dimple in her right cheek. "Good." He kissed that spot and then dragged his lips to hers. "My goal is to keep you happy."

"I am happy." She settled her head against his chest again. "This whole month has been a dream."

"It has," he agreed, tracing his fingertips along her arm. It was a dream he didn't want to wake up from anytime soon.

The thought filled him with an urgency to get going, to move forward with her, to take the next step. Which meant he had to get out of bed. "I probably should go out there and help your grandpa." The man had been very patient about his tardy morning appearances, but today August had an important item on the agenda with Poppa.

"Okay." Leila pouted but scooted away from him. "Since it's Saturday, I can come and help in the vineyard too—"

"You stay here and relax." He kissed her lips once more before hauling himself out of bed. "You've been working hard too. You deserve some downtime."

"Maybe I'll make you a nice late breakfast." She propped herself up on her elbows. "When can you be back?"

"I could take a break around ten." He pulled on his jeans and a sweatshirt, and then sat on the edge of the bed. "I'd love to share breakfast with you." He'd love to share every breakfast with her for the rest of his life, which meant he'd best get going. "Don't go to too much trouble, though." He kissed her once more. "It's supposed to be your day off."

"I like going to trouble for you." She sat up, the covers falling away from her naked body and tempting him to forget heading out that door. "Besides, we likely won't have any other alone time today, with the family picnic happening later this afternoon."

"Right." Everyone from both of their families would be gathering at the ranch later that afternoon. "But I'll bet we could sneak away for a while."

"Not a chance, given how much your nieces and nephew love to spend time with their uncle Auggie." She lay back down. "Besides, I love your family."

"I do too. Most of the time." Even with his brother constantly hounding him to propose to Leila. He swore Wes sent him at least five text messages a day asking if they were engaged for real yet. His answer was always the same.

Not yet, but soon.

"All right, my love." He stared into her eyes. "I'll see you a little bit later."

There went that smile again. "Not too much later."

"I'll come back as soon as I can." He rose from the bed and grabbed his coat, forcing himself to walk out the door before he gave in to temptation and got back in bed with her.

In the last several weeks, the mornings had grown much colder. He stepped outside and followed the frost-encrusted path to the west, taking in the view of the fiery-yellow aspen trees that blanketed the mountainsides. He'd forgotten how beautiful fall was in Colorado, how much his father had loved this time of year.

Back when they were young, his dad would take the family on weekend hikes to go leaf peeping. They'd spend hours searching for the best trees to serve as a backdrop to their family pictures.

His father would hoist him up onto his shoulders so August could pick some of the best leaves to take home as a souvenir. He'd loved being that tall, sitting on his father's shoulders.

The cold, crisp fall air brought him back to those days. Lately, memories of his father came easier. Talking with Leila and his mom and siblings had brought his dad back to life for him, and now he couldn't wait to have kids of his own to continue his dad's legacy.

August pulled a beanie out of his pocket and yanked it down over his ears. Before long, the snow would be flying, and he and Leila would be entering a different season together. He was ready to take the next step. He'd been ready since he'd kissed Lei at the AppleFest.

He moved faster through the chardonnays and finally found Poppa already hard at work with the pruning shears.

"Good morning, son." The man paused from his work and greeted August with a handshake like he had every morning for the last month. "It's a cold one today, boy. I heard we've got snow in the forecast next week."

Their conversation started out this way every morning—with talk about the weather. August knew from experience a farmer had to be obsessed with what was happening in the skies. But today, he had other things on his mind. "Yeah, you can feel the change in the air."

There were many changes coming. He picked up the other pair of shears lying in the cart nearby. "Speaking of changes, I wanted to talk to you about something."

The man came to work alongside him. "You can talk to me about anything."

"You know how much I love your granddaughter. She means everything to me."

"You don't have to tell me that." Poppa snipped branches and tossed them into the cart. "Nonna and me, we couldn't be happier for the both of you."

"Thank you." He hadn't expected emotion to choke him up,

but her grandparents could've easily held a grudge against him instead of opening their hearts the way they had. They'd been the ones to walk with Leila through the aftermath when he'd abandoned her the first time. And they'd had the most to lose when Kingston had tried to take over the winery. Yet they'd been so generous with offering him a place in their family.

"Your support means a lot to us." He stopped working. "I know I haven't always been faithful to my promises, but I've learned from those mistakes and I'm a different man now."

Poppa set his shears in the cart as though he knew this moment deserved his entire focus. "I see that change in you, son. It takes a lot of courage to own up to things. We couldn't be more thrilled to have you back in all of our lives."

Damn, his eyes were stinging. "I'm ready to marry her, if she'll have me." He'd been ready the day they'd arrived back from California, but he'd wanted to let them all settle in. "I'll devote my whole life to her. She'll never have to wonder how much I love her." Because of where they'd been, he wouldn't take Leila for granted. "So, I am officially asking for your blessing to put that ring on her finger."

"Well, it's about time." Poppa chuckled. "She was getting a little antsy, if you want to know the truth."

August laughed too. "She wasn't the only one."

He patted the ring he'd been carrying in his pocket since before California. Now he had to figure out the perfect time to ask the most important question of his life.

* * *

Leila tried to focus on the spreadsheet in front of her, tallying the newest orders that had come through, but her gaze kept drifting to the window.

Lately, she couldn't focus on anything for more than five minutes without her mind wandering to August. She wouldn't mind having him to herself all evening, but there would be a lot of people around at the picnic.

Regina weaved herself around Leila's legs, purring and meow-ing. "What do you think?" Leila picked up the cat, cradling her in her lap. "Will Auggie and I be able to sneak away from the party to be alone?"

Not that she wanted to avoid his family. Now that there were no more lies to manage, she loved spending time with Mara and Jane and sweet Charlee. But still, her relationship with August felt new and exhilarating, and she liked going to bed early with him.

An e-mail dinged on her computer, drawing her attention back to her work. But instead of another wine club order, this one was from August.

Dearest Lei,

Want to sneak away from your desk early and meet me in the pasture before the chaos starts? Knievel and I will be waiting.

The simple request brought a smile to her face. She wasn't sure she'd stopped smiling even once over the last month.

"Sorry, Regina." She set the cat on the floor and closed her laptop. "I have a secret rendezvous to get to."

After shutting off the lights, she hurried out the door and locked up the office. Regina followed her out the pet door, veering off into the grass as though she'd caught a mouse's scent.

Leila drove to the Harding Ranch, enjoying the scenes from a perfect fall day—the golden aspen leaves fluttering to the ground, the highest peaks in the distance frosted with a layer of fresh snow. Instead of parking at the main lodge, she continued on down the rutted dirt road and parked near the barn.

August already stood at the fence with Knievel, wearing his cowboy hat and the grin he seemed to save for her alone.

Funny, she'd thought she loved him so much back in high school, but truthfully, she hadn't even known what love was. Yes, she'd cared for him deeply, but the love she had for him now ran through her blood, giving her insatiable energy and hope. It drove her to move faster, her feet slightly clumsy on the uneven ground as she entered the pasture through the gate.

He took her hands in his and pulled her in for a kiss. "Hey."

"Hi." He made her breathless every time he touched her. "I'm so glad you e-mailed."

He grinned. "I knew you'd be working on your day off."

"I'm not sure there's such a thing as a day off around the winery." But their hard work had already started to pay off. They were building up their wine club; they were regenerating the vines and preparing for the future. They didn't have extra money, but they had enough. They had everything in just being together.

"Knievel and I have something to show you. Want to take a little ride?"

"I would love to." She accepted his help climbing onto the back of the horse, and then he pulled himself up behind her. "I've never ridden bareback." But she had to admit, she enjoyed the feel of August's strong chest against her back.

"We don't have far to go." He secured one arm around her waist, holding her close while he steered the reins with the other.

They ambled out of the pasture to the path around the lake while she smoothed her hand on Knievel's mane. "He's such a beautiful horse."

"And you're such a beautiful woman," Auggie uttered against her neck. He kissed the spot under her ear that made her moan.

"How far are we going?" she asked weakly. She couldn't kiss him the way she wanted to up on this horse.

"Almost there." He guided the horse into the trees at the lake's edge. In a small clearing, he'd set up a bistro table with a bottle of wine and a platter of cheeses and grapes.

"Wow." She admired the spread. "And here I thought you summoned me so we could fool around."

"I'm always hoping we can fool around." He dismounted the horse and then helped her slide to the ground before setting his hands on her hips and drawing her close. "We don't have too much time before our families come looking for us, though, and I have plans." His eyebrows rose mysteriously.

"Plans, huh?" Her heart lifted. "What kind of plans?"

"Plans to eat a little." He took her hand and led her to one of the chairs, pulling it out for her. "Plans to drink a little."

While August poured her a glass of wine, Leila popped a few grapes into her mouth. "That's it? Plans to eat and drink?"

His grin overtook his eyes, bringing those crinkles in the corners she knew and loved. "Okay. There's more. I wanted to get you alone so I could tell you I love you more than anything." He lowered to his knee in front of her. "I had this whole plan to take you on another romantic overnight date in Denver—for real this time—but I can't wait that long." He pulled a small box out of his pocket and opened it. "Marry me, Lei. As soon as possible. Let's start to build the future we always talked about together."

"Auggie..." Tears ran hot down her cheeks as she studied the beautiful simplicity of the emerald-cut diamond with a gasp. "That's Nonna's ring."

"It is." He caressed her left hand. "Poppa first offered it to me right after we said we were getting married."

She laughed. "I still can't believe you went along with my harebrained idea."

"I can't say I regret one minute of pretending to be your fiancé." He carefully took the ring out of the box and slipped it onto her left ring finger. "Our engagement may have started out as a ruse, but I love you, Lei. I never stopped loving you." He kissed her knuckles. "You were the woman I compared everyone else to, the woman I never thought I deserved."

"I've always loved you too," she whispered. "Always. You are the only man I've ever fully loved. The only man I *will* ever fully love. And I'm dying to marry you."

Auggie stood with a whoop and pulled her to her feet, dancing her around their space. "I swear the ring has been burning a hole in my pocket since your grandfather gave it to me. I couldn't wait to give it to you."

"I'm glad you didn't wait." Leila wrapped her arms around his neck, swaying her hips with his in time to their own music. "No more waiting." She said the words between small kisses. "Let's go to a beach and get married as soon as possible."

"Exactly what I was thinking." He lowered her into a dip and then brought her back up, twirling her around.

Leila held onto him, laughing and out of breath. "We're getting married!" She was marrying August Harding. "I can't believe—"

Her fiancé's phone broke out into song.

"Great," August muttered. "That's Wes's ring." Leila stepped away so he could answer.

"Where are you two?" she heard his brother ask through the speaker. "We're getting all the food ready. Ryan said Leila's Jeep was here."

"We'll be right there." Auggie ended the call and shoved the phone into his pocket. "Where were we?" He pulled Leila back to him.

"You told them we'd be right there," she murmured, holding off his kiss to tease him. "We should probably help."

He dipped his lips to her neck. "We're too busy to help."

"I think you're right," she half whispered.

"Uncle Auggie!" Ryan's shout came from a distance. "Where are you?"

August groaned. "I guess our moment is over."

"For now." She stood on her tiptoes to reach his lips once more before they were found. "But there will be many more moments."

"Countless moments," he murmured. "A whole future full of them."

"Seriously, Uncle Auggie! I'm never gonna find you." Ryan's voice was much closer.

August held a finger against his lips with a smile, telling her to stay quiet. Then he took her hand and they led Knievel toward the kid's voice. At exactly the right moment, they rushed out of the trees and onto the path. Auggie ambushed Ryan, sweeping him up into his arms and then hoisting the kid onto his shoulders.

Ryan squealed and cheered. "I knew it! I knew you were around here. My dad told me to come this way."

"I'm glad he did." August set Ryan on Knievel's back and handed him the reins.

"Yes! A horsey ride! Giddy up!" the boy called.

Smiling, August collected Lei to his side, and they walked Ryan and Knievel back to the pasture, dropping the horse off before heading for the lake's beach to see their families.

Jane and Toby were fussing with all the baby stuff—the diaper bag and stroller to keep Charlee contained. Mara was chatting with Nonna, Papa, and Wes's family near the picnic tables.

Ryan ran ahead of them. "I found them! They were having some secret picnic in the woods. But I brought them back!"

"Here we go." August held Leila's hand tightly in his and stopped walking. "You ready for this?"

She looked at the crew in front of them with tears in her eyes— at Mara and Nonna and Poppa. At Wes and Thea, who was just starting to show. At Ryan, who couldn't seem to sit still, and his lovely older sister, Olivia. At Jane and Toby, who were too busy doting on Charlee to notice much of anything else. At Sam, who was pouring wine, of course. This was their family. Messy and loud and chaotic, but also their support system.

"I'm ready."

Wes approached them first. "A secret picnic, huh?" His gaze went right to Leila's left hand. "Holy shit! You finally asked her to marry you!"

"That's a quarter in the jar," Ryan called.

Leila laughed through her tears. "Yep." She held up her left hand for all to see. "It's official!"

"What!" Mara pushed her way past everyone else to wrap them both in a hug. "I can't believe this! I mean, I knew you would get engaged, but I thought I'd have to wait forever."

"We're done waiting," Auggie told her.

Jane all but moved Mara out of the way to hug them. "I knew this would happen when I saw you two at the AppleFest!"

"Now we can finally talk about something else at our house," Toby joked. He shook August's hand. "Congrats, guys."

"Thank you." Leila had started to cry again, but she didn't wipe her tears away. They were happy ones.

"Way to go, man." Wes pulled August in for a literal bro hug. "I knew you had it in you." He shifted to hug Leila. "Welcome to the family!"

"Thank you." Oh, these tears. She wasn't sure they'd ever stop.

"Can we eat now?" Ryan looked down at them all impatiently. "I'm hungry."

"Sure, we can eat." Auggie took her hand again, and together they led the way to the picnic tables where her grandparents still stood, Poppa's arm around Nonna's shoulders.

Chaos erupted as everyone else got the food organized, but Leila tugged August to her grandparents. She hugged them both tightly to her, never wanting to let go. "Thank you for showing us what love could look like."

"After seeing the kind of relationship you two have, we'll never settle for anything less," Auggie added.

Nonna wiped her eyes and kissed both of their cheeks. "Everything you two have been through only makes your love stronger."

"Welcome to the family, son." Poppa initiated August into the Valentino clan with kisses on both of his cheeks.

"Nonna." Ryan wandered to them and tugged on her sleeve. "You should eat. Ladies first," the boy said solemnly.

"Why, thank you." Nonna allowed Ryan to escort her to the food table with Poppa following a few steps behind. "You're such a gentleman."

"I'm a cowboy," Ryan informed her. "Like my dad and my uncle Auggie. Cowboys are *always* gentlemen."

That they were. Leila slipped her hand back into August's and nudged him in the opposite direction.

He shot her a curious look. "Where are we going?"

"To your cabin." Or at least to the cabin Mara had offered him. They hadn't spent much time there since he'd been staying in her cottage.

A wicked grin heated his eyes. "Think they'll miss us?"

Leila paused and looked over her shoulder. Everyone was too busy dishing up food, talking and laughing and discussing the prospects of a wedding to even notice they'd stepped away. It was a wonderful sight.

She smiled at him, squeezing his hand. "They won't miss us. And I don't want to miss this moment with you." The first beautiful moment of the rest of their lives.

August isn't the first Harding sibling
to find love at Silverado Lake...

When shy and sensible Jane Harding is paired up
with the rodeo's sexiest bull-rider Toby Garrett
for her best friend's wedding, she's prepared for
disaster. But this sweet-talking cowboy is
determined to show her the passion between them
is worth braving any odds.

Read Jane and Toby's story in *First
Kiss with a Cowboy*!

Available Now

About the Author

Sara Richardson grew up chasing adventure in Colorado's rugged mountains. She's climbed to the top of a fourteen-thousand-foot peak at midnight, swum through class IV rapids, completed her wilderness first aid certification, and spent seven days at a time tromping through the wilderness with a thirty-pound backpack strapped to her shoulders. Eventually, Sara did the responsible thing and got an education in writing and journalism. After a brief stint in the corporate writing world, she stopped ignoring the voices in her head and started writing fiction. Now she uses her experience as a mountain adventure guide to write stories that incorporate adventure with romance. Sara lives and plays in the Upper Midwest, where she still indulges her adventurous spirit, with her saint of a husband and two sons.

You can learn more at:

SaraRichardson.net

Twitter @SaraR_Books

Facebook.com/SaraRichardsonBooks

Instagram @SaraRichardsonBooks

For a bonus story from another author that you'll love, please turn the page to read *Sunrise Ranch* by Carolyn Brown.

Bonnie Malloy never really knew the meaning of home. She and her mom moved around so much when she was young that she was never able put down roots, and she got to the point where she never wanted to. But now she has a chance to run her very own Texas ranch, and she just discovered two half sisters she never knew about. The three women couldn't be more different, but Abby Joy and Shiloh have shown Bonnie how it feels to truly be part of a family.

The only catch is that to inherit the ranch, Bonnie must stay there for a whole year. Worse yet, she has to live with cowboy Rusty Dawson—and he thinks the property is rightfully his. Each becomes determined to drive the other out...until they realize just how much they enjoy being together. But is the woman known for going wherever the wind takes her really ready to settle down once and for all?

FOREVER

Chapter One

Three little monkeys jumping on a bed.

The song echoed through Bonnie's head, but it brought about a good memory. Her mother had read that book about the little monkeys to her so many times that Bonnie had memorized it before she was three years old and knew when Vivien left out a single word. Maybe the memory was so strong because her mama soon left off reading to her, and there weren't many other books in their trailer house.

Bonnie smiled as she picked up her bottle of beer and took a long drink from it. "Three sassy sisters livin' on a ranch," she singsonged. "One got married and went away. Two sassy sisters livin' on a ranch, one got married and went away. One sassy sister livin' on a ranch"—she paused—"it's mine now. All I have to do is sit still for another six months and it's mine, and then I can sell it and go wherever I want. Whatever I decide I'll never have to get up at five o'clock in the morning to feed cows in the cold or heat again. Do I go east or west? Both have a beach. All I need is a sign to point me in the right direction."

The sun dipped below the crest of the Palo Duro Canyon, leaving streaks of purple, red, pink, and orange in its wake. Black

Angus cattle grazed in the pasture between the Malloy ranch house and the horizon. A gentle breeze wafted the scent of red roses and honeysuckle across the porch.

The sun set every evening. Cattle roamed around the pastures in search of green grass every day. Flowers bloomed in June in the panhandle of Texas. Not a single sign in any of that.

"Hey, we're here," Abby Joy and Shiloh yelled at the same time as they came around the end of the house.

Bonnie looked up toward the fluffy white clouds moving slowly as the breeze shifted them across the sky. "Is this my sign?"

Six months before, the three half sisters had showed up at the Malloy Ranch to attend Ezra Malloy's funeral. He was the father they'd never met, the one who'd sent each of their mothers away when she'd given birth to a daughter instead of a son. Then he'd left a will saying that all three daughters had to come back to the Palo Duro Canyon and live together on his ranch for a year if they wanted a share of the Malloy Ranch. If one of them moved away for any reason—love, misery, contention with the other two sisters—then she got a small lump sum of money, but not a share of his prized two thousand acres of land at the bottom of the Palo Duro Canyon.

With both sisters now married and moved away in the last six months, Bonnie was the last one standing. All she had to do was live on the ranch until the end of the year, and every bit of the red dirt, cactus, wildflowers, and scrub oak trees belonged to her. If she moved away from the ranch early, for any reason, then the whole shebang went to Rusty Dawson, the ranch foreman and evidently the closest thing to a son that Ezra ever had. Unless that cowboy had enough money in his pocket or credit at the bank, he could forget owning the ranch, because Bonnie had full intentions of selling it to the highest bidder.

She'd liked Rusty from the first time she laid eyes on him. He'd taught her and her sisters how to run a ranch—at least what he could in six months. At first, he'd seemed resigned to the fact that one or all of Ezra's daughters would own the place and had voiced his wishes to stay on as foreman at the end of a year. That had been the fun Rusty. After Abby Joy had married and left the ranch, Bonnie had seen a slight change in him—nothing so visible or even verbal, except for a hungry look in his eyes. Now that Shiloh had married Waylon and moved across the road to his ranch, he had changed even more.

Tall and just a little on the lanky side, he had dark hair, mossy green eyes that seemed even bigger behind his black-framed glasses, and a real nice smile. It didn't matter how handsome he was, he was out of luck if he thought he could get rid of Bonnie and inherit the ranch. No, sir! She'd already given up six months of her life and was willing to give up six more to have the money to reclaim her wings. She'd never planned to stay in this god-forsaken place to begin with, and now that her sisters were gone, she and Rusty were about to lock horns when it came to the ranch.

Abby Joy sank down into a chair and tucked a strand of blond hair back up into her ponytail. Even pregnant, she still had that military posture—back straight as a board, shoulders squared off.

Shiloh, the only dark-haired sister in the trio, headed off to the kitchen. "Got lemonade made?"

"There's a pitcher in the refrigerator. There's also cold beers and a bottle of wine. Take your choice," Bonnie answered.

"Lemonade for me please," Abby Joy yelled.

Shiloh brought out two tall glasses filled with ice and lemonade. She handed one to Abby Joy and then sat down in a lawn chair on the other side of Bonnie. "Everything sure looks different now than it did last winter when we got here, doesn't it?"

"Are we talkin' about Abby Joy's big old pregnant belly?" Shiloh teased.

"I think she meant the ranch," Abby Joy shot back. "I thought I'd dropped off the face of the earth into hell when I drove past Silverton that day. This was the most desolate place I'd ever seen, and I'd done tours in Afghanistan. If I hadn't been so damned hungry, I wouldn't have even come up here to the house after the funeral, but I heard someone mention food."

Bonnie laughed out loud. "I was starving too, but I sure didn't want y'all to know that."

"Why not?" Shiloh asked.

"I thought you'd look down on me even worse if you thought I was so poor I couldn't even buy food," she answered, "but I was."

Abby Joy took a sip of her drink and nodded. "I looked down the row at y'all at Ezra's funeral and figured I'd outlast both of you, but I got to admit that I was just a little scared of you, Bonnie. You looked like you could kill us all with that stone-cold stare of yours."

"I felt the same about y'all, and now you've both moved away." Bonnie drank down part of her beer.

"Yep." Abby Joy smiled. "I was the smart one. I left when I figured out right quick that love meant more than any money I would get from staying on the ranch."

"That old bastard Ezra treated all of our mothers like breeding heifers, not wives," Shiloh chimed in. "I've come a long way toward forgiving him, but he'll never be a father to me."

Abby Joy shook her head. "He's more like a sperm donor, isn't he?"

"That's kind of the way I feel, so why would I want this ranch?" Bonnie asked. "If he'd done right by us, or any one of us, then the ranch would mean something, but he didn't, so why shouldn't I just sell the damned place and get on with my life. I'm not like you two. I didn't get to settle down and grow up in one place. Mama moved whenever the mood struck her, so I'm used to traveling."

"You've got six months to decide what you want," Abby Joy said. "Give it some time. Don't rush into anything, but if you ever do decide you don't want your name attached to anything that Ezra had, you can come live with me."

"Are either of you sorry that you left?" Bonnie asked.

"Not me!" Shiloh turned up her glass of lemonade and took several gulps. "I was having second thoughts about staying on the ranch those last few weeks, but Abby Joy can't have you all the time if you leave. I get you at least half of the year."

Bonnie smiled. "I'm not stayin', and I'm probably not moving in with either of you, but I appreciate the offer. I'm going to sell the place and travel. I will come see you real often, though. I don't want us to ever be apart for very long at one time..." Bonnie downed the rest of her beer and stood up. "Getting you two for sisters was definitely the one good thing Ezra did for us."

Bonnie pulled both her sisters in for a group hug, then stepped back and slapped at a mosquito on her arm. "These damn bugs are horrible this time of year."

"Everything's bigger in Texas," Shiloh joked.

"It's all that moisture we got in the spring." Abby Joy pushed up out of her chair and led the way into the kitchen. "Come July, Cooper says that we'll be begging for rain and even a mosquito or two."

"Not me." Shiloh picked up the dirty glasses and the beer bottle and followed her sister. "This canyon grows mosquitoes as big as buzzards. I don't believe that they'll all be dead in a month. They'll be hiding up in the rock formations, and they'll swoop down on us and suck all our blood out when we're not looking."

Was the fact that her half sisters had figured out love meant more to them than the ranch the sign she was looking for? Abby Joy had given up her right to the place when she married Cooper Wilson, a cowboy rancher whose land was right next to the Malloy Ranch. Shiloh had married Waylon Stephens, the cowboy who owned the ranch across the road from the Malloy place, just a few weeks ago. From what Bonnie could see, neither of her sisters had a single regret for the decision they'd made.

But finding love and settling down wasn't the right thing for Bonnie. She was born to fly, not grow roots in the canyon, and by the time New Year's Day rolled around, she would spread her wings and take off. Maybe she'd start with going to Florida or

California to see the ocean. She loved bringing up the site for a little hotel in the panhandle of Florida and listening to the sound of the ocean waves.

"Wouldn't it be something, after everything is said and done, if Rusty bought this place when I sell it?" Bonnie picked up the pitcher of lemonade and a platter of cookies and carried them to the living room.

"Wouldn't it be poetic justice if all Rusty's children were all daughters?" Shiloh plopped down on the sofa and picked up two cookies.

"Serve Ezra right for throwing away his own daughters." Abby Joy eased down into a rocking chair and reached for a cookie. "Y'all ever wonder why he brought us back anyway? He didn't want us when we were born because we weren't boys, so why would he even give us a chance to inherit his ranch?"

At least once a week, the sisters had an evening at one place or another, and tonight was Bonnie's turn. She might be the one who'd showed up at the ranch six months before with her things crammed into plastic bags, but she knew how to be a good hostess.

Shiloh raised her glass. "To all of us for not killing each other, like Ezra probably wanted."

"Hear, hear!" Bonnie said as all three sisters clinked their glasses together.

* * *

Rusty Dawson stopped at the small cemetery on the way home from his weekly poker game with several of the area ranchers. That night Cooper, Waylon, and Jackson Bailey had been over at Cooper's place, and they'd all four played until almost midnight. Rusty had walked away five dollars richer, which was unusual for him. Usually, he was at least a dollar or two in the hole when the last hand was played.

He sat down on a bench that faced Ezra's grave and stared at the inscription on the tombstone for a long time. By the light of the moon, it was just obscure dark lines. So much had happened in the six months since the man died and his daughters had showed up at the ranch. Pictures from the day of the funeral flashed through his mind. Abby Joy had arrived just seconds before the graveside service began. She'd shown up in full camouflage and combat boots, and she'd snapped to attention and nodded smartly when it was her turn to walk past the casket. He'd always wondered if maybe she was showing Ezra that she was every bit as brave and tough as any son he might've produced. Shiloh was already there, of course. She looked like she'd just walked away from a line dance in a bar like the Sugar Shack up on the other end of the Canyon—pearl snap shirt that hugged her curves, starched jeans, Tony Lama boots, and a black Stetson hat.

Bonnie, the youngest of the sisters, had put a little extra beat in his heart from the first time he laid eyes on her. She drove up in an old rattletrap of a truck with duct tape holding the passenger-side window together, tires so bald that he was amazed she hadn't had a blowout on the trip, and rusted-out fenders. She was wearing tight jeans, a leather jacket, and some kind of lace-up boots. A fake diamond sparkled on the side of her nose. He figured anyone with such a sassy attitude would surely be the one who inherited the place, and he was beginning to believe he'd been right.

You just going to lay down, roll over, and let her have it, or are you going to fight for what I meant for you to have? Ezra's voice was so clean in Rusty's head that he whipped around to see if the old guy's ghost haunted the cemetery. If you want the ranch, run her off it and take it for your own. Anything worth having is worth fighting for.

At first, Rusty had hoped the sisters would all hate each other and disappear so that he could mourn for his old friend and boss in private. But they had all three moved right in and dug in their heels for what looked like was going to be the duration.

"You shouldn't have sent them away, Ezra. They've all got your traits, and I mean more than just your blue eyes. They're determined and hardworking and don't mind speakin' their minds. Bonnie is the only one left now." Rusty removed his glasses, rubbed at his tired, burning eyes, and shook his head. "But you're right. It's time I gave Bonnie a run for her money. That ranch is the only real home I've known. And I love this canyon. I couldn't stand seeing her sell it to some strangers, after all my years of hard work. If she's still here at Christmas, by damn, it won't be because I didn't try."

An owl hooted off in the distance and a coyote answered it. Crickets and tree frogs had set up a chorus all around him. He found himself feeling angry with Ezra for the first time—after all, the old guy had promised him the ranch. He was trying to put his feelings into words when Martha, one of the three dogs that lived on the ranch, cold-nosed him on the hand. He jumped a good foot up off the bench and came back down with a thud. His glasses flew off and landed at the base of the tombstone. He retrieved them, blew the dust away from the lenses, and then put them back on.

"Dammit!" he muttered as he scratched the dog's ears. "You scared the crap out of me. Come on, you can ride up to the house with me."

The dog jumped into the truck as soon as Rusty opened the truck door. She rode in the passenger seat until he reached the house, and then licked him across the face as she bounded across his lap, hopped out of the vehicle, and ran to the porch.

"I thought she might have come to meet you," Bonnie said from the shadows. "Did you win or lose tonight?"

"Came away five dollars richer." Rusty joined her on the swing. "Couple more nights winnin' like this, and I'll have the money saved up to buy a square foot of this place when you sell it."

"Who told you that I'm selling out when I inherit the ranch?" She frowned.

"Of all y'all, you are the one who'd never make a rancher. You're the hardest working of the three and you soaked up what I've taught you, but I can see it in your eyes..." He took a deep breath.

"You can't see anything in my eyes," she argued. "I'm the best damn poker player among all of us. Get out the cards, and I'll prove it to you."

"No, thanks. I'm going to hold on to the five bucks I won tonight," Rusty said. "But, honey, you'll light a shuck out of here so fast at the end of this year that your sisters will wonder if you were ever even here. You never intended on staying any longer than you have to."

"Bullshit!" Bonnie smarted off. "You don't know me at all, and it would take more than six months to figure out a damn thing about me. I'll tell you this much, though, when and if I do sell this ranch, you better have more than five dollars in your pocket."

He crossed his arms over his chest. "I've been saving for a few years, and I've got good credit."

Bonnie glared at him for several seconds and then smiled. "Maybe I won't sell it at all. It will be mine to do with whatever I damn well please, and since it adjoins Abby Joy's place, and is right across the road from Shiloh's, I may divide it between the two of them."

Let Mr. Smarty-Cowboy roll that idea around in his brain. Bonnie had no intention of doing such a thing, but if Rusty wanted to play hard ball, she'd get out the bat and catcher's mitt.

"I'll talk to Cooper and Waylon, and buy it from them," Rusty said.

"I may look like I don't know anything to you, but, honey, I do know how to hire a lawyer that will put it in writing that my sisters can't sell it to anyone, and especially not you." She flashed an even meaner look at him.

Rusty grinned and smiled at her in a condescending way that she'd never seen before. "I figure you'll be gone long before you have to make those decisions. I've seen the antsy in you lately. You won't last six more months. I'm going to bed. You better be up early in the morning. We're going to be in the hay field when the sun comes up. With the spring rain we had, it looks like it might be a good one."

"Not me." She yawned. "Ezra's rules said that I don't have to do one thing but be here. I get a paycheck every week whether I lift a finger or not. Remember what the will said? So tomorrow morning I plan to sleep in as long as I want, and then maybe do my toenails. Oh, and you can get your own breakfast, too. I'll have a bowl of cereal when I decide to get up."

Chapter Two

Ezra hadn't believed in spending money on what he called frivolous things, so the old ranch house did not have central heat and air. A fireplace provided warmth in the winter, and a couple of window units worked well enough to keep the temperature out of the triple digits in the summer. The small bunkhouse where Rusty stayed was about the same, but it only had one window unit, and it only cooled his bedroom.

He paced the floor from the living room with bunk beds lining three of the walls, to the kitchen, through his bedroom, going from hot to cool several times. He was so angry with himself for letting Bonnie get under his skin. If her mother was anything at all like her then he couldn't blame Ezra for sending her away. Damned women—all of the species anyway—and damn Ezra for not letting him have the ranch like he'd said he would.

You want it, work for it. Ezra's gruff old voice popped back into his head.

"I did," Rusty growled.

Rusty hadn't grown up in the lap of luxury. He'd worked hard for everything he ever had. He'd gone into foster care when he was so little that he didn't even remember his parents. He was told that they both went to prison on drug charges and had died before he was in school. He ran away from the last foster home when he was fourteen, lied about his age, and got a job on a ranch. He'd been doing that kind of work ever since. Ezra had lured him away from Jackson Bailey after Rusty had been working over at the Lonesome Canyon Ranch a couple of years.

"We even had central air and heat in the bunkhouse over there, but Ezra paid better, and he hinted that since he didn't have a son to leave his ranch to, that I would inherit this place someday." He opened the ancient and rusted refrigerator and took out a gallon of milk.

He poured a glassful and continued to talk to himself. "Ezra demanded more hours out of me, but I didn't mind the work, since I was getting a paycheck and got plenty of food, and I had the run of the bunkhouse. He even let me decide who to hire for summer help, and . . ." He sighed. "Malloy Ranch would be mine when Ezra passed on."

He stared out the kitchen window after he finished drinking his milk. A huge moon hung in the sky right over the bunkhouse. Stars danced around it, and a few clouds shifted from one side to the other, blocking out a little light some of the time. All three dogs had rushed inside the second they had the opportunity, and Martha nosed his bare foot.

"One of you should stay at the house and protect Bonnie," he scolded them and then laughed. "Though she's tough enough that she don't need anyone to take care of her. What do you think, Vivien? Can she chew up railroad spikes and spit out staples? That's what Ezra said about her mama." He stooped down and scratched the ears of the part Catahoula dog that had been named for Bonnie's mother. The dog yipped and went to stretch out on the cool hardwood floor with Martha right behind her. Polly, the dog named for Shiloh's mother, stuck around begging for doggy treats.

"Lot of help you are," Rusty muttered as he gave her a Milk-Bone.

* * *

When the alarm went off the next morning, he rolled over to see three sets of eyes peering up at him over the side of the bed. "How'd it get to be morning so quick?"

All the dogs turned around and raced toward the door. He pushed back the covers and hurried across the large living room to let them out. In another week, there would be ten hired hands living here, mostly teenage boys he'd have to shake out of the bunk beds lining the walls every morning. When the boys arrived, the dogs would be perfectly happy to sleep outside.

Rusty dressed in work jeans, a faded chambray shirt that he left open at the throat, a faded T-shirt showing underneath, and a pair of tan work boots. He made himself a couple of peanut butter sandwiches, poured a thermos full of coffee, and filled a large cooler with sweet tea and ice. Then he put together three bologna sandwiches and shoved them into a plastic bag.

When he reached the field that morning, the sun was just rising over the eastern crest of the canyon.

"Sunrise Ranch," he muttered. "I'm going to own this ranch if I have to mortgage my soul and all three of those dogs to get it, and I'm going to rename the place Sunrise Ranch. It has a good ring to it, and Ezra can just weep and moan about it. He should've done right by me."

Don't you dare change the name of this place. Ezra's gruff old voice scolded him. *It started off as Malloy Ranch back at Texas statehood days, and by damn, it will stay that way until the crack of doom.*

Rusty knotted his hands into fists. He'd worked hard for Ezra, had given him an honest day's work for what he got paid. Ezra was dead. He could name the ranch whatever he pleased. When Ezra got sick and barely had the energy to go from his recliner to the kitchen, Rusty had run both the ranch and the house for the old guy. Then a week or so before he died, he'd called in the lawyer and changed his will. Rusty had been disappointed, but Ezra assured him that his daughters were like their worthless mothers and wouldn't last a week on the ranch.

Guess who was wrong, he thought as he crawled up into the tractor, ate his peanut butter sandwiches for breakfast, and waited for good daylight to begin his day.

* * *

Bonnie planned on keeping her word and sleeping until noon, but she had a restless night and was more than ready to crawl out of bed at five o'clock that morning. She ate a bowl of cereal and two muffins, then packed a lunch to take to the field. If she was honest, she missed Rusty coming in to eat with her that morning, but that didn't mean she wasn't still mad at him for his arrogance the night before.

What about your stubborn pride? Shiloh's voice whispered in her head. *Y'all are just alike. Neither one of you will give an inch.*

"I'm up, and I'm going to the field. That's giving a mile, not an inch," Bonnie said as she grabbed her sack and jug of sweet tea. "Stay on your side of the barbed wire, sister. I don't need your advice. I can take care of myself."

From day one, Bonnie had never given a damn what Ezra wanted done. He hadn't even cared enough to take a look at her when she was born, her mother had told her, and he hadn't been around to see one single solitary accomplishment in her life, so he didn't deserve the right to call her daughter after he was dead.

As she crawled up into the driver's seat of the tractor that she usually drove, she remembered that Loretta, Jackson Bailey's wife from the adjoining ranch to the north, had welcomed them to the canyon, and said, "It's kind of bare right now, but in a few weeks, when the wildflowers pop up, it will be lovely. Blue-bonnets, wild daisies, coreopsis, and flowering cactus sure give it a different look. And trust me when I say it grows on you. The sunsets and sunrises are beautiful, and pretty soon, you'll wonder why you ever wanted to live anywhere else."

Bonnie had admired Loretta's flaming red hair and her sweet smile, but she'd thought that the woman had rocks for brains. There was no way this barren place would ever grow on her. She would stick around for a year just to prove to those two bitchy half sisters who were looking down on her that she could hold her own. But Loretta had been right. The place might not have grown on her, but it did have a kind of beauty in the spring and early summer, and she'd come to love her sisters.

"Damn it to hell!" She slapped the steering wheel and then started up the tractor's engine. "I promised myself that I wouldn't stay six months ago, and I never go back on a promise I make to myself, but now a part of me wants to stay here, and that would mean being tied down."

Her mind went back to that first day she'd been in the canyon. Ezra's funeral was over and the neighbor, Jackson, had brought a copy of Ezra's will for each of the sisters to keep, and one for Rusty. He had cut past the legal jargon and told them that Rusty would pay each of them on Friday evening for forty hours of work at minimum wage. Room and board would be provided free of charge. Rusty would bring in staples once a week, but if they wanted anything other than what he had bought, they would have to buy it themselves.

Bonnie hadn't been expecting a salary, so that had made her happy. No way would she ever let either of her sisters know that she'd spent her last dollar on enough gas to get her to the funeral. She kept her mouth shut and listened as Jackson went on to tell them that they would get their salary whether they sat on the porch and did nothing or whether they pitched in and learned the business of ranching. It made no difference and was their decision.

"I should be doing that today just to prove to Rusty that I can," she muttered, "but it sounded too boring, and besides if I'm going to get a good price for this place, it should be kept up. God only knows that Rusty can't do it by himself."

Jackson had said that Rusty would teach them the ranching business, if they had a mind to learn. Then he'd told them that whichever daughter was still on the ranch one year from that day would inherit the whole place. If anyone left before the year was up, they got a one-time, lump sum payment from Ezra's estate, but they would relinquish any and all rights to the ranch. Abby Joy and Shiloh hadn't been allowed to disclose what their inheritance was when they'd left. For all Bonnie knew, it was anywhere from $500 to $50,000.

At noon she parked the tractor and got out of the cab. After doing a few stretching exercises and rolling the kinks out of her neck, she picked up her sack lunch and sat down under a shade tree. She'd only taken the first bite when Rusty joined her.

"What are you thinkin' about?" he asked. "You look like you're ready to fight a wild bull with nothing but a willow switch."

"Just going over in my mind what Jackson told us that first day I was here," she said honestly, but she didn't tell Rusty that she'd fought against an attraction for him since day one. No way was she going to admit that, not when they had crossed horns over the ranch like a couple of rangy old bulls. She admired his work ethic—getting up at the crack of dawn seven days a week to take care of things—but she also liked his kindness. Add that to his eyes and the way he filled out his jeans, and it was dang hard to fight the feelings that had grown for him.

"That was a strange time for sure," Rusty said.

"You didn't like any of us so well, did you?" she asked.

"I didn't figure any of you would last a week. Abby Joy would get tired of it, and Shiloh was way too prissy for ranchin'. I was wrong about all of you. I figured you'd sit on the porch and draw your pay. Never figured you'd pitch in and learn a damned thing, but y'all got out there doing your best," he chuckled. "But I could also see that the other two were determined to learn, and you were just passing time. You don't give a damn about this place."

"Nope, I don't," she admitted. "Only reason I learned anything at all was out of sheer boredom and to show my sisters that they weren't better than me. Why'd you come over here anyway? I thought we were mad at each other."

"Only shade tree around here," he replied.

"I was here first," she protested.

"Too bad." He shrugged.

She tipped up her chin and looked down her nose at him. "I'm going to take a lot of pleasure in getting out of this place."

"Then I'll get the whole shade tree to myself," he smarted off.

There weren't many times she'd been alone with Rusty. She stole a glance over at him. Bulging biceps, a flat tummy under a chambray work shirt that was wet with sweat. That some woman hadn't snatched him up already was a miracle. She'd have to be very careful in the next months to not let anyone know about the little flutters in her heart whenever he was around.

"You've gone all quiet again," Rusty said.

"Was Ezra a controlling person?" she asked.

"Where'd that question come from?"

"You probably knew him better than anyone, so tell me more about him?" she said.

"Oh, hell, yeah, and mean as a rattlesnake," Rusty said. "I mean, he named the dogs after your mothers, so that ought to tell you something. He always told me he was leaving the ranch to me. Then a week before he died, he called the lawyer and changed his will."

"He called you the son he never had," Bonnie said. "Was that to make us feel less worthy of the Malloy name? I just can't wrap my mind around why he changed his will and brought us here. If I could figure out why, then maybe I'd find some peace before I leave Texas. Seems like every time I think of him, all I feel is anger, and a little bit of fear that I might be like him in some way. Most of the time I don't even like my mother, but I love her. I can't imagine even liking Ezra."

Rusty shrugged. "That old fart had his own ways. He was good to me, and for that I loved him, but what he did to you girls was wrong. I'm mad at him this morning, so I don't want to talk about him."

"Why?" Bonnie was stunned.

Rusty never had anything but praise for Ezra.

"He popped into my head and fussed at me when I said I might change the name of the ranch, and it made me even madder when he changed his will," Rusty said.

"What were you going to change the name to?" she asked, "And how would Ezra feel about that? I thought y'all were best buddies."

"Sunrise Ranch," Rusty answered. "I love the way the sun comes up over the crest of the canyon every morning." Rusty paused. "Sometimes I can hear his voice in my head, and it's good advice, but he was on one of his mean streaks this morning."

Bonnie pulled a banana from her sack and peeled it. "My mama does that all the time. Out of nowhere, she pops into my head and has something to say about what I'm doin'. Most of the time it's to tell me that I'm not smart enough to do something. It makes me so mad that I make it my mission to prove her wrong. I'm glad you stood up to him, even if he's dead and just a voice in your head. Sunrise Ranch has a nice sound to it. Maybe you'll come up with the highest bid after all, since you said you'd change the name to something nice."

"One more cup of tea, and then I'm going to work. You have a choice in what you do. I don't," he said.

"You could move off the ranch. I bet I could kick any mesquite bush between here and Silverton and a dozen foremen would come running out lookin' for a job," she said.

"And wouldn't a one of them be as good as I am." He settled his dusty old straw hat on his head and left without even looking back.

"Little egotistical there," she called out.

He waved over his shoulder but still didn't turn around.

You've met your match. Her mother was in her head again, and this time she was laughing out loud. Bonnie heaved a long sigh and wondered if he'd felt the same attraction and little shocks of desire that she did when they were together. If so, why was he holding back? Should she talk to her sisters about the way she felt?

She shook her head as she finished off the last sip of her tea. No, she wouldn't talk to anyone about anything until she sorted it all out herself. She might find that the old saying about being out of sight, out of mind worked in this instance.

Chapter Three

Rusty had no intentions of going to the Sugar Shack on Saturday night, not after spending the whole day sitting in a tractor seat. He was dog-tired and ready to throw back in Ezra's old recliner and watch *Longmire* on television. Ezra had bought the DVDs of both that and *Justified*, and Rusty had watched them many times. But neither show held his attention, and he was bored. He'd gotten soft in the past six months. Any old time he wanted company he could go up to the ranch house and visit with the sisters.

He went into the bathroom, where he stared at his reflection in the mirror. Light brown hair that needed cutting, a couple of days' worth of scruff on his face. "I am a loner," he whispered. "I don't need a gaggle of women around me to keep me company."

He picked up his razor and shaved, then took a shower and put on a pair of pajama pants. He opened a can of chili, poured it into a bowl, and warmed it in the microwave. Once that was done, he poured himself a glass of sweet tea, and carried both to the living room. He set it on the end table beside his recliner and settled in to watch something on Netflix. At the end of the first episode of *The Ranch*, he realized he hadn't been paying enough attention to it to even know what had happened, so he got up and turned off the television.

Feeling cooped up, he went outside to sit on the porch and pet the dogs, but they weren't anywhere to be found. "Probably at the ranch house," he muttered. "Since women came onto the ranch, they're gettin' plumb spoiled."

So are you. Ezra's voice was back in his head. *Since them girls came around, you've gotten spoiled to having company all the time.*

"Maybe so," Rusty agreed. "So what?"

Ezra didn't have an answer for that.

Rusty walked from the bunkhouse to the ranch house and found the dogs lyin' on the porch—right where he figured they would be. Martha opened one eye and yipped one time. Vivien and Polly didn't even bother to do that much.

"I'm going to the Sugar Shack," he announced and headed back to the bunkhouse to get dressed. "Maybe I'll feel better after a few beers and when I dance some leather off of my boots."

* * *

Bonnie's thoughts all through the day had been constantly on the ranch and the insane attraction she'd felt for Rusty. It seemed even stronger since they were the only ones left on the ranch. She had no intentions of ever doing anything about it, so why wouldn't it just disappear? Too bad there wasn't a delete button for times like this, or for just time in general. Push the button and the chemistry she felt for her foreman would disappear. Push it again, and a whole year would disappear. She'd be on a beach somewhere in a cute little bar—hell, she might even own the bar—drinking a margarita and dancing with handsome beach boys.

She'd been restless after she finished cutting hay all day, so she'd gone to the grocery store in Claude to buy food for the week. She was pushing her cart toward the checkout counter when the message came over the PA system saying that the store would be closing in fifteen minutes. "Bring your purchases to the front of the store, please."

Evidently she was the last remaining person in the store, because no one else was pushing a cart toward one of the three cashiers. Bonnie unloaded her cart onto the conveyor belt and then stuck the ranch credit card into the machine to pay for everything.

"Been a long day," she said in the way of conversation.

"Yep, and I can't wait to get home, get my boots on, and go to the Sugar Shack for some excitement," the woman said. "The place don't get hoppin' until about nine, so I'll get there at just about the right time."

Bonnie just nodded. No way did she have enough energy to go to the Sugar Shack this evening, and besides, the last time she had gone there, she had had Shiloh with her. Going alone just didn't sound like much fun.

On the trip back down into the canyon, her thoughts went back to the Malloy Ranch again. "I've got to get away from the forest so I can see the trees, as Mama used to tell me when I was fretting about something. Maybe I will go to the Sugar Shack, have a beer, do a little line dancing, and not think about anything but having a good time."

Now that's my girl. That pesky voice that sounded like her mother's was back.

"You've always put having a good time ahead of everything else," Bonnie muttered as she turned off the highway and down the lane to the ranch. She just shook her head when she passed the cemetery where Ezra was buried. "How on earth the two of you ever got together is a mystery that I'll probably never understand."

She parked her truck and unloaded the groceries. The dogs were all waiting on the front porch, so she promised them that she'd bring out a surprise in a few minutes as she headed into the house. She put away the perishables, kicked off her shoes, and put on her only pair of cowboy boots. When she'd tucked the legs of her jeans down into them, she picked up a package wrapped in white butcher paper and took three big soup bones out to the dogs.

"See, I didn't forget you ladies," she said. "Y'all are welcome to carry these back to the bunkhouse. Rusty might even let you bring them inside if you promise to keep them on the floor."

She balled up the butcher paper and threw it into the bed of her beat-up truck. Then she got behind the wheel and headed back down the lane, made a right-hand turn out onto the highway, and traveled a few miles before making another turn. The Sugar Shack was in an old wooden building with a wide front porch, and the whole place looked like it had been sprayed down with that pink medicine Bonnie's mama had given her for a stomachache when she was a little girl. She could hear the jukebox music blasting away before she even got out of her vehicle. Tips of cigarettes flared red as a row of cowboys leaned against the front of the building and sucked in drags.

She walked through a haze of smoke on the way into the bar and got a few catcalls and offers from guys who were willing to put out their cigarettes if she'd dance with them. She'd grown up around folks a lot rougher than these cowboys, so she just ignored them, paid her cover fee, and went inside. Most of the place was dimly lit, but the bar area was at least semibright. She located an empty barstool and slid onto it, not paying a bit of attention to who was sitting in the one right next to her.

"What are you doin' here?" Rusty asked.

"I decided that I've been thinkin' about serious things way too much. I just need to have some fun, so here I am." She motioned for the bartender to bring her a beer. "What about you? You lookin' to get lucky tonight?" Saying the words caused a shot of jealousy to shoot through her heart.

"Maybe," he answered. "Are you?"

"Never know what beer and dancing might cause," she answered with a shrug.

The bartender brought her beer, and she tipped up the bottle and took a long drink.

A good-looking dark-haired cowboy tapped her on the shoulder. When she looked up, she recognized him as one of the guys who worked over on her brother-in-law's ranch.

"Want to dance?" he asked as Jason Aldean's "She's Country" came on the jukebox.

"Sure!" She handed her beer to Rusty. "Finish it before it gets warm."

"Don't know if you remember me, but I'm Lake, and I work for Cooper." He took her hand and led her out onto the dance floor. He swung her out a way, then brought her back to his chest and began a fast two-step and swing dance combination. "This song sounds like it's about you," he said. "You ain't afraid to stay country like you was born and raised."

"I'm glad you noticed," she teased with a hip wiggle when he spun her out the next time. She glanced over at the bar to see if Rusty was even watching, only to see nothing but empty barstools. With a quick glance over Lake's shoulder, she saw that Rusty was on the floor hugged up to a cute little brunette so tight that air couldn't get between them.

The next song was "Down to the Honkytonk" by Jake Owen. One of the lines said something about him having a girl that went bat shit crazy on tequila.

"Do you get silly on tequila?" Lake asked as he kept Bonnie on the dance floor.

"Honey, I could drink you under the table any day of the week," she answered.

Before Lake could disagree with her, Rusty tapped him on the shoulder and took his place with Bonnie.

"Why'd you do that?" she asked.

"He's a player," Rusty said. "You don't want to get mixed up with him. He's only interested in one-night stands."

Rusty was by far the smoothest cowboy she'd ever two-stepped with. When that song ended, he took her by the hand and led her back to the bar. Having her hand in his caused little shots of desire to run through her body, but that didn't surprise her so much. Dancing with him was one more thing she'd have to be careful about.

"You're not the boss of me," she protested.

"Nope, I'm not," he said. "But I will warn you of danger when it's right under your nose."

"Like a big brother?" she asked.

"Something like that," he chuckled.

* * *

Rusty wondered if Bonnie felt the heat between them like he did. He'd been attracted to her wild, free spirit from the first time he saw her, and that had grown through the months. He'd never let her know that, though—not when he had to run her off to even get a chance at the ranch.

She was staring right into his eyes, and then a woman touched him on the arm. "I've got a bone to pick with you, Rusty Dawson. You snuck out of the house without even tellin' me goodbye last month, and you never called me. I'm not just a one-night stand. I'm a good woman, and you're a bastard. I've waited four whole weeks to hear from you."

"You're drunk, Sandy," he said.

"Yeah, but I'll be sober tomorrow, and you'll still be a bastard." She turned her attention toward Bonnie. "You're one of Ezra's daughters, ain't you? Well, honey," she draped an arm around Bonnie's shoulders, "Rusty is just like Ezra, bastard to the bone. Don't let yourself get mixed up with him."

"Let's get out of here," Rusty said.

"I agree," Bonnie said.

"You'll wish you'd listened to me"—Sandy slurred her words—"because I know what I'm talkin' about. He might marry you, but it'll only be to get the ranch. He'll never be faithful. Every time your turn your back, he'll be lookin' to get some on the side. You mark my words."

"I'm so sorry about that," Rusty said as he walked across the parking lot with her. "She was drunk off her ass. I took her home, put her to bed, and left. She got the impression that we'd slept together, but we didn't."

"Hey, you don't owe me any apologies," Bonnie told him. "We all make mistakes."

"Tell me about yours." He grinned.

"I would if we had some of Ezra's moonshine, but that's all gone, so..." She shrugged.

"It's not Ezra's, but I've got a pint of blackberry 'shine in the bunkhouse. Want to share a few shots with me, and talk about all our mistakes?" He caged her with an arm on each side of her against the door of her truck.

"Are you flirtin' with me?" she asked bluntly.

He removed his hands and shook his head. "Nope. With all the noise around us, I had to lean in real close so you could hear me."

"You really think gettin' me drunk would make me tell all my secrets?" She giggled. "Honey, I'm not one of them sad drunks who talks about how the world's not treating her right. I'm a happy drunk, one who don't give a damn what she says or does." She was remembering the night that she and her two sisters had gotten drunk on the last of Ezra's 'shine. Or at least Shiloh and Abby Joy did—she herself had enough 'shine sense to take a few sips and leave it alone, being as how she'd made the stuff herself back in Kentucky, and she knew what a kick it had.

"I like a happy drunk." Rusty smiled.

"Well, then, let's just get to it." She ducked under his arm and came up on the other side. "I'll follow you to the bunkhouse. In the morning, if you can make it to the house, I'll sure enough brew up my hangover cure for you."

"Who says I'll have a hangover?" he teased.

"You will have one like you've never had before when I get finished making you a couple of real blackberry bombs." She got into her truck and slammed the door shut.

When they arrived at the ranch, all three dogs followed their vehicles to the bunkhouse. Once inside, Martha flopped down on the cool floor in front of the sofa. Vivien followed Rusty into the kitchen, and Polly headed for the rug in front of the fireplace.

"I guess they're our chaperones." Bonnie followed Rusty into the kitchen.

He got the blackberry moonshine and two shot glasses down from the cabinet, set them on the table, and started to pour.

"Oh, no, you don't." She hip-bumped him out of the way. "If we're going to have a real drink, then I'll do the mixin'." She reached for a bottle of tequila. "Looks like you're about out of this."

"That and this pint of 'shine and six beers in the refrigerator is all that's left in the bunkhouse. I don't keep any alcohol in here when the summer help arrives. They're mostly underage, and I sure don't want to get tossed in jail for giving liquor to a minor," Rusty said.

"Then let's do this up right." Bonnie poured a cup of moonshine into a blender, added all of the tequila, and a twist of lemon. She put a few cubes of ice into the blender and punched chop, then hit stop when its contents were smoothie texture. She carried the blender and the two glasses into the living room.

"We were going to talk about mistakes. You go first." She settled down right in the middle of the well-worn sofa, set the blender on the coffee table, and poured two shots.

He took one of the glasses from her, threw back its contents like a shot of whiskey, and held out his glass to be refilled. "I ran away from the last foster home when I was fourteen and went to work on a ranch. I wish I'd finished high school and taken some business courses. Ezra took care of the finances, and it's been a struggle for me to learn how to operate the computer and do all that. Your turn."

She drank her bomb and said, "I got in with a bad group in eastern Kentucky. We got caught growing pot."

"Did you do jail time?" he asked.

"No, it was worse than that," she told him.

"I'm listening." He refilled her glass.

"In the county I was living in at the time, one family owned the pot business, and no one cultivated marijuana without their permission—and they didn't give it to kids. They caught us harvesting it, took it all from us, and went to our parents. We didn't get taken to jail, but our folks had to pay them the equivalent of a fine. Mama had to cough up five hundred dollars, and I had to work as a waitress all summer to pay her back."

She'd downed that bomb, so he made her another one. "Surely you made more than that in three months."

Bonnie threw back the drink and held out her glass for more. Memories were stirred up in her mind that she thought she'd buried too deep to ever surface, and they brought about the same hurt feelings as they had all those years ago. If her mother could get her hands on a dollar, she'd figure out a way to rationalize taking it. Bonnie's feelings or needs seldom if ever played into the grand scheme of anything. "Yep, and she called the rest of the money I made the interest and the lesson—depending on whether she was drunk or high herself. Your turn."

They switched back and forth with their tales of woe until finally Bonnie leaned her head back on the sofa and began to snore. Rusty gently carried her to his bedroom, laid her on the bed, and covered her with a quilt. She roused up, moaned, and threw her hand over her eyes.

He stretched out beside her and whispered, "Shhh... just sleep."

* * *

Bonnie was jerked awake the next morning when Vivien licked her hand that was dangling over the side of the bed. She opened her eyes wide, looked around, and didn't recognize a single thing other than the dog that was named for her mother. The light stung her eyes. Her head pounded so hard that she could hear every heartbeat in it.

"Good mornin'." Rusty brought in a tray with pancakes and coffee. "We've overslept. It's too late to go to church, so evidently we won't be able to ask forgiveness for our sins."

"I don't know about you, but I don't believe I did anything I have to repent for." She sat up in bed, checked to be sure she was wearing clothes, and threw back the quilt. "I only had a few sips from a shot of blackberry bomb."

"I had about three of those wicked bombs you brewed up. You drank the rest of that blender full." He put the tray over her lap and sat down beside her.

"Well, at least you didn't sneak out in the middle of the night and leave me like you did that Sandy woman. Are you going to call me?" Her tone was saccharine.

He poured syrup on the pancakes, cut into them, and took a bite.

"I thought this was my breakfast," she said.

"It's ours to share, like we did all our mistakes last night." He handed her the fork and his hand brushed against hers. His gentle touch sent sensations coursing through her body that made her want to throw off the sheet and drag him right back into bed with her.

She took a bite and wondered what in the hell she'd shared with him. Did she tell him about the sorry sucker who'd talked her out of her virginity and then told everyone in high school about it the next day? Did she tell him that she'd never been so glad to go home that evening and find her mother packing the car to move again?

"So, what did I share?" she asked.

"I know about you trying to grow pot." Compared to all the other scrapes she'd been in, that wasn't so bad.

"So, we exchanged a few stories, got drunk, and now we're sharing pancakes. That doesn't change jack crap about this ranch," she said.

"Nope, it sure doesn't. I might make breakfast, but I'm still going to do my best to make you hate this place and leave before Christmas," he said.

"Give it your best shot, cowboy," she told him.

Chapter Four

Bonnie was on her way out the door when her phone rang. The noise startled her so badly she fumbled when she tried to fetch it from her hip pocket and dropped it on the floor. Breathless, she finally answered it on the fourth ring.

"Hello, Shiloh," she said.

"Why weren't you in church this morning?" Shiloh asked.

"Overslept," Bonnie answered.

"You're out of breath. What were you doing?"

I got drunk and had a hangover and woke up in Rusty's bed, she thought and smiled. But she said, "I was on my way outside when the phone rang. It startled me."

"Abby Joy and I are going to Amarillo this afternoon. Want to go with us? We're leaving in about half an hour."

Rusty walked up behind her. "I'm going out to check the hay we cut yesterday. Want to go with me?"

"Did I hear someone say something in the background?" Shiloh asked.

"Rusty came in the back door and wanted to know if I wanted to go to the pasture with him, but I'd rather go shopping. I'll see you in thirty," Bonnie said.

"Hello to him. See you in thirty. Oh, and tell Rusty, the guys are watching the bull riding on television at Abby Joy's if he wants to go over there." Shiloh ended the call.

Bonnie turned around to find him so close that his warm breath tickled the side of her cheek. "You're invited to Cooper's to watch bull riding."

All those damned moonshine bombs had to be the reason he affected her the way he did that morning. Sure, she'd had a little secret crush on him, but she'd never had to fight against the desire to take a step forward and kiss him. "I'm going shopping with my sisters."

He brushed a sweet kiss across her cheek. "Thanks for the evening and the night."

Her legs felt like they had no bones. Her pulse began to race, and her heart thumped against her ribs. "You can sweet-talk me, feed me breakfast, or get me drunk, and I'm still not going to let you have this ranch unless you're the highest bidder."

He chuckled. "But I will keep trying until the very last second. Bring home a couple of steaks, and I'll grill them for us tonight."

"There are two in the fridge"—she waved over her shoulder—"that I bought in Claude last evening."

"Y'all have fun," he called out just as she slammed the door of her truck.

She gave him a thumbs-up sign.

"What in the hell have I done?" she moaned as she drove the short distance from the bunkhouse to the ranch house. "I haven't been that drunk in years. It's a wonder I didn't do something totally stupid, like have sex with him."

She took a quick shower and washed her hair, dried off in a hurry, and threw on a pair of clean jeans and a shirt. She usually let her hair dry naturally, but that afternoon she used a blow dryer before she whipped it up in a ponytail. Her phone rang just as she picked up her lipstick.

"Where are you?" she asked when she saw Abby Joy's name

pop up on the screen. "I thought y'all said thirty minutes. I've been ready for a while now."

"We just passed the cemetery," Abby Joy said.

"I'm headed out now. You don't even have to honk." She ended the call and hurriedly put on her lipstick.

She'd just picked up her purse when she remembered that she hadn't fed the dogs, so she hurried back inside and filled their bowl with dry food. She thought her head would explode when she bent over and hoped that she'd remembered to refill the aspirin bottle that she carried in her purse. She took her time crossing the yard, but her head was still pounding when she got into the backseat of her sister's van.

"You're flushed like you've been runnin' around in circles," Shiloh said.

"I don't think it's from runnin'." Abby Joy shook her head as she backed the van out of the driveway. "She wasn't in church this morning, and she's glowing. I heard someone say that she was at the Sugar Shack last night and got into a little catfight with Sandy Hamilton. I betcha they were arguing over some good-lookin' cowboy, and our sister won. That look on her face"—Abby Joy looked up at her in the rearview—"tells me she brought that cowboy home with her, and the two of them had sex."

Shiloh turned around in her seat as far as the seat belt would allow and stared at her youngest sister. "Is that true? Who was it? Is he still in the house? What is Rusty goin' to think of that?" She fired off questions too fast for anyone to keep up with.

Bonnie shook her head and then grabbed it with both hands. "I don't kiss and tell. No one is in the house or was last night. I don't think I need Rusty's permission to bring a man home if I want to. After all, in six months the ranch will belong to me, and he'll be working for me if I decide to keep it."

What was the matter with her anyway? She had no intention of keeping the ranch. The moment it was in her hands, she planned to have a Realtor put a sign out beside the road announcing that it was for sale.

"What makes you think he'll stick around? If you decide to stick around, you'd better be putting out some feelers for a new foreman," Shiloh said.

While Bonnie was mulling that over in her head, Abby Joy spoke up. "You went home with someone, didn't you? No one glows like you are right now if they haven't had sex for the first time since Christmas." She glanced up at her youngest sister in the rearview mirror again.

"Or unless they're pregnant," Shiloh said. "The both of you are glowing. I'm beginning to feel left out. Y'all are going to have babies that will grow up together, and my poor little children will be so much younger that they'll get picked on by their older cousins."

Bonnie wanted children someday, but not right now. She had some heavy decisions to make about her life, and a pregnancy at this point would complicate the hell out of things. Her upbringing had taught her that when she got ready to have kids she would settle down in one place. She damn sure wouldn't jerk them out of school in the middle of a semester. Bonnie had lost count after twenty at how many schools she'd attended from kindergarten through graduation.

"You got something to tell us, little sister?" Abby Joy asked.

"I am not pregnant, and I'm glowing because I just got out of a hot shower, and y'all are making me blush," Bonnie said.

"Good God!" Shiloh gasped. "Bonnie blushing? I didn't think she had it in her to do that."

"Don't make me laugh." Abby Joy giggled. "With this baby lyin' heavy on my bladder, if I laugh too hard we'll be turning around and goin' back home to get me a pair of dry underwear."

Bonnie crossed her arms over her chest. "Y'all are bad sisters today."

"We wouldn't be if you'd tell us who you went home with last night," Shiloh told her.

"I left the Sugar Shack and came home. End of story," Bonnie said.

"Well, dammit!" Shiloh sighed. "I wanted to hear a more exciting story than that on the way to the mall."

"Three sassy sisters livin' on a ranch, one got married and went away. Two sassy sisters livin' on a ranch, one got married and went away. One sassy sister livin' on a ranch, she's all confused and don't know what to do..." Bonnie said. "Is that story good enough for you?"

"Double dammit!" Abby Joy swore. "Now I've got that worm in my head about the little monkeys."

"Good." Bonnie smiled. "Serves y'all right. I hope that song haunts you all day."

"Seriously," Shiloh said, "have you given some thought to what you intend to do about the ranch?"

"Yes, but I've got a question for both of you." Bonnie nodded. "Y'all fell in love with someone and left, so evidently, it isn't hard to move off the ranch. But do you have any regrets now that time has passed? Both of you could have been in love and still put off leaving until the year was up. You could have even spent a night away at a time now and then, like Shiloh did when Waylon was hurt. As long as you didn't actually move away, both of you could have still been in for a share of the ranch."

"I don't have a single regret," Abby Joy answered without hesitation. "But then, I was in love with Cooper, and love trumps all the dirt in Texas in my books."

"I don't have regrets either," Shiloh said. "Both of you know, I was having doubts about staying on the ranch anyway. Following the terms of that will made me feel like Ezra had control over my life, and even if I had half ownership with you, Bonnie, it was"— she paused—"I can't explain the feeling, but I can tell you that when I made up my mind to leave, it felt like the chains dropped off my heart. Like Abby Joy, I was in love with Waylon, so that had a bearing on it, I'm sure, but I was relieved that Ezra wasn't running my life anymore."

"He really was an old sumbitch, wasn't he?" Bonnie whispered. "Do you wonder why he made his will the way he did? Why would he even care if we ever knew each other? I mean"—she took a deep breath and let it out in a whoosh—"I'm glad we have gotten acquainted, but why?"

"Can't answer that," Abby Joy replied. "I'm glad I came to the funeral, and that y'all did too, but understanding why Ezra did anything he did is impossible, and I've tried."

"Me too." Shiloh nodded.

"Thanks for being honest." Bonnie turned to look out the side window. She tried to imagine simply moving off the ranch and relinquishing all her rights to it to Rusty, but she didn't want to leave him. They made a great team, and he needed her right now, here in the busy season.

* * *

Rusty knocked on the door of Cooper's ranch house and then poked his head inside. "Where are y'all at?"

"In the living room," Cooper called out. "Come on in. The bareback bronc riding is about to begin. Bull riding comes after that."

Rusty carried a six-pack of cold beer through the kitchen and the foyer and into the living room where Cooper and Waylon were already stretched out in a couple of recliners. He twisted the top off two bottles and handed one to each of them. Then he sat down on the sofa, propped his boots on an oversize hassock, and uncapped a beer for himself.

"Heard you didn't close down the Sugar Shack last night," Cooper said. "You sick or something?"

"Nope, just got bored with it. Sandy was drunk." Rusty took a long drink of his beer.

"Sandy's always drunk. Woman can't hold her liquor any better than she can a boyfriend." Waylon muted the commercial.

"She's clingy and thinks if you buy her a drink, you're in love with her and about to propose." Cooper nodded. "I told you not to ever get involved with her, Rusty."

"I didn't, but I can't convince her of that," he groaned.

Waylon hit the red button on the remote to turn the sound back on. "Damn, I wish I was still doin' the rodeo rounds. I liked the sounds of the crowd, the thrill of the rides, all of it."

"Marriage changes a cowboy," Cooper said.

"Yep, it does," Waylon agreed. "And when it comes down to the line, I'd rather be married as out there bustin' up bones and spendin' time in emergency rooms. Since I got that concussion a few weeks ago in the wreck, I'd be afraid to ride anyway. I don't ever want to get to where I wouldn't know Shiloh."

"Wait until you've got a baby comin' along." Cooper combed back his dark hair with his fingertips. "That *really* changes everything. I sure enough feel my responsibility to keep healthy. I'm not even running for sheriff next election. I'm just going to ranch."

The commercial ended and the bronc riding event started. All three guys yelled for their favorite contestant, who was trying to make it all the way to the National Professional Rodeo in Las Vegas in December.

Rusty slumped down on the sofa and watched one event after another, but his thoughts wandered back to the Malloy Ranch. Cooper had inherited the Lucky Seven from his grandparents. Waylon had started off with a small spread and renamed it the Wildflower Ranch. Then the elderly lady next door to his place died and left him her small acreage. When he and Shiloh got married, she doubled the size of their acreage by buying the adjoining ranch to the south.

Rusty loved living in the canyon. He'd put down roots at the Malloy Ranch. He finally belonged somewhere. About all he could do at this point was hope that when Bonnie sold the place, he was the high bidder and that a bank would back him.

Chapter Five

The next morning the window served as a picture frame for the most beautiful sunrise Bonnie had ever seen. She threw off the covers and stared out at the gorgeous sight for a long time before she finally got dressed and headed toward the kitchen. She was halfway down the hall when she got a whiff of cinnamon blended with the aroma of coffee.

"Good mornin'," Rusty said. "I made cinnamon toast for breakfast. Looks like we're goin' to have a good day to get the hay raked and baled."

Was this his new trick to get rid of her—be nice so she'd feel sorry for him and give him the ranch for a fraction of its price? Well, he was dead wrong, if that's what he thought.

"So this is how we're going to play it, is it?" She poured a cup of coffee and carried it to the table.

"Play what?" he asked. "I was hungry for cinnamon toast and we usually have breakfast together if we're not fighting."

"I was afraid things would be awkward between us after the bombs on Saturday night," she answered.

"Why would things be weird?" Rusty set a whole cookie sheet full of cinnamon toast on the table and then poured himself a cup of coffee and took a seat.

His long legs brushed against hers under the table, and heat spread through her body like she was standing next to a raging bonfire. He bowed his head to say grace. Lord have mercy! How was she supposed to keep a divine thought in her head while he said a short prayer with his leg touching hers?

"Amen," he said, "and now let's eat and talk about why you think we should act any different than we did before. We're consenting adults and we both had a bit to drink. Now we're ranchers and we've got work to do."

No wonder Mama never remarried, Bonnie thought. Vivien's words came back to her in a flash. *Men are impossible to live with for any length of time. You just have a good time with 'em and then shove 'em out the door and go find another one. The thrill and excitement don't last long. Ezra Malloy proved that to me, and I ain't never forgot that lesson.*

Bonnie had heard that speech so many times when she and her mother were together that it was branded on her brain. She might not agree with her mama, but it had been a long time since she'd talked to her, so she made a mental note to give Vivien a call later that day.

"I'm thinking about leaving. If you aren't going to sell me the place when you inherit, I need to get some feelers out there for another job. Cooper already has a foreman, but he said he'd hire me as a hand, and so did Jackson."

"No! You can't do that!" Bonnie gasped.

"Yes, I can and yes, I will. No use in waiting around, and then bein' jobless. Ranchers don't need many hands in the dead of winter. It would be easier to get one now and get settled into a place by Christmas," Rusty said.

Bonnie laid her toast down and picked up her coffee. If Rusty left, she'd be lost. She'd learned a lot in the last six months, but sweet Jesus, she couldn't run the ranch without him, not even with the summer help arriving in the next few days.

"Please don't do that," she whispered.

"I like you," he said, "a lot. When y'all first arrived here, I could see that you had spunk and determination. You've worked hard to learn this business. But with your decision to leave and sell out, it's time for me to take my dogs and move on to another job."

Bonnie set her coffee down and shook her finger at him. "You're not taking the dogs. They belong on this ranch."

"Those dogs were left to me in the will, so they're mine," Rusty told her. "Get serious. Whoever buys the place will bring in their own dogs, and they probably will fight with Vivien, Polly, and Martha. And, honey," he dragged out the endearment to at least six syllables, "those dogs go with me. They're mine." He pushed back from the table. "I'm going out to the field to rake the hay. I'll see you this evening."

"Will you be here tomorrow?" she asked.

"Will you?" he shot over his shoulder as he settled his straw hat on his head and slammed the screen door.

Vivien's drunk voice popped into her head again. *Men! Can't live with 'em, and it's against the law to shoot 'em.*

"Why is it against the law to shoot them?" Bonnie muttered as she picked up a second piece of toast. "We could have a season on them, say once every five years. One day only, women could buy a tag like when I hunted deer in Kentucky. Red tag could be shoot to kill for cheaters and beaters. Blue tag could be a grazing shot for drunks and—"

Her mother's special ring tone interrupted her. "Hello, Mama, I was going to call you after breakfast."

"Great minds and all that crap." Vivien chuckled. "So how are things there? Looks like you're going to own a ranch before too many months, don't it?"

"Not if I leave," she said.

"Holy smokin' shit!" Vivien gasped. "You just made me spew coffee all over the table. You've beat both your half sisters out for the ranch. You'd be a fool to give up now. You deserve that place after the way Ezra did me and you."

"I didn't earn it, Mama, but if I'm honest with myself, Rusty really should have it. He put up with Ezra for years and took care of him when he was sick," Bonnie said.

"You *did* earn it. You've done without things other girls had, and you've had to work for everything you needed—and so did I," Vivien told her.

"Why'd you marry him?" Bonnie asked. "Did you love him? Was he charming? Did he make you feel good about yourself? What drew you two together?"

There was a long silence before Vivien answered. "I was in one of my phases when I thought I wanted to live in the wilds. Ezra was not charming. He was crude and downright salty, but he had a ranch, and at that time I didn't want to go back to Texas or Kentucky. I wanted to settle down and have a family, and Ezra wanted a son. I didn't love him, but we tolerated each other fairly well until you were born. I never went back to the ranch after I gave birth to you. He packed up all my personal things and had them shipped back to where my mother was living at the time. I left the hospital with you in my arms, a bus ticket, and a checkbook with a deposit equal to the prenup agreement, which was ten thousand dollars."

"Did you know I had two half sisters?" she asked.

"Of course, I did," Vivien sighed. "He never mentioned them, but that's a small community down there in the canyon, so I knew."

"Why didn't you tell me?" Bonnie could feel anger rising up from her toes. "I had a right to know that, don't you think?"

"What good would it have done? I didn't know where they were living or even what their names were," Vivien answered. "And I damn sure didn't want to know their mothers. From what I heard, they were both on the hoity-toity side."

"Why didn't you ask for half the ranch?" Bonnie tried to push the anger down, but it didn't work.

"I signed a prenup. If I didn't produce a son, then I got ten grand and a bus ticket out of the canyon," she answered. "Figured I had a fifty-fifty chance, and I lost the bet."

"So I'm just the by-product of a bet?" Bonnie's voice went all high and squeaky.

"I know that tone, and I don't like it, so goodbye." Vivien ended the call.

Bonnie wanted to throw the phone at the wall, but she shoved it into her hip pocket and stood up so quickly that she knocked her chair over. She stomped across the kitchen floor to the back door, didn't even look back at the chair or the remainder of the toast and her half-empty cup of coffee on the table.

She'd wanted to talk to her mother about these feelings she had for Rusty, but the conversation had sure enough taken a different path. "So, Mama, the ultimate love 'em and leave 'em, married Ezra for money and security, not love," she fumed as she got into her old truck and drove out to the hay field. "She hasn't changed much, except she's given up on security, and now it's a good time she looks for. Even at her age now, she's always looking out for thrills, and when she gets bored with whoever is providing her with drama and fun, she goes on the prowl for another one."

Rusty was in the adjoining field, and although she couldn't see his face, she wondered if he was as angry as she was. Or maybe he was using his man powers and simply putting it out of his mind, like brushing a piece of lint from the shoulder of his jacket. Sweet Jesus! She had to persuade him to stay throughout the summer and fall at the very least.

Bonnie parked her truck, rolled down the windows, and was still mumbling to herself when she opened the door to the cab of the tractor. A blast of heat that had the faint aroma of sweat and the smell of dogs hit her in the face. She hopped up into the driver's seat, turned on the engine, and adjusted the air conditioner.

"He can go if he wants to. I can hire another foreman, and the summer help will be here next week, but he's damn sure not takin' the dogs," she declared as she put the tractor in gear and started raking the hay into windrows. She wiped tears from her cheeks. She didn't want him to leave, and it had a helluva lot more to do with her feelings for him than it did with finding another foreman. There, she'd admitted it—she wanted more out of the cowboy than just having him as a foreman or even as a friend.

* * *

When Bonnie stormed across the distance between her truck and the tractor, Rusty could tell by her body language that the woman was still angry. Women were such strange critters. He thought she'd be happy that he was leaving the ranch.

All of the sisters had been fast learners, but Bonnie had been the one who'd caught on to everything the fastest. Maybe it was because she'd had a hardscrabble life, and hadn't ever been handed everything. Abby Joy had showed up with her stuff in duffel bags, and Shiloh with monogrammed luggage. Bonnie had arrived with her things packed in plastic Walmart bags, and not once had she let her older half sisters intimidate her.

She could run the ranch standing on her head in ashes, Rusty thought, *and do a fine job of it. She don't need me anymore. In the last six months she's learned plenty enough to do the job until she can get a foreman.*

His phone rang, and he grabbed it without even looking at the name on the screen. "Hello, you ready to talk this through?" he asked.

"No, but maybe we should." Waylon chuckled.

"Sorry, I thought you were Bonnie. We had an argument this morning," Rusty told him.

"Over what, if you don't mind me asking?" Waylon asked.

"Me leaving the ranch in the next few weeks," Rusty replied.

"I'll gladly give you a job and pay you more than you're making over there. I could use an extra foreman with all the new property," Waylon said.

"Thanks for the offer. The idea just came to me this morning that I should probably leave the place, and I want to think on it a couple of weeks," Rusty said.

"Don't jump into anything without sleeping on it would be my advice, but I'd hire you in a minute if you make that decision," Waylon said. "But the reason I called is that Shiloh and I are having a little barbecue for our hired hands tomorrow evening.

We wanted to invite you and Bonnie. Cooper and Abby Joy are coming for sure. She's been craving barbecued ribs."

"I never turn down ribs," Rusty said. "What time and what can I bring?"

"You can bring a six-pack of beer. Shiloh says she's asking Bonnie to bring baked beans." Waylon chuckled again.

"What's so funny?" Rusty snapped.

"Just thinking about the arguments Shiloh and I had before we admitted we were in love. It was a tough time, but seems like we all have to go through it until we admit to our feelings. That's what Shiloh told me later when we talked about those days. I'm thinkin' maybe you and Bonnie might be fighting over more than that ranch," Waylon answered.

"Me and Bonnie in love," Rusty sputtered. "That's not damn likely."

"Just tellin' you about me and Shiloh. I'm putting you down for a six-pack of beer, but if y'all are still fightin', then maybe you should bring a pint of something harder." This time Waylon laughed out loud.

"I'll bring a damned twelve-pack," Rusty growled. "And you better make extra ribs because I eat a lot when I'm aggravated."

"I'll get another rack, then. See you tomorrow night." Waylon ended the call.

Rusty tossed the phone over on the passenger's seat. He had the offer of a really good job, and he would still be in the area with all his friends. Maybe whoever bought Malloy Ranch would hate the place, and he'd have the opportunity to buy it again sometime on down the road. All he had to do was load up his truck, move across the road, and settle into Waylon's new bunkhouse. He wouldn't have a room all to himself, but he'd have a place to lay his head at night.

At noon, he parked the tractor and noticed that Bonnie had done the same. They each got into their vehicles without even a simple wave, like they always did when they were heading back to the house for dinner.

If that was the way she wanted to be, then Rusty would give her enough space to cool off. He didn't even slow down when he passed the house but drove straight to the bunkhouse. All three dogs waited on the porch, and he bent down to pet each one of them. When he straightened up and went inside, they followed him.

He headed straight to the refrigerator, took out a gallon of sweet tea, and drank at least a pint straight from the container. He could almost hear Ezra laughing and telling him that a woman wasn't worth forgetting to take water or tea to the field with him. He put the voice out of his head while he made himself a ham and cheese sandwich. When he'd gotten out potato chips and pickles, he sat down at the table and bowed his head, but he was too agitated to pray.

Finally, he looked up at the ceiling and said, "God, why did you make women so damned stubborn? Pardon the cuss word. And by the way, thanks for the food."

No booming voice came down to answer his question, but one of the dogs cold-nosed his hand and made him almost jump out of his chair. "Are you trying to tell me something, Vivien?" he asked the mutt.

She whimpered and wagged her tail on the floor.

"Is the woman you're named after as bullheaded as her daughter?" He took another long drink of tea and then picked up his sandwich. "I'd rather be eating with her, you know. I've always looked forward to an hour in the middle of the day when we could talk about anything and everything. She's always been the easiest one for me to visit with."

Vivien laid a paw on his foot and yipped.

"Why is she bein' so damned hard to get along with? Is it because she misses her sisters? Or maybe because she's been havin' to work so hard? Well, that's ranchin' in a nutshell, and if she don't like it, maybe she should sell out," he said between bites.

He finished his meal and headed back to the field, driving slowly because all three dogs were running along beside the truck. Dust floated across and through the barbed wire fence from where Bonnie was already back at work. When he got out of his vehicle, he sneezed twice on the way to the tractor, but the dogs stayed right with him. He opened the cab door, and they all three got inside. Two shared the passenger's seat, and Vivien curled up on the floorboard.

"Hmmmph!" Rusty said as he started the engine. "She's got rocks for brains if she thinks I'm leaving a single one of you behind. We'll go to court if we have to."

Chapter Six

Any other time, Bonnie would have suggested that she and Rusty ride over to the Wildflower Ranch together, but not that Tuesday evening. They hadn't even spoken to each other since the day before, and she wasn't going to take the first step toward reconciliation. Not when he threatened her with the dogs.

She had spent a restless night, and that morning when she awoke, she had trouble separating reality from the visions she'd had in her sleep. Tears ran down her cheeks as she sat up in bed and wondered if she'd gotten the sign she'd asked for in the form of dreams. In the first one she'd crammed all her clothing into one big black garbage bag and the other small things she'd accumulated since she'd been on the Malloy Ranch into a box. She'd put them in the back of her truck and was driving past the cemetery when she saw Ezra sitting on the top of his tombstone. With a big grin on his face, a wicked mean look in his eyes, he waved goodbye to her.

Ezra had won. All three girls had lost. Plain and simple.

She couldn't let him win. She just couldn't.

In the second dream, there was snow on the ground, and both sisters, Abby Joy and Shiloh, stood on the porch as she drove away. She watched them in the mirror and realized that they would grow closer and closer to each other, while she'd just be a stranger who dropped in every few months or years to say hello.

Ezra had won a second time. He'd put the sisters together only to split them up again.

Bonnie punched her pillow several times. She couldn't let him win, and she damn sure couldn't leave her sisters behind. What if they needed her? What if she needed them like she had several times in the past months?

"Dammit!" she muttered as she wiped even more tears away with the edge of the bedsheet. "When did I put down such deep roots?"

About half angry with herself for letting herself become so vulnerable that she'd let other people deep into her heart, she threw back the covers and crawled out of bed.

· She spent the entire day going back and forth from trying to convince herself that she was crazy for letting two dreams affect her whole life, to being honest with herself and admitting that they had been signs. She wasn't a lot closer to making a final decision when the day ended, and she went back to the ranch house that evening. She took a long shower, dressed in clean jeans and a sleeveless shirt, and carried her baked beans out to the truck. The vehicle looked like crap on the outside, but it had new tires, bought with her first couple of weeks' paychecks back in the winter. "You've been a faithful old friend. No way I'm goin' to turn my back on you now." She set her big bowl of baked beans on the seat beside her and put the pecan pie she'd whipped up the night before on the floorboard on the passenger side. "If you could talk, would you tell me to tell Rusty to get on down the road and not let the door hit him in the ass? Or would you tell me to settle down and call this place home."

She shot a dirty look through the gate of the small family cemetery where Ezra was buried and drove on across the road to her sister's place. She discovered that she had a choice—park right beside Rusty's truck or go all the way to the end of the line of cars and trucks. No way was she going to let him think that he'd intimidated her. She pulled in beside his vehicle, got out, and circled around behind the bed of her truck. She opened the passenger door, and suddenly both Waylon and Cooper were right there to help. One picked up the pie and the other the beans.

She caught a quick glimpse of Rusty sitting in the shadows when she mounted the porch steps, but she didn't acknowledge his presence. "Hello, everyone."

"Miz Bonnie." A few of the hired hands tipped their hats.

"Howdy." A couple more raised a beer bottle.

Out of the corner of her eye, she saw that Rusty didn't do either one, which told her that he was still every bit as angry as she was. She passed Waylon and Cooper coming through the kitchen door on their way back out to the porch. Abby Joy and Shiloh were busy at the stove, so Bonnie grabbed an apron from a hook, slipped it over her head, and asked what she could do to help.

"The corn bread should be done." Shiloh pointed at the stove. "If you'll get it out of the oven and cut it into squares, we should be ready to put it on the table and call everyone in for supper. The pie looks amazing. Thanks for bringing it. Abby Joy made a cobbler, and I whipped up a cream puff cake, so we should have plenty."

"I'll get a few glasses of tea poured up," Abby Joy said.

"I assume we're doing this buffet style?" Bonnie shoved her hands into two oven mitts and pulled the big pan of corn bread from the oven.

"Yep, and before all those guys get in our way, tell me what's going on with you and Rusty. He's pouting and you've got that look on your face that you had right after Ezra's funeral," Abby Joy said.

"Waylon said they're fighting," Shiloh informed her older sister.

"Over what?" Abby Joy asked.

"The dogs," Bonnie answered.

"Why would you fight over the dogs? Didn't Ezra leave them to Rusty in his will?" Abby Joy clamped a hand over her mouth. "Is he moving off the ranch? Good God, girl, what will you do?"

"She's tough." Shiloh picked up a knife and cut the pie into ten pieces. "She'll hire a new foreman and keep runnin' the place. Waylon said he offered him a job, so if he leaves, the dogs will just be across the road."

"That's not why we're really fighting." Bonnie sighed. "I've been thinkin' about it all day long while I sat in a tractor. It's just something to fight about because neither of us will face our feelings."

"And what's that supposed to mean?" Shiloh asked.

"That we're attracted to each other and have been for months," Bonnie blurted out.

Shiloh winked at Abby Joy.

"What's the winking all about?" Bonnie cut the corn bread and made a pyramid of it on a platter with the squares.

"We saw the attraction between the two of you the first week we were at the ranch," Abby Joy told her.

"We've just been waiting for y'all to figure it out for yourselves," Shiloh added. "So, give us the short version of what caused the fight." She carried a bowl of coleslaw to the dining room table.

"We've been arguing about me selling the ranch for a week now. And now he's saying that he might as well leave, since it'll be hard to find a job on a ranch in the wintertime. Then he said he was taking the dogs. I don't want him to leave, and I'm terrified about putting down roots. What if I got my mama's genes and after six months me and Rusty got ourselves in a relationship, and then I decided that I wanted to sell out and leave. He was good to teach us and help us learn, and Ezra was a sumbitch for going back on his word about leavin' the ranch to Rusty."

"Then why are you arguing with yourself about selling it to him?" Shiloh asked.

"Hell, if I know." Bonnie shrugged. "I'm so damned confused I don't know whether to wind my butt or scratch my watch as my mama used to say." She went on to tell them about the two dreams.

"The dogs just gave you something to argue about when you're really angry with yourselves because you can't figure out what it is you want to do and why. And, honey, I believe in dreams. Mama used to tell me that God has visited folks in dreams since the beginning of time, and when He speaks, we should listen," Abby Joy said.

Cooper came into the kitchen, walked up behind Abby Joy, and slipped his arms around her. "It sure smells good in here. Is it about time to call in the hungry guys?"

Abby Joy turned around and kissed him on the cheek. "Bonnie will have the corn bread on the table in about five seconds, so go on and tell them it's ready."

"Yes, ma'am." Cooper bent and brushed a kiss across his wife's lips. "And thanks to all three of you ladies for all you've done."

Bonnie had barely set the platter of corn bread on the table when the men started filing inside the house. Rusty was the last one in the line, and he stood back against the wall. Waylon removed his cowboy hat and bowed his head. The rest of the cowboys did the same.

When he'd said "Amen" at the end of the very short grace, Shiloh kissed him on the cheek.

In that moment, Bonnie began to doubt whether she really wanted to sell the ranch and travel or if she wanted what her sisters both had, roots and someone to love them.

"We don't have room for everyone to sit down in the house, but we've set up a couple of long tables out in the backyard," Shiloh said. "The silverware and napkins are already out there."

"Man, this looks good," Cooper said.

"Smells good too. I haven't had anything but sandwiches for two days." Rusty stepped forward, picked up a plate, and began to load it.

Bonnie shot a mean look across the table at him, but his eyes were on the food and the evil glare was wasted. Fixing her own plate, she wondered if he'd missed coming to the ranch house to eat with her as much as she'd missed having him there.

How on earth Rusty got behind her was a mystery, but suddenly, he was there, and he whispered softly in her ear, "We need to talk, don't you think?"

His warm breath on the soft part of her neck sent shivers down her spine. "You're not taking those dogs away from their home," she said. "They were raised on the ranch, and they'd be miserable anywhere else. I'll stay right there and never leave before you take them away. I won't even sell it until they've all passed away, and then I'm going to bury them right on top of Ezra. That way he'll have all three of his wives in the same grave with him."

"Let's talk about all of this tomorrow." Rusty set his plate down on the first table they came to.

"Where and when?" she asked.

"Neutral place," he answered. "In the barn at six o'clock."

"I'll be there." With a curt nod, she walked on past him and sat down at the second table with Abby Joy, Cooper, and a handful of hired hands.

"What was that all about?" Abby Joy whispered.

"Just setting up a meeting so we can talk," Bonnie answered.

"You've got a job right here anytime you want to move," Abby Joy said. "Just promise me you won't get a wild hare and leave the canyon. Sisters should stick together, and besides, this baby"— she laid her hand on her bulging stomach—"needs his aunts. I don't know a blessed thing about babies, so I'll need all the help I can get too."

Bonnie made up her mind right then and there to stick around until the dogs had all died, and so that she could be an aunt to Abby Joy's baby. Bonnie missed having family in her life, so she couldn't very well deny her little niece the same. "I promise."

She glanced over at the other table, where Shiloh and Waylon were sitting with the rest of the hired hands. Her mind went back to that first day when Cooper had told them that they'd need more than one napkin because the chicken was greasy. She had been glad that her two older half sisters weren't bashful when it came to food. On first impression, Shiloh had seemed pretty prissy, and the older sister was without a doubt a force to be reckoned with, but when they all three gathered around in the kitchen that cold day, all three of them hadn't had any qualms about food.

Abby Joy bumped her on the arm. "What are you thinkin' about? You've hardly touched your barbecue, and I know you like it a lot."

"I've been thinkin' about our first day together a lot lately," she answered.

"You mean at Ezra's funeral?" Cooper asked. "I couldn't believe that all three of you showed up looking like you did at his graveside service."

"Oh?" Abby Joy raised an eyebrow.

"Think about it," Cooper chuckled. "You looked like you'd just come out of a war zone in all that camouflage and your combat boots. Shiloh, over there"—he nodded her way—"looked like she'd just left a rodeo, and I wasn't sure if you were a biker or a punk rocker, Bonnie."

"I couldn't believe those two were my sisters, either." Bonnie giggled. "I figured that Abby Joy was like Ezra, and Shiloh had to take after her mother, and that neither of them would last two days on a ranch. Shiloh would be afraid she'd break a fingernail, and Abby Joy would be…"

"I'd be what?" Abby Joy asked.

"Bored to tears on a ranch after the life you'd led in the military," Bonnie finished. "I didn't even know Ezra, but from what Mama told me when she was drinking too much and bitchin' about him, I figured you were the most like him."

"Hey, now, I'm the least like Ezra of all of us," Abby Joy declared.

Suddenly Bonnie had that antsy feeling that she only got when someone was staring at her. She glanced over at the other table and locked eyes with Rusty. She wished that she could fall into those sexy green eyes all the way to the bottom of his soul and find out what his real feelings were. Waylon nudged him with a shoulder, and he looked away just about the same time Abby Joy poked her on the arm with her forefinger.

"You don't have a smart-ass remark about me being the least like Ezra?" Abby Joy asked.

"Nope, but I've got a question for Cooper. You liked Ezra, right?"

Cooper nodded. "He was an eccentric old codger, but he was smart as a whip when it came to ranchin'. All of us around these parts could depend on him for advice—other than when it came to women."

"Guess that answers my question fairly well," Bonnie said. "Thanks."

Cooper's head bobbed in a quick nod, and then he changed the subject. "These beans are great. What's your secret?"

"A tablespoon of mustard," Bonnie answered. "It cuts the sweet of the brown sugar and ketchup."

And a little argument is good for a relationship, like mustard is good for beans. Her mother's voice popped into her head. *It cuts all that sweetness of flirting and sex. Every couple has to endure a few tests to see if the relationship will withstand the long journey.*

That just might be the smartest advice you have ever given me, Mama, Bonnie thought. *Why don't you apply it to your own relationships?*

Chapter Seven

Bonnie was sitting on a bale of hay in the corner of the barn, ready for their talk, when Rusty arrived. Several strands of blond hair had escaped from her ponytail and were stuck to her sweaty face. Pieces of hay were still stuck to her clothing from hauling bales from the field to the barn all day. With no one else to help, and refusing to work together, they'd each loaded their own truck bed full, driven it to the barn, and then unloaded and stacked it there. They'd gotten in what they'd baled the day before, and tomorrow, they'd move to another field and start cutting what was ready there.

"Why didn't Ezra ever get the machinery to make those big round bales?" She removed her work gloves and laid them beside her.

"He was old school." Rusty sat down on the running board of her truck. "He said that ranchers wasted enough hay to make half a dozen small bales with what they lost on every one they left out in the weather. I think that once we were set up the waste would be worth it in the long run because we'd save a ton of money in the summer." When Ezra was alive, Rusty wouldn't have doubted anything the old man said.

"How would that be saving money?" she asked.

"We wouldn't be payin' the summer help wages," he answered. "But we're really not here to talk about hay, are we?"

"No, but after loading and hauling this all day, I'm all for buying the new stuff for the big bales," she said. "I'll go first. The argument over the dogs was just so we didn't have to face the real problem, which is the fact that I really do like you. One minute we're arguing, and the next we get along pretty good. I don't know if you're just pretending to be nice so I'll sell you the ranch, or if you feel the same sparks I do when you're in the same room with me." She pushed a strand of hair from her sweaty face.

He was speechless at her honesty. "I like you too. Always have felt a connection between us, but I'm having second thoughts about this place. I've had a love-hate connection to the ranch. Seems like it's tainted when it comes to relationships. I don't care if I had ten daughters and no sons, I'd never send them away, and they'd all inherit an equal share of whatever I had when my days on this earth came to an end. And Ezra shouldn't have treated his wives the way he did. Far as I could tell, none of them did a thing wrong, and it wasn't their fault their first child wasn't a son. The second one might have been."

"You won't get an argument out of me on any of what you just said," Bonnie agreed, "but a ranch is basically just dirt and grass. Is it really worth losing a friend, or the love of your life, over? Neither of my older sisters thought it was."

"Sometimes the place is just dirt if we don't get rain when we need it." Rusty chuckled. "When y'all first got here, you were sure enough ready to put on the gloves and go to war for the ranch, and now all you can talk about is selling it and gettin' the hell out of Dodge, or the Palo Duro Canyon, as this case is."

"Yep, but then we bonded, and now I feel pretty alone. It's not the first time. Every time Mama moved us, I had this same feeling of not knowing anyone. I hated walking into a new school three or four times a year," she said. "But not putting down roots is part of me now, and I don't know if I can stay in one place and be happy, Rusty. I'm afraid to even give it a try, but my heart has grown roots here and I have sisters who are living close by. Plus, you and I need to make the decisions about what happens on this place. Ezra is gone, and he doesn't get a say-so anymore."

Rusty moved over to sit beside her. "No, he doesn't, but he's buried right here on the property."

"He left you his knowledge of ranchin'." Bonnie nudged him with her shoulder. "I inherited his blue eyes and stubborn will. That's all he should get credit for."

"If you stay, and I hope you do," Rusty said, "what will you tell your kids about him someday? You do realize he'll be their grandfather."

"I'll tell them the absolute truth, and then I'll tell them that they have a father who is amazing and loves them, even if their grandfather wasn't a nice person," she answered.

"How can you make that kind of statement when you have no idea who the father of your kids will be?" Rusty turned and studied her face.

"Because I won't ever marry until I can find a man that I can truly say is amazing and that will love our children. I grew up without a father, for no other reason than I wasn't a boy. My kids, boys or girls, are going to have a daddy to love them, protect them, and provide for them, or I won't have a husband," Bonnie declared with so much conviction that Rusty could have sworn the temperature in the hot barn rose a few more degrees.

"Now, let's talk about you," Rusty said. "Are you staying or leaving?"

"Staying. I can't let Ezra win, and besides, I kind of like having roots, now that I realize how it feels," she answered. "Let's make a deal. We both stay until Christmas and see where this attraction between us goes. No rush. No hurry. But I want to talk to that lawyer who set up Ezra's will. Think you could arrange a meeting with him?"

"What do you want to talk to him about?" Rusty frowned.

"I want to understand a little more about the way the will is written," she answered. "Then we'll be ready for another talk. When can we visit with him?"

"I'll call him tomorrow morning and set up an appointment," Rusty answered. "Now we should be ready to talk honestly about *us*. I've missed you the last two days." He scooted over closer to her.

"I wouldn't want to run this place without you." She turned so they were facing each other. "And I like having you around. I missed you too."

He cupped her face in his hands and their lips met in a fiery kiss that warmed the barn right up to a full ninety-plus degrees. His hands trembled and his pulse raced when the kiss ended.

"So, we're good then?" He wanted to kiss her again, just to see if the second one stirred his feelings as much as the first one.

"Yes, we're good." She laid her head on his shoulder. "Can we go over this one more time, though? We've agreed that neither of us will leave the ranch, but we haven't talked about the dogs."

"According to the will, they are mine," he said, "but I'm willing to share them with you as long as you stay on the place." He leaned back and frowned. "Are you keeping me around just so you don't have to give up the dogs?"

She reached up and ruffled his dark hair. "You're smarter than you look."

He grabbed her hand and brought it to his lips to kiss each knuckle. "I've got lots of surprises to show you, since you've said you'll stick around for a while."

Chapter Eight

On the day of Ezra's funeral, Jackson Bailey had served as executor to Ezra's estate and handed each of the sisters a copy of his will. Bonnie shoved hers into the bottom dresser drawer in her new bedroom and never gave it another minute's thought. When she awoke on Thursday morning, the first thing she did was go straight to the dresser and get the blue binder.

She padded barefoot to the kitchen, where she made a pot of coffee and then sat down at the table to try to make heads and tails out of the legalese its pages contained. Most of it was so deep that she couldn't understand a word of it, but the language that said the sisters had to stay on the ranch for a year to share it was plain enough. If two of them left, it went to the third one—kind of like the last girl standing. Bonnie would have to have the lawyer verify what she thought that meant, but if it did, everything could change in a hurry. Because the way she read it said that if she was the last one on the ranch, then it went to her, even before the year was up.

"Good mornin'." Rusty came into the kitchen by the back door. "What have you got there? Coffee smells good. Let's have ham and cinnamon toast for breakfast."

"Ezra's will," she answered. "That sounds fine."

"I'll call that lawyer about nine. That's usually when businesses open up in Claude. Don't get your hopes up. He's an old guy, maybe Ezra's age or older, and he pretty much keeps hours when he wants to." Rusty poured two mugs of coffee and brought them to the table. "What's got you worried about it? I thought it was pretty straightforward."

"I can't understand anything I'm reading, but I wanted to at least have looked at it before we go into town to see the lawyer." She pushed it to the middle of the table. "What's on the agenda for today?" But then she cocked her head to one side and listened intently. "That sounds like a car or maybe a truck."

"I thought it was a tractor with a bad engine problem coming up the lane," Rusty said.

"Are we expecting company?" Bonnie asked.

She pushed back her chair and frowned as she started toward the door. When she stepped outside, she could see the dust boiling up as the old blue pickup truck drove down the lane. She heard the door open and close behind her and felt Rusty's presence even before he laid a hand on her shoulder.

"Friend of yours?" he asked.

"Holy crap on a cracker!" Bonnie sighed. "That would be my mother, arriving without notice. I guess she sold her car and got a truck." *Could the morning get any worse?* she thought as she took a step back. "Mama?"

"I've come to rescue you," Vivien yelled as she got out of the truck and jogged across the yard. A tall blond woman, she was so thin that Bonnie used to tell her to put rocks in her pockets to keep a strong wind from blowing her away. She looked every one of her fifty-three years, but then she lived on cigarettes, coffee, booze, and an occasional joint or two.

Vivien opened up her arms, and Bonnie walked into them.

"I don't need or want to be rescued," she said. "Mama, meet Rusty. Rusty, this is my mother, Vivien Malloy."

"I'll stick around until tomorrow and maybe you'll change your mind." Vivien took in the house and surrounding area in one sweeping glance. "This place ain't changed since you was a baby."

Vivien released her daughter from the hug. "You don't have to live like this another day, darlin'. I've changed my mind about you staying here to get his worthless piece of dirt. I want you to take whatever the money is offered in the will and go with me to California. If this old truck won't make it, we'll stop and get another one or finish the trip on the bus."

Bonnie folded her arms over her chest and stepped in front of the door. "I'm not going anywhere."

Vivien looked rougher than usual. Her eyes were bloodshot, and her hair hung in limp strings. She reeked of whiskey and marijuana and smelled like she hadn't had a bath in a week.

"Have you been drinking and driving again?"

"Yep, but I didn't get caught, so it's all right." Vivien giggled. "And yes, I had a joint or two to relax me on the long drive, and now I'm coming down off it. You know what that means—munchies. What's in the kitchen?"

"We haven't had breakfast yet, and we'll be glad to have you join us. We were about to make cinnamon toast and fry up some ham to go with it. The coffee is ready. You ladies can have a cup and visit while I get the food ready. Come on in and make yourself at home." Rusty held the door open.

"So, you're Rusty," Vivien said as she pushed her way inside. "I need to clean up a bit. Don't worry about me. I still remember where everything is located in this godforsaken place."

"In my wildest imagination I can't see Ezra married to her," Rusty whispered as he got down a loaf of bread and began to slather butter on each piece.

Bonnie got a slice of ham out of the refrigerator. "Her favorite men have been bikers who stick around for a few weeks or maybe even a couple of months and then they get into a big fight and we usually wind up moving somewhere else."

"And even after you got out of school, you moved with her?" Rusty asked.

Bonnie nodded. "I hold down a job better than she does, so she needed me."

"That's called an enabler." Rusty shook a mixture of cinnamon and sugar over the buttered bread and slid it into the oven.

"Well, well, ain't this cozy?" Vivien arrived back in the kitchen. "I don't remember Ezra ever helping me cook a damn thing. You sure ain't related to him in any way, Rusty."

She wore a pair of Bonnie's newest jeans, one of her shirts, and she'd changed out her ratty sneakers for Bonnie's cowboy boots.

"You are welcome to take my things without asking," Bonnie said in a saccharine tone.

"Thank you." Vivien poured herself a mug of coffee and added three heaping spoonfuls of sugar. "I knew you wouldn't mind. We'll be traveling together anyway and sharing hotel rooms, so it's not like you won't get them back."

"I'm not going anywhere," Bonnie reaffirmed. "Why are you going to California? You've always stuck around Kentucky and east Texas."

"About two months ago, Big Ben came into the bar where I've been working since you left Kentucky. We hit it off." Vivien shrugged. "And then he cheated on me. I've always wanted to see the ocean, and you talked about it when you was a kid, so I sold everything I had and headed this way. With what you'll get, surely, we can get out there and rent us a trailer. We can always find a job as bartenders. Come on, Bonnie, have some sense. This damned ranch ruined my life. Don't let it tear yours up, too."

Bonnie sat down at the table beside her mother and laid a hand on Vivien's arm. "Mama, you need to slow down. Why don't you stay a few days here with me and forget about California?"

Vivien jerked her arm free. "Honey, this is *my* life. I'll live it the way I want to. If you're smart, you'll come with me and do the same. It's exciting. Settling down ain't in my blood. I was glad that Ezra kicked us out. I would've probably left him before long anyway. I damn sure wasn't happy being here or being pregnant, and I vowed after you was born I'd never go through that again, not even to give him a son and get part of this ranch."

"You are going to get yourself killed," Bonnie scolded.

Vivien shook her head. "Maybe, but I'll die happy, not withered up on a worthless ranch doing something I hate. Rusty, darlin', if she stays with you when I leave, you just remember whose daughter she is before you go gettin' involved with her. What the hell good could come out of me and Ezra Malloy? You just think about that."

"I don't believe that our heritage determines our future," Rusty said. "Bonnie, if you'll take a step to the side, I'll get the toast out of the oven, and we can eat breakfast."

"And that's real sweet of you, Mama, to say that about me. Maybe I've done something you've never been willing to do—like change for the better," Bonnie said through clenched teeth.

"You always were a smart-ass. Got that from your daddy," Vivien told her. "You wouldn't have a denim jacket around here somewhere, would you?"

Bonnie realized she would be relieved when her mother had breakfast and left. One minute she wanted to cry for her mother's bad choices in life; the next she wanted to send to her bedroom without supper to punish her.

"Why do you want a denim jacket?" Bonnie asked.

"They say it gets cool in the evenings in California, and I left in such a hurry that I didn't pack a coat." Vivien heaped her plate with three pieces of toast and a big chunk of the ham slice.

"Why'd you leave so fast?" Bonnie asked and then shook her head slowly. "You took all of that biker's money when you headed west, didn't you? Like you used to do when I was a little girl and you got tired of living with some guy."

"And his bag of pot and two bottles of whiskey. I drove all night to get here," she said. "And I came to get my baby girl so I can take her to see the ocean like she always wanted."

"No thanks," Bonnie said. "I like the ranchin' business too well to leave it."

"I swear to God, she's just like Ezra," Vivien said.

"I can call Cooper," Rusty whispered just for Bonnie's ears. "After all, he is still the county sheriff until the election is over."

Bonnie shook her head and turned her attention back to Vivien, who was eating so fast that she couldn't have enjoyed the food. "You think Big Bill will follow you here?"

"No, he'll just cut his losses and move in with that hussy from the bar that he's been flirtin' with. And it's Big Ben, not Big Bill. Come on, Bonnie. Let's go see whoever we need to talk to and get your money. Between us we can have a good time," Vivien said.

"For the last time," Bonnie said, "the answer is no." She couldn't help but wonder what the answer might have been a few days before if Vivien had arrived with the same offer.

Bonnie remembered the dreams again and the empty feeling she had when she left her sisters behind. She didn't ever want to experience that in real life.

And this is your third sign, that niggling little voice in her head said. *Your mother is offering you freedom. You need to make up your mind for sure about what you want, and never look back.*

"Your loss," Vivien said as matter-of-factly as if she were discussing whether or not Bonnie should have a beer or a shot of whiskey with her.

"More coffee, anyone?" Rusty asked as he brought the second pan of toast to the table and sat down.

"Hey, where is everyone?" Shiloh yelled from the front door.

"In the kitchen," Bonnie called out.

"Who's here?" Abby Joy's voice preceded her into the kitchen.

Vivien looked up from the table and smiled when they entered the room. "I'm Vivien, Bonnie's mother."

"These are my sisters, Shiloh and Abby Joy," Bonnie said.

"Half sisters," Vivien corrected her. "Glad to meet y'all."

"Same here." Shiloh and Abby Joy said in unison.

"We were taking the morning off to run into Amarillo to grocery shop. We stopped by to see if you want to go, but since you've got company..." Shiloh let the sentence trail off.

"Give me time to finish eating and then I'll be leaving. You should never miss a chance to get off this ranch, Bonnie. Even if it's just to go for groceries," Vivien said.

Shiloh poured herself a cup of coffee and sat down at the kitchen table. "So what brings you back to the canyon, Miz Vivien?"

"My daughter," Vivien answered and picked up another piece of toast. "I thought she'd be tired of this place, and she'd jump at the chance to go with me to California. Maybe y'all can talk sense to her."

Bonnie could have sworn that the look Shiloh shot her way was one of pure understanding. But how could her sister know anything about the way Bonnie and Vivien had lived? Both of them had had a fairly stable life.

"We don't know what we'd do without her." Abby Joy pulled up a chair and sat down. "I'm having a baby soon, and my child is going to need her aunts to be close by, and I need her to help me. I don't know anything about babies."

"Neither does she," Vivien said.

"But she knows me, and she can calm me down when I get scared." Abby Joy smiled.

Bonnie could have hugged her sister for saying that.

"And she promised she'd stay close to us even if she didn't stay on this ranch. We've kind of grown to like having siblings," Shiloh said.

Vivien glanced up at Bonnie. "You're going to be sorry. Every evening, I'll watch the sun set over the ocean, and you could be with me."

"You're playin' a dangerous game," Bonnie warned her. "We have lovely sunsets right here, and you can get sober and clean, maybe even learn to put down some roots like I have."

"That ain't for me." Vivien shook her head. "But, honey, I'll call and check in when I get my new job. Maybe you and your boyfriend"—she nodded toward Rusty—"can come out and visit me. You know how I hate goodbyes, so don't follow me to the door and wave and all that crap. We'll keep in touch. See you later." She stood up, finished off the last swallow of coffee, and grinned. "You wouldn't have a spare bottle of Jim Beam for me to take along on the trip, would you?"

"No, I do not," Bonnie said quickly.

"Never know the answer if you don't ask." Vivien waved as she left the house. In a couple of minutes, Bonnie heard the front door slam and then she let out a loud whoosh of breath that she didn't even realize she'd been holding.

"I'm sorry." Bonnie looked straight at Rusty. "I owe you a big thank-you and an apology."

"You are welcome, but you don't have to be sorry." He stood up and carried empty plates to the sink. "I'm going to the barn to change the tire on the tractor you use. You ladies probably have a lot to talk about." His eyes twinkled. "Hey, I'm special. Now I've met both your parents."

"That's not saying a lot, now is it?" she told him.

Rusty shot her a grin and strode out the door with a wave.

"Had your mom been drinkin'?" Abby Joy asked. "Her eyes were bloodshot."

"She drove all night from Kentucky and is damn lucky she didn't get stopped for drunk driving and drugs, but that's my mama. I have to love her, but nothing says I have to like her all the time," she said. "I'd forgotten how crazy she can be. Do y'all ever wonder what it was in Ezra that made our mothers marry him? From what we saw of that old man in the casket, I can't see why any woman would want to vow to love him forever."

"I've wondered the same thing about my mother," Abby Joy said. "Since we never knew him, we'll never know the answer to that question."

"Do you think she'll get all the way to the West Coast in that truck?" Shiloh asked.

"If she doesn't, there's lots of biker bars and truck stops between here and there. She'll find a way." Bonnie crossed her arms on the table and laid her head down. "Someday I'm going to get a message that says she's been killed unless she cleans up her act. God, I'm scared to death of..." She didn't finish.

"That wouldn't be your fault," Abby Joy said.

Shiloh patted her on the shoulder. "She's living a daredevil life and it has consequences."

"Not her. I'm scared to ever have children," Bonnie said. "She told Rusty that I didn't have anything to draw on, and she's right. Look at my parents—Ezra and Vivien. At least y'all had good mothers to balance out what Ezra donated to the gene pool."

"Maybe you take a lesson from them on how not to be," Shiloh offered. "Are you trying to tell me something?"

"If I'm pregnant, it'll be the new baby Jesus. I haven't had sex since I got here," Bonnie said bluntly. "I'm just saying that any man in his right mind would never want a relationship with me if they truly understood my background."

"Don't be thinkin' that," Shiloh said. "I've seen the love you shower on a baby calf, or even the dogs. You'll be a great mother."

"Amen." Abby Joy added her two cents. "And besides, we've all got each other to help us learn the ropes on parenthood. I, for one, am glad that you didn't let your mother talk you into leaving us. We've proved that we belong together right here in this canyon."

"Yep," Shiloh said.

"Thank you both." Bonnie raised her head and wiped away the tears flowing down her cheeks. "Right now, I can't imagine living anywhere else."

"Well, that's settled," Abby Joy declared. "So now let's get on with some grocery shopping and talking about these sparks I keep feeling between you and Rusty."

"Good Lord!" Bonnie said. "One thing at a time. I need to process all this before I move on to my feelings for Rusty."

"At least you admit and recognize that the feelings are there, so that's a start." Abby Joy reached for the last piece of toast.

"And that's a big step for me," Bonnie admitted.

Chapter Nine

Bonnie had a lot of time to think as she drove a tractor around the field that afternoon. Rusty was just over the barbed wire fence on the next twenty acres cutting hay, just like she was doing—like they'd both done the day before. The difference was that they weren't fighting now, and every so often, they were even close enough to wave at each other.

In between those times, she replayed the morning over and over again in her mind. It was so surreal that she could almost believe it had never happened—that it was just a bad nightmare. Of all the crazy stunts Vivien had ever pulled, this one was the most insane. Bonnie slapped the steering wheel with both hands when she realized that her mother was the very reason Rusty might want to be with *her*?

"It better not be because you felt sorry for me. I don't want your pity," she muttered.

Her phone rang, and she picked it up from the passenger seat. When her mother's name came up, she answered immediately. "Did you change your mind? Where are you? I'll come get you."

"Hell, no, I ain't changed my mind," Vivien said. "I'm on my way to California. I'm not about to change my mind. I'm stopped at a roadside rest outside of Clovis to catch a catnap in the bed of the truck. I brought along a sleeping bag, and I'm dog-tired. I'm calling to ask you one more time to come with me."

"Answer is still no. I'm happy right here where I am, Mama, but I'll drive to Clovis and get *you* if you'll change your mind. You can work with us here on the place or get a job in Claude or somewhere close and just live here if you don't want to do ranch work," Bonnie told her.

"No, thanks. I washed my hands of that place when you was born," Vivien said. "Rusty seems like a good guy, but Ezra trained him, so keep that in mind. Make him sign a prenup before you marry him so he don't steal half the place from you. Even good men ain't to be trusted. You be real careful. There ain't no such thing as an honest man."

Bonnie sucked in a long breath to say something else, but then she realized that her mother had hung up on her. She slapped the steering wheel again, stopped the engine, and got out of the tractor. Tears ran down her cheeks—Lord have mercy! She'd cried more in the past few days than she had in her whole life put together. She shook her fist at the sky. Just when she thought she had left the past behind her, its ugly old head had popped right up again, coming at her this time as doubts and fears. Cooper and Waylon were good, honest men for sure, and so was Rusty. Her mother was wrong—she just flat out had to be.

She caught a movement in her peripheral vision but didn't realize it was Rusty until he and all three dogs surrounded her. He took her in his arms and eased the two of them down on the ground. "What's the matter? Is it Shiloh or Abby Joy?"

"It's Mama." She sobbed into his chest.

"Is she hurt? Did she change her mind?" He rattled off questions too fast for her to comprehend, much less answer.

Even after meeting her and after knowing now exactly what kind of mother Bonnie had, he was still concerned for the woman. For some strange reason, that was the final little bit of what it took to convince Bonnie that she was right where she belonged and gave her the courage to admit her feelings.

"Mama is fine. She just wanted to give me one more chance to go with her." Bonnie dried her eyes with the back of her hand.

Rusty laid his hands on her shoulders and looked deeply into her eyes. "Please don't go."

"I couldn't if I wanted to, which I don't," she whispered without blinking. "It would be too painful to leave this ranch, my sisters, and most of all, you. I love you, Rusty," she admitted. "It's too soon to say it, but there it is. I figured it out a few days ago, and I'm tired of fighting the feeling. I don't want to go another day, or even another hour, without saying the words. I think I fell in love with you right there on that first day, but ..."

He put his fingers over her lips. "There are no buts in real love, only ands. I love you, Bonnie, and I don't give a damn who your parents were. We don't have to be the by-products of our parents, darlin'. I'm a foster child, and I don't even remember my folks. We can build our own life right here in this place. We can take steps forward and never look over our shoulder at the past. And, honey, I believe I felt the same about you from the beginning, but I didn't want you to think it was just to get this place."

"Okay." She managed a weak smile through the tears. "I love you, and I'm never letting my mother or anyone else make me doubt myself again."

Rusty pulled her close to his chest. "What are we going to do about this?"

"Live together on this place for six months and figure it out a day at a time?" she suggested.

"That sounds good to me." He tipped up her chin for a long kiss that left her breathless.

"Maybe you could even move your things back into the ranch house?" She might be moving too fast, but she didn't want to waste time she could be spending with Rusty.

Vivien wedged her way between them and licked Bonnie's hand. "Somehow I feel like this dog loves me more than my mother does. Do you realize you're the first person who's ever said those three words to me, Rusty?" Tears began to stream down her cheeks, again.

He brushed a sweet kiss across her forehead. "I believe you're the first who ever said them to me, too. And, I promise to tell you every day that I love you. Now, tell me what caused these tears." He pulled a red bandanna from his pocket and dried her cheeks.

"I've had to be tough my whole life, and I don't like to cry because it's a sign of weakness, but I'm so happy that I figured out where I belong. These are happy tears, Rusty."

He tucked the bandanna back into his hip pocket and slipped an arm under her shoulders. "I'd never be so stupid as to think that you were weak."

"Thank you," she whispered. "I meant it when I said I love you, but"—she stopped and shook her head—"it goes deeper than that. I can't explain it."

"It's more like a soul mate kind of thing then, right?" he asked.

"That's right, and I like the feeling." She finally smiled.

"So do I, darlin'." He kissed her one more time.

Chapter Ten

Six months later

Bonnie awoke to find Rusty propped up on an elbow staring at her. She smiled and reached up to run a hand over his unshaven face. "Happy wedding day. Are we ready for this?"

"I hope so." He grinned. "There's a lot of people that's goin' to be mad as hell if we ain't at the church this afternoon at about two o'clock. They're going to have to wade through more than a foot of snow just to get to their trucks, but Cooper and Waylon said they'd take care of clearing the porch of the church and sidewalk."

"It's supposed to be bad luck for the bride and groom to see each other on their wedding day." He toyed with a strand of her hair. "Do you think maybe we should have just gone to the courthouse?"

"Nope. I've always wanted a wedding," Bonnie assured him. "I want to see the look in your eyes when I walk down the aisle, and I want to hold that memory in my heart forever."

"There's no way you could be more beautiful than you are right now." He pulled her lips to his for the first morning kiss. "Think your mother will show up and surprise you?"

"It would be a big surprise all right." Bonnie threw back the covers and got out of bed. "She's still runnin' with that motor-cycle gang, and they've joined up with more bikers somewhere up near the Canadian border in Washington. She called yesterday and tried to talk me into gettin' on a plane and coming out there to live with them."

Rusty got out of bed and picked up a pair of jeans. Bonnie stopped what she was doing and stared at his fine naked body— all hardened muscles, a broad chest, and a heart inside that was so full of love for her that sometimes she still found it hard to believe. In only a few hours, she'd have a piece of paper that said he belonged to her. She full well intended to frame it and set it up on the mantel above the fireplace in the living room for the whole world to see.

"I'm a lucky woman," she whispered.

"What was that?" Rusty asked.

"I said I'm one lucky woman," she repeated.

"Not as lucky as I am." He grinned and rounded the end of the bed to take her in his arms. "I'd like to go back to bed with you, but we're kind of on a tight schedule here. We've got brunch at Shiloh's, and then we're supposed to go straight to the church."

"And Abby Joy says once I step foot in the church, I can't see you anymore until the wedding." She tugged on her jeans and stomped her feet down into her boots. "Let's go get the feeding chores done and then head over to Shiloh's."

"Lovers forever." She held up a pinky.

"Married couple from today until death parts us." He wrapped his pinky around hers.

"Ranchers together." They both said it at the same time and held up three fingers.

* * *

Rusty looked out over the congregation that Wednesday after-noon and thought again that New Year's Day was a strange day

for a wedding, but there was no way he was going to argue with
Bonnie. She wanted the ceremony to be on the very day when she
took ownership of the ranch. After her mother had come for that
crazy visit, they'd signed papers back in the summer, and those
papers said that on the day they married, the Malloy Ranch would
belong to the two of them—and that on that very day, the name of
the place would be changed to Sunrise Ranch.

The pianist began to play "The Rose," and Shiloh came
down the center aisle with her arm looped in Waylon's. Abby
Joy and Cooper followed behind them. In less than an hour,
Rusty would have two sisters-in-law and two brothers-in-law—
he'd have family for the first time in his life. The preacher raised
his arms for everyone to stand, and the pianist began to play the
traditional wedding march. The double doors at the back of the
church opened, and Bonnie came down the aisle alone. Jackson
Bailey had offered to escort her, but she had refused. She told
Rusty that she was giving herself to him in marriage, and she
didn't need anyone else to do that for her.

She was wearing a lovely white lace dress that stopped at her
ankles. Peeking out from under its hem were the same biker boots
that she'd worn a year ago on that very first day that Rusty had laid
eyes on her. *The day that I fell in love with her if I'm being honest
about the whole thing,* he thought. His eyes met hers, and he
couldn't wait for her to reach the front of the church. He met her
halfway back down the aisle and hugged her tightly to his chest.

"I'm the luckiest man alive this day," he whispered.

"I'd say we've made our own luck," she said. "Now let's go
get married so we can tell the whole world about this baby we're
going to have in four months."

He tucked her free hand into his, and together, they stepped
up in front of the preacher. She handed her bouquet to Shiloh
and turned to face Rusty, just like they'd rehearsed, but the night
before, she hadn't looked so much like an angel straight from the
courts of heaven. Suddenly, he was tongue-tied and was glad that
he'd written his vows on a piece of paper.

* * *

The party for just the wedding party after the reception was held at the newly named Sunrise Ranch. While the ladies were in the bedroom helping Bonnie get out of her fancy lace dress and into a pair of jeans, Rusty slipped away and walked down to the cemetery. The wind whistled through the bare tree branches and blew powdery snow up from the ground, which chilled the bare skin on his face. He pulled the collar of his fleece-lined jacket up to keep his ears warm and bent his head against the cold.

The gate into the cemetery squeaked loudly as if it were competing with the noise of tree limbs rattling against each other. He wasn't aware that the dogs had followed him until he had brushed away the snow and sat down on the bench in front of Ezra's tombstone, and the three of them gathered around him.

"My faithful old friends." He took time to pat each of them on the head with a gloved hand. "We've come together to tell him goodbye, haven't we?"

He sat there for a full minute before he began to talk to the tombstone, which was half covered by a drift of snow. "I'm here again, Ezra. It was a year ago today that we put you in the ground, and I doubt that you would believe how much things have changed. Why you did what you did is still a mystery to me, but I have to admit, there's three cowboys in this part of the canyon now who are mighty glad that you did it for whatever reason. When Abby Joy got married and left the ranch, the other two sisters came right here and talked to you. When Shiloh did the same, Bonnie came to talk to you. I figure now that everything is settled, it's my turn."

He patted the bench, and all three dogs jumped up on it with him.

"They never knew I saw them make their journey here, and I'll never know what they said to you, but I don't imagine any one of them was telling you that she loved you. I may never come back here again except when it's time to mow and keep the cemetery cleaned up. I owe you that much. But this will be our last conversation. Abby Joy has a beautiful little son, and Shiloh will be having a boy in a few months, so you see if you'd kept either of them around, you would have had a grandson to leave your ranch to, and it would most likely remain the Malloy Ranch. Bonnie and I got married today, and we're having a daughter. We just found out yesterday that it's a girl, and we're so excited about her. I don't care if we have all girls or if they want to be ranchers when they grow up or not. I can't imagine some of them not wanting to take over for me and Bonnie when we get old, but that will be their choice. One thing for damned sure, they won't be sent out into the world to fend for themselves like your daughters were. They'll be raised right here on Sunrise Ranch. And another thing just as sure, they will be loved." Rusty ran out of words and sat silent for a time. "I just wanted to tell you that, Ezra, and to thank you for giving me a job, because now I have a family. Goodbye, now, and I don't know why I should, after the way you treated folks while you were here, but I hope you find peace somewhere along your eternal journey, because you sure brought happiness to a lot of us, whether you intended to or not."

He stood up and started back toward the house, the dogs following at his heels. When he closed the gate, it didn't squeak. The wind had stopped blowing and everything was eerily quiet. He looked up at the moon hanging in the sky just in time to see a shooting star streak across the darkness.

* * *

When everyone had left that evening, Bonnie slumped down on the sofa beside Rusty. "It was a wonderful day in spite of the snow." She sighed.

"You were a beautiful bride, and now you're *my* gorgeous wife," he said. "Maybe in the spring we can sneak away for a honeymoon." He took her hand in his and kissed her knuckles, one by one.

"Honey, in the spring I'll either be nine months pregnant or we'll already have a pretty little daughter. Our honeymoon will be right here in this house, starting tonight and lasting through all eternity," she told him. "Where did you disappear to while I was changing clothes?"

"I went to talk to Ezra and tell him that we'd changed the name of the ranch," he said. "Our new sign will be hung over the cattle guard as soon as the weather clears up. I forgot to tell him that."

She snuggled in closer to his side. "Shiloh and I've had a few talks with him during this past year."

"I know." He nodded. "Guess what? I saw a shooting star on the way back to the house."

"What did you wish for?" she asked.

"That you would always love me as much as you do right now," he said.

"Darlin', that was a wasted wish." She smiled.

"Oh? So, you're not going to love me always?"

She shifted her position until she was sitting in his lap. "No, I'm just not going to love you as much as I do right now. I plan to love you more every single moment of every single day. You had that already, so you should have wished for something else."

"A new tractor, maybe?" He brushed a kiss across her lips.

"Why not?" She grinned. "Sunrise Ranch could always use a new tractor."

About the Author

Carolyn Brown is a *New York Times* and *USA Today* bestselling romance author and RITA finalist who has sold more than eight million books. She presently writes both women's fiction and cowboy romance. She lives in southern Oklahoma with her husband, a former English teacher who is the author of nine mystery novels. They have three children and enough grandchildren to keep them young.

You can learn more at:

CarolynBrownBooks.com

Twitter @TheCarolynBrown

Facebook.com/CarolynBrownBooks

Instagram @CarolynBrownBooks

Find more heartwarming fun from Carolyn Brown!

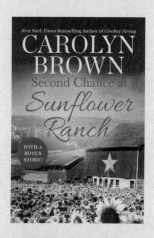

Available Early 2022

Enjoy the best of the West with these handsome, rugged cowboys!

TEXAS HOMECOMING
by Carolyn Brown

Dr. Cody Ryan is back in Honey Grove, Texas, much to the delight of everyone at Sunflower Ranch—everyone except the veterinarian, Dr. Stephanie O'Dell. So he can't believe his fate when a sudden blizzard forces them to take shelter together in an old barn. Cody's barely seen his childhood crush since he left, so why is she being so cold? As they confront the feelings between them, it's clear the fire keeping them warm isn't the only source of sparks. But once the storm passes, will Stevie and Cody finally give love a chance?

SECOND CHANCE AT SUNFLOWER RANCH
by Carolyn Brown

Jesse Ryan is shocked to return home after twenty years and find the woman he could never forget had given birth to a little girl about nine months after he'd left—*his* little girl. As a single mom, the last thing Addy Hall needs is Jesse complicating her life even further, especially since she's always had a crush on the handsome cowboy. But the more time she spends with him, the more she wonders what might happen if they finally became the family for which she'd always hoped. **Includes the bonus novella *Small Town Charm*!**

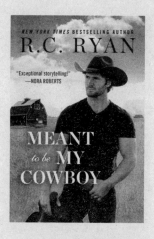

MEANT TO BE MY COWBOY
by R.C. Ryan

Fresh off a bad breakup, Annie Dempsey has rules for her new life in Devil's Door, Wyoming: no romance, no drama, and steer clear of the Merrick clan—her family's sworn enemies. But when a charming stranger steps in to protect Annie from a sudden threat, rules fly out the window. Because her mystery hero is...Jonah Merrick. As she hides from a dangerous pursuer at Jonah's ranch, they can't deny the chemistry pulling them closer together. But can they put their family rivalry aside to make room for love instead?

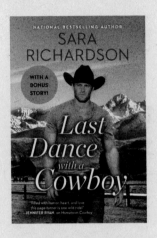

LAST DANCE WITH A COWBOY
by Sara Richardson

Leila Valentino will do anything to keep her grandparents' Colorado winery afloat. Even partner with August Harding, the first—and last—man to break her heart. The cowboy's investment offer could save the business, but her grandparents have no idea how close they are to going under. So Leila insists August pretend he's back in town for *her*. When their faux relationship starts feeling for real, a second chance seems possible—but can August convince Leila that this time he's not walking away? **With a bonus story by Carolyn Brown!**

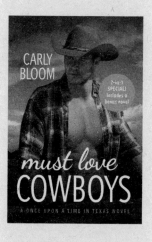

MUST LOVE COWBOYS
by Carly Bloom

Alice Martin doesn't regret putting her career as a librarian above personal relationships—but when cowboy Beau Montgomery comes to her for help, Alice decides to see what she's been missing. She agrees to help Beau improve his reading skills if he'll be her date to an upcoming wedding. But when the town's gossip mill gets going, they're forced into a fake romance to keep their deal a secret. And soon Alice is seeing Beau in a whole new way...**Includes the bonus novel *Big Bad Cowboy*!**